VINCE FLYNN

THE THIRD OPTION

A MITCH RAPP NOVEL

$9.99 U.S.
$12.99 CAN.

"What thriller readers live for."
(*Kirkus Reviews*)

Don't miss the next installment
in the Mitch Rapp series

VINCE FLYNN'S
LETHAL AGENT
A Mitch Rapp Novel by Kyle Mills

Coming in hardcover
from Emily Bestler Books

ISBN 978-1-9821-2106-8

$9.99 U.S./$12.99 Can.

Praise for *Red War*

"Outstanding. . . . Mills is writing at the top of his game in this nail-biter."

—*Publishers Weekly* (starred review)

"In the world of black-ops thrillers, Mitch Rapp remains the gold standard. Mills has embraced the high-concept-thriller style and continues to exceed expectations."

—*Booklist* (starred review)

"Events lead to a dramatic, you-got-your-money's-worth conclusion. Good, escapist fun."

—*Kirkus* Reviews

"The characters drive the story and Mitch Rapp continues to be a mainstay of the modern techno-thriller."

—*New York Journal of Books*

Praise for *Enemy of the State*

"In the world of black-ops thrillers, Mitch Rapp continues to be among the best of the best."

—*Booklist* (starred review)

"Series fans and newcomers alike will watch in wonder as Mitch Rapp executes a clever plan that leads to an explosive climax."

—*Publishers Weekly*

"This novel perfectly combines geo-politics, covert operations, and the backstory of the characters. Readers can close their eyes and remember past books written by Vince Flynn and will not skip a beat with Kyle Mills at the helm."

—*Crimespree Magazine*

Praise for *Order to Kill*

"This series continues to be the best of the best in the high-adventure, action-heavy thriller field. . . . Flynn's name, Flynn's characters, and Mills's skill will take this one to the top of the charts, territory already familiar to Mitch Rapp."

—*Booklist* (starred review)

"Just as compelling as when Flynn was doing the writing. . . . Satisfied fans will hope that Mills will fulfill their continuing Mitch Rapp needs far into the future."

—*Publishers Weekly* (starred review)

"Flynn is a master, maybe *the* master, of thrillers in which the pages seem to turn themselves."

—Bookreporter.com

"What thriller readers live for: tense and dramatic with a nice twist."

—*Kirkus* Reviews

Praise for *The Survivor*

"The biggest compliment one can give Mills is that it's totally unclear where Flynn's work ends and his begins, in *The Survivor*."

—*San Jose Mercury News*

"Mills has created a wonderful tribute to Flynn while also writing a great novel. While thriller readers and fans miss Flynn, Mills was the perfect choice, and Rapp will continue in good hands."

—*Associated Press*

"Mills perfectly treads the line of bringing his own considerable talent and style to the table while being respectful of the source material and seemingly channeling Flynn's own voice."

—Bookreporter.com

"*The Survivor* is truly a magnificent book."

—*San Diego Book Review*

"The book is vintage Flynn/Rapp."

—*The Post and Courier* (Charleston, SC)

"Superb. . . . the greatest post-9/11 series going."

—*Providence Journal*

**The Last Man Kill Shot American Assassin
Pursuit of Honor Extreme Measures Protect and Defend
Act of Treason Consent to Kill Memorial Day
Executive Power Separation of Power The Third Option
Transfer of Power Term Limits**

"Complex, chilling, and satisfying."

—*The Cleveland Plain Dealer*

"Just fabulous."

—Rush Limbaugh

"Spectacular and exceptionally timely."

—*The Providence Journal*

"A Rambo perfectly suited for the war on terror."

—*The Washington Times*

"Pure high-powered exhilaration."

—*Lansing State Journal*

"Suspenseful . . . satisfying and totally unexpected."

—*The Roanoke Times*

Novels by Vince Flynn

And by Kyle Mills

VINCE FLYNN

THE THIRD OPTION

POCKET BOOKS

New York London Toronto Sydney New Delhi

Pocket Books
An Imprint of Simon & Schuster, Inc.
1230 Avenue of the Americas
New York, NY 10020

This book is a work of fiction. Any references to historical events, real people, or real places are used fictitiously. Other names, characters, places, and events are products of the author's imagination, and any resemblance to actual events or places or persons living or dead is entirely coincidental.

This Pocket Books paperback edition July 2019

POCKET and colophon are registered trademarks of Simon & Schuster, Inc.

For information about special discounts for bulk purchases, please contact Simon & Schuster Special Sales at 1-866-506-1949 or business@simonandschuster.com.

The Simon & Schuster Speakers Bureau can bring authors to your live event. For more information, or to book an event, contact the Simon & Schuster Speakers Bureau at 1-866-248-3049 or visit our website at www.simonspeakers.com.

Manufactured in the United States of America

10   9   8   7   6   5   4   3   2   1

ISBN 978-1-9821-2106-8
ISBN 978-1-4391-9512-3 (pbk)
ISBN 978-0-7434-5158-1 (ebook)

THE
THIRD
OPTION

PRELUDE

There exists in America a silent and invisible order made up of former soldiers, intelligence officers, and diplomats. In Washington, they are everywhere and they are nowhere. The average person never sees them, never pauses to think about them, never notices the hand they may have had in a seemingly ordinary death. Most people never stop to think twice about the drug overdose of a lobbyist reported on page B-2 of the *Washington Post*'s Metro section, or the suicide of a colonel in the United States Army, or the fatal mugging of a White House staffer.

Average Americans are too busy living their lives to look beyond the headlines and wonder what secrets these people may have taken to their graves. Among those in the know, eyebrows are raised and even a few quiet questions asked, but ultimately a blind eye is turned, and life goes on. To seek answers from this dark community is a very dangerous thing. It is the world of covert operations, a very real but unseen part of our government's foreign and sometimes domestic policy. It is bigger than any one person. It is *the third option,* and it is one that is not always used by wise and honorable men.

1

Through the darkness the man moved from tree to tree, working his way toward the large house. The nineteenth-century estate, forty miles south of Hamburg, Germany, spanned one hundred and twelve acres of beautiful rolling forest and farmland and was designed after the Grand Trianon at Versailles in France. It had been commissioned by Heinrich Hagenmiller in 1872 to win further favor with William I of Prussia, the newly crowned German emperor. Portions of it had been sold off over the years as it became too expensive to maintain so much land.

The man walking silently through the woods had already studied hundreds of photographs of the property and its owner. Some of the photos were snapped from satellites orbiting the earth thousands of miles up, but most were taken by the surveillance team that had been in place for the last week.

The assassin had arrived from America only this afternoon and wanted to see with his own eyes what he was up against. Photographs were a good start, but they were no substitute for being there in person. The collar of his black leather jacket was flipped up around his neck to ward off the bite of the cold fall evening. The temperature had dropped twenty degrees since sunset.

For the second time since leaving the cottage, he stopped dead in his tracks and listened. He thought he had heard something behind him. The narrow path he trod was covered with a fresh bed of golden pine needles. It was a cloudy night, and with the thick canopy above, very little light reached the place where he stood. He moved to the path's edge and slowly looked back. Without his night-vision scope, he could see no more than ten feet.

Mitch Rapp had been trying not to use the scope. He wanted to make sure he could find his way down the path without it, but something was telling him he wasn't alone. Rapp extracted a 9-mm Glock automatic from his pocket and quietly screwed a suppresser onto the end of it. Then he grabbed a four-inch tubular pocket scope, flipped the operating switch on, and held it up to his right eye. The path before him was instantly illuminated with a strange green light. Rapp scanned the area, checking not only the path but his flanks. The pocket scope penetrated the dark shadows that his eyes could not. He paid particular attention to the base of the trees that bordered the path. He was looking for the telltale shoe of someone who was seeking to conceal himself.

After five minutes of patiently waiting, Rapp began to wonder if it wasn't a deer or some other creature that had made the noise. After five more minutes, he reluctantly gave in to the conclusion that he had heard an animal of the four-legged variety rather than two-. Rapp put the pocket scope away but decided to keep his gun out. He had not made it to the ripe old age of thirty-two by being careless and sloppy. Like any true professional, he knew when the time was right to take chances and when to cut and run.

Rapp continued down the path for another quarter of a mile. He could see the lights of the house up ahead and decided to go the rest of the way through the underbrush. Silently, he maneuvered through the thickets, bending branches out of his way and ducking under others. As he approached the edge of the forest, he heard the snap of a twig under his foot and quickly moved to his left, placing a tree directly between himself and the house. A kennel of hunting dogs, not more than a hundred yards away, erupted in alarm. Rapp silently swore at himself and remained perfectly still. This was why he needed to check things out on his own. Amazingly, no one had told him that there were dogs. The canines grew louder, their barks turning to howls, and then a door opened. A deep voice yelled in German for the beasts to be quiet. The man repeated himself two more times, and finally the dogs settled.

Rapp slid an eye out from behind the tree and looked at the kennel. The hunting dogs were wired, pacing back and forth. They would be a problem. Not as bad as trained guard dogs, but their senses were still naturally keen. He stood at the edge of the forest listening and watching, taking everything in. He didn't like what he saw. There was a lot of open space between the forest and the house. There were some gardens that he could weave his way through, but it would be hard to stay silent on the paths of crushed rock. The dogs would

Item(s)	Total

San Francisco : [2017] (Checkout)
39082123088848   21/Aug/2019

Generally have more fun (Checkout)
and aholstfig heat thigh thigh steep
Yeah uhyuh to ship in the mouning chart yeah
Babe : why of to report : why I show i
the happiness project (Checkout)
39082121758088   21/Aug/2019

(Checkout)
Adult Paperback - southwood 2018
37082121758088   21/Aug/2019

(Checkout)
Adult Paperback - southwood 2018
39082123028258   21/Aug/2019

August 05, 2019 01 18

August 06, 2019 01:18

39065153658529   27/Aug/2019
Adult Paperback - Southwood, 2018
(CheckOut)

39065153655442   27/Aug/2019
Adult Paperback - Southwood, 2018
(CheckOut)

39065157494798   27/Aug/2019
The happiness project : or, why I spent a
year trying to sing in the morning, clean my
closets, fight right, read Aristotle, and
generally have more fun (CheckOut)

39065153066848   27/Aug/2019
San Francisco, [2017] (CheckOut)

Total	**4 Item(s)**

make approaching from the south very difficult. Surveillance cameras covered the other avenues, and there was twice the open space to traverse. The only good news was that there were no pressure pads, microwave beams, or motion sensors to deal with.

Officially, Mitch Rapp had nothing to do with the U.S. government. Unofficially, he had been working for the CIA since graduating from Syracuse University more than a decade ago. Rapp had been selected to join a highly secretive counterterrorism group known as the Orion Team. The CIA had honed Rapp's raw athleticism and intelligence into a lethal efficiency. The few people he allowed to get close to him knew him as a successful entrepreneur who had started a small computer consulting business that required frequent travel. To keep things legitimate, Rapp often did conduct business while abroad, but not on this trip. He had been sent to kill a man. A man who had already been warned twice.

Rapp studied the area for almost thirty minutes. When he had seen enough, he started back, but not down the path. If someone was in the woods, there was no sense in walking right into a trap. Rapp quietly picked his way through the underbrush for several hundred yards to the south. He stopped three times and checked his compass to make sure he was headed in the right direction. From the intelligence summary, he knew there was another footpath due south of the one he had come in on. Both paths entered the estate from a narrow dirt road and ran roughly parallel to each other.

Rapp almost missed the second footpath. It appeared

less frequented than the first one and was overgrown. From there he worked his way back to the curving dirt road. When he reached it, he knelt down and extracted his pocket scope. For several minutes he scanned the road and listened. When he was sure no one else was about, he began walking south.

Rapp had been doing this for almost ten years, and he was ready to get out. In fact, this probably would be his last job. He had met the right woman the previous spring, and it was time to settle down. The CIA did not want to let him go, but that was tough. He had already given enough. Ten years of doing what he did for a living was a lifetime. He was lucky to be getting out in one piece and with a marginally sound mind.

A little more than a mile down the road, Rapp came upon a small cottage. The shades were drawn, and smoke drifted from the chimney. He approached the door, knocked twice, paused for a second, and then knocked three more times. It opened two inches, and an eye appeared. When the man saw that it was Rapp, he opened the door all the way. Mitch stepped into the sparsely furnished room and began to unbutton his leather jacket. The man who had let him in locked the door behind him.

The cottage had knotty pine walls that had been painted white and three-inch plank floorboards that were covered with shiny green paint. Brightly colored oval throw rugs were scattered about the floor, and the furniture was old and solid. The walls were adorned with local folk art and some old black-and-white photographs. Under normal circumstances it would be a great place to spend a cozy fall weekend reading a good book by the fire and taking long walks through the forest.

At the kitchen table a woman sat wearing headphones. On the table in front of her was about a quarter of a million dollars in high-tech surveillance equipment. All of the gear was contained in two beat-up black Samsonite suitcases. If anyone were to stop by the cottage, the cases could be closed and moved off the table in seconds.

Rapp had never met the man and woman before. He knew them only as Tom and Jane Hoffman. They were in their mid-forties, and as far as Rapp could tell, they were married. The Hoffmans had stopped in two countries before arriving in Frankfurt. Their tickets had been purchased under assumed names with matching credit cards and passports provided by their contact. They were also given their standard fee of ten thousand dollars for a week's work, paid up-front in cash. They were told someone would be joining them and, as always, not to ask any questions.

All of their equipment was waiting for them when they arrived at the cottage, and they started right in on the surveillance of the estate and its owner. Several days after arriving at the cottage, they were paid a visit by a man known to them only as the professor. They were given an additional twenty-five thousand dollars and were told they would receive another twenty-five thousand dollars when they completed the mission. He had given them a quick briefing on the man who would be joining them. He did not tell them the man's real name, only that he was extremely competent.

Tom Hoffman poured Rapp a cup of coffee and brought it to him by the roaring fieldstone fireplace. "So, what'd ya think?"

Rapp shrugged his shoulders and looked at Hoffman's face. His complexion was neutral, not flushed like Rapp's from being out in the cold night air. In response to the question, he said, "It's not going to be easy." Rapp had already checked the woman's face and shoes. Neither of these people had been outside. It must have been a deer that he had heard in the woods.

"It rarely is," noted the stocky Hoffman, who took a drink from his own mug once again while trying to get a read on the stranger before him. The six-foot-one muscular man whom he knew only as Carl moved like a big cat—soft on his feet. There was nothing clumsy about him. His face was tanned and lined from long hours spent outdoors. His jet-black hair was thick and just starting to gray around the temples, and there was a thin scar on his cheek that ran from his ear down to his jaw.

Rapp looked away from Hoffman and into the fire. He knew he was being sized up. Mitch had already done the same with both of them and would continue to do so up until the moment they parted. He looked back into the fire and focused on the plan. He knew the tendency in these situations was to try to come up with something that was truly ingenious—a plan that would bypass all of the security and get him in and out without being noticed. This was not necessarily a bad path to take if you had enough time to prepare, but as of right now they had about twenty-three hours to draw the whole thing up and pull it off. With that in mind, Rapp had already begun thinking of a strategy.

Turning away from the fire, he asked the woman, "Jane, how many people are invited to this party tomorrow night?"

"About fifty."

Rapp ran a hand through his black hair, grabbed the back of his neck, and squeezed. After staring into the fire for a long moment, he announced, "I have an idea."

THE FIRST SIGNS of morning were showing in the east. The black sky was turning gray, and patches of fog wafted from ponds as the cool fall air mixed with summer's leftover warmth. The pristine Maryland morning was interrupted by a dull thumping noise in the distance. Two Marines walking patrol on the Jeep road by the west fence instinctively searched for the source of the sound. With M-16s slung over their shoulders, they craned their necks skyward, both knowing what was approaching without having to see it. Within seconds they also knew it wasn't a military bird. The telltale thumping was far too quiet. The white helicopter buzzed in over the trees and headed for the interior of the camp. The Marines followed it for a second and then continued with their patrol, both assuming the civilian bird was delivering one of the president's golf partners.

The Bell JetRanger continued on an easterly heading toward the camp's water tower. Just in front of the tower was a clearing with a cement landing pad. The bird slowed and floated smoothly toward the ground, its struts coming to rest right on the mark. The pilot shut the turbine engine down, and the rotors began to lose momentum. A black Suburban was parked on the nearby road, and several men in dark suits and ties stood by watching as the visitor stepped out of the helicopter.

Dr. Irene Kennedy grabbed her briefcase and headed for the truck. Her shoulder-length brown hair was pulled back in a ponytail, and she was wearing a crisp blue shirt. Kennedy clutched the lapels of her tan suit against the cool air. When she reached the Suburban, an army officer extended his hand. "Welcome to Camp David, Dr. Kennedy."

The forty-year-old employee of the Central Intelligence Agency took the officer's hand and said, "Thank you, Colonel."

Kennedy's official role was as director of the CIA's Counterterrorism Center. Unofficially, she headed up the Orion Team, an organization born in secrecy out of a need to go on the offensive against terrorism. In the early eighties the United States was stung hard by a slew of terrorist attacks, most notably the bombing of the U.S. embassy and Marine barracks in Beirut. Despite the millions of dollars and assets allocated to fight terrorism, after the attacks, things only got worse. The decade ended with the downing of Pan Am Flight 103 and the deaths of hundreds of innocent civilians. The Lockerbie disaster moved some of the most powerful individuals in Washington to take drastic measures. They agreed it was time to take the war to the terrorists. The first option of diplomacy wasn't doing the job, and the second option of military force was ill suited to fight an enemy that lived and worked among innocent civilians, so America's leaders were left with only one choice: the third option. Covert action would be taken. Money would be funneled into black operations that would never see the light of day, much less congressional oversight or the scrutiny of the press. A clandestine war would be mounted, and the hunters would become the hunted.

The ride took just a few minutes, and no one spoke. When they arrived at Aspen Lodge, Kennedy got out and walked up the porch steps, past two Secret Service agents, and into the president's quarters. The colonel escorted Kennedy down the hall to the president's study and knocked on the open door frame.

"Mr. President, Dr. Kennedy is here."

President Robert Xavier Hayes sat behind his desk sipping a cup of coffee and reading Friday morning's edition of the *Washington Post*. A pair of black-rimmed reading spectacles sat perched on the end of his nose, and when Kennedy entered he looked up from the print and over the top of his cheaters. Hayes immediately closed the paper and said, "Thank you, Colonel." He then rose from his chair and walked over to a small circular table where he gestured for Kennedy to sit.

Hayes was dressed for his morning golf match, wearing a pair of khaki pants, a plain blue golf shirt, and a pullover vest. He set his mug down on the table and poured a second cup for Kennedy. After placing it in front of her, he sat and asked, "How is Director Stansfield?"

"He's . . ." Kennedy grasped to come up with the appropriate word to describe her boss's failing health, "as well as could be expected."

Hayes nodded. Thomas Stansfield was a very private man. He had been with the CIA from its very inception, and it appeared he would be with it to the very end of his own life. The seventy-nine-year-old spymaster had just been diagnosed with cancer, and the doctors were giving him less than six months.

The president turned his attention to the more immediate matter. "How are things proceeding in Germany?"

"On track. Mitch arrived last night and gave me a full report before I left this morning."

When Kennedy had briefed the president on the operation earlier in the week, the one thing Hayes had made crystal-clear was that there would be no green light unless Rapp was involved. The closed meeting between the president and Kennedy was one of many they had had in the last five months, all in an effort to harass, frustrate, destabilize, and, if possible, kill one person. That fortunate individual was Saddam Hussein.

Long before President Hayes had taken office, Saddam was a source of irritation to the West, but more recently he had done something that directly affected the fifty-eight-year-old president of the United States. The previous spring, a group of terrorists had attacked the White House and killed dozens of Secret Service agents and several civilians. In the midst of the attack, President Hayes was evacuated to his underground bunker, where he sat for the next three days, cut off from the rest of his government. The siege was ended, thanks to the bold actions of Mitch Rapp and a few select members of the intelligence, law enforcement, and Special Forces communities.

After the attack the United States was left with two pieces of information that pointed to the Iraqi leader. There was a problem, however, with bringing this information to the United Nations or the international courts. The first piece of evidence was obtained from a foreign intelligence service that was none too eager to have its methods exposed to international scrutiny, and the second was gathered through the use of covert action—the third option. How that information was extracted would be deemed reprehensible by all but a few.

In short, they had some very reliable information that Saddam had funded the terrorists, but they could never make the facts public because that would expose their own methods. And as President Hayes had already noted to an inner circle of advisors, there was no guarantee the UN would do anything once it was confronted with the facts. After intense debate by President Hayes, Director Stansfield of the CIA, and General Flood, the chairman of the Joint Chiefs, the three had decided they had little choice but to go after Saddam on a covert level. At its core, that's what this meeting was all about.

President Hayes leaned forward and placed his coffee mug on the table. He was eager to hear Rapp's take on the situation in Germany. Hayes had discovered that where others failed, Rapp had a way of making things happen. "What does Mitch think?"

"He thinks that given the short notice and the security around the target, we would be better off opting for a more direct approach." Kennedy went on to give the president a brief overview of the plan.

When she was finished Hayes sat back and folded his arms across his chest, his expression thoughtful. Kennedy watched him and kept her own expression neutral, just as her boss would do.

Hayes mulled things over for another ten seconds and then said, "What if they did it . . ." The president stopped because Kennedy was already shaking her head.

"Mitch doesn't respond well to advice given from three thousand miles away."

The president nodded. After the White House incident the previous spring, Hayes had read up on Rapp. It was almost always his way or the highway, and while this could be a concern, one could hardly argue with the man's record of success. He had a history of getting the job done, often when no one else even dared to take it. Hayes suppressed his urge to be an armchair quarterback and instead decided to remind Kennedy of what was at stake.

"Do Mitch and the others know they are on their own?"

Kennedy nodded.

"I mean really on their own. If anything goes wrong, we will deny any knowledge of the situation and of who they are. We have to. Our relationship with Germany could not withstand something like this, nor, for that matter, could my presidency."

Kennedy nodded understandingly. "Sir, Mitch is good. He'll have all of his backups in place by this evening, and if things get too tight, he knows not to force it."

The president stared at her for a moment and then nodded. "All right. You have my authority to go ahead with this, but you know where we stand, Irene. If it blows up, we never had this meeting, and we didn't have the five or six meetings before, either. You had no knowledge of these events, and neither did anyone else at the Agency." Hayes shook his head. "I hate to do this to Mitch, but there's no choice. He is way out there working without a net, and if he falls, we can't do a thing to help him."

2

Rapp had taken a five-mile run around noon, but other than that he had stayed in the cottage the entire day. He needed the jog to stay loose, to take the edge off of all the coffee he had consumed. He had communicated directly with Irene Kennedy several times via a STU III, MX3030 Comsat. The voice-secure satellite phone was his only direct link to Washington. No one else knew he and the Hoffmans were in Germany, and no one could. If the mission went off without a hitch, his masters would need complete deniability, and if the mission fell apart, they would need it even more.

Rapp's plan for the evening had required certain purchases. Earlier in the day Tom Hoffman had driven into Hamburg with a shopping list. Hoffman had been very careful about where he bought the various items, never buying more than one thing in the same neighborhood and always avoiding store surveillance cameras.

Night had arrived, and Rapp was sitting at the kitchen table with the Hoffmans going over each detail for what seemed like the hundredth time. The Hoffmans were very thorough in this regard. They had come up with a concise tactical operation order, clearly defining the mission down to the last detail. Rapp had worked with enough Special Forces types that he could tell that one or both of them had been with one of the military's elite units.

All notes would be burned before they left the cottage. The primary, secondary, and third radio frequencies all had to be memorized; the same went for the escape and evasion routes, passwords, and codes. Maps could be carried, but no markings could be made on them. All of their fake credentials were placed in flash bags. If things went really wrong, all they had to do was pull a string on the bag and its contents would be incinerated. Weapons were checked, rechecked, and checked again.

Rapp had a hard time putting his finger on it, but he didn't have a good feeling about this one. He reminded himself that there had been a mission early in his career about which he had felt great, and before all was said and done, a dozen U.S. commandos were dead. Ever since then he rarely felt confident about any mission, but there was something unusual that was gnawing at him about this one. Rapp could sense that he was losing a little bit of his edge. He had been an angry man for so many years, and he had always used that anger to sharpen his focus.

That anger was born in the aftermath of the Pan Am Lockerbie disaster. At the time, Rapp was attending Syracuse University. Thirty-five of his fellow students had died in the terrorist attack, and one of them was his girlfriend. During this period of intense grieving, Rapp was approached by the CIA. The Agency had dangled the prospect of revenge in Rapp's face, and he had jumped. The target of that revenge became Rafique Aziz, the person behind the terrorist attack on Pan Am Flight 103. Rapp had spent the last decade hunting the terrorist and had finally come face to face with him the previous spring. Aziz was now dead, and the anger was gone.

It had been replaced with something very different—an emotion Rapp didn't know he could still feel. Anna Rielly was now his focus, and what he felt for her was the opposite of hatred. She was one in a million. The type of woman who made you want to be a better man, and Rapp desperately wanted to be a better man. He wanted to put his life with the CIA behind him and move on.

Jane Hoffman removed her headphones and announced, "The first guests have arrived."

Rapp looked at his watch. It was five minutes to eight, about two and a half hours before show time. It was time to check in with Kennedy one more time. Rapp grabbed the COMSAT mobile phone by the handle and carried it to the bedroom.

IF DR. IRENE Kennedy had bothered to look out the window of her seventh-floor office, she would have noticed that the fall colors of the Potomac River Valley were at their peak. Unfortunately, there hadn't been much time of late to stop and take in life's little pleasures. Langley was on shaky ground—under assault from both external and internal forces. Word had leaked that Thomas Stansfield, the director of the CIA, was in poor health. The critics on Capitol Hill smelled blood and were on the move, and from within the Agency, massive egos were maneuvering for the directorship. Kennedy, never one to get involved in politics, was doing her best to stay out of the line of fire, but it was proving almost impossible. It was no secret that she and the director were very close.

Washington was a town that loved drama and gossip, and no one loved it more than the politicians. With the delight of brooding Shakespearean characters, they had started their deathwatch. Several of them had gone so far as to call, feigning concern for Stansfield and his children. Kennedy wasn't naive. Stansfield had taught her well. No one on Capitol Hill liked her boss. Many of the senators and representatives respected him, but none of them liked him. The seventy-nine-year-old director had never let any of them get close enough. As the deputy director of operations and then director of Central Intelligence, Stansfield had been the keeper of Washington's secrets for more than two decades. No one knew exactly how much he knew, and no one really wanted to find out. Some people were actually worried that he had been building thick dossiers on all of Washington's elite, so that upon his death he could wreak havoc from the grave.

This was not going to happen. Stansfield's entire professional life had been centered on keeping secrets. He was not about to break with that. This, of course, was of no comfort to those in Washington who had committed the most egregious sins. It was of no comfort because they couldn't imagine possessing such valuable information and not using it.

It was painful for Kennedy to cope with the slow death of her mentor, but she had to focus on the job at hand. The Orion Team had been given the go-ahead by the president of the United States to assassinate a private citizen, and not just any private citizen. Kennedy stared at the black-and-white photograph clipped to the dossier on her desk. The man was Count Heinrich Hagenmiller V, a German industrialist and cousin to the Krupp family. The fact that President Hayes was willing to authorize the assassination of a private citizen of one of America's closest allies spoke volumes about his new commitment to fight terrorism at every level.

Hagenmiller and his companies had first landed on the CIA's radar screen back in the early nineties. At the time, Kennedy was working on a project known as the Rabta II operation. Rabta II was a worldwide effort by the Agency to prevent Muammar al-Qaddafi from building a facility capable of producing biological, chemical, and nuclear weapons. The operation received its name from the original weapons facility that Qaddafi was building in the late eighties. The plant was located in the town of Rabta in northern Libya. In 1990, just before it was to start production, President Bush threatened to use air strikes and publicly identified the European companies that had helped build the factory. One of those companies was Hagenmiller Engineering.

Rather than see his dream bombed to the ground, Qaddafi closed the plant and began searching for a new place to set up shop. In early 1992, the CIA discovered the site of his new weapons plant. The Libyan dictator was trying to build the plant deep inside a mountain.

Once the facility was complete, it would be impregnable to everything except a direct strike by a nuclear warhead.

In an effort to stall the completion of the facility, the CIA launched Rabta II. They identified all equipment, technology, and personnel that would be crucial to the construction of the facility. With the help of its allies, the United States placed an embargo on all the items on the list. But as with all embargoes, Qaddafi and his people found ways around it. Since the inception of the operation, Hagenmiller Engineering and its subsidiaries had popped up several times. Each time they claimed they had no idea whom they were selling their goods to and walked away without even a token fine from the German government. Heinrich Hagenmiller was well connected. With Qaddafi fading from the international scene and seeming to mellow with age, the United States did not press the issue with the German government.

Kennedy flipped through the dossier, looking at a series of photos and the translated conversations that Hagenmiller had had with his newfound business associates. It was this new relationship that most concerned the CIA. Hagenmiller Engineering was, among many things, a manufacturer of high-tech lathes and other engineering components crucial to the building of a nuclear bomb.

On the next page were photos of the count's various homes. A brownstone in one of Hamburg's oldest neighborhoods, the family's estate an hour to the south, and a mountain retreat in Switzerland. Hagenmiller's family had rich royal roots and a lot of debt. Five months earlier Kennedy had consulted her counterpart in German foreign intelligence, the BFV, and he had told her the United States wasn't the only country inquiring about the count. He had recently received calls from the Israelis and the British. When questioned by the BFV just three months ago, Hagenmiller had sworn that he would personally oversee the sale of all sensitive equipment.

Kennedy didn't buy Hagenmiller's new promise and put him under the microscope. Hackers from the CIA compromised Hagenmiller Engineering's computer system and looked into the count's personal finances. A picture began to form of a man who had squandered the family's fortune. He was on his fourth wife, and the first three hadn't let him off easy. The heavy costs of maintaining the family's properties and his jet-setter lifestyle had drained the nest egg.

Two weeks earlier Kennedy had sent a tactical reconnaissance team to Germany to put Hagenmiller under twenty-four-hour surveillance. The team followed the count to Switzerland, and that was when things got really interesting. Kennedy studied a series of photos taken from the woods near Hagenmiller's mountain retreat. Some of the shots were grainy, but several of them were clear enough to make out the man Hagenmiller was meeting with. He was Abdullah Khatami. Khatami was a general in the Iraqi army, the man in charge of rebuilding its nuclear weapons program. He was also Saddam Hussein's cousin, and like many of Saddam's closest followers, he had grown a thick black mustache.

There were more incriminating photos, of Hagenmiller taking a briefcase from Khatami and then shaking hands. After their meeting was concluded, Hagenmiller drove to Geneva with his bodyguards and deposited the money in his bank. The following day the CIA's hackers got into the bank's computer system and discovered that five million dollars had been deposited in Hagenmiller's account.

Kennedy immediately ordered surveillance stepped up and went to the president with the mounting evidence. Hayes was looking for ways to fight Saddam but wanted to be absolutely sure that the count wasn't being duped. Kennedy's people found irrefutable evidence the following day. Sources had told them that at eleven o'clock this evening, Hamburg time, a staged break-in would occur at the Hagenmiller Engineering warehouse. Four computerized lathes and a variety of other equipment used in the production of highly sophisticated nuclear components would be stolen and loaded onto a waiting freighter at the German port of Cuxhaven.

Kennedy laid out the evidence before the president. Hagenmiller had already been warned twice and had promised he would personally make sure it didn't happen again. Despite the warnings and the promise, he was still willing to sell highly sensitive equipment to a person who was the world's number one sponsor of terrorism and who had sworn to wipe America off the face of the planet if given the chance. Hagenmiller had rolled the dice, and he was about to lose. President Hayes gave Kennedy the go-ahead. He had one requirement, however. With something as delicate as this, he wanted Mitch Rapp to be on the ground calling the shots.

Kennedy's phone rang, and she picked it up.

"Everything is in place."

She recognized the voice as Rapp's. "Give me a quick update."

Rapp ran down the checklist of developments and explained the final touches they had added to the plan. Kennedy listened and asked very few questions.

When Rapp was done, he asked, "If I miss him tonight, will I get another chance?"

"I doubt it. The second TRT is in place by the warehouse. As soon as the tangos show up, they will anonymously alert the German authorities and then follow until an arrest is made. Once that happens, the cat will be out of the bag on Hagenmiller, and there will be too many eyes watching him."

"Yeah, I agree." The TRT that Kennedy was referring to was a tactical reconnaissance team. They were the ones who had discovered the theft that was to occur at eleven P.M. Rapp knew that they were in place, but they did not know that Rapp was in the country.

Rapp said, "You need to alert us if the tangos move on the warehouse before eleven. The timing on this is crucial. We can't be pulling up to Hagenmiller's at the same time the police are on the phone telling him that he's been robbed. He expects to hear from the authorities tonight, and for the element of surprise, it's best that we are the first people to contact him."

"Understood." There was a moment of silence, and then Kennedy asked, "What's your gut telling you on this one?"

Rapp gripped the handset and looked around the

small bedroom, not sure if Kennedy was asking for the sake of asking or if she really wanted to know. Rapp replied tentatively. "I'm not sure. I would have liked a little more time to prep, but that's usually the case."

Rapp didn't sound like his confident self, and Kennedy picked up on it. "If it doesn't look good, don't force it."

"I know."

"No one back here is going to second-guess you."

Rapp laughed quietly. "That's never worried me before, why would it now?"

"You know what I mean. Just be careful."

"I always am." He was on autopilot.

"Anything else?" asked Kennedy.

"Yeah." Rapp paused. "This is it."

"What do you mean?"

"I'm done. This is the last one."

Kennedy knew this was coming, but now wasn't the time to talk about it. Mitch Rapp was a valuable asset, perhaps the most valuable asset on the team. It would not be easy to let him go. "We'll talk about it when you get back."

In a firm tone, Rapp said, "It's not up for debate."

"We'll talk."

"I'm serious."

Kennedy sighed into the receiver. It seemed as if the walls were closing in. One more thing to worry about. "There are some things you need to know before you make that decision."

Rapp read a little too far into the comment and said, "What in the hell is that supposed to mean?"

"Nothing." Kennedy sighed. She needed some sleep, she needed to spend some time with her son, and she needed to put things in order with Stansfield before he died. The fabric was starting to fray. "I just need to bring you up to speed on what's going on around here."

Rapp sensed that she was a little frazzled, which for Kennedy was a rarity. "All right. We'll talk when I get back."

"Thank you."

"No problem."

"Anything else?"

Rapp tried to think if he had missed anything. "Nope."

"All right . . . good luck, and keep me in the loop."

"You got it." Rapp placed the handset back in the cradle and ended the call. Leaning toward the window, he pulled back the curtain and looked out into the dark night. He couldn't shake the feeling in his stomach. Something wasn't right.

3

Senator Clark picked up the gavel, almost as an afterthought, and let it fall to the wooden block. Members of his committee were already out of their chairs and headed for the door. It was very unusual for senators to be working at all on a Friday, let alone into the late afternoon. But Washington was in the midst of a fall budget battle, and everybody was putting in the extra hours to try to find a way around the impending impasse. As was often the case, the Republicans wanted a tax break and the Democrats wanted to increase spending. The president, for a change, was actually trying to broker a compromise rather than exploit the situation, but neither party was willing to budge. The town was more partisan than ever. The polarization of special interests had left little room in the middle. You were either part of the solution or part of the problem. It was no longer okay to hold certain beliefs, no matter how well thought out. If you disagreed, you were the enemy. It had become a town of absolutes, and Senator Clark didn't like it. He had got into politics because it was the next mountain to climb, not because he enjoyed stubborn, senseless partisan agendas. It was beneath him, and it wasn't worth his time.

Hank Clark had been in the United States Senate for twenty-two years. He had thrown his hat into the ring after the Nixon resignation. Trust in politicians was at an all-time low, and the people of Arizona wanted an outsider. Someone who had made a name for himself. Hank Clark was their man. The new businessman of the West. A true self-made millionaire.

Henry Thomas Clark was born in Albuquerque, New Mexico, in 1941. His father failed at almost every business he tried, and with each failure his mother seemed to crawl a little further into the bottle. Vodka was her preference at first, poured liberally into screwdrivers and bloody marys. When times were really rough, she would drink bad whiskey and even a little Mad Dog 20/20. While Mom drank, Dad tried his hand at every nickel-and-dime job he could get. He sold ranching equipment, vacuum cleaners, used cars, aluminum siding, even windmills at one point. He failed miserably at each and every one of them, just as he had failed as a husband and a father. When Hank was eleven, his father quit for good. He went out back, behind their rented mobile home, and blew his brains out.

In a way, young Hank was relieved. With his father gone, he went after life with a determination to succeed. Hank took every spare job he could find and spent the next seven years trying to sober up his mother and find a way out of poverty. Fortunately for Hank, he had been blessed with many of the fine qualities his father lacked. He was good with people, was a tireless worker, and had an arm that could throw a wicked curve ball. That was Hank's ticket out. After high school he accepted a full ride to play baseball for the ASU Sundevils. Hank was a three-time all-Pac 10 pitcher and would have had a shot at the big leagues if it wasn't for a car accident his senior year. After college he took a job working for a resort in Scottsdale. It was at that resort, in the booming Phoenix suburb, where Hank Clark started to meet the right people. People who had vision. People who knew how to speculate on real estate.

At twenty-four Hank left the resort and went to work as a runner for a developer he had met. He loved helping to bring the deals together. He loved watching people with focus do something with their money. And most importantly, he loved the commissions. By the age of thirty Hank had made his first million, and by thirty-five he was worth more than twenty million dollars. Big, tall Hank Clark was the toast of Phoenix. The developer with the Midas touch. He had climbed one mountain, and now it was time for another.

That next mountain was politics, and after almost a quarter of a century Clark had decided it was insurmountable by any ethical means. The way to win in politics was to gain an edge over one's opponent and to do it by any means necessary, without letting him know what you were up to. Hank Clark wanted to be president, and he had been working toward that goal since the day he arrived in Washington in 1976.

As the senator rose from his chair, one of the committee's staffers approached and whispered, "Chairman Rudin is waiting for you in the bubble."

Clark nodded and handed the man his briefing book and materials. "Please take that back to my office for me." He then worked his way toward the door, wishing his fellow senators and their staffers a good weekend as he went. Hank Clark was the chairman of the Senate Select Committee on Intelligence. Most of the senators wanted to serve on the Armed Services, Appropriations, or Judiciary committees that got a lot of attention from the press. The intelligence committee wasn't one that they fought to get on, as it did much of its work behind closed doors.

The Senate Select Committee on Intelligence and the House Permanent Select Committee on Intelligence were charged with the oversight of the entire U.S. intelligence community, most notably the Central Intelligence Agency, the National Security Agency, and the National Reconnaissance Office. Clark was the man who kept an eye on the keepers of the secrets, and he had been methodically and quietly storing those secrets away.

Senator Clark left the committee room and started down the hall of the Hart Office Building. He smiled and nodded to the people he passed. Clark was a good politician. He made everyone feel special, even his enemies. He turned the corner, opened a door, and stepped into a small reception area. A Capitol Hill police officer was sitting on a stool next to a second door on the other side of the room. The man looked up and said, "Good afternoon, Mr. Chairman."

Clark offered an affable smile. "How are you holding up, Roy?"

"The old back is sore, sir, but I think I can make it another hour."

"Good." Clark patted him on the shoulder and punched in his code to the cipher lock beside the door. At the sound of the lock being released, he opened the door and stepped into room SH 219. Room 219 was one of the most secure rooms on the Hill. It was entirely encased in steel, making it impossible for electromagnetic waves to enter or leave. The room itself was divided into smaller rooms, each elevated off the floor so technicians could sweep beneath for bugs.

Senator Clark continued down the hall, passing several of the glass-enclosed briefing rooms, where the senators and a few select staffers received briefings from the various intelligence agencies. Near the end of the hall he approached another door with a touch pad. Clark punched in his personal five-digit code, and the door hissed as its airtight seal relaxed. He entered the elevated room and closed the door, the gasket expanding once again to its airtight position. Black blinds covered the room's four glass walls, and a sleek black oval conference table occupied the center of the fifteen-by-twenty-five-foot space. There was a place at the table for each of the committee's fifteen members. The glass-covered table had individual reading lamps for each senator and a computer monitor mounted at an angle under the glass. The room was dark except for one lone light at the far end.

From where he was standing, Senator Clark could see the thin, bony fingers of his counterpart in the House. Congressman Albert Rudin's hands were placed on the table under the soft light of one of the fifteen modern black lamps. Clark could barely make out Rudin's profile in the shadows, but it didn't matter. He had it memorized, and that profile could belong to one of only two people: either Congressman Albert Rudin, the chairman of the House Select Committee on Intelligence, or Ichabod Crane.

Clark continued to the far end of the room. "Good afternoon, Al."

Rudin didn't respond; and Clark didn't expect him to. Al Rudin was probably the most socially retarded politician in Washington. Clark grabbed a glass from the credenza behind the congressman and filled it with a couple of shots of Johnnie Walker scotch. The senator waved the drink in front of Rudin and asked if he'd like some. Rudin gruffly shook his head.

Albert Rudin was in his seventeenth term as a United States congressman. He was a Democrat to the bone and hated absolutely every single Republican in town with the possible exception of Senator Hank Clark. Rudin was a tireless party hack. He did whatever it took to perpetuate the party. If the party was embarrassed by a scandal where they were clearly in the wrong, it was Al Rudin they paraded out in front of the cameras. It was pretty much the same rhetoric every time. The Republicans want to starve your children, they want to give a tax break to their wealthy friends, they want to kick your parents out of their nursing home—it made no difference that the reporters were asking questions about possible felonies committed by a fellow Democrat; to Rudin, it was good versus evil. He represented good, and the Republicans represented evil, and the truth mattered not. This was a marathon, not a simple jog around the block. It was about beating the Republicans.

Hank Clark sank into the leather chair two over from Rudin and turned on the small reading lamp. After taking a long sip from his drink, he put his feet up on the chair between them and let out a long sigh. Clark weighed two-hundred-sixty pounds, and at six foot five he needed to take a load off his tired bones.

Rudin leaned over and said, "I'm worried about Langley."

Clark looked at him passively and thought, *No shit. When aren't you worried about Langley?* Rudin was obsessed with the CIA. If he had it his way, the Agency would be mothballed like an old battleship and placed in the Smithsonian. Despite thinking it, and wanting to say it just once, Clark was far too smart to let a sarcastic impulse get the best of him. It had taken him years to gain Rudin's confidence, and he wasn't going to piss it all away for one small moment of personal satisfaction.

Instead, Clark nodded thoughtfully and said, "Tell me what's on your mind."

Rudin shifted uncomfortably in his chair. "I don't want another insider to take over when Stansfield dies. Your committee should never have confirmed him in the first place." Rudin's face twisted in disgust as he talked about Thomas Stansfield. "We need to bring someone in who can clean that place up."

Clark nodded and said, "I agree," even though he didn't. He thought of reminding Rudin that Stansfield had been confirmed by a Democratic-controlled committee but thought it was best to keep him as calm as possible.

"The president is in love with that damn Irene Kennedy, and I know that bastard Stansfield is going to recommend her as his successor." Rudin shook his head. His deeply lined leathery skin turned red with anger. "And once she's nominated, it's over. The press and everybody in my party"—Rudin pointed a bony finger at Clark—"and yours is going to want to jump all over the idea of having a woman as the director of Central Intelligence." Rudin didn't want his position to be construed as politically incorrect, so he added, "Not that I would mind a woman, but not Stansfield's protégée. We have to do something to stop that from happening, and we have to take care of it before the president gets the ball rolling. Once that happens, we're screwed."

Clark studied Rudin for a moment and nodded slowly as if the crass old man had just imparted a rare pearl of wisdom. It was so easy to play him. "I've been keeping an eye on Kennedy, and I think she just might self-destruct before the process gets that far."

Rudin eyed the big man sitting next to him. "What information do you have that I don't?"

Clark let a big old grin crease his face and raised his drink. "If you're good to me, Albert, I just might let you see someday."

Rudin was mad at himself for asking the question. He knew firsthand that Hank Clark liked to keep tabs on people, friend and foe alike.

The old congressman from Connecticut scratched

his nose and asked, "What type of information are we talking about? Is it personal or professional?"

Clark smiled. "I think it would be considered professional."

Rudin scowled. He hated begging for details. Besides, he had learned a long time ago that Clark would tell him only when he was ready and not a moment before. Sniveling for info would do no good.

"I assume you will let me know when the time is right."

Clark nodded as he took a drink. "I'll keep you in the loop, Albert."

4

Mitch Rapp put the finishing touches on his makeup. A rinse dye had turned his black eyebrows and hair light brown. Special contacts transformed his dark brown eyes to blue, and the makeup made his olive complexion more pale. Rapp looked down at the black suit jacket and long black leather overcoat on the bed and checked his equipment one last time. The leather overcoat contained hidden compartments that were loaded with Rapp's premission laundry list. Near the bottom of the knee-length overcoat were three passports and ten thousand dollars in cash of various European currencies. One passport was American. It had Rapp's real photograph, an alias, and stamps indicating that he had entered the country through Dresden. The second passport was French and contained a photograph of Rapp with a goatee and short hair, and the third passport was Egyptian and contained no photograph. Each passport had a matching credit card. They were his way out of Germany if something went wrong. No one at Langley knew about them. If things fell apart, Rapp wanted to be able to disappear.

Rapp had memorized most of the main roads and railway lines that would get him out of the area, but he carried a tiny GPS unit the size of a deck of cards to make sure he knew his exact location. A matte-black combat knife was concealed in the right sleeve of the jacket, and four extra clips of 9-mm ammunition were stashed away in various places. In the back of the jacket was the newest model in the Motorola Saber line of handheld encrypted radios. To wear a headset in an urban environment was too obvious, so Rapp had developed a system. Threaded through the lining of the jacket were wires that led to a small speaker in the left collar, a microphone in the lapel, and volume and frequency controls in the sleeves. The jacket had a few other goodies that Rapp had ordered, bringing the total weight of the garment to twenty-three pounds.

His current credentials were in the left pocket of the suit coat. For this evening Rapp would be Carl Schnell of the Bundeskriminalant, or BKA. To its counterparts in English-speaking countries the organization was known as the Federal Office of Criminal Investigation. It was Germany's version of the FBI. The credentials would be his way past security and into the house.

Rapp grabbed his leather shoulder holster and put it on over his white dress shirt. Slung under his right arm was a 9-mm Glock pistol. The serial number had been removed from the weapon. Two extra clips of ammunition were stashed in the holster's pockets under his left arm. Each clip held fifteen rounds, and with four more clips stashed in the leather overcoat, Rapp had enough for a small battle. It was all for backup. He was planning on getting the job done with one shot.

Rapp slid on a pair of well-worn black leather gloves and picked up the long, sleek, silenced Ruger Mk II from the bed. It fired a .22-caliber cartridge and was almost completely silent. Its only drawback was that it was thirteen inches long. Rapp slid it into the specially designed pocket on the front right side of the overcoat and put on both jackets and a black fedora.

When he walked into the other room the Hoffmans were giving the cottage a once-over, wiping any areas where they might have left fingerprints. Rapp had already done the same in his room. When they were finished they grabbed two bulletproof vests and strapped them on before donning their overcoats.

Tom Hoffman looked at Rapp and asked, "Are you wearing any body armor?"

Rapp shook his head, frowning at the question, and said, "Come on, let's saddle up."

Taking his duffel bag, Rapp walked into the dark night and adjusted the brim of his hat. He stared up at the night sky and hoped this would be the last time. No matter how much he wanted it, though, something told him it wouldn't be.

Several moments later the Hoffmans came out of the cottage, and the three of them got into the maroon Audi sedan. All of the electronic surveillance and communications equipment was stowed in the trunk. Tom Hoffman was behind the wheel, and Jane was in the passenger seat. Mitch Rapp was in back. The Audi rolled gently down the rutted dirt road. It was pitch black in the forest, the trees blocking out what little moonlight there was. Rapp looked out the side window.

Even with the car's headlights on, he could see no more than twenty feet into the woods.

When they reached the paved road Rapp swallowed hard. The show was on, and they'd be at the front gate within minutes. His reservations about the mission had not gone away. He watched Tom Hoffman bring his right hand up and press his earpiece. He was plugged into the gear in the trunk and was monitoring the local police channels. Hoffman was to stay with the car, and Rapp and Jane Hoffman were to enter the house. Rapp needed one of the Hoffmans to come with him. They spoke flawless German, which he did not. His other reason for wanting to bring the wife with him was that a woman would be less threatening to Hagenmiller and his security. This was the one part of his plan that Tom Hoffman had protested. He wanted to be the one to go with Rapp.

Rapp was a little bit thrown by the intensity with which the man had challenged this. He had repeatedly stated that he would be more comfortable if he were the one who entered the house with Rapp. When pressed for a logical reason, Tom Hoffman couldn't come up with one. Again, something didn't seem quite right to Rapp. It was his mission, and he was calling the shots. He told the Hoffmans that he had the authority to pull the plug at any moment, and if they didn't agree with his plan, he would love nothing more than to call it quits. Rapp knew that the Hoffmans wouldn't get the second half of their money until they completed the mission, and he wanted to see just how badly they wanted that cash. He got his answer when they dropped the issue as if it had never meant a thing from the start.

Up ahead, a well-lit stone gatehouse came into view, and the sedan began to slow. Rapp checked his watch. It was nine minutes past eleven. The count would be surprised. Hagenmiller was sure to have gone over the timetables in his head. He wouldn't expect the police to show up in person at the estate this early but, rather, that they would simply call an hour or two after the break-in.

The sedan turned off the road and pulled up to the tall, ornate wrought-iron gate. A large man dressed in a dark suit and carrying a clipboard stepped from the gatehouse to the right side of the car. Rapp had already slid over to the left side to avoid getting his photograph taken from the surveillance camera mounted above the door to the gatehouse. He had also pulled the brim of his fedora down, making it difficult for the guard to get a good look at him. He took an immediate inventory of the man and noted the bulge on his right hip. It could be either a radio or a gun. Rapp decided it was probably a gun.

Jane Hoffman had her window down and was retrieving her forged Federal Office of Criminal Investigation ID. When the guard saw the badge, he stopped and didn't come any closer. In Germany, the former land of the Gestapo, the BKA commanded people's attention. Rapp was counting on this to get them in and out without too many questions. Jane Hoffman began to speak to the guard in a firm tone. The guard nodded and said that he would have to call up to the house first. She shook her head and told him that they did not wish to be announced. This had all been anticipated and rehearsed. The guard politely told her that Herr Hagenmiller was entertaining and that he would have to call up to the house before he could let them in.

She consented, but on the condition that he let them in and then make the call. Fortunately, the guard nodded and retreated to the stone building. The huge wrought-iron gate began to slide open, and the sedan sped forward. Rapp kept his eyes on the guard in the gatehouse as they passed. He was already on the phone.

"Step on it. The sooner we get there, the better."

The Audi accelerated up the winding asphalt driveway. When they came around the second bend, the house was visible, its white stone façade bathed in bright lights. Rapp had both hands on the front seats and was peering out the window. The place reminded him of some of the estates that had been built in Newport, Rhode Island, at the turn of the century.

Tom Hoffman slowed the car as it rounded the drive and came to a stop directly in front of two stone lions and a butler. Rapp got out of the car on the driver's side and looked at the huge marble fountain of Poseidon, water spewing from his trident. How fitting, he thought. The father of Orion. His eyes scanned an area to the left where a cluster of limousines were parked, the chauffeurs standing around talking. Beyond the limousines were about a dozen sports cars and luxury sedans. Rapp assumed they belonged to the less haughty guests. He filed away the existence of the cars and turned his attention to the house. He listened while Jane Hoffman spoke to the butler and showed him her ID. Rapp worked his way around the rear of the car, his eyes scanning the windows of the mansion. To the right was the ballroom. Through the three large windows, Rapp could see groups of men in tuxedos and women in full-length gowns drinking, talking, and smoking. He faintly heard what he thought must be a string quartet and couldn't help thinking to himself that this would be a party they would never forget.

Rapp shoved his BKA credentials in the butler's face and waved for Jane to follow. The butler was protesting vehemently as Rapp started up the steps. He couldn't understand everything the man was saying, but it was something about using a different entrance. Rapp continued to ignore him. He went up the first three steps and started across a tiled terrace that contained a fountain on the left and the right. Jane Hoffman appeared at his side, and the butler raced ahead of them. When they reached the large two wooden doors of the main entrance, the butler stopped and put his hands out like a traffic cop. Rapp had already sized the man up and checked him for weapons. There was no need to kill him; he had done nothing wrong. If needed, a quick jab to the chin would easily put the servant out of commission.

Rapp listened as the butler pleaded with Jane Hoffman. As expected, he was recommending that they wait in the study for Herr Hagenmiller. She conceded to the request but told the butler that they would wait no more than one minute, not a second longer. If Herr Hagenmiller did not come to them, they would go question him in front of his guests. The butler nodded over and over in an attempt to make it crystal clear that he knew exactly what they wanted. They knew that the man would prefer anything to having two BKA agents burst into his employer's private party.

The doors were opened, and they stepped into the huge foyer of the nineteen-thousand-square-foot mansion. Straight ahead a heart-shaped marble staircase led to the second story, and to the right a massive pair of ten-foot oak French doors led to the ballroom. Standing in front of the doors was an equally massive man. Rapp eyed the bodyguard from head to toe. It would take more than a jab to put this one out of commission. Rapp had seen the slab of beef in the surveillance photos. Hagenmiller wasn't the smartest man in town, but he also wasn't an outright idiot. He knew enough to have some protection when dealing with someone as unstable as Saddam Hussein.

The butler gestured to the left, to another set of large French doors. Rapp knew from the floor plans that they led to the study. When Rapp and Hoffman started for the door, the butler moved ahead and showed them the way. Once they were inside, he told them to wait and closed the doors. Rapp looked at Hoffman briefly and then checked out the room. It was more like a library than a study. There was a spiral staircase in the opposite corner that led to a balcony which ran along the three interior walls. Old leather-bound books filled the shelves up top, and down below were quite a few more. Elaborately framed oil paintings, some as tall as Rapp and others no bigger than his hand, adorned every square inch of the walls that weren't occupied by the bookshelves. On the far wall a roaring fire burned in the room's ornate fireplace. Rapp was not an art expert, but the collection of paintings had to be worth millions. Rapp turned his attention to the furniture and then the rugs. Everything in the room, with the exception of a few lamps, looked to be at least a hundred years old.

That's great, Rapp thought to himself. *The guy is born into the lucky sperm club, pisses away his inheritance, and then, rather than auction off some of his expensive possessions, he decides to sell highly sensitive technology to a sadistically crazed psychopath who would love nothing more than to drop a nuclear bomb on New York City. This prick deserves to die.*

Rapp checked his watch. Two minutes and three seconds had elapsed since they had come through the gate. Rapp glanced out one of the room's two large windows that looked down onto the main driveway. Tom Hoffman was standing beside the Audi, the engine still running. Hoffman gave Rapp a quick wave, and Rapp returned the gesture. Rapp looked at his watch again. They had been in the den for thirty-eight seconds. Rapp had set the limit at two minutes. After that, he would go find the count. There was no sense in letting him get on the phone and try to find out what was going on. Rapp walked across the room and put one eye up to the small gap in the middle of the French doors. At first he couldn't see much, and then he realized why. The beefy bodyguard had taken up his post outside the study and was blocking his view.

Rapp stepped back and frowned, trying to think of ways to take the bodyguard out without having to kill him. To knock him out, he'd have to get close, and with a neck as thick as the bodyguard's, Rapp's best shot might serve only to enrage the man. The last thing he wanted to do was get into a wrestling match. Rapp decided he would keep his distance and play it by ear.

It was nearing the three-minute mark when the study doors opened and Heinrich Hagenmiller V entered the room. He was holding a glass of champagne in one hand and a cigarette in the other. Obviously, no one had bothered to tell the count that smoking had become impolitic. Take away the man's hand-tailored tuxedo, his Rolex, his slicked-back hair, and his chin tuck, and he was no different from any other terrorist.

To Rapp's dismay, a second man followed the count into the room. He was about the same age and size as Hagenmiller and was also wearing a tuxedo. The walking mountain of a bodyguard also entered, and then the butler left, closing the doors for privacy.

With a look of complete shock, the count asked why in the world the BKA would be paying him a house call. Jane Hoffman began answering Hagenmiller in his native tongue, going along with the cover story they had rehearsed. Not more than two lines into it, the second man stepped forward and announced forcefully that he was the count's attorney and that he would like to see some ID.

Rapp was following the conversation closely, but he had kept most of his attention on the bodyguard. The man stood like a sphinx off to the side, his arms folded across his chest. Hoffman was between Rapp and the door. Directly across from Rapp was the count, and on his right were the lawyer and the bodyguard. When the lawyer stepped forward and asked to see credentials, Rapp made up his mind. Every second they hung around was a chance for something to go wrong.

As he started to slide his left hand into his jacket, Rapp glanced to his right to see Jane Hoffman pulling out her fake BKA identification. His hand eased into the hidden pocket and grasped the Ruger Mk II. Turning his body to the left, he extracted the silenced .22-caliber and extended his arm.

The count was no more than four feet away from the tip of the extended weapon. Rapp squeezed the trigger once, and a bullet spat from the end of the long black barrel. Instantly, a red dot appeared between the count's neatly trimmed eyebrows. Rapp did not pause to watch the man fall—he knew he was already dead. He switched the Ruger from his left hand to his right, took one step forward, and delivered a vicious left hook to the attorney's jaw. The man tumbled to the side and back, almost taking out the bodyguard as his unconscious body rolled across the floor. With the Ruger still in his right hand, Rapp took a step back, gaining some distance between himself and the bodyguard. The man was already taking his first step toward him, reaching for his gun.

Rapp yelled, "Halt!" but the bodyguard kept reaching.

He had only a split second to think. He fired a second shot—this one hit the bodyguard in the wrist, and his heavy semiautomatic pistol thudded to the floor. The man instantly bent over in pain, grabbing his wrist with his other hand. Rapp took two big steps and kicked at the man's face as if he were punting a football. The blow sent the three-hundred-pound bodyguard reeling back, land-

ing him on top of a small wooden end table with a porce-
lain lamp delicately perched atop its polished wood
surface. The lamp shattered as it hit the wood floor, and
the table splintered into a dozen pieces under the weight
of the heavy man.

Rapp pushed Hoffman out of the way and bounded
for the door. Just as he got there, it opened, and the small
head of the butler appeared. Rapp grabbed the man by
the tie and yanked him into the room. Taking the butt
end of the Ruger, he smashed it down on the butler's
temple with far less force than he normally would have.
The butler's eyes rolled back into his head, and his knees
went limp. Rapp released his grip from the man's throat
and let him slump to the floor. Next, he stuck his head
into the hallway to see if anybody was watching and then
closed and locked the door.

He moved across the room like a machine. His first
priority was the bodyguard. After grabbing three pairs of
plastic flex cuffs from his pocket, he turned to hand one
of them to Jane Hoffman and froze in his tracks.

In that one fleeting moment, Rapp couldn't believe
what he was seeing. The words fell from his lips in slow
motion. "What in the hell are you doing?"

Rapp barely got the words out of his mouth before
Jane Hoffman fired the first shot from the end of the
suppressed Heckler & Koch P7. The 9-mm parabellum
round hit Rapp square in the chest and put him back on
his heels. The second shot propelled him back over the
legs of the bodyguard. The air was gone from his lungs
as his ass hit the floor, and his upper body fell back,
sending his head with a whiplash effect toward the bot-

tom rung of a wooden library ladder. Rapp's head hit with tremendous force, his eyes rolled back into his head, and his entire body went limp.

Jane Hoffman's heart was racing, and her hands were shaking. It was her husband who was supposed to be in here, and she was supposed to be out in the car. With her gloved hand, she picked up Rapp's Ruger from the floor and shot the bodyguard twice in the chest. She tossed the Ruger over by Rapp's body and then detached the silencer from the end of her pistol. When she was done, she placed her own gun in the bodyguard's hand. Grabbing a small canister from her pocket, she sprayed a fine mist of gunpowder residue onto the bodyguard's hand so it would appear that he had fired the weapon. She stood and backed up. She was looking for something. On the floor by her right foot, she found it: the bodyguard's Heckler & Koch pistol. She picked it up and put it in her holster.

Relieved to be done, she ran to the door, unlocked it, and stepped out into the foyer. She walked quickly to the front door, the joyous sounds of the party spilling forth from the ballroom, no one the wiser to what had just happened. Jane Hoffman was outside and down the steps in seconds. Her husband was nervously waiting for her behind the wheel of the sedan, and the second she was in the car, he sped down the driveway.

5

The man stood near the edge of the forest not more than a hundred yards from where Rapp had been the night before. From his elevated position, he could clearly see the front of the mansion. He had one hand against his left ear and was holding a small pair of binoculars in his right hand. A coil ran from his earpiece down under the collar of his dark brown jacket and was attached to a Motorola Saber encrypted radio. He listened with great interest to what was going on inside the house. It had already started. He had heard the surprise in Rapp's voice at the sudden turn of events. Now he was waiting for the woman to exit the mansion. If she didn't make it out alive, that was fine, but if she was merely wounded, that was not acceptable. No one could be left alive to talk. He was under strict orders.

It had to look as if Rapp had been killed by the bodyguard. Hagenmiller must die first and then Rapp. If the Jansens could pull it off and make things look convincing, they would live. If they screwed up in the slightest way, they would be eliminated. That was why he was there—to manage the situation closely.

The bearded man standing in the woods was a former employee of the CIA. He was known by a few close friends as the Professor. His real name was Peter Cameron. At first glance, he was not the type of person you would expect to find in this line of work. In his late forties and a good thirty pounds overweight, he was not about to get physical with an adversary. But that had never been his style. Cameron managed situations from a discreet distance, and if he needed to intercede, it was always done with his right index finger, not his fists. He was an expert marksman and believed fervently that the easiest way to kill a man was with a bullet. More often than not, though, he was a voyeur—a man who worked behind the scenes and watched from the shadows. Cameron dispatched the assassins, and more and more, he had enjoyed the thrill of going into the field and watching things develop. It was far more interesting than sitting behind a desk at Langley and getting briefed via satellite uplink. Cameron needed to be on top of every detail, and he couldn't do that from the other side of the Atlantic. A lot was riding on this mission. An incredible amount, really.

Cameron had heard murmurs about the man they called Iron Man, and *if* the stories were only half true, Mitch Rapp was amazing. Cameron admired him for his skill and determination. In a raw egotistical way, he was excited about being the person responsible for taking down someone as strong as Rapp. Yes, there was a little bit of guilt involved in killing an asset who had served the Agency so well, but like many others, Rapp was just another pawn, another foot soldier, who in the end was expendable. History was full of them, and in truth, that was why Cameron had left Langley. He had been shown the path by someone who truly valued his talents, someone who was willing to reward him for his years of hard work.

Cameron tensed as he saw the front door of the mansion open. He brought the binoculars up to his eyes and zeroed in on the area. He breathed a slight sigh of relief as he saw Beth Jansen race down the steps and into the waiting car. As the Audi sped away, Cameron checked the front door to make sure no one was following, and then he watched the car go down the winding driveway. As it neared the gate, Cameron could hear the horn honk and see the headlights flash. Before the car had come to a complete stop, the gate opened. When the car pulled onto the road, Cameron nodded his approval and turned his attention back to the mansion. He watched it for several minutes, looking for a sign that the murders had been discovered. There was nothing.

Pleased with the results, Cameron placed the binoculars in his pocket and began to pick his way through the branches and undergrowth. A few seconds later, he found one of the walking paths and started for the dirt road. Unlike the previous evening, he was the only one in the forest tonight. That had been close. He had almost blown it. His ego had gotten the best of him, and he had decided to try to stalk Rapp. His skills in the forest were amateurish compared with Rapp's. He didn't even get close. Cameron had followed him with night-vision goggles, and when he was barely close enough to see Rapp, the man had stopped and disappeared into the forest. Cameron had stood frozen for more than twenty minutes, afraid that Rapp was doubling back on him. It was the first time he had felt true fear in many years.

Cameron would have liked to have gone up against Rapp in an urban environment. He felt confident he would have the advantage on the busy streets of Washington, where he had practiced his spy craft for decades. That would have been a real pleasure, to have hunted Rapp in Washington. Cameron smiled and shook his head as he walked—happy that the mission was a success and a little disappointed that he would never again experience the thrill of stalking Rapp.

As Cameron neared the dirt road, he veered off the path and found his transportation. Underneath some camouflage netting was a black BMW K 1200LT motorcycle. Cameron folded up the netting and placed it in one of the saddlebags. Then, after wheeling the bike back out onto the path, he put on a helmet and started the sleek machine. Its powerful headlamp lit up the path ahead. As it purred to life, he climbed on and slipped the bike into gear. Cameron slowly moved onto the dirt road and turned toward the cottage, in the opposite direction from the way the Jansens were headed. If everything went according to plan, he'd see them at the airstrip in another twenty minutes. The mission was a success.

HIS EYELIDS FLUTTERED and then snapped open. Mitch Rapp tried to focus, but his vision was blurred. His senses were coming back slowly, one at a time, like a computer booting up programs. His sense of smell came on-line first, the burnt odor of gunpowder filling his nostrils, and then there was a thumping noise, coming from where he did not know. Slowly, he let out a noise that started as a groan and ended as a growl. Rapp tried to move, but the pain was excruciating—in both his head and his chest.

He lay on his back staring up at the ceiling, trying to figure out where he was and what was wrong. The glaze on his eyes began to clear, and then it hit him. Rapp's first reaction was to try to sit up. His head was barely an inch off the floor when sharp pains shot through his chest, forcing him to give up. Looking back at the ceiling, he brought his right hand up to his chest and felt under the folds of the heavy black leather coat. He pulled his gloved hand out and looked at it for signs of blood. The leather was dry—no blood. Forcing himself to ignore the pain, Rapp rolled onto his left side, and from there he got up on one knee and looked around the room.

"That fucking bitch," he mumbled to himself. His head was still cloudy, but things were coming back to him. Rapp ran his fingers along the outside of the leather jacket and felt the two slugs that had been caught by the Kevlar liner. Rapp remembered them asking him in the cottage if he was wearing any body armor. The way they asked the question at the time seemed unusual, and now he knew why. *Thank God she didn't shoot me in the head,* he thought.

Remembering that he had started his stopwatch when they passed through the gate, Rapp looked at the watch to find out how much time had passed. He stared in disbelief as he realized he had been out for nearly four minutes. A new sense of urgency kicked in as he looked at the other bodies strewn about the room. Rapp started to stand and had to reach out and grab the edge of the desk to keep from falling over. When he'd steadied himself, he checked the back of his head and was confronted with a black leather glove shiny with blood. He looked at the floor where he'd been, and sure enough, there was a pool of blood the size of a dinner plate. Rapp cursed as he looked around the room. If things weren't bad enough, he now had to clean up his blood; leaving it behind would be worse than a thousand sets of fingerprints. Rapp knew he had to move, and move fast, if he was going to make it out. There were a lot of questions to be answered, but they would all have to wait. Right now, it was Psychology 101—Maslow's Hierarchy of Needs—*survival.*

Ignoring the stabbing pain in his chest and the throbbing welt on the back of his head, he knelt down and picked up his Ruger pistol. While grabbing the gun, he noticed the bodyguard had been shot. Rapp filed it away and moved on, checking the room for any other evidence that might tie him to Hagenmiller's death. He checked the lawyer and the butler and was relieved to find that they were still breathing. He moved to the main doors, locked them, and then went to the windows to check the driveway below. As he expected, the Audi was gone. With his back against the wall, Rapp looked around the room and scrambled to come up with a plan. He needed to get rid of the blood, and just wiping it up wouldn't do the trick. Fear of getting caught was helping to clear his mind. After a few seconds his eyes fell on the fireplace, and then he looked around at all of the expensive artwork. He didn't want to do it, but he saw no other solution. Rapp recalled the mansion's floor plan and looked to the study's other set of doors. They led to the game room and then through another door to the solarium. From there he could get outside onto the grounds near where the limousines and cars were parked. The decision was made in a split second.

Rapp moved across the room to a collection of crystal bottles sitting in the middle of a sterling silver tray. He pulled the top off one of the bottles, brought it under his nose, and got a stiff whiff of cognac. Rapp took a swig from the bottle and then walked over to the pool of blood, dousing the area and then the bodies of Hagenmiller and the bodyguard. With the remaining bottles he began soaking the rug, curtains, and whatever else he could think of. He raced over to the fireplace, took a stick of kindling from an old brass kettle, and stuck it into the flames. Seconds later the skinny piece of birch was aglow. Rapp took one lap around the room, lighting everything that had been doused in alcohol, and then tossed the stick of wood into the far corner.

Rapp grabbed the butler by the shirt collar and dragged him across the floor to the doors by the game room. He did the same with the lawyer, who was starting to stir. Flames were licking their way up the wall, and the heat was rising rapidly. Rapp burst through the doors into the game room and dragged the two men in with him. He stopped for just a second to catch his breath, worried that one of his ribs was probably broken. He told himself there was nothing he could do about it right now and then moved to lock the doors to the study from the inside. He took one last look around—the bodies were completely engulfed in flames, and the fire was spreading rapidly. Rapp pulled the door shut and ran across the long room, past the billiards table, the stuffed heads of exotic animals, a suit of armor, and finally an antique wood bar.

He stopped at the next door, listened for a second, then opened it and checked the hallway. To his right he could hear voices coming from the general direction of the kitchen and the main hallway. He stepped into the hallway, pulling the door closed behind him, and moved quickly through the open glass doors of the solarium.

The room was an annex that had been added thirty years after the original construction. The three exterior walls were dominated by large sheets of paned glass that ran fifteen feet from the floor to the ceiling. Plants and wicker furniture were arranged in various patterns to give visitors the impression of walking through a garden. Bright lights shone down from above so the guests could take in the brilliance of the room from the circular drive as they arrived and departed.

Rapp quickly extinguished the lights and checked back down the hall toward the kitchen. There were still no signs that the fire had been discovered. He moved across the solarium, crouching behind various plants. When he reached one of the patio doors, he looked beyond a row of hedges where a group of limousines were parked. The drivers stood around smoking and playing cards. Rapp needed to get past them to the other cars that had been driven by the guests. He hoped a valet might have been kind enough to leave the keys in the ignition.

The shouts came from the direction of the kitchen at first, and then almost instantly the limousine drivers noticed something was wrong. The drivers ran toward the front door of the mansion to investigate. Rapp sprang from the solarium and ran across the patio, his chest aching with each breath of air. He went down the steps to the crushed-rock driveway, shot to the right, and ran past the limousines. The first car he passed was a Jaguar. Rapp didn't bother to check for keys. He needed something that would blend in a little better, preferably something that was made in Germany. Next was a red Mercedes-Benz; he passed on that one, too, but stopped at the third, a black Mercedes coupe. Rapp breathed a sigh of relief as the door opened and he saw the keys dangling from the ignition.

The car started, and Rapp eyed the gas gauge as it rose to two-thirds of a tank. He was in luck. Rapp shifted the car into first gear, and instead of pulling out onto the driveway, he turned the opposite way onto the grass. He drove the car across the side lawn toward the rear of the house. He looked over to his right to see if anyone had noticed him. Everyone appeared to be focused on the fire. The headlights lit the way as the sporty car picked up speed across the level, plush lawn. Rapp got a little too anxious with the accelerator several times, and the wheels spun out on the dew-covered grass.

Rapp never went anywhere without an escape plan,

and this was no exception. From the moment he arrived, he had started memorizing avenues of escape. He knew where the adjoining roads led, the nearest train stations and airfields, anything that would help him get away as quickly as possible if things went wrong—and something had gone horribly wrong tonight. He couldn't even begin to imagine how he had been set up. Rapp smashed his fist down on the leather steering wheel and swore at himself for ignoring the warning signs that were now so obvious.

He turned the car onto one of the walking paths that cut through the large garden in the backyard. It occurred to him that the roof-mounted security cameras were undoubtedly recording his movements, but he discarded the worry after only a second. The fire would keep everyone busy for quite some time. He reached the end of the large garden, and the car gained speed as it cut across another large swatch of grass and the tires found the soft gravel of a horse trail. Rapp shifted the car into third gear and then fourth. With the car climbing above sixty miles an hour, he checked the odometer and noted how far he would have to travel before the first turn.

The road rolled down and away from the mansion, and Rapp kept his focus on the path ahead, heading for the small bridge that would get him over a creek that separated the manicured lawn from the forest. Moments later, the car flew over a short wood bridge, its side mirrors inches away from clipping the railings. Rapp slowed, looking for a turn that, according to the satellite photos he'd studied, should be coming up on his right. Rapp glimpsed the fork and, downshifting, shot up a small hill and into the woods.

It was a little over a mile to the first paved road. Rapp eased off the accelerator, reminding himself that the twenty or thirty seconds gained by racing through the woods would be quickly negated if he slammed into a tree. As the car bounced its way along the winding, rutted path, Rapp began to run through his options. Denmark was one hundred miles to the north, and the Netherlands was one hundred miles due west. Rapp wasn't crazy about going to either country. The subtle nuances of their language and culture were not second nature to him as they were in the countries to the south. Italy was an option. There was someone in Milan, someone who had been special to him once. Kennedy knew about her. She was former Mossad, Israeli intelligence, and still might be, for all Rapp knew. People in his line of work were never fully retired. Intelligence agencies had a way of hanging on to you whether you wanted them to or not. But Rapp could trust her. They had a bond that went beyond oaths to countries and organizations. They were the same person. Rapp knew he couldn't go to her, though. Not now, not with Anna in the picture. If he went to Milan, he would end up in her bed. Milan would have to be a last resort.

France was the best choice. Rapp had safe deposit boxes in Paris, Marseille, and Lyon. Boxes no one at the Agency knew about. In France, there were friends he had made through his consulting business and his days as a triathlete, people he could trust from a life he had intentionally kept secret from his handlers. Not even Kennedy knew about the precautions he had set up.

Rapp downshifted into second gear and maneuvered the car through a sharp turn. The road snapped back around to the left and continued its meandering way through the forest. As he plotted the course ahead, he thought about Irene Kennedy. What was it in her voice when they had talked? Could it have been guilt over sending him to his death? Rapp shook his head. That was impossible. They were like family. Kennedy would never set him up. It had to be someone else, but who? Very few people knew about the Orion Team, and even fewer knew about this mission.

The car finally reached the firm traction of black asphalt. Rapp looked to the north and then the south. He hesitated for only a second and then turned the car toward Hanover, away from Hamburg. The E4 autobahn was only four miles away, and once he got there, Rapp could be on the other side of Hanover in less than forty minutes. From there, it was another hour and a half to Frankfurt. With the fire raging back at the estate, it would take at least an hour, he hoped, for them to discover that the car he was driving was missing, and even then they might not realize the importance of it. One thing was certain, however: when the German federal police found out that the assassins had gained access to the estate by posing as BKA agents, a dragnet would be thrown the likes of which the country probably hadn't seen since the old divided days of east and west. Radios moved much faster than cars, and that meant he might have to part company with his new wheels before Frankfurt.

The car flew down the road at more than eighty miles an hour. Rapp ignored the pain in his chest and his throbbing headache and focused on the problem. He had to disappear. He had to get out of Germany and find out who in the hell had set him up. A frightening thought gripped Rapp, driving him to near panic. Cursing, he pushed the accelerator all the way to the floor. There was a problem that needed to be dealt with immediately. Rapp weighed the risks of making the call from his digital phone. No, there were too many security issues. As much as he hated the delay, the call would have to wait.

6

Anna Rielly unlocked the front door of the small cottage-style home. Behind her, the day's final shadows were stretching across the rolling Maryland countryside. She was happy to be out of the city after another hectic week of following the president. When she took the job as White House correspondent for NBC, she had never fully imagined how much running around it would entail. She stepped into the entryway, setting her black purse and an overnight bag down on the bench to her right. As she hung her coat in the closet, she noticed one of Mitch's draped over the banister and hung it up, too.

Rielly grinned to herself as she started up the stairs. Mitch Rapp had lived alone for too many years. In the master bedroom, she dropped her overnight bag to the hardwood floor with a thump and began working the buttons of her blue blouse. She walked over to the French doors that looked out over the Chesapeake Bay and sighed. Rielly doubted she would ever tire of the view. She adored the cottage—it spoke volumes about the man she had fallen in love with—the man she wanted to spend the rest of her life with. Rielly stripped down to

her underwear and discarded her bra with the hope that
she wouldn't have to put one back on until she left for
work on Monday morning.

She looked out at the bay, enjoying the last reflections
of Friday's light, and then glimpsed herself in the closet
mirror to her right. At thirty, her body was even better
than when she had played volleyball for the University of
Michigan. She knew this was in great part the result of a
diet that was completely void of junk food, three or four
weekly workouts, and, most importantly, her mother's
genes. There was one other thing that had added more
than a little extra tone in the waning months of summer.
Rielly brought her right arm up into a curl and smiled at
the definition of her biceps. Then she ran a hand along
her rock-hard right thigh and traced a finger along the
vertical line that separated the hamstring from the quad-
riceps. As part of her new commitment to enjoy life
more, she had purchased a Mastercraft ski boat back in
June. Rielly, a Chicago native, had spent her summers on
Lake Poygan in Wisconsin and was slaloming by the age
of six. Mitch and Anna had spent a good three months
carving up the glassy early-morning and late-evening
water of the bay. There was no workout she could think
of that could so tire the body and at the same time so
awaken the mind.

Anna slid her hands around to her waist and tried to
stick out as much belly as her little frame would allow.
A soft smile covered her face as she imagined herself
pregnant. Her best friend was due in four months, and
Anna called to get daily updates. Mitch had whispered
his hopes of a baby in her ear on more than one occa-

sion, and she had always responded the same way, telling him that he had his priorities in the wrong order. Marriage came first and then the baby.

Rielly threw on a pair of old faded Levi's, brown leather Cole-Haan slides, and one of Mitch's worn and tattered sweatshirts. After grabbing a black scrunchie from the drawer of the bedside night table, she pulled her brown hair back in a ponytail and started downstairs. Mitch had gutted the first floor of the cottage, getting rid of the dining room and creating a space that flowed from kitchen to eating area to family room. Rielly went into the kitchen, grabbed a beer from the fridge, and then realized she had forgotten her book upstairs. She ran up, got the book, came back down, and went out onto the deck. She stood at the railing for a moment, looking out over the water, savoring the cold beer.

Sinking back into one of the Adirondack chairs, she crossed her legs and opened her book. A coworker had talked Rielly into joining a book club when she moved to D.C. At the time, she thought it would be a good idea. She was looking for ways to restore some normalcy to her life after the tragic events that had taken place at the White House during the first days of her new posting. Now, after five straight book club selections, she wasn't so sure she could handle another novel about a dysfunctional woman whose life was a mess because her father never gave her the attention she deserved. The first month it was great, the second it was okay, the third was tolerable, the fourth barely tolerable, and this fifth was going to be her last try. The group was meeting on Monday night, and Rielly hadn't even had time to read the jacket copy. After a big swig of beer, she cracked the book and started in.

Five minutes later, Rielly finished the first chapter and closed the book. The author had just described in graphic detail how she had watched her father beat her mother to within an inch of her life when she was just six years old. Not another one, Rielly told herself. As she got out of the chair, she decided she would have to miss the meeting on Monday night. Anna headed back into the living room with her beer and put the book back on the shelf. She scanned the CD collection and decided on a live Dave Matthews album. With beer in hand, she began searching the bookshelves for something else. Mitch read a book a week and had built up a big collection of both fiction and nonfiction. After only a few minutes, she hit pay dirt. Nelson DeMille's newest novel sat on the shelf with all of his previous works. She headed for the fridge to grab another beer and then back out onto the porch. One of DeMille's smart-ass, wisecracking heroes was exactly what she was in the mood for.

It was the perfect thing to take her mind off Mitch, where he was, and what he was doing. He had promised her that this would be it. This was his last mission, and then they would go about the business of leading normal lives. Rielly looked out at the calming waters of the Chesapeake with her green eyes and said a quick prayer for Mitch; that he was all right and that he would return to her by morning's first light. Rielly opened the book and started in—determined to lose herself in its pages.

* * *

THE SIGNS HAD caused him to rethink his plans. One never succeeded in this business without taking risks, but the trick was knowing how far to push it. If he blew past Hanover, there was no turning back. There would be a one-hour window during which he would be stuck on the autobahn, racing to make it to Essen, where he could ditch the car. If the call went out over police radio, he'd be a sitting duck. Another sign appeared on his right indicating that the exit for the Hanover international airport lay one kilometer ahead.

Rapp was used to operating alone. He had no need to discuss his options with anyone. His mind ran quickly down the list in almost the same way a naval aviator runs down his list of options when an engine flames out sixty miles from the deck of a carrier. There was no reason to panic—it was just a problem to be solved as quickly and efficiently as possible. Rapp checked his mirrors and flipped the turn signal up. As the Mercedes banked through the exit, he pulled the brim of his hat down another inch. Airports were always loaded with surveillance cameras, and after they found the car, the tapes would be reviewed by Germany's best counterterrorism experts.

His breathing had calmed over the last thirty minutes. Rapp was pretty confident that his ribs were bruised but not broken. If it were the latter, his breathing would be short and extremely painful. He followed the signs to the parking garage and stopped at the green gate to grab his ticket. To his right, under a large halogen light pole, Rapp noted the tinted bubble of a surveillance pod. Inside the dark plexiglas, he knew a camera was recording his arrival. Rapp rolled the window down and with his gloved hand grabbed the time-stamped ticket. When the gate's arm popped up, he shifted the car into first and started up the spiraled concrete ramp. He passed the first and second levels and pulled into the third. Driving slowly up and down the aisles, he checked for more surveillance cameras and was pleased to discover none. Rapp backed the car into a spot between two other Mercedes and rolled the driver's-side window down several inches. Then, leaving the keys on the floor of the front seat, he got out and left the car unlocked. With any luck, it would be stolen before the police could find it, but he doubted it. Following the signs to the terminal, Rapp intentionally walked with a limp and hunched shoulders. With the brim of his hat down, he kept a lookout for more cameras.

As he entered the terminal, he saw several instantly. They were right where they always were, high above and looking down on the masses of people. Unfortunately, the masses weren't there at a quarter past midnight. When they found the car, they would discover him on the tapes shortly thereafter. That was why he was walking with a limp and hunched shoulders. For good measure, he wrapped his right arm across his body and let his left arm hang limp. This served two purposes: first, to disguise his height and walk; second, to make them think he was wounded. Maybe they would waste some of their resources looking for him in clinics.

He looked for the baggage claim signs and took the

escalator down one more level. Only one of the carousels was crowded with passengers from a recent arrival; the others were empty. Rapp went to the busy carousel, meandered about for a minute as if he was looking for his wife, and then walked out the door to the cab stand. Seven cabs were lined up, and when Rapp raised his hand, the first one in line pulled up twenty feet to his spot on the curb. Rapp sank into the back seat and pulled out his wallet. A quick glance at the dashboard told him the tank was full. In German he asked the man how much it would cost to take him to Essen, about an hour and a half one way. The cab driver smiled at the opportunity. Rapp paid the man and thanked him with a good tip. Before replacing his wallet, he took out some additional cash. As he eased back into the seat, his left hand slid under his jacket and found the grip of his 9-mm Glock.

The car pulled away from the curb, and the cab driver radioed his dispatcher that he had a fare to Essen and would check in after he dropped off his passenger. When they had cleared the airport and were back on the autobahn, Rapp slid forward, switching his gun from his left hand to his right. He placed the tip of the pistol against the back of the driver's head and in German told him to keep both hands on the steering wheel.

The driver, a tall, thin man who was close to forty, stiffened at the sudden development but kept his hands on the steering wheel. The man was a heavy smoker. Rapp could smell it on his clothes and his hair.

"If you do exactly as I say, nothing will happen to you. If you fuck up, just once, I'll put a bullet in your head and dump you in a ditch." Rapp didn't raise his voice; he wasn't sure what words to stress in German, so he pressed the tip of the gun into the man's head and said, "Am I making myself clear?"

The driver nodded his head slowly. "Good," Rapp replied. With his left hand, he took the cash he'd held and stuck it in front of the man's face. "Take it. We are not going to Essen. You're taking me to Frankfurt."

After taking the money, the cab driver nodded slowly, and Rapp pulled the gun back an inch, allowing the man to straighten his head. Rapp checked the driver's credentials on the glove box. His name was Geoffrey Herman.

"Geoffrey, you're going too slow. Speed it up, and keep your eyes on the road." Rapp watched the speedometer and asked, "Ever had this happen before?"

The driver nodded his head and croaked his reply through a pair of parched lips.

This was a good development. The man had walked through the desert and survived. "Well, I can promise you this. If you do everything I say, nothing will happen to you. I will get out of your cab, and you will have made a lot of money for driving someone to Frankfurt. If you try anything funny, you're dead. That's our deal. No negotiating."

Geoffrey nodded enthusiastically, but he was still obviously terrified. Rapp knew he had to calm him down so they wouldn't get into an accident. "Why don't you have a cigarette and relax? We've got a long drive ahead of us."

The driver nervously fished for his smokes and lit

one up. Now came the interesting part for Rapp. He had a little more than two hours to cultivate a bond with this man. Mitch didn't like to kill people, and he would do everything possible to avoid having to off this poor sap. There was nothing Geoffrey could give the police that they couldn't get off the surveillance tapes at the airport. The only reason to kill him would be to buy more time, and Rapp hoped to do that in another way.

"Where are you from, Geoffrey?"

"Hamburg."

"What brought you to Hanover?"

Still a little nervous, he replied flatly, "I didn't like Hamburg."

The conversation got better over the next hour and a half. As Rapp probed, the driver loosened up. He was getting a good picture of who Geoffrey Herman was. They passed several police cruisers parked on the side of the autobahn. Each time, Rapp watched Geoffrey to make sure he did nothing to alert them. The driver kept his hands on the steering wheel and his eyes straight ahead. Rapp learned that Geoffrey was divorced and lived alone. He owned the cab, and he liked working nights. It allowed him to enjoy his days and do as he pleased. He was also a recovered alcoholic, and he reasoned that it helped keep him out of the bars in the evenings. The most important thing Rapp learned was that Geoffrey Herman was a convicted felon. He had spent two years in prison for robbery and had no love for the law. Rapp couldn't have been happier with the news.

It was almost two in the morning when Geoffrey announced that he should call his dispatcher. He had told her he would check in after he dropped his fare off in Essen. Rapp thought about it momentarily and asked, "Do you have to go back to the airport, or are you done for the night?"

"I'm done when I want to be done. I own the cab."

Geoffrey should not have offered that piece of information so freely, Rapp thought. "Would it be unusual for you to call it a night at this time?"

"Not at all. You were my last fare of the night."

Rapp took a second to think it over and said, "Go ahead and call in. Tell them everything went well, and you're going to call it a night."

Rapp watched Geoffrey dial the number on his cell phone and leaned forward to listen to the conversation. The female dispatcher sounded genuinely tired and disinterested. The call lasted no more than ten seconds. After they said goodbye, Rapp took the phone and turned it off. Watching Geoffrey's face closely, he asked, "Was that your normal dispatcher?"

Without hesitation, he nodded yes. "Her name is Sheila. I've worked with her for five years."

Sinking back into the seat, Rapp breathed a sigh of relief. The BKA had yet to pick up his trail. If they had, they would have tried to keep Geoffrey on the phone. Rapp looked at the map on his lap and thought now might be one of those times he could push it. "Geoffrey, have you spent much time in southern Germany?"

7

Irene Kennedy awoke to strange sounds that could only be coming from one thing: cartoons. This had become a Saturday morning ritual. Young Thomas, or Tommy, as he was called by most of his peers, was six. The days of him calling for her when he woke up were gone. In a strange way, she missed it. He was always at his best in the morning, affectionate and cuddly. She preferred the extra hour of sleep on Saturdays, but every once in a while, she wouldn't mind having to get out of bed and rub his back and kiss him until he was ready to get out from under the covers. He was too old for that stuff now, he had told her. He had an independent streak that no doubt had come from Kennedy herself.

She sat up in bed and swung her feet onto the floor. The bedside clock told her it was 7:58. Kennedy was simple in most regards. Her pajamas for as long as she could remember were either flannel pants or boxers and whatever large T-shirt happened to be available. She was thin, maybe too thin. It wasn't intentional; she just wasn't a big eater.

In the bathroom, she turned on the water and pulled

her straight brown hair into a ponytail. After scrubbing her face with a washcloth and soap for a good three minutes, she brushed her teeth and went down the hall to find Tommy right where she thought he'd be—sitting four feet in front of the TV in his pajamas, completely entranced by the Power Rangers blowing buildings apart. Kennedy walked around the couch and kissed the top of his head.

"Good morning, honey."

Tommy mumbled something that his mother couldn't quite understand and kept his eyes focused on the screen. Kennedy rubbed his head, picked up his empty cereal bowl, and headed into the kitchen. On her way past the table, she grabbed the milk and put it back in the fridge. After placing her son's bowl and spoon in the sink, she started the coffee maker and grabbed a banana.

As she leaned against the counter, her thoughts turned to Rapp. The anonymous tip to the German authorities about the freighter had gone as planned. For good measure, they had also alerted the media. That way, the BKA wouldn't be able to downplay the story. As far as what had happened with Hagenmiller, Kennedy was in the dark. The Counterterrorism Center had the ability to monitor events from afar, and with the help of the Global Operations Center, there wasn't a news story that could break without them being informed in fifteen minutes or less. The problem with this particular story was that Kennedy had to play dumb. She couldn't let even her closest people in the CT know that she had any idea that Hagenmiller was going to be taken out.

Kennedy finished the banana and told Tommy to turn off the TV and get dressed. He reluctantly obeyed, and fifteen minutes later they were out the door—Kennedy with two cups of coffee and Tommy with his football and rubber Godzilla. Waiting for them in the driveway was a dark blue Ford Crown Victoria with their driver, Harry Peterson, from the Agency's Office of Security. Irene and Tommy got in the back seat and said good morning. Kennedy handed Harry the fresh cup of coffee, and they were on their way.

Kennedy had resisted getting a driver. She lived less than ten minutes from Langley and at first saw it as an intrusion into her private life. Unfortunately, though, the previous summer the *Washington Post* had done a profile on her titled "The Most Powerful Woman in the CIA." Kennedy had not cooperated with the interview, and the president himself had asked them not to pursue the story. But the *Post* went ahead and did it anyway. She wanted nothing to do with the limelight, and more directly she wanted the people she was hunting to know as little about her as possible.

The fallout from the story was predictable. The threats started to roll in. Thomas Stansfield moved decisively. He ordered a security system for Kennedy's home and gave her a driver. The CIA monitored the security system, and at least once a night, a CIA security team would drive by the house and check things out. Kennedy was also given a pager with a panic button. She was ordered to have it on, or next to her, twenty-four hours a day.

Tommy was at that age where there was no such

thing as an inappropriate question. He had glimpsed Harry Peterson's gun one day while the two of them were playing catch in the driveway, waiting for Irene to come out. Tommy had asked to see the gun, and Harry resisted his natural instinct to say no. Harry was fifty-one and had learned that the last thing you wanted to do with a young boy was to make something taboo. It only served to pique their curiosity. Harry showed him the gun, gave him a very stern lecture about safety, and let him touch it. Later on, during the drive into Langley, Tommy had blurted out the question, "How many bad guys have you killed?"

Irene had wondered the same thing many times but had, of course, never asked the question. Men like Harry Peterson didn't fall into this line of work when they grew bored with selling copiers. They were typically former military types, cops, or covert operators who were a little too old to be crawling around rooftops in some Third World hellhole.

The car pulled up in front of the Old Headquarters Building. The OHB was completed in 1963, and the New Headquarters Building was finished in 1991. The two buildings combined had more than 2.5 million square feet of office space. Irene and Tommy entered the building and stopped at the security checkpoint. Irene signed Tommy in, and the guard gave him a visitor's badge that restricted him to the common areas down one level. After she scanned her own badge, mother and son went through the turnstile and downstairs.

Like all of the other modern government agencies,

the CIA had become sensitive, inclusive, and caring. Full day-care services were offered six days a week. Kennedy only used them on Saturday mornings, and Tommy actually liked it. He had gotten to know some of the other kids, and they typically enjoyed their Saturdays together building and then destroying things. Kennedy signed him in with Joanne, the weekend den mother, and then resisted the urge to kiss Tommy on the head. His friends were watching. She had been severely reprimanded on several occasions for committing this egregious act of affection in front of the guys. Instead, she waved and said she'd be back down for lunch.

Kennedy went back to the elevators and took one up to the sixth floor. In 1986, Ronald Reagan signed a presidential finding that authorized the CIA to identify terrorists who had committed crimes against American citizens and help bring them to the United States to stand trial. Later that year, the Counterterrorism Center was born. Its purpose: to coordinate the fight against terrorism, not just within the CIA but also with other federal agencies. Cooperation with other agencies, especially the FBI, was not something that had been encouraged throughout the CIA's history. This was a first, and there were many individuals among the old guard who saw this new relationship with the FBI as a sign that the end of the world was near.

Next to the door was a simple sign with black letters that read "Counterterrorism Center." Before punching her code into the cipher lock, Kennedy paused, collected her thoughts, and pushed. The room's main features were its projection screens and a large two-tiered rectangular conference table. The middle of the conference table was raised several feet. Underneath it sat a vast array of computer monitors, secure faxes, and phones. This mess in the middle of the room was the nerve center. This was where the case officers sat and coordinated information and activities with allies and other U.S. government organizations. The room was a cross between a network news control room and an air traffic control tower.

The first face Kennedy saw was that of Tom Lee, the CTC's deputy director and Kennedy's number two. Lee was speaking with two of the case officers who had been working on the Hagenmiller case. When he saw her, Lee cut off the two case officers and crossed the room to Kennedy. Halfway there, he jerked his head in the direction of her office.

The two converged outside Kennedy's door, and Lee gave his best "You're not going to believe what happened" look. Kennedy and Lee got along well. Both were quiet, even-tempered intellectuals. As was traditional with the deputy director slot at the CTC, Lee was not an employee of the CIA. He was FBI. This was the brave new world that the Counterterrorism Center had pioneered. Under Kennedy's command were employees of the Federal Bureau of Investigation, the Secret Service, the National Security Agency, the Drug Enforcement Administration, the Bureau of Alcohol, Tobacco and Firearms, the Defense Intelligence Agency, the Pentagon, the State Department, the Justice Department, and scientists from the Centers for Disease Control and Lawrence Livermore. Fifteen years earlier, not even the heads of these agencies would have been allowed to view the classified material that these mid-level analysts were able to.

Lee closed the door and placed his hands on his hips. Bureau all the way, he was wearing a suit and tie, even on a Saturday morning, though at least he had taken his jacket off. The CTC tended to be a little looser on the dress code than the rest of Langley. Most of the case officers out in the pen were wearing jeans. Lee was a native of Seattle, though his parents had immigrated from Korea. He had graduated from the University of Washington with a double major in accounting and computer science.

Kennedy set her bag down and asked, "What's wrong?"

Lee shook his head slowly. "We think Count Hagenmiller was killed last night."

Kennedy's eyebrows shot up. "Really?"

"Yes . . . really." Lee studied Kennedy for a sign that she might know more than she was letting on. He had his suspicions that Kennedy and her beloved Agency didn't always tell him what was going on. On a certain level he respected this, but there were times when it made him a little nervous. As was always the case, her expression betrayed nothing.

After sitting down in her ugly government-issue chair that was covered in some mystery gray fabric, she asked, "What do you mean, we think?"

"We are not entirely sure what is going on at this point. What we do know is that several Hamburg TV stations are reporting that a fire broke out at the Hagen-miller estate last night. The damage was extensive. We know from NSA intercepts that two bodies were dis-covered in the ashes. Both were badly burned. They presume that one is the count and the other is his body-guard."

"I assume we can rule out an accident?"

Lee nodded. "As we've discussed . . . we're paid to be paranoid. Even with that in mind, the odds that a burn-ing log rolled out of the fireplace and then tackled and killed the count aren't good."

"I'd have to agree." Kennedy grabbed her coffee. "What's our early assessment?"

"That's a good question. Our first thought was that Saddam ordered the hit for . . . take your pick of reasons. Hagenmiller screwed him somehow, maybe Saddam thought he blew the whistle on the heist. Maybe Saddam wanted all of the equipment for half the dough. Who knows? Saddam is the obvious candidate, but we have another interesting development." Lee pulled up a chair and sat. "About an hour ago, our fax machine started humming. The BKA has put out a bulletin on three indi-viduals. Two men and one woman, all Caucasian. Sally just got off the phone with her contact at the BKA, and they are fuming." Lee was referring to one of the case of-ficers who dealt with the European Union and the various law enforcement agencies that helped with counterterror-ism. "Supposedly, these three individuals gained access to the Hagenmiller estate last night by posing as agents from the BKA. They have them on tape arriving in one car, and this is where it starts to get a little weird. Two of them get out of the car and go into the house. One man and one woman. A couple of minutes later, the woman comes running out and jumps into the car, and she and the driver leave. Now, about five minutes pass, and all of a sudden the fire starts. At about the same time, they have the third guy on tape leaving the house from a side door. He steals a car and leaves the estate by a back road. They found the car that he stole in the parking garage at the Hanover airport about two hours ago. They have him on airport surveillance catching a cab and have put out a nationwide bulletin for the vehicle."

Kennedy tried to remain calm. "What about the other car?"

"No word on it yet."

She took a sip of coffee and focused on concealing the fear that was clawing at her gut. "Any other developments?"

"One." Lee's face took on an exhausted look. "The secretary of state called five minutes ago."

Kennedy didn't like the sound of this. She set her coffee mug back on the desk.

"It appears that he and Hagenmiller are, or in the count's case I should say were, avid art collectors. They have many mutual friends . . . a list that reads like a who's who of foreign dignitaries and royalty. The secretary of state said that he knows we had the count under surveillance and that he would like us to cooperate with the German authorities in apprehending the assassins." Lee leaned back and added, "Apparently, a very valuable collection of art was destroyed in the fire."

"You're kidding me?"

"No. I guess some very well-known and valuable originals were lost."

"No." Kennedy frowned in a rare show of emotion. "He told you he knows that we had the count under surveillance and that he wants us to cooperate with the BKA."

"Yes."

"And just how does he know we had him under surveillance?"

"I don't know."

"Do you have any ideas?"

Lee thought about it for a second and said, "Maybe."

"Make it a priority to find out, please." Kennedy reached for her phone. "In the meantime, I'd better see what I can do to head the secretary off before he does any more damage."

8

It was noon, it was fall, it was Saturday, and if you were a native Washingtonian, it was the best time of the year to be in the nation's capital. Spring was nice, but it brought too many tourists and the dreadful humidity of the Potomac River Valley. In the fall, the air was crisp, the colors were vibrant, and in neighborhoods all around the city, the coeds were back and excited about another year away from Mom and Dad. As Peter Cameron walked hurriedly around the south side of Washington Circle, he thought of none of this. He wished he could be out enjoying the gorgeous Saturday afternoon, but there were more urgent issues at hand.

Cameron had been back in the States for only a few hours, and in that time he had discovered some very bothersome information. He and the Jansens had left Germany just after midnight from a small airfield on the outskirts of Hamburg. Then they flew to Meaux Esbly, another small airfield an hour from Paris. Cameron took the first flight for New York out of Charles De Gaulle in the morning, and the Jansens left from Orly and were to fly nonstop to Mexico City. From there they were to take a flight to Los Angeles and then home to Denver.

Cameron reached the northwest side of Washington Circle and continued up Pennsylvania Avenue. He had just left his small office at George Washington University. Cameron had worked at the CIA from 1974 to 1998. During his last year at Langley, he had been approached by someone who presented him with a job opportunity that would increase his income five-fold and allow him to dabble, free of congressional oversight, in something he really enjoyed. Part of the package was a professorship at GW that required about ten hours a week and paid as much as his old job at Langley. The class was about the CIA, it met three times a week, and he had two full-time teacher's assistants. There were other consulting jobs that came along with his new package and some cash bonuses for doing exactly what he was doing right now.

At 25th Street, Cameron took a right and headed halfway up the block before ducking into the Columbia Hospital for Women. He approached a row of pay phones. Three were being used, and two were not. Cameron plugged in the proper change and dialed a number. When the voice answered on the other end, Cameron brought his fingers up and pinched his larynx. His voice sounded scratchy and a pitch higher.

"I need a cab."

The voice on the other end asked, "How fast, how far, and how many passengers?"

"In an hour. Twenty miles, domestic, and four passengers."

There was barely a pause on the other end, then the reply, "Site four in sixty minutes. Anything else?"

It took Cameron an extra second to remember that site four was the Montgomery County Airpark, and then he replied, "No." He hung up the phone and left the hospital. He hated using phones. It came from years of knowing firsthand the capabilities of the NSA and the CIA, but there was little choice, given the urgency of what he had to do. Cameron had just left one of the computer labs at George Washington. He rarely used his office computer to surf the Web, and when he worked out of the labs, he tried to use a different computer each time. He had also obtained a list of students with Internet accounts and their passwords. The Internet was the strange new world, and the laws protecting privacy on it hadn't yet made it into the infancy stage. Virtually every law enforcement, military, and intelligence agency monitored the Web searching for patterns of suspected spies, terrorists, and criminals.

Cameron turned onto M Street and headed west toward Georgetown. Just twenty minutes ago, he had used the account of a sophomore who was majoring in international business to surf the Web. It was the top story with all of the German newspapers and TV stations. The *London Times* had even posted it. Cameron had expected the Hagenmiller assassination to be fairly high-profile. That was part of the plan. But what he didn't expect to see was that the German authorities were seeking three individuals. Not two but three. When he had left the estate, there had been no fire, let alone a fire that would go on to destroy half of the century-old mansion. The stories also reported that the remains of two badly burned bodies had been found in the smoldering wreckage. Beth Jansen had specifically said three bodies, not two. Hagenmiller, the bodyguard, and Rapp. Something was wrong, and Cameron thought he knew what it was.

He was starting to sweat. He unzipped his blue jacket as he crossed over Rock Creek and flapped it open several times to let his body heat escape. The parkway below was crowded with bikers and joggers. Cameron pushed on across the bridge, cursing the fact that instead of enjoying the day and relishing a job well done, plus a sizable cash deposit in one of his offshore accounts, he now had to deal with these incompetents.

At 29th Street, Cameron found another pay phone and punched in a number. He said, "Hey, I've got a tee time in an hour. Can you make it?"

The person hesitated and then said, "An hour might be pushing it. Where are we playing?"

"Montgomery Village Golf Club."

There was another pause. "Is it a tough track?"

"It can be, but I think you can handle it."

"Do we have a foursome?"

"No." Cameron looked over his shoulder. "We could use two more, and make sure they're good sticks. And I don't want to play with any strangers."

"Got it. I'll meet you out there in ninety minutes."

Cameron hung up the phone and headed up 29th Street. The cobblestone sidewalk was steep and heaved from tree roots. A sheen of sweat coated his face, and his beard was starting to itch. His apartment was at the top of the hill on Q Street. It was only six blocks, but all of it was uphill. The forty-eight-year-old veteran of the CIA cursed himself for the extra weight he'd allowed to build around his abdomen. When this was over, he would check into one of those high-class spas where they flushed all of the crap out of you and the weight just melted away. That's what he needed—to be pampered and surrounded by beautiful people. For the first time ever, he had the money to enjoy the finer things in life.

But first he needed to take care of this loose end. Up the hill Cameron trudged. By the time he reached Dumbarton, the jacket was off, and the pits of his button-down shirt were soaked through. The two bags he needed were already packed, and his car was parked in a rented garage two blocks away. Downhill, thank God. He would have to stop at one of the safe deposit boxes and get cash for the freelancers. No one in this line of work came cheap. He would, of course, ask his employer to reimburse him later, and with any luck he would be able to retrieve the money he'd paid the Jansens. Cameron debated for several seconds whether or not he should send word to his employer. As he crossed the intersection at O Street, he decided against it. The man hated shoddy work and loved people with initiative. He would take care of the problem on his own and then give him a complete accounting of the events. The Jansens had to go. If Irene Kennedy got her hands on them before he did, his employer would have an aneurysm. Cameron might have to disappear for a while. Maybe forever.

* * *

THEY HAD ARRIVED in Freiburg at ten minutes to six in the morning. The city of a little more than two hundred thousand was just starting to stir. During the night's journey, Rapp had discarded his silenced Ruger and encrypted radio as they passed over a bridge near Stuttgart. He had also burned the BKA credentials and several other documents. Rapp had been to Freiburg once before in his mid-twenties. He had picked it randomly as a place to disappear between assignments. His memories of the city in the middle of the Black Forest were good ones. The plan back then was to stay one week, but he ended up staying for two. He had arrived before the annual Hocks Festival. Freiburg was a big cyclist town, and it didn't take long for Rapp to hook up with one of the clubs. He spent his days racing through the forest and river valleys with a pack of crazed cyclists who enjoyed the pain almost as much as he did, and his nights drinking great German beer and chasing beautiful German women. There would be none of that on this trip.

Rapp had found a spot near the Munsterplatz, the town's marketplace, and ditched the cab. Farmers and craftsmen were already arriving to set up their stands for the busy Saturday morning crowd. Rapp and Geoffrey had set off on foot. A mile later, they walked into a small inn called the Zum Roten Baren. Geoffrey had followed Rapp's instructions perfectly. He told the man behind the front desk that they had driven down from Frankfurt to spend the weekend hiking and that they had planned to come down the night before but had to work late, so instead they got up early and drove down.

The elderly innkeeper seemed to buy the story. Rapp had instructed Geoffrey to pay for two nights in advance with cash. The innkeeper happily took the money and gave them a room without checking IDs, which pleased Rapp all the more. Up in the room, Rapp gave Geoffrey the money he'd promised, blindfolded him, and tied him securely to the bed. Before leaving, Rapp went over Geoffrey's story with him one final time. "Just lie on the bed and try to sleep. When the housekeeper discovers you, have them call the police and tell them the whole story. Tell them I threatened to kill you if you didn't cooperate, just like we discussed in the car."

Geoffrey nodded one last time, and Rapp placed a gag over his mouth. With Geoffrey safely tucked away, Rapp stripped nude and took out his blue contacts. His eyes screamed relief as soon as the foreign objects were removed. In the shower, he washed and rinsed his hair five times to get all of the brown out. He tried not to irritate the cut on the back of his head, but it was impossible. When he got out of the shower, he left the water running and cleaned as much of the blood off the back collar of his dress shirt as he could.

After dressing, he went back into the bathroom, turned off the water in the shower, and cleaned the drain trap of hair. He threw all of the towels into a white plastic laundry bag that the inn provided and checked the room one more time. As he left the room, Rapp placed the Do Not Disturb sign on the door and closed it.

It was 6:45 by the time he left the inn by a side door. Rapp walked two miles across town to the area by the

Albert Ludwig University. On the way, he dropped the plastic bag containing the towels in a Dumpster behind a restaurant and stopped at two separate drugstores and a hotel gift shop. When he reached the university, it was after 7:30, and the temperature was in the sixties. Rapp found the student commons and scouted it out until he found a bathroom that was private enough. It was unisex and on the third floor. He locked the door and went to work. Taking the clippers he had bought at the first drugstore, he put an inch-and-a-half guard on the end, plugged it into the outlet, leaned over the sink, and started buzzing his thick black hair. Then he put a half-inch guard on and buzzed the sides and back of his head. Again, he cleaned up the hair and then put on a blue T-shirt that had a picture of Freiburg's most famous landmark, the Munster Cathedral. Over that Rapp put on a plain gray sweatshirt. He also wore a pair of tan shorts, white sweat socks, and blue shoes. His clothes and shoes from the night before were bundled up and shoved into a canvas shopping bag. Everything else went into a large green backpack that he had bought at the second drugstore, with the exception of the Glock pistol, which he shoved into the waistband of his shorts and covered with the bulky sweatshirt.

It was a huge relief to get out of the clothes. He had wanted to do it much earlier, but he didn't want Geoffrey to see his transformation. Rapp left the university and found a bakery just blocks away. He was famished and devoured several pastries, a croissant, and a bottle of orange juice. Next he found a coffee shop and killed another twenty minutes sipping a piping-hot blend. At five minutes to nine, he started out for his next destination.

The bike shop was almost exactly as Rapp remembered it. The enthusiasts and club members were already milling about in front of the small shop in their brightly colored, tight-fitting Lycra outfits waiting for the order to mount their bikes. Rapp picked his way through the crowd and into the shop. Bicycles hung from virtually every inch of the ceiling and lined the walls. Rapp approached the counter and asked for help in French. A man behind the counter directed him to a young woman with long black hair. The woman was French. He quickly found out that she was from Metz and was spending the school year studying abroad at the University of Freiburg.

As they looked at bikes, Rapp asked her if they still ran the loop on Saturdays. The woman said it had grown more popular than ever. Freiburg was in Tour de France country. The loop was a route that went northwest to the ancient fortress city of Breissach and then across the Rhine into France. From there, the cyclists would race down the French side of the river and cross back over at Mullheim, Ottmarsheim, or Basel, Switzerland. On a good Saturday, hundreds of brightly clad Swiss, French, and German cyclists raced the loop. Rapp was looking forward to the fact that the border guards let the packs of riders cross over without checking their passports. He remembered this part of Europe being very open, even during the Cold War. From Freiburg, France lay just fifteen miles to the east, and Basel was less than fifty miles to the southwest. The border crossings were low-key because of the heavy volume of people who lived in one country and worked in another. But, as Rapp had seen in other countries, there was no doubt that the security at crossings could be ratcheted up at a moment's notice.

After reviewing the selection of bikes, he chose a classic mint green used Bianchi. He also purchased saddlebags, a fanny pack, and a riding outfit complete with shoes, a small white cap, and a pair of Oakley racing glasses. Using the backpack that he had already purchased would not work. He would stick out like a sore thumb. Rapp paid for everything in cash. He wanted to hold off on using the credit card as long as possible. The woman showed him to a tiny bathroom in the basement of the shop, and Rapp put on his new outfit. Into the innermost pocket of the fanny pack he put the gun, one extra clip of ammunition, a silencer, and his stash of francs, deutsch marks, and pounds. In the outer pocket he put his French passport and several hundred francs. Everything that was to be discarded was put back into the backpack. He kept his new clothes.

When he got back upstairs, the riders were getting ready to leave. Rapp rolled up his clothes into tight balls and shoved them into the saddlebags of his new bike. He told the helpful young woman that he would be back in one minute. Holding up his backpack, he said he had to give it to a friend. Waddling in his hard-soled black biking shoes, he disappeared around the corner. A half block away, he found a trash can, lifted the top bag, and shoved the backpack in. There were better ways to do this, but he was short on time.

Back at the bike shop, the pack of thirty-plus cyclists

were starting to pull away. Rapp thanked the young French woman for her help and wheeled his Bianchi out onto the cobblestone street. Two blocks later, he caught up to the rear of the group and settled in. Rapp was much more than a cycling enthusiast. He no longer competed professionally, but it wasn't many years ago that he had been one of the world's top-ranked triathletes. He had won the Ironman in Hawaii and posted three top five finishes in what was the sport's greatest annual event. Then his work with the CIA had picked up considerably, and the hectic and unpredictable schedule had forced him to give up competition. But he still swam, jogged, and biked at least five days a week.

It was 9:36 when they rolled out of town. Rapp stayed at the back. His legs felt good, but his chest hurt a little. The pain made him think of the previous night's events, and he began to try to analyze what the hell had happened. Who could have been behind the Hoffmans' little stunt? The chances that the Hoffmans had acted alone were all but impossible. Rapp had never met them; he could see no motive they would have for killing him. A very select few knew of his relationship with the CIA, and even fewer knew about his recent mission. He knew of one for sure and assumed the other two. The person in the easiest position to arrange for the Hoffmans to take him out was the one person he thought he could always trust. Rapp didn't like it one bit. It shook his faith to the core, and it ran counter to everything his instincts had ever told him, but the shitty reality was that Irene Kennedy was suspect number one. Rapp didn't want to believe it. He wanted desperately to believe anything else, but for the moment there wasn't any other answer. He would have to get back to the States and find out for himself. And he would start with the Hoffmans. He would need help in tracking them down, but he knew just the person to ask.

As they rounded a turn, Rapp got his first glimpse of the Rhine and straight ahead the old Celtic fortress of Breisach. The town was situated on an eighty-meter-high rock plateau that was one of the earth's most natural military positions. From the ridge the road fell off into the valley. The riders went into full crouches and pumped their legs. The speed of the group topped forty miles per hour. Riding at the back, Rapp drafted off the riders in front of him and searched for the bridge that would take them over the Rhine. He didn't like what he saw. The row of vehicles backed up at the checkpoint stretched for what looked to be at least a mile. *Stay cool,* he told himself. *You don't look anything like the person they're searching for, you have a visa and a European Union identity card that no one knows about, and you're traveling in a group.*

Rapp dropped his bike into the lowest gear and picked up the pace. He easily passed nine cyclists and settled into a spot closer to the middle of the group. Three minutes later, they were on a shoulder passing the cars that were in line to cross the bridge. Rapp took a drink from his water bottle and kept his eyes peeled for anything that might be useful if he had to turn around and head back. The group began to slow, but not much. Rapp used the opportunity to spin his fanny pack around so he could get into it if he needed to. For either the passport or the gun.

A group of French cyclists passed them going the other way. Most of the cyclists waved, but a few shouted taunts back and forth across the roadway. Up ahead, Rapp saw a border patrol officer standing on the shoulder and waving his hands for the cyclists to stop. The lead cyclist began shouting at the man while they were still some fifty yards away. Rapp couldn't understand what he was saying but noticed that he was pointing back at the pack of French cyclists who were racing off in the other direction. A second officer appeared and intervened. By the time they reached the bridge, the officers were gesturing for them to continue through. As Rapp passed them, he heard the second officer shout encouragement. Thank God for national pride.

When they reached the other side, Rapp breathed a huge sigh of relief. The hard part was behind him. The peloton moved west for a quarter of a mile. Rapp allowed himself to fall to the back of the pack, and when they turned to the south, he peeled off and went straight. A road sign told him that Colmar was twelve kilometers ahead; most of it, he knew, was uphill. Rapp put his head down and picked up the pace. His first priority was to find a computer, and then he had a train to catch.

9

Death was coming. It had been, of course, since the day he was born on his parents' farm outside Stoneville, South Dakota, in 1920, but now it was upon him. Death had its bony fingers wrapped around his small, frail body and wasn't about to let go. It was the natural progression of things. A beginning and an end. Surprisingly, this didn't bother him. He had lived a long life. Much longer than most. He had seen and heard things that very few others had. The sacrifices he had made for his country would be remembered by few, and again this didn't bother him. His life had been lived in the shadows, and as the Information Age exploded, he had grown increasingly comfortable with his relative anonymity.

Thomas Stansfield was a private man, as was fitting for the person who ran the world's most famous, and infamous, intelligence agency. He had chosen to die at home surrounded by his daughters and grandchildren. The doctors had tried to talk him into surgery and radiation therapy, but Stansfield declined. The best they could give him at his age was another year or two, and that was if he survived having three-quarters of his liver removed. There was a good chance that he would never recover from the surgery. His wife, Sara, had passed away four years ago, and Thomas missed her dearly. Her death, more than anything, probably contributed to his decision not to fight. What was the sense? He had lived seventy-nine good years and was for the most part alone. The other big reason not to fight was his daughters. He did not want them to have to put their lives on hold for two years to watch him gradually wither away. If he were younger, things might be different, but he was tired. He wanted to die in privacy, with his mind and dignity intact.

A hospital bed had been moved into the study on the first floor of his home. The modest three-thousand-square-foot colonial sat on two wooded acres overlooking the Potomac River. In the spring, they could sit in the backyard and watch the water rush over Stublefield Falls, but now, in the fall, it was barely a trickle. Stansfield sat in his favorite leather chair, and looked admiringly out the window at the fall colors. How appropriate it was to die this time of the year, he thought. At least, Robert Frost would think so.

Sally, his eldest daughter, was in town from San Diego taking care of him. His other daughter, Sue, was to arrive on Wednesday from Sacramento. Their plan was to stay with him to the end. The five grandkids had been out two weekends before to spend some time with Grandpa before he was too far gone to enjoy it. The oldest was seventeen, and the youngest was five. The weekend had been painful but necessary. There had been a lot of tears.

Today Sally had helped him get dressed for a visitor. He was wearing a pair of tan slacks, a light blue button-down, and a gray cardigan. His white hair was parted to the side and combed back. Iowa was slugging it out with Penn State on the TV, but Stansfield wasn't paying attention to the game. He was worried about a phone call he had received. He wanted to put everything in order before he passed. The grandkids were taken care of. Trusts had been set up for college and grad school if they chose, but nothing else. There would be no sports cars or boats, no toys to make them weak. The house would easily fetch a million, not bad considering he had bought the land for two thousand dollars back in 1952. And there were other investments, of course. A person would have had to be a fool not to have capitalized on some of the information that had come across Thomas Stansfield's desk over the years. The daughters would get the bulk of the estate, and he didn't worry for a moment about whether the money would be used wisely.

What did worry Thomas Stansfield was the CIA. Things were not in order, and they were beginning to show signs of being worse than he had thought. No one outside Stansfield's family had been allowed to look behind the curtain he had pulled across his life. There was one exception, and that was Irene Kennedy. Stansfield thought of her as his third daughter. She was, he believed, the most talented and crucially important person working for the CIA. This made her a big target for a lot of people, and Stansfield was worried that when he was gone, his enemies would do their best to destroy her.

★ ★ ★

SALLY ESCORTED DR. Kennedy into the study and then closed the door on her way out. Irene approached Stansfield's chair and kissed him on the forehead. This was a new thing for them, since the cancer had been discovered. At the time, they had quietly mused over death's habit of bringing one's true feelings to the surface. Kennedy took the chair across from her boss and asked him how he felt.

"Pretty good, but let's not worry about me. There's nothing we can do about that." Stansfield studied her for a moment and asked, "What's wrong?"

Kennedy wasn't exactly sure where to start, and after a brief hesitation, she said, "The operation we were running in Germany last night . . ."

"Yes."

"Things didn't go exactly as planned."

"How bad?"

"Mitch hasn't reported in yet, and the BKA has put out a continentwide bulletin on three individuals they believe are responsible for the death of Count Hagenmiller."

"This was expected."

"Yes, it was, but some other things have transpired." Kennedy went on to describe the fire and the strange piece of information they had intercepted from the BKA—that it appeared Rapp left the mansion after the Hoffmans and had to steal a car to get away.

When she was done, Stansfield said, "It sounds to me as if something didn't go according to plan. My guess is that Mitch told the Hoffmans to make a break for it and he'd lay down a diversion."

Kennedy nodded. "That's what I thought at first, but Mitch hasn't checked in, and I just recently received a message from the Hoffmans. They"—Kennedy shook her head—"said the target was achieved, but an asset was lost in the process."

"Mitch."

With a sad, slow nod, Kennedy said, "Yes."

"What about this third individual the BKA has on tape?"

"We haven't been able to get any further information on that."

Stansfield sat back, a little surprised. He would have thought Irene fully capable of verifying the report through several channels. "Why?"

"There's another problem that has arisen. When I arrived at the CTC this morning, Tom Lee informed me that Secretary Midleton was looking for me."

This caused the frail Stansfield to sit up a bit in his chair. The secretary of state had no business calling his director of counterterrorism without going through him first. "What did Mr. Midleton want?"

"It appears he and the count shared the same passion: fine art."

Stansfield looked out the window, making the connection. He knew that the arrogant secretary of state was very proud of his private art collection. Stansfield remembered a profile that had been done by the *New Yorker* discussing the renaissance man's fifty-million-dollar collection. "Why would he call you?"

"The message said that he knows we had the count under observation and that any information we can give the German authorities would be greatly appreciated."

"How would he know we had the count under surveillance?"

Kennedy shrugged at the obvious. "It would appear we have a leak."

"Or a mole."

"Yes."

"Any ideas?"

"Not at the moment, but Tom Lee was as disturbed by it as me. He said he was going to look into it."

"Can you trust Mr. Lee?" asked an always cautious Stansfield.

"I think so, but I will, of course, do some checking on my own."

"Good. Have you told the president about Mitch?"

"No. I'd like to know exactly what's going on first."

"I agree. I assume you haven't used our contacts at the BKA because you don't want to draw any more attention to the CTC."

"Yes. I'm trying to collect as much passive information as possible. The NSA is keeping us busy with intercepts. So far, our plan is working. Most of the people in the CTC think Saddam had Hagenmiller killed. A couple even think the Israelis may have done it. The Hagenmillers were Nazis during World War Two, and they were selling very sensitive equipment to one of Israel's most dangerous enemies. There was plenty of motive. I think some of my more streetwise people might suspect that we had a hand in it, but they're not saying anything, nor will they." Kennedy frowned. "If people find out that we had him under surveillance, it won't look good."

"I agree. I will take care of Secretary Midleton. How are you going to find out about Mitch?"

"The Hoffmans are due back in the States this evening. I'm going to fly to Denver and debrief them personally."

"Who are you bringing?"

"No one. I've dealt with them before. I can handle it myself."

Stansfield gave her a look of admonishment. Kennedy had very limited field experience.

Kennedy read her boss's expression and said defensively, "This is my mess, and I'll be the one to clean it up. Besides, the fewer people we get involved, the better."

Stansfield shook his head. "The last thing you need right now is to leave town and draw attention to yourself. Besides, contract agents like the Hoffmans tend to get a little jumpy when an operation goes badly. I will send some people to take care of it."

Kennedy conceded the point. "What would you like me to do?"

Stansfield thought about it for a moment. "Hope that the Hoffmans are wrong and Mitch is alive." Stansfield saw by Kennedy's expression that his words didn't have their intended effect. "Don't worry about Mitch. This is what he's best at. He'll find his way back to us all by himself." The director of Central Intelligence inched forward in his chair, and his gray eyes peered into Kennedy's. "I want you to find out where Secretary Midleton is getting his information, and I want you to do it as quickly and quietly as possible."

RAYS OF SUNLIGHT floated through the kitchen window of Liz and Michael O'Rourke's Georgetown brownstone. Liz O'Rourke pecked away at her laptop. A glass of cranapple juice sat on her left, and on her right was a structurally unsound stack of documents and files that looked as if they might plummet to the floor any minute. Her yellow Lab, Duke, was lying in front of the patio door, napping in the warm sunlight. The former newspaper reporter was at peace. Everything about the setting was perfect except the absence of coffee. And considering the fact that she was five months pregnant, it was a happy trade.

Liz was working on her first book. It was titled *America's Most Corrupt Politicians.* Since her husband of less than a year was a U.S. congressman, she was using her maiden name, Scarlatti, not that Michael would have objected to using O'Rourke. She just thought it was the prudent thing to do. With the help of a friend who was a literary agent, she had inked a deal with a New York publisher based on a ten-page book proposal. The side job, as she referred to it, made quitting the newspaper an easy decision. Her husband came from some fairly big money. Liz didn't need to work, but she wanted to. At thirty-one, she knew if she stopped cold turkey, she'd go nuts.

She was wearing a pair of gray sweats and a small blue New York Yankees T-shirt that barely covered her belly button. The little baby-T drove Michael nuts. He loved it when she wore it around the house, but if she so much as stepped out to get the newspaper in it, he gave her a concerned fatherly look. Liz was just finishing a paragraph when she heard the jingle of Duke's dog tags. Peeking over the top of the laptop, she saw her husband's best friend staring at the front door. The sound of keys in the lock caused him to yelp and jump to his feet. Down the hall he went. The dog was named after John Wayne, and now there was talk of another. She feared that the next one would be called Vince after the legendary Packers coach. Liz's big problem with this was that her father was named Vince, and she really didn't think he'd take well to sharing his name with the family dog.

The clock on the kitchen wall read 12:32. With a raised eyebrow, Liz noted that her husband was only thirty-two minutes late. He was getting better. While she counted how many pages she had written, she listened to the boys express their love and mutual admiration for each other. If it wasn't for the fact that Michael was very good at showering her with affection, too, she would be really jealous.

A moment later, her thirty-three-year-old husband appeared in the kitchen with the grin of a five-year-old on his face. O'Rourke had been a U.S. Marine and captain of his hockey team at the University of Minnesota. Despite his stern appearance, he was a real softy. He slid around the back of Liz's chair and brushed her hair over to one side. He kissed her cheek just once and then moved on to her neck while his hands found her exposed and bulging belly. Duke came down the hall to watch and wait his turn. Liz reached back and ran her hands through Michael's hair, kissing him on the cheek and moaning in his ear. His hands slid up, and he gently cupped his wife's breasts.

"Lunch or sex?" he whispered in her ear.

"Both."

"Which one first?" He kissed her neck some more.

"I don't care . . . mm . . . you decide."

Michael did not expect Liz's sex drive to increase with her pregnancy, but it was nonetheless a pleasant surprise. "If we don't leave now, my bet is we won't leave for the rest of the day."

"And what's wrong with that?"

"We don't have any food."

"Is that my fault?" Liz said a little defensively.

"Noooooo." Michael smiled as he drew out the word. "Not you, Princess." He had taken to calling her by her royal moniker when he wanted to tease her. That's what Big Vince liked to call his daughter. "We only live six blocks from a grocery store, and you quit your job a month ago."

Liz withdrew her arms. "How many grocery stores do you pass on your way to and from work every day?"

"Nope. I'm not going to let you do it." He stood and walked around to one of the other chairs. Shaking his head and grinning, he said, "We already talked about this. You said you'd do it. You said it would give you an excuse to get out from behind that computer."

"But I'm pregnant." Liz put on her best pouty look.

"Nice try . . . I'm not falling for it. Come on. Let's go

down to Einstein's. I'm dying for a tuna melt and a big cup of java."

"What about the sex?"

"Later. I need a little sustenance. You've been wearing me out lately."

"Poor baby."

Duke edged his snout under his owner's hand, and Michael started petting him. "Are you going to take off our son's T-shirt and put on some adult clothes so we can get going? I'm really hungry."

"Son's T-shirt." Liz nodded while she thought of a retort. "That's a really funny one, Michael. Have you been working on it all morning?"

"Nope." He grinned. "I thought of it right here on the spot. Completely impromptu."

"Well, none of the neighbors seemed to mind it when I took Duke for a walk around the block earlier."

"You took Duke for a walk in that T-shirt?" The smile was gone.

Liz stared at him for a while and then smiled. "No, I didn't, but if you keep giving me shit about it, I might."

Michael nodded. "You win. But I don't think it's a good idea for you to keep raiding the baby shower presents. If someone sees you wearing the kid's clothes, they'll really think you've lost it."

Liz smiled. "Another funny one. Let me check my e-mail, and then we'll go."

She hit the AOL icon, and the computer started the dial-up. After a series of squeals and whistles, the laptop beeped and the computer announced, "You've got mail." Liz clicked on the mailbox icon, and a sec-

ond later the electronic message appeared on her
screen.

Dear Liz,

*I hope all is well. I need you and Michael to do me a
favor, and please don't ask any questions. Call Bella at
the cottage, and tell her you really need to talk to her.
Whatever you do, don't mention my involvement or
name over the phone. Something has gone wrong, and I
need her to stay with you for a few days. When she gets
to your house, you can tell her that I'm safe, that I apologize, and I will explain everything when I get home.
Under no circumstance are you to let her go back to the
cottage or her apartment. Tell Michael to exercise caution
and call Scott C. if he needs help.*

Sincerely,
Syracuse

P.S. I know all about Seamus, Michael, and Scott C.

She could barely believe what she was reading. Bella
was Annabella Rielly, her best friend, and Syracuse had
to be Anna's boyfriend, Mitch Rapp. She feared she
might know who Scott C. was, and if she was right, just
how in the hell did Mitch Rapp know about that
dreaded chapter in her family's history? Liz looked up
from the screen in disbelief, her perfect Saturday afternoon ruined.

"Honey, I think you'd better take a look at this."

10

Peter Cameron sat in one of the plush leather seats of the brand-new Cessna 750 Citation X executive jet. The plane could be configured to carry up to twelve passengers, but for this trip there were only four, not counting the pilots. A woman and two men were sitting at a small table studying maps and photographs. Cameron had withheld the Jansens' full profiles. The less these people knew, the better. As far as Cameron was concerned, the less everybody knew, the better. This problem needed to be dealt with swiftly. Like the first twenty-four hours following the outbreak of a disease, this next day was crucial. Nip it in the ass now, and everything would be fine. Leave any unfinished business on the table, and things could spin out of control.

One of the men got up and came over. He sat down across from Cameron so he could study him. His name was Gus Villaume. To a few people in his line of work, he was known as the Frog. A French Canadian from Montréal, Villaume had worked for the CIA in the seventies and early eighties as an agent inside the Dassault Aviation Company. In 1986, he had decided to break out on his own and work as a freelancer. The money was much better, and his work hours were whatever he chose.

Villaume studied Cameron with his hawklike eyes. The Frog had wondered about this Cameron for some time. He was competent enough but a little too quick to use force. He was a yes man, Villaume guessed. Someone else was giving him orders. The way the former civil servant threw money around, it was obvious that his boss was an individual with substantial financial assets. The unknown identity of Cameron's employer was beginning to bother Villaume. When working among thieves, knowledge of that sort could be used as insurance if things got bad.

Villaume stroked the edges of his black mustache and asked Cameron, "So, who are these two individuals?"

"Nobody. They were asked to do a job, they blew it, and now they have to pay."

Villaume noticed how Cameron used a casual tone as if these people were being fired for lack of performance. "So now they die?"

"They knew what they were getting into."

Holding up two black-and-white photographs, Villaume asked, "This is all you can give me? No background on them?"

"You don't need any more information. It's going to be an easy job. In and out."

Villaume studied Cameron's face. "I'll be the judge of how easy the job will be."

"If it'll make you feel any better, I'm planning on taking the shots."

This caused a smile to fall across the other man's face. Leaning back, he said, "Really?"

"Yes, *really*. Why does that amuse you so much?"

"I've never seen you get your hands dirty before, let alone kill someone."

Cameron let his displeasure show. "There's a lot you don't know about me, Gus."

"I'm sure there is, but all the same, I'd like to know more about these two targets."

"All you need to know is that this will be easy, and you're going to be paid well." Cameron's voice had taken on an agitated tone.

Villaume kept his own tone even. "I will not take my team into a situation without more information. If you refuse, we'll get off this plane when we land in Colorado Springs and take the first plane back to Washington."

Cameron didn't like that idea at all. "For Christ sake, Gus, if I thought this thing was going to be messy, I would have called Duser."

Villaume looked over at his two team members for a brief second. The reference to Jeff Duser had got their attention. Duser was a former U.S. Marine who had been court-martialed and run out of the Corps for a list of offenses too long to recap. A decade later, the sadist was well into his thirties but seemed mentally still stuck in his teens. He and his crew of pumped-up cronies were about as subtle as a sledgehammer. How he had ended up in this line of work Villaume had yet to figure out, but he had a good idea that the man sitting across from him had something to do with it. Duser was not well respected by other freelancers. As a general rule, contracts were to be carried out in as quiet a manner as possible. If possible, a hit should be made to look like a suicide, or, given the right situation, the body should simply disappear.

"Maybe you should call Duser . . . that way, you can guarantee front-page coverage in Sunday's *Denver Post.*"

"What is that supposed to mean?"

"Peter, if you need me to explain that to you"—Villaume shook his head—"you should find a new line of work."

"Hey, Duser and his boys get results."

"And headlines."

"I'm not going to sit here and argue with you, Gus. This job is a cakewalk. Maybe you're getting too old for this."

Villaume kept his stare focused on Cameron's dark pupils. At fifty-two, he had lost very little, and what was gone in terms of physical ability he had more than made up for in increased knowledge and instinct. And at this moment, his instincts were telling him that Cameron was lying. Villaume had learned long ago that in this line of work, you should use great caution before you threaten another business associate. Once that hand was shown, there was no taking it back, and it often forced the other person to make plans of his or her own. It was clear that Cameron was a man who could not be trusted. The Frog did not like it, but it was time to raise the ante.

"I will ask this question one last time. If you don't give me an answer, our participation in this mission is over. If you spread any false rumors about why we backed out, I will have Mario pay you a visit." Villaume glanced over at the large man sitting on the other side of the aisle. He had one continuous eyebrow that ran across an incredibly large head attached to a neck and body that weren't any smaller.

Cameron squirmed in his seat and looked over at Mario Lukas. The man gave him the creeps. Half Frankenstein, half Baby Huey, he followed Villaume as if he were the second coming. Cameron had no doubt he would be dead within seconds of Villaume giving the word. Cameron decided it wasn't a good idea to fight this particular battle. Villaume and his people could be dealt with later.

As if this was all a giant waste of time, Cameron asked, "What would you like to know?"

Villaume responded with a fake smile. "Are they cops?"

"No."

"Do they have any military experience?"

Cameron paused. "Yes."

"Both of them?"

"Yes."

"Which branch?"

There was more hesitation on Cameron's part. "Army."

"Any Special Forces training?"

"I can't get into that."

Villaume scoffed. "The hell you can't."

"I've given you all of the information you need." Cameron held up his sat phone. "If you want out, tell me right now, and I'll call Duser."

Villaume studied him. He had little doubt that Cameron was full of it. This whole thing was a rush job. Calling his bluff, he said, "Go ahead. Call him."

Cameron looked at the phone for a moment and then swore under his breath. "Fine, Gus." He shifted in his seat, saying, "God, you're a pain in the ass sometimes." Throwing his arms up in surrender, he said, "Ask away."

Cameron's slithery ways had Villaume's antenna way up. "Peter, I have been doing this for almost thirty years, and the only thing that has kept me alive is my thoroughness. Jerk my chain one more time, try to bluff me like you just did with that threatened phone call, or God forbid you're dumb enough to withhold information from me . . . like the fact that these two have spent time at Fort Bragg." Villaume shook his head, and the hawk eyes burrowed in on the plump Cameron. Pointing at the Professor, he said, "You might end up in a tragic accident with that brand-new car of yours."

THE FORD EXPLORER raced across the cement tarmac of the Essex Skypark and pulled up alongside the Learjet. The driver was in a hurry. Kevin Hackett had called to tell him a storm front was moving in, and if they wanted to make it to Denver by sundown, they'd better step on it. Scott Coleman lifted the back hatch of the truck and grabbed two metal cases. He ran them over to the plane and handed them to Dan Stroble, one of his former SEAL Team Six members. Coleman went back for a large duffel bag and then parked the truck over by one of the hangars. Running back across the tarmac, he looked at the water of the Back River just east of Baltimore. White-caps were starting to form, and the few boats that were out were getting tossed around. The sky to the north was dark. It looked as if they would just make it.

A gust of wind whipped across the long runway, catching the bill of Coleman's ball cap. Before it could be whisked away, his left hand clamped down on top of it, and he sprinted the last forty feet to the jet. Coleman hopped up through the small hatch and pulled it closed behind him. Poking his head into the cockpit, he asked, "Are we are all set, Kev?"

Hackett nodded. "As soon as you strap in."

Coleman took off his faded olive bush jacket, revealing a rock-solid physique. Handing the jacket to Stroble, he asked, "Is the gear stowed?"

"Yep."

"All right. Buckle up, and we're out of here."

Coleman squeezed himself into the copilot seat, slipped on his shoulder straps, and donned a headset. Hackett had arrived an hour earlier, filed a flight plan, and prepped the plane. Coleman ran down a quick check of the instruments while Hackett maneuvered the medium-range executive jet into takeoff position. They stopped at the south end of the runway and looked right into the teeth of the oncoming storm. Curtains of rain were falling in at least three different areas to the north and east. With no time to waste, Hackett increased the power to the twin jet engines and released the brakes. The small eight-passenger jet rolled down the runway and lifted effortlessly into the air. Moments later, raindrops started to pelt the windshield, the wipers came on, and the craft banked to the west, passing over the northern end of Baltimore. Two minutes later, the rain was behind them. The agile craft quickly gained altitude, and at fifteen thousand feet, they broke through the clouds and were greeted by a bright sun that they would be flying straight into for the next three hours.

Coleman looked over his shoulder and asked Stroble to grab his sunglasses. Both Stroble and Hackett had served under Coleman when he had commanded SEAL Team Six. The three of them had been through the wringer together. They had enjoyed their years in the Navy, but they sure as hell didn't miss the shitty pay and dog-and-pony bullshit. They answered to nobody but themselves now and were very selective about the jobs they took—most of them legitimate. Their company, SEAL Demolition and Salvage Corporation, did much of its work abroad. Between contracts, they helped train law enforcement divers from the various counties and cities that bordered the Chesapeake Bay.

Scott Coleman wasn't sure which category this job would eventually fall into. The only thing illegal about it so far was that their fee had been wired into a bank in the Caribbean, where it would avoid detection by the IRS, or anyone else who might be of a mind to track the full activities of the SEAL Demolition and Salvage Corporation.

The old man was dying. That was plain enough to see. Coleman was a little surprised at how this had affected him. He hadn't known Thomas Stansfield for long, but his admiration for him was genuine. In Coleman's line of work, it was hard not to put the old spy-master on a bit of a pedestal. Stansfield had been one of the original covert operators. During World War II, his services were sought after by Wild Bill Donovan and the OSS. As one of the famed Jedburgh team leaders, Stansfield had been dropped into Nazi-occupied Norway during the war to help organize resistance. He had been battle-tested in the field for many years before taking a job behind a desk, a rare thing in Washington. The CIA, and thus America, was about to be dealt a serious blow by the loss of the wise old man.

Coleman's recent business relationship with the head of the CIA was more than a little strange. Several years earlier, Coleman had taken certain political matters into his own hands. He had spent a good portion of his life trotting around the globe, eliminating people who were deemed a threat to the national security of the United States. On one of those missions, he had lost half of his team, only to learn later that the mission had been compromised by a senator with an affinity for booze and women. Coleman left the Navy in disgust when his commanders refused to tell him the name of the man who had compromised the mission. A short while later, he learned from his friend Congressman Michael O'Rourke who the guilty party was. The event changed Coleman's life. He began asking the question: *Who is a bigger threat to my country, a terrorist ten thousand miles away or the corrupt self-serving politician down the street?* Coleman became involved in an intricate plot to correct the course of the government in Washington. Before the affair was over, a half dozen politicians had been assassinated, and their plan to restore some honor to politics had been hijacked by a cabal of Washington insiders. In the end, Coleman killed two of the cabal's leaders, and a cease-fire was negotiated by Director Stansfield and Congressman O'Rourke. Both parties agreed that it would be best for the country never to know the details of what had happened and who had been involved.

At first, the deal was one of mutually assured destruction. Neither party could harm the other for fear that the real story would be sent to the press. This was how Coleman had become a freelancer for the director of the CIA—the men needed each other. The relationship was strange at first, but they had grown to trust and respect each other.

When they reached their cruising altitude, Hackett engaged the autopilot and turned to Coleman. "So, are you going to tell us what the hell is going on?"

Stroble heard the question and got out of his seat. He kneeled down in the doorway to the cabin to listen to Coleman. "There was an operation, and something went wrong. Two of the players are due back in the country tonight, and we are to collect them and bring them back to Washington."

"I assume they don't know we're coming." Stroble looked to his boss.

"No." Anticipating the next question, Coleman asked him to grab his black duffel bag. From it, he retrieved two large folders. In the business, they were referred to as jackets. He handed one to Stroble and kept the other for himself. "Stansfield was kind enough to provide us with a little background information." Coleman flipped open the folder and looked at a black-and-white photograph of one of their pickups. The man looked vaguely familiar. His real name was Jim Jansen. He was from Pittsburgh and had entered the Army right out of high school in 1974. After serving in Germany, he came back and went through Ranger School. The next stop was Korea and then the Green Berets, where he led an A-team and, Coleman already knew, met his wife, the other person they would be picking up. By the time gaps in Jansen's personnel records, Coleman could tell that he'd been sheep-dipped by the Agency on at least three occasions during his years in the Special Forces. *Sheep-dipping* was a term used by the folks down at Fort Bragg when the CIA borrowed their warriors for missions that were not recorded in their regular jackets. Coleman skipped ahead to see if there was any mention of what Jansen had done for the CIA. As he expected, there wasn't.

Coleman and Stroble continued to study the jackets and shared the important details they found with Hackett. None of what they read surprised them. It was not uncommon for retired Special Forces types to work for Langley both officially and unofficially.

Hackett eyeballed the plane's instruments and checked to make sure the autopilot was functioning properly. As his eyes danced over the dials and digital readouts, he said, "As usual, the Culinary Institute of America is not giving us the full story." Hackett was not a big fan of the CIA and liked to refer to it by the name of America's most well-known chef school.

"And what makes you say that?"

"If this is such an easy op, then why are they sending us? Why not send a couple of their own people out to

Colorado, or, better yet, why not call them on the phone and bring them in?"

"I never said it was going to be easy. Stansfield told me something didn't feel right about this one, and that's why he called us."

"Did he tell you what in the hell these two did to get into hot water?" asked Hackett.

Coleman looked to Stroble first and then to Hackett. "Do you guys remember Iron Man?"

Hackett's eyes opened wide, and Stroble let out a nervous laugh. "How could I ever forget him?" answered the latter. "He's a one-man army."

"Fuckin' James Bond," mumbled Hackett.

"Well, the Jansens"—Coleman held up the folder that had been in his lap—"were working with Iron Man on a very delicate operation. Apparently, things didn't go off as planned. The Jansens reported that they had nailed the target, but Iron Man had been lost."

"What?" asked a disbelieving Stroble.

"The Jansens were on the run and didn't have time to get into details, but they reported that Iron Man is dead."

Hackett shook his sun-bleached blond head. "Back to my original point. I still don't see why they need us."

"Because Stansfield has conflicting information about whether or not Iron Man is still with us."

"I'm not sure I understand," said Stroble.

"Stansfield couldn't get into it other than to say that he has other sources who say Iron Man is still alive."

"And," added Hackett, "this op was run without the official knowledge of the president and the Congress, and that's why they called us."

"I would assume that's the case."

Hackett, continuing in his pessimistic mood, said, "Well, I just hope we don't bump into Iron Man while we're out in Colorado. People have a habit of dying when he's around."

Coleman took the file and slapped it across Hackett's chest. "People used to say the same thing about us. Read this, and try to relax. I'm telling you right now, this is not going to be a big deal. We'll move slow and cautious, all right?" Hackett nodded and took the file.

Looking out the window of the jet, Coleman's thoughts turned to a night several months ago. He had been at an Orioles baseball game with a date when he'd bumped into an old friend and his wife. They were sitting out in right field, having a beer and a hot dog. When the old friend went to introduce the other couple they were with, Coleman almost dropped his beer. There, sitting across the table, was someone he hadn't seen since he'd left the SEALs. At first he wasn't sure. Not at something as benign as a baseball game. But at second glance he knew it was him. He could see the recognition in his eyes. They were the darkest, most alert eyes he had ever seen, and they belonged to a living legend in the world of black operations. Coleman had seen him operate in the field twice and had heard others utter his name with a shake of their heads. He was at home in almost any city in the Middle East and much of Europe. He was perhaps America's best assassin, and there he was sitting at a baseball game with a beautiful young reporter. It was almost too surreal to believe, but it was him, and now they were about to cross paths again.

11

M ichael O'Rourke was tense. As tense as he'd
been in several years. He clutched the
leather steering wheel of his Chevy Tahoe
with white knuckles, and as his eyes peered ahead, his
mind searched for answers. He adored Anna Rielly.
There wasn't much not to like about her. She'd been his
wife's best friend since college, and she'd been a good
one. They had been elated when she called the previous
spring to tell them she was going to be NBC's new
White House correspondent. That elation lasted less
than a week.

On Rielly's first day at work, she had been caught up
in a terrorist attack that had almost cost her her life. A
dozen Secret Service officers and agents had been killed
in the attack, and in the ensuing drama that unfolded,
Bill Schwartz, the president's national security advisor,
was killed as well as his secretary and several others.
The hostage standoff was ended after a bold takedown
by the FBI's Hostage Rescue Team. At least, that had
been the story reported in the press.

As a member of the House Select Committee on Intelligence, O'Rourke was privy to information that even

his fellow representatives were not. The official position taken by the White House after the hostage crisis was that SEAL Team Six and other counterterrorism units were used in an advisory role during the crisis and nothing else. *Other counterterrorism units* was code for Delta Force—the Army's ultra-secret Special Forces unit. The Pentagon still refused to admit the group's existence, even though it was the focus of dozens of books and several feature-length movies. O'Rourke knew that the Pentagon's Special Forces units had played a much bigger role than just advising. They had both been involved in the takedown, and the SEALs had actually lost two members. In the interest of keeping the right-wing nuts from going ballistic, the FBI's HRT was given the full credit for the bold and successful operation.

As O'Rourke looked back on the dramatic events that had unfolded the previous spring, it occurred to him that it wasn't long after the White House crisis that he and his wife had been introduced to Anna Rielly's new boyfriend. O'Rourke hadn't noticed it at first, but as they spent more time with him, he started to see little things. Every time they went out for dinner, he would suggest some off-the-beaten-path location, and he would always sit facing the door. On the few occasions where this hadn't been possible, he would spend a fair amount of the evening looking over his shoulder as new patrons would enter. The way he carried himself, the way his eyes were constantly taking inventory of his surroundings—Liz hadn't noticed it, though she had with her own husband. Michael O'Rourke was a former Marine, and, like many leathernecks, he wasn't known for his subtle ways.

The difference between Rapp and O'Rourke was that Rapp was much smoother. In O'Rourke's mind, his own hyper-awareness served two purposes. The first was to know his surroundings, and the second was to let others know that he knew what they were up to. This helped serve as a deterrent.

With Rapp, there was no attempt to deter. O'Rourke had wondered on more than one occasion if the Syracuse University grad was a spook. He owned a business that allowed him to travel extensively throughout Europe and the Middle East, both of his parents were dead, and he had no ties that O'Rourke could see to the local community other than Anna.

It was in late August when O'Rourke became convinced that Rapp was much more than a computer consultant. They had been at a Baltimore Orioles game with Anna and Mitch when they had bumped into a blast from the past—Scott Coleman, retired lieutenant commander United States Navy and former CO of SEAL Team Six. O'Rourke and Coleman had a colorful history, parts of which O'Rourke wished he could forget.

O'Rourke had seen it in their eyes when the two men were introduced. Coleman, who O'Rourke could easily say was one of the most unflappable people he had ever met, looked as if he had seen a ghost when he was introduced to Rapp. It lasted for a second tops, and then Coleman quickly recovered, but O'Rourke had seen it. Rapp, of course, showed nothing. Not even the slightest hint that he and the former Navy SEAL had any connection, but Coleman had flinched.

O'Rourke had said nothing to his wife, and he hadn't

lifted a finger to try to confirm his suspicions. As a member of the House Intelligence Committee, O'Rourke knew that to start asking around about such individuals could raise unwanted attention, and O'Rourke was trying his best to maintain a low profile. He had his own secrets to hide.

Now, whether he liked it or not, he would have to start asking questions. Mitch Rapp was much more than a computer salesman, that was for certain. The very fact that he knew there was a relationship between his grandfather and Scott Coleman said that he had access to some very delicate and highly classified information.

O'Rourke exited off of Route 50 midway between Bowie and Annapolis. The thought of how his wife looked when he'd left made him cringe. Almost six months pregnant, everything going smooth, and now this. Stress was bad, that's what the doctor and the nurses had told them over and over. The look of fright on her face was right there as he backed out of their short driveway. He had left her with Duke and his Detonics pocket 9-mm. The gun was small and fit perfectly in her hand. She had fired it on at least ten different occasions. There had been a time in the early stages of their relationship when she would have freaked out over a kitchen knife, let alone a gun, but some unwanted circumstances had changed her opinions.

O'Rourke knew the look of fear on her face was not for herself. Liz was a tough woman, and she would be locked in a home that had recently undergone an eleven thousand dollar security upgrade. The look of fear was for him. They had called Anna's apartment and Rapp's house and had gotten the answering machines at both. Rather than send her husband to investigate, Liz had wanted to call the police. Michael explained to her why this wasn't a good idea, and she had reluctantly agreed after a good five minutes of heated debate. It was during this time that she had announced her intention to come with him. This initiated another five minutes of debate that made the first five look calm. It finally ended when Liz doubled over with a severe abdominal cramp. Her maternal instincts won out, and she realized Michael would be better off without her.

Michael promised that he would call her before he pulled up to Rapp's house and stay on the phone with her the whole time he was there. He was about to do just that when his mobile phone rang. O'Rourke grabbed it from the center console and said, "Hello."

"Where are you?"

"I'm almost there."

"You said you were going to call."

Michael ignored that and instead asked, "How are you feeling?"

"Better. I think I should have come with you."

Again, he ignored her as he turned the dark green truck onto the road that Rapp lived off. "How is Duke?"

"Duke's fine. He's sitting right next to me on the couch eating popcorn."

O'Rourke shook his head and stopped at the end of Rapp's driveway. Duke was supposed to be a hunter, not a house dog. They had gone around and around on this, and as in most of their little battles, he had lost.

O'Rourke scanned the tree-lined street for cars and saw none. Just as he turned into the driveway, the rain started falling. It was coming down hard. O'Rourke pinched the phone between his ear and shoulder while he turned the wipers on.

"Shit."

"What's wrong?"

"Nothing. It just started raining very hard." O'Rourke sighted Anna Rielly's car and asked, "Anna drives a little BMW, right?"

"Yes. Is it there?"

"Yeah. When was the last time you tried calling her?"

"Just before I called you."

O'Rourke looked over at the small house. The sky had grown dark with the falling rain, but there were no lights on. Things didn't look so good. "Honey, I'm going to have to get out and take a look."

"Michael, I don't think that's a good idea." Liz's voice sounded panicked. "I think you should wait right there until the police show up."

"Take it easy. I'm just going to look in the windows. If anything happens, call the cops, and then call that other number I gave you."

"Michael, please be careful, and don't do anything stupid."

O'Rourke promised he would try to do one and not the other and then made a dash for the small front porch. His hair and jacket were wet by the time he reached cover. After shaking the water from his head, he reached under his jacket and pulled out a .45-caliber Colt pistol. He couldn't see any signs of Anna through the small window on the front door, so he pressed the doorbell with the tip of the pistol. O'Rourke waited several seconds and then pressed it again. He could hear the bell ring somewhere inside.

"What do you see?"

O'Rourke tried to look through one of the larger windows to the right of the door, but the shades were drawn. "Nothing."

"Is there any broken glass or toppled furniture?"

O'Rourke peered through the small window. "No." His face was inches away from the glass when he saw something move. Startled, he dropped the phone and jumped back, bringing the gun up in both hands. O'Rourke stood off to the side of the door, his heart racing, trying to decide if he should pick up the phone or find better cover. The frightened squawking of his wife's voice won out, and he snatched the phone from the floor just as the front door swung open.

12

Peter Cameron was having his doubts about calling on Villaume. The man was a little too independent for his liking. He was right about Duser, though. What carpet bombing was to air strikes, Duser was to black ops. The man and his people liked to bring a lot of firepower to the party and weren't afraid to use it. Villaume, although he was very adept at keeping a low profile, presented an entirely different problem. He lacked loyalty, and not just to his adopted country but also to his faithful employer of thirty years—the CIA.

Cameron looked out the front window of the rented van and watched the road. It was a quarter to five in the evening, and the afternoon sun was throwing long shadows off the peaks of the mountains. The van was backed into a spot near the office of the Buffalo Bill Motel. It was a quaint twelve-room motel on the outskirts of Evergreen, Colorado. Evergreen was a beautiful town in the mountains forty minutes due west of Denver. It was surrounded on all sides by huge hills that anywhere other than the Rockies would have been referred to as mountains. A half dozen creeks sliced through the hills from all sides and met in the middle of town. In the last decade, Evergreen had fought a battle that towns just like it had fought across the nation. Multimillion-dollar homes were being thrown up and golf courses developed. The place now sported four coffee shops and one of the nicest post offices in the country. The old-time locals were torn between increased wealth, provided by all of the dollars their new neighbors threw into the town, and the loss of their serenity.

Peter Cameron could care less about any of this. He was waiting in the van as Villaume had instructed. Villaume was inside the manager's office taking care of things, and he had told Cameron on no fewer than three occasions that he wasn't to leave the van. Cameron was getting sick of being treated like a neophyte. He had been in the intelligence business for almost as long as the Frog. Granted, he didn't have as much practical field experience, but it wasn't as if this was rocket science.

Villaume had split the group into two upon arriving in Colorado Springs. A van and a Jeep Cherokee had been rented from National Car Rental with the aid of false IDs and credit cards. He and Cameron had driven up in the van, and Mario Lukas and Mary Juarez had taken the Jeep. Lukas and Juarez were up in the mountains right now scouting out the Jansens' A-frame. If they saw anything unusual, they were to report in right away; otherwise, they were to set up the surveillance equipment and go to dinner. At no time did Villaume want anyone to see the four of them together.

The Jansens' flight wasn't due until nine, so they had plenty of time to get things ready. Villaume came back out to the van with keys in hand and moved the vehicle down to the far end of the motel. The two men grabbed some of the equipment and moved it into the room. Cameron dropped his stuff on one of the beds and took a look around. The floor was covered with ugly seventies orange shag carpeting, the bedspreads were a shiny rust color and looked to be made of some highly flammable fabric, and wagon wheels served as headboards for the two twin beds. The room's art consisted of a cheap print of Buffalo Bill and an ashtray shaped like a six-shooter.

Villaume popped one of the case's clasps and said, "It ain't the Ritz, but it'll do." After taking out a detailed map of the area, he unfolded it and stuck it to the wall with four thumb tacks. Next, he popped open two metallic briefcases and readied the equipment. Mario and Mary were to set up four directional parabolic microphones and a digital camera. Mary had also come up with the idea to set up a microwave tripwire. The Jansens, like most people in their line of work, had chosen their lair carefully. It was near the top of the mountain with only one home above it. Their house sat a good hundred yards off the main road. Mary Juarez was going to set up the invisible tripwire twenty yards in on the Jansens' driveway. If anyone decided to make a visit, they'd know.

Villaume looked back at the map after the equipment was powered up. Pointing to it, he said, "They picked this town well. There's only one road that comes in and out of this canyon. Only one road that leads up to their place. We might be able to use it against them, but if anything goes wrong, we're trapped."

Cameron stood back and studied the map, his arms folded across his chest and one hand scratching his beard. "I see your point. How far is it back to Interstate Seventy?"

"About eight miles."

"And then how far to Denver?"

"Straight down the hill for about twenty minutes, and then we should be able to get lost in the city."

"What about heading out of town to the south?"

Villaume looked at the map. "I think it's even worse. We might be able to find some back road to turn off on and hide out for a while, but unless you can get a helicopter to come get us, we're trapped."

Frowning, Cameron surveyed the map for any other options. There were none. "We can't afford getting tangled up with any cops. Thirty minutes on two roads." Cameron shook his head. "They'll have us on TV before we reach Denver."

Villaume didn't like where he thought Cameron might be going with this, so he stayed quiet. Cameron stared at the map for a while longer and then casually announced, "If we have any run-ins with the cops, we'll have to dispose of them."

"You mean kill them." Villaume hated the way desk jockeys liked to come up with antiseptic terms like *dispose* and *eliminate*. Call a spade a spade.

Cameron shrugged. "I see no other choice."

"I'll be the judge of that." Villaume stared at Cameron. He was really beginning to question his judgment in letting this man come along. "You still haven't told me what you want to do with the two targets. Are we going to kill them right away, or do you want to talk to them?"

Cameron hadn't thought that one through yet. "I still haven't decided. As you've repeatedly pointed out, it would be nice to avoid a scene. It would, in fact, be best if they just disappeared forever."

"Can your person at the airport take them out if need be?"

"I gave him instructions to follow from a very discreet distance, and only as far as the exit to Evergreen."

"You didn't answer my question."

Cameron stared back at him, not entirely enthralled with Villaume's abruptness. "'No' is the answer to your question."

"Well, if that's the case, I would let them get settled into their house, listen to what they have to say, and then take them just before sunrise."

Cameron nodded. "That's what I was thinking."

Villaume grinned slightly. *You are so full of shit,* he thought to himself. *You've never had an original idea in your life.*

Cameron saw the smirk on Villaume's face, and he didn't like it. The man needed to learn to respect his employers a little more. When this whole thing was over, he just might have to look into eliminating the Frog and his people. Duser would probably do it for half the normal fee. Duser hated the Frog as much as or more than Cameron did. The Professor grinned back at Villaume and decided a phone call to Duser would tie things up nicely.

★ ★ ★

AT THE COLORADO Springs airport, Scott Coleman, Kevin Hackett, and Dan Stroble were loading their gear into a rented silver Chevrolet Suburban. Hackett had made arrangements to leave the Learjet overnight and have the tanks topped off. As with the group that had landed two hours before them, everything was paid for with credit cards that did not bear their real names.

Hackett was the detail man and always had been. Back on SEAL Team Six, when Coleman needed to overcome a unique logistical problem, Hackett's talents were usually called on. He had the patience and the ability to deal with the minutest of details, whereas Coleman was much more suited to deal with the big picture. It was a relationship that had served them very well over the years. There were times, however, when Hackett's attention to detail bordered on whining.

With everything loaded up, the three former SEALs climbed into the Suburban and left the airport. It took about fifteen minutes to get through the Springs, and then they were on Interstate 25, driving with the rest of the traffic at eighty miles an hour. Stroble, who had spent a lot of time in the area, was driving the SUV. He had explained to the others that it was better to take the Interstate up to Denver and cut over than to take the winding Highway 67 through the foothills.

Hackett was in back pecking away at his four thousand dollar laptop. The computer had a tiny digital phone built in and could access the Internet without a hard line. One of his great assets was his computer skills. Hackett liked to say there was very little you couldn't find over the Internet. Instead of having to stop at a convenience store to buy a map of the Evergreen area and risk getting caught on video, he could simply go on-line and find all the information they needed. Within five minutes, he had printed out eight pages of information on a tiny portable printer the size of a rolling pin.

Hackett handed the sheets to Coleman and went to work on his next project. As he pecked away at the keys, he asked for the third time since leaving Baltimore, "Why did Stansfield call on us instead of using someone within the Agency?"

Coleman lowered the sheets and stared out the front window of the truck. "You know the answer to that, Kevin."

Stroble was hunched over the steering wheel, trying to get a good look at the sky. Weather in the mountains was a tricky thing. It could be seventy and sunny one minute and thirty and snowing the next. Glancing at the rearview mirror, he said, "If you've got a problem, state it, but you're starting to get on my nerves, Kevin."

This is how conversations went between Stroble and Hackett. Coleman barely noticed it anymore, he'd been around them for so long. They were like brothers. One minute, they could be throwing punches, and the next, they could be sharing a beer and laughing. They hadn't swung at each other in a while, but they still got in some pretty heated arguments. The two had been best friends since entering Basic Underwater Demolition School with the SEALs twelve years earlier. They had been paired up as swim buddies during the grueling sixteen-week course that was designed to weed out all but the most devoted. Sleep deprivation, hazing, torturous runs on sandy beaches, and freezing midnight swims were all part of an elaborate testing process to find the toughest warriors. When the real shooting started, quitting wasn't an option.

"What's bothering me"—Hackett pushed his round glasses up on his nose—"is that I don't think this is just some milk run. I think they were doing something outside official channels and it went wrong."

"No shit, Sherlock," Stroble replied. "The man wouldn't have called on us otherwise." Hackett could really be an old woman sometimes.

"What you're missing is when things go wrong, they like to cover their tracks. Today we are the people who are sent to fix this problem; tomorrow we might be the problem."

"What in the hell is that supposed to mean?" asked Stroble.

Hackett kept typing. "We don't know what the Jansens were doing, but you can bet if it involved Iron Man, it was some serious shit. Some shit that didn't go off the way they planned it. When that happens, our beloved Culinary Institute of America has a history of making people disappear."

"You're paranoid," scoffed Stroble.

"That's what you said that time in Libya."

Libya was a bad memory that none of them liked to conjure up. Stroble clutched the steering wheel and mumbled, "You're paranoid every time we run an op."

Hackett hesitated and then replied in an icy tone, "That's bullshit, and you know it." It was all he had to say.

The two men in the front seat were well aware of Hackett's sixth sense.

Coleman turned sideways and looked at Hackett questioningly. He had seen a lot of weird stuff in the thirty-nine years he'd been alive. Most of it as a SEAL. Some of it he could explain, but much of it was beyond the realm of proven science. How one warrior could walk through a dense jungle and literally smell an ambush before the team walked into it was inexplicable. Hackett was one such individual. As a leader, Coleman had learned to respect these intuitions.

"Talk to me."

Hackett shrugged his shoulders. "I've been getting the willies . . . like I've lived through all of this already, but I know I haven't. I've never been to Evergreen, but I know what it looks like. I've never been to the Jansens' house, but I know what it looks like."

"Like it was in a dream?"

"Yeah."

"What else?"

"Something bad is going to happen at that house. I don't know what, but something bad is going to happen."

Stroble grimaced and looked out across the landscape. "Shit." The word was not uttered mockingly but with dread of what lay ahead.

Coleman nodded at Hackett and said, "All right. We'll play this cool. We'll take it real slow and scout things out before we move. If you're still getting your bad vibes in the morning, we'll have to come up with a different plan. Are we all in agreement?" The other two men nodded.

13

Anna Rielly sat on the couch, her arms wrapped around her legs, pulling them tight against her chest. Her best friend had been attempting to console her for the better part of an hour, while Michael O'Rourke alternated between sitting and pacing back and forth in front of the couch. The rain falling outside only added to the dreary mood inside the O'Rourkes' Georgetown home.

After getting over the initial shock of finding her best friend's husband on the front porch of her boyfriend's house holding a gun in his hand, Rielly had listened long enough to understand that Michael O'Rourke didn't want to talk about whatever was bothering him while they were still at Rapp's house. He had handed Anna the mobile phone, and Liz had quickly explained to her that she should listen to Michael and follow him back to Georgetown immediately.

Anna had known instantly that it had something to do with Mitch. She had tried to ask, but again Michael made it clear that they shouldn't talk about it until they got back to the city. This tactic did not work. Anna became understandably upset, and he was forced to tell her that Mitch was all right. This calmed her down just enough to get her into the car and under way, but that was about it. By the time they got back to the O'Rourkes' house, she was a mess.

It took a good thirty minutes for Liz to calm her down, and as far as Michael was concerned, very little useful information came out during this time. Anna would not answer Liz's questions, and the few times that Michael had tried to steer the conversation, his wife had given him a look that told him to butt out. Anna repeatedly stated that she couldn't talk about what Mitch might be involved in. The only point she conceded was that Rapp's computer consulting business was, in fact, legitimate.

O'Rourke grew increasingly frustrated with the way things were going. He wanted answers, and felt he deserved them. This was, after all, something that he did not bring on himself, much as the events involving Scott Coleman and his grandfather had been something he did not bring on himself. O'Rourke paused and thought about that one for a moment. He knew he wasn't being entirely honest. If he had kept his mouth shut and not informed Scott Coleman about a certain senator's complicity in getting a dozen Navy SEALs killed, that whole problem never would have developed. He had learned a hard lesson from that one. Keep your mouth shut. Secrets are better left in the dark. In a way, this was the only thing that was keeping him from taking off the kid gloves. Maybe it was better if he didn't know what Mitch Rapp was really up to?

This line of reasoning only took the congressman so

far, and then it ran into a dead end. The reality was that he was already involved, and it was not by his or his wife's choice. It was Mitch Rapp who had sent the e-mail and asked for help. They deserved a few answers. O'Rourke needed to know what he was now involved in, and if Anna wasn't willing to give the answers, he would go elsewhere.

O'Rourke stood and walked toward the foyer. The rain was coming down in sheets. Looking back at his wife and Rielly, he said, "Anna, I need you to answer some questions." Choosing his next words carefully, he added, "And I need you to answer them truthfully."

Liz O'Rourke looked up at her husband with a scowl on her face. "Michael, I think your questions can wait."

They were going to have it out, and at this point Michael didn't care. It would be his Irish temper against her Italian temper. It had happened before, and it would happen again. They never got physical, and they always made up. Until today, the last five months had been a constant stream of "yes, dears." This, Michael knew, was because of his wife's anointed state of pregnancy. For the most part, Liz ran the show. She was a tough-minded woman, and this, among a long list of things, was why he had married her. But just as she had her strengths, he had his, too. And he feared they were in an area where he had significantly more experience than his wife.

"Do you remember," Michael said in a stern voice, "what happened right here in this house not so long ago?" Michael pointed at the floor. "You went to the store, and when you came back, I was gone."

Liz O'Rourke's big brown eyes looked up at her husband, and she swallowed hard. The memory was more like a nightmare. Thanks to Michael's grandfather and Scott Coleman, her husband had come within inches of losing his life. On the night in question, Michael had been abducted from this very house and taken to the home of one of the most powerful men in Washington. He had been brutally beaten and interrogated, and if it hadn't been for the quick actions of CIA Director Thomas Stansfield, Michael wouldn't be standing here right now.

"Liz." Michael lowered his voice. "We have been dragged into this through no fault of our own. A certain dark chapter in our past has been dredged up and dangled in front of our faces." He slowly shook his head. "And I honestly don't know if Scott Coleman's name was mentioned as a threat or merely an honest suggestion, but I need some answers. Can you understand that?"

Liz looked apprehensive, but she nodded. Michael walked over to the chair and sat. With hands folded and his elbows resting on his knees, he looked at Anna and said, "I know Mitch is much, much more than a computer consultant, and I'm guessing from the way you've been acting since I picked you up at his house that you also know he's more than just a simple computer consultant."

She didn't deny nor confirm the accusation, so O'Rourke took it as a yes. "For him to send Liz that e-mail means one of three things." Michael began ticking the options off on his fingers. "First, he's a spy for us and quite possible a former Navy SEAL." Rielly's tear-filled eyes squinted in a questioning manner at the SEAL comment. "Second, he's a spy for someone else. Or third, he's involved in something illegal like drugs."

Anna shook her head vigorously at the last suggestion.

"Does he work for the CIA?"

"I don't want to talk about this." Rielly gestured with her hands for Michael to stop.

"How about the Pentagon?" he persisted.

"Don't ask any more questions."

"Is it the NSA?"

"Michael, no. I told you I can't talk about this." Rielly buried her face in her hands. "Just please leave me alone." Anna wanted everything to stop. Her head was throbbing. All she wanted was to have Mitch home and safe. She'd been having nightmares about this very thing for the last two months. In every single one of those dreams, Mitch was dead, and it scared her in a way she had never experienced. It was unbearable to think that she could come this far, find the man she wanted to spend the rest of her life with, and then lose him.

Before telling her his real story, Mitch had made Anna promise that she would never discuss what he did for the CIA. Not even with her parents and surely not a U.S. congressman. But Mitch had reached out from wherever he was and contacted Liz and Michael. Anna didn't know what to do.

"Why don't you ask Mitch yourself?"

Michael ignored her and said, "Anna, you know what I do for a living. I can pick up a phone and have someone from the CIA sitting in this room within an hour. It's re-quired by law. I sit on the House Select Committee on Intelligence, and they have to answer to us. I could go down to the Hill right now, and with my security clearance I could start digging. I will probably set off some alarms at Langley and the Pentagon and God only knows where else, but people will have to answer my questions."

Anna lifted her head and looked at O'Rourke. "Michael, I'm begging you, just leave it alone until you can talk to Mitch."

"I can't do that," he said, firmly shaking his head. "Mitch dumped this in our laps, and in the process he has dredged up some stuff that I would really prefer be kept buried. I need to know how he knows about that stuff, and I need to know now."

"I can't tell you. I promised."

O'Rourke took in a deep breath and then let it out in a frustrated moan. He wasn't getting anywhere. Rielly was every bit as stubborn as his wife. Changing tactics, he asked, "Do you think it's fair to my family that Mitch has dumped this on us? He's obviously in some serious shit if he's worried about your safety." Leaning closer to Rielly, he said, "I think I know what Mitch does for a living, and this is not some game." O'Rourke pointed to himself. "I know. I've been there. Dark-clad men, in the middle of the night with silenced weapons, making people disappear without a trace. That's why he got hold of us. There is no other reason. He's worried about your safety. Now, would you please answer my questions? I need and deserve to know what we've been involved in."

Rielly's tears fell even harder, and she blew her nose on a tissue. "I can't. I made a promise."

O'Rourke was getting really frustrated. Tears be

damned, he pushed ahead. "Mitch wanted us to bring you here because he's afraid someone will try to get their hands on you so they can get to him. I have no problem protecting you. I love you, and Liz loves you, but for Christ sake, we're now in danger, too. If you won't answer my questions, I'm going to be forced to start digging."

Rielly began to cry so hard she shook. Liz pulled her close and held her tight. She looked at her husband with the most disgusted expression he had ever seen. He opened his mouth to speak, but Liz stuck her hand out. "Don't say another word."

O'Rourke stood and out of sheer frustration said, "This is a bunch of bullshit."

A second later, Anna Rielly was up and walking across the room. "I'm sorry . . . I'm so sorry I got you involved in this." She continued into the foyer and grabbed her jacket.

Liz O'Rourke was right on her heels. As she passed her six-foot-two-inch, two-hundred-fifteen-pound husband, she delivered a forearm shiver that moved him back a step.

"Anna, where do you think you're going?" shouted Liz.

"I'm leaving. It's not fair to have gotten you involved in this. I made the choice to fall in love with him, not you. You shouldn't have to go through this."

Liz grabbed her best friend by the arm and swung her back toward the stairs. Pushing her up the steps, she said, "You are staying right here until I know you're safe!" Rielly began to protest, but Liz would have none of it. She continued pushing her old college roommate up the stairs. On the fourth step, Liz stopped and glared at her husband.

Michael started to say, "I was only . . ."

"Don't even try to explain yourself!" snapped Liz. "I am so disappointed in you right now, I don't even want to look at you!" With that, the two women were up the stairs and gone.

Michael watched them go and then smacked himself in the forehead with the palm of his hand. On his way into the kitchen, he threw a dozen well-punctuated swear words at himself and then threw in a few more for good measure. Michael yanked the refrigerator door open and grabbed a bottle of beer. He took a big swig and leaned back against the counter. Duke came up and sat in front of him. O'Rourke looked down at the yellow Lab and said, "It's just you and me, buddy."

After taking another gulp of beer, O'Rourke shook his head in sheer frustration. It really sucked knowing that even though you were right, you were wrong. Every single thing he had just said in the other room was right, but because they didn't like the way he said it, he was now wrong and would pay the price. O'Rourke let out a loud moan and thought, *Give 'em an hour, and then go upstairs and apologize.*

In the meantime, there was one thing he could do. O'Rourke walked over to the phone on the kitchen wall and grabbed it. Opening the cupboard, he glanced down a phone list until he found the right number. A short while later, a woman answered on the other end.

"Capitol Hill Police Department. How may I direct your call?"

"Watch commander, please."

There were two clicks on the line, and then another female voice came on. "This is Sergeant Hall."

"Sergeant, this is Congressman O'Rourke. How are you doing tonight?"

"Just fine, and you, sir?"

"Well . . . I just got a weird phone call. The second one in two days."

"Did they threaten bodily harm?"

"Yeah, the standard stuff. I wouldn't bother you, but my wife is pregnant, and she doesn't need the stress right now." O'Rourke pinched the bridge of his nose. If the watch commander only knew how true that was.

"Would you like me to have a unit check up on you throughout the night?"

"That would be great. Do you need the address?"

"Nope. I've got it right here on the screen. You're in Georgetown just off Wisconsin."

"That's correct."

"We'll take care of it, sir. Someone will be by every hour, and if there are any more problems, don't hesitate to call."

"I won't. Thank you, Sergeant." O'Rourke placed the phone back in the cradle and paused. He was tempted to make another call, but considering the trouble he had already gotten himself in tonight, he decided against it. They would be safe in the house with the new security measures. Beyond that, he would sleep on the couch with Duke and his Remington 12-gauge shotgun. They would be fine for the night, and then, he hoped, tomorrow would bring more answers and less emotion.

14

The birds were chirping, and the sky was slowly showing signs of morning. A thin bank of clouds obscured the top of Mount Evans due west of where he was sitting. The house was at eight thousand feet, some six thousand feet short of the mountain's summit. Scott Coleman could see why people moved here. The thick pines and aspen-laden hills, towering mountains, icy creeks, and glassy ponds enveloped one with an awesome sense of calmness. Like being in one of the great European cathedrals, you were left with the feeling that you were in the presence of the creator. Coleman was an ocean man. He had always been and always would be, but he could clearly see why others chose the mountains.

Coleman was sitting on the deck of an A-frame cabin located at the top of Prospect Drive. From his perch, he could see the Jansens' house several hundred feet below and across a large ravine. Hackett had found the cabin on the Internet. It had been a relatively simple task. First, he had legitimately accessed the Pentagon's computer network and retrieved detailed elevation maps of Evergreen. From there, Hackett located the Jansens' house and picked four streets that would offer a good position to set up surveillance. Next, he searched the local real estate and property management Web pages. It took about fifteen minutes to find the house at the top of Prospect Drive. It was listed under the Weekend Getaway section of the Evergreen Leasing and Management Company. The company specialized in helping owners rent their mountain retreats when they wouldn't be using them. Hackett had very little trouble hacking his way past the site's security measures. Once in, it took less than a minute to find that the cabin was available, and with a little more work he retrieved the combination for the lock box.

Coleman was wrapped in a camouflage sleeping bag and sitting in a deck chair with his blue baseball hat pulled down tight over his blond hair. On the table next to him was a night-vision scope and a pair of binoculars. Unfortunately, they were too far away to use the directional microphone they had brought. Stroble and Hackett were in the living room sleeping on the floor. Around eleven o'clock the previous evening, the Jansens had been dropped off by an airport shuttle van. The three former SEALs had watched them for about an hour and then settled into two-hour shifts. Coleman was in the final minutes of his 4:00-to-6:00 watch. The three men had agreed on a plan of sorts. They would see how the morning went and then phone the Jansens and give them the choice of meeting them in town for a chat or inviting them up to their house. If the latter was the case, Stroble would be positioned in a spot of his choice with his trusted and robust Galil sniper rifle.

Coleman was to bring the Jansens back to Washington, whether they wanted to come or not, and killing them was to be avoided if at all possible. They had talked the night before about jumping the Jansens at dawn. Stroble had pointed out that they'd been traveling for the better part of a day and would be tired and disoriented. His vote was to hit them at first light and get it over with. Nothing cute. Strap on the body armor, tactical vests, and goggles, grab the silenced MP-5s and a few flash-bangs, and bust down the front door. This was classic Stroble. Hit the target hard, and hit it fast.

Hackett saw very little virtue in his friend's plan. Plus, he was still getting his bad vibe. Coleman, for his part, was intent on returning to Washington with his two men and the Jansens. He wanted everyone alive and no one in Evergreen the wiser that three very lethal individuals had spent a night in their perfect little town.

The former SEAL Team Six commander knew from experience that once you started setting off flash-bangs and breaking down doors, things could get out of hand. Plus, they weren't dealing with a couple of teenage ragheads. The Jansens were highly trained army commandos, and they were on their home turf. They would surely have weapons nearby, and this was what really bothered Coleman. He and his men weren't trained in policing action. They were trained to kill. It had been hammered into them during thousands of hours of close-quarters battle, or CQB as it was known in the counterterrorism trade. If someone had a gun, they were trained to shoot them in the head, not the arm. Three shots to the head, and then move on to the next target. It was not hard for Coleman to envision a scenario where one of the Jansens, or both, reached for a weapon in the middle of the raid. If that happened, the Jansens would be dead, and there was a chance, though a slim one, that one of them would also get shot. Nope, thought Coleman. There was no reason to get anyone killed.

It was getting light now. The sun was still not up, but he could see the Jansens' house clearly. Coleman looked behind him. Hanging from the wall of the cabin was a circular white thermometer with a mountain lion in the middle. The temperature was a crisp fifty-two degrees. Coleman stretched his arms above his head and looked at his watch. It was 6:02, time to wake up Hackett and let him keep an eye on things for a few hours. As Coleman stood, he looked down for one last check. He was about to head into the cabin when the front door of the Jansens' house opened, and a man walked out. Coleman snatched the binoculars from the table and brought Jim Jansen into focus just before he entered the detached two-car garage.

This was a little unexpected. In the still mountain air, Coleman could hear the car start even though it was more than a half a mile away. Next came the brake lights, and then the car backed out of the garage. Coleman walked quickly to the sliding glass door and flung it open. "Get your asses up, you two! Jansen's on the move." Coleman went back to the railing and watched as the Subaru station wagon turned around in the driveway. Jansen got out, opened the back hatch, and then ran back into the house, leaving the car running.

Coleman started for the living room. He didn't like what he saw.

PETER CAMERON WASN'T the only person who thought of logging onto the Internet to check up on what had happened in Germany. At one in the morning, Jim Jansen had signed onto his AOL account. His wife was sound asleep, but he was restless. They had just made a lot of money, and he wanted to go someplace remote and warm, so he and his wife could relax. Jansen knew Kennedy would want to debrief them. That was all part of the plan. Since Iron Man wasn't around, there wouldn't be anybody else to contradict their story. After the debriefing, they would have to go someplace nice and hide out for a few weeks. The work that he and his wife did paid great, but it was absolutely draining. Looking back on it, he could honestly say if they were offered the same amount of money to do this job again, they would turn it down. Iron Man had made him nervous. The man had sensed that something was up, despite all of the planning they had done. His wife had told him in detail about what had happened in the house—the way Iron Man had shot Hagenmiller and disabled the bodyguard. They had been lucky that Beth had killed him so easily.

Jansen started with the *London Times*. The European press would have had a full day to cover the story, and he figured there was a decent chance that the *Times* might mention the assassination of Count Hagenmiller in its Sunday edition. When the German authorities figured out that Iron Man was an American, the story would be front-page news everywhere, but that would take a while.

Jansen was pleasantly surprised to find the headline "Germans Believe Count Was Assassinated" plastered across the front page. He couldn't help feeling a little excited over the high-profile treatment of the case. By the second paragraph, the excitement was replaced by confusion. There was no fire when they had left the estate. By the fifth paragraph, the confusion had deepened, and by the end of the article, it had been replaced entirely by fear.

He had followed the story right up to the point where it said a man and a woman posing as BKA agents had left the estate in a maroon Audi sedan at approximately 11:15 P.M. and had not been seen since. Then there was the mention of a third individual who left approximately five minutes later in a car that was stolen from one of the guests attending the count's party. Jansen's heartbeat picked up as he read on. The stolen car had been tracked to the Hanover airport. From there, the article jumped to a cab driver who was found bound and gagged in a hotel in Freiburg, Germany. Based on the detailed account that the driver had given the police, there could be little doubt that the man who had held him at gunpoint was none other than Iron Man.

Jansen had raced into the bedroom in a panic and got his wife up. He asked her again exactly where she had shot the operative they knew only as Iron Man. It didn't take long for the two of them to figure out that he must have been wearing a bulletproof vest and had not told them. It was a stupid mistake. Jim Jansen wanted to strangle his wife for not putting a third bullet in the man's head. This was the exact reason he was supposed to be the trigger man.

What they had to do was glaringly obvious. They had to run, and they had to run fast and far. When the man they had ambushed in Germany made his way back to the United States, he would tell Irene Kennedy everything, and she would understandably give him all the information he needed to track them down. Jim Jansen had very little doubt about the outcome of that confrontation. The Jansens would last right up until they gave up who had hired them, and then they would be killed the proper way—a bullet to the head.

WHILE JIM AND Beth Jansen raced around their house gathering the things they would need for quite possibly the rest of their lives, they didn't realize that there was a far more imminent threat sitting in room ten of the Buffalo Bill Motel. Peter Cameron had listened to every word the Jansens uttered, and it had given him ample time to plan and get things into place. With a little luck and cooperation from the Jansens, he would be back in Washington by noon.

Cameron was extremely efficient with virtually every firearm there was. It didn't matter if it was a pistol, a shotgun, or a rifle. In his early twenties, he had gone to a gun club in rural Virginia with another employee of the CIA and was exposed to competition shooting for the first time. Over a period of years, this had turned from a passion into an obsession. Cameron was the top pistol shooter in his club and one of the best on the East Coast.

He was very proficient at skeet shooting and was deadly accurate with a rifle. All of this shooting, however, was done under controlled conditions.

Cameron's pride and joy was his gun collection. Over the years, he had steadily built it up to the point where it now totaled more than a hundred pieces. Since he had bought them wisely and they had appreciated greatly over the last two decades, the collection was now worth a small fortune.

Despite all of this, Cameron was deeply embarrassed by one fact. He had never killed another human. Villaume was right—Cameron had always sent someone else to do the dirty work. Now that Cameron had officially broken with the CIA, and he was dealing with hired killers like Villaume and Duser, he felt it was time to make a statement. This was how he had rationalized his decision to be the one to pull the trigger on the Jansens. He was in a dangerous line of work where a peer's respect for one's talents could someday mean the difference between life and death. Deep down inside, however, Cameron knew the real reason. He had wondered for years what it would be like. He had spent thousands of hours shooting at inanimate targets with weapons that were designed to kill living things. Many of them designed specifically to kill human beings. The competitions had always taken place under closely controlled and regulated circumstances. The only variables were often the wind and the humidity. His passion had never been taken to that final level, and now it was time.

Cameron, it turned out, was beginning to realize it was a good idea he had brought Villaume along for the job instead of Duser. The man was a meticulous planner, like himself, and in the end someone with far more practical field experience. Cameron had brought two handguns, a sniping rifle, an assault rifle, and a submachine gun. He had had it in his head that he would take the Jansens from a safe distance of five hundred to six hundred meters with his Walther WA 2000 sniping rifle. Villaume didn't like this idea. The Walther fired a .300 Winchester Magnum cartridge, and the shot would sound like a cannon up in the mountains. They wanted to get in and out of Evergreen without attracting any attention. Villaume, used to trying to make things easier rather than more difficult, had pointed out to Cameron that they could take up a position two-hundred meters from the Jansens' front door.

At 4:45, the van stopped half a mile down the road from the Jansens' house. Villaume and Cameron got out and started their trek up the mountain. Lukas and Juarez pulled the van off the road and onto a small trail, where they monitored the surveillance devices and waited. If Cameron failed, and the Jansens got past, they were to block the road with the van and hose down the Jansens' vehicle with their silenced MP-5s.

It had taken Cameron and Villaume longer than they had wanted to get into position. Villaume was not happy about this. At fifty-two, he was far from in top shape, but compared with Cameron, he felt like an Olympic decathlete. At least, he seemed to know his weapons, Villaume thought. It was almost 5:30 by the time they settled into their spot underneath a towering pine tree. They were on the other side of the Jansens' driveway and down a bit toward the road. They had a clear view of both the house and the garage. Cameron had planned his first kill meticulously and brought everything that would give him an edge. In addition to the bed of soft needles that he was lying on, he had brought a padded mat and a roll. He was wearing a camouflage sniping suit and was nestled in behind a Stoner SR-25 assault rifle. Threaded onto the end of the weapon's free-floating barrel was a customized silencer, and attached to the fore end was a spring-operated bipod for added stability. In essence, the weapon was an M-16 modified to act as a sniper support weapon. Unlike the M-16, though, it fired a heavier 7.62-mm cartridge. The weapon could be fired in single shot or burst mode. Cameron had the selector switch on single shot and was looking through the times-six telescopic sight.

When Jansen appeared from the house at 6:00 A.M., Cameron was not surprised. Mary Juarez had already informed them that it sounded as if they were ready to leave. The warning didn't help. Cameron's heart began to beat harder even before the front door opened. Despite the cool morning air, sweat formed on his brow, and his breathing became short. Cameron swung the rifle from left to right as Jansen walked to the garage. The cross hairs stayed centered on the side of the target's head for less than half the trek. Cameron couldn't believe how nervous he was. His normally steady aim was anything but. Talking himself down, he reminded himself of the backup that was in place. If he missed, everything would be fine. Lukas and Juarez would take care of things.

This approach did not work. Cameron knew he had a relatively easy shot, and if he missed it, Villaume would see it as proof of his amateur status. When the car started to back out of the garage, Cameron took a moment to close his eyes and wipe a layer of sweat from his forehead. Counting backward from one hundred, he concentrated on his breathing in an attempt to slow his pulse. Everything needed to be brought back down into the zone, and he would be fine.

Villaume whispered in his ear, "I'll let you know if the woman comes out. Keep the guy in your sights." The car backed out of the garage and turned around in the driveway. When the driver jumped out and ran back into the house, Villaume said, "This is it. When he comes back out, wait as long as you can to shoot until she comes out, but don't let him get behind the wheel. We don't want to have to shoot up the car if we don't have to."

Cameron did not reply. He felt better. His breathing and pulse had slowed. He could feel himself falling into the zone. The cross hairs stayed centered on the open front door. He kept counting down, slower and slower. His breaths were shallow and taken through the nose. When Jim Jansen appeared on the porch a minute later, Cameron was not startled. He simply followed the man as he walked toward the rear of the wagon. After throwing several bags in the back, Jansen reached up and slammed the tailgate closed. The action left his face perfectly bisected in the black cross hairs of the scope. Cameron's right forefinger sat poised over the cold trigger of the Stoner rifle. He heard Villaume start to speak, and at that moment the target turned his head toward the front door. Cameron knew immediately what Villaume was saying, and without waiting another second, he squeezed the trigger in one smooth, constant motion.

SCOTT COLEMAN BROUGHT the pair of binoculars to his eyes and looked down on the Jansens' house. It looked as if they were getting ready to go someplace, and it appeared they were in a hurry. Keeping the binoculars up, he turned his head toward the sliding glass door and in a hushed voice said, "Dan, get the truck out of the garage. We'll come back and sanitize the place later."

If they hurried, they could beat them down to the main road and block them from getting into town. If things could be handled peacefully, they could talk them into coming back to Washington. If they couldn't cut them off, they'd have to follow, and things could get tricky.

Coleman watched as Jim Jansen came back out of the house and threw two large duffel bags into the back of the Subaru station wagon. Jansen's mouth was opening, as if to say something, and then his body lurched violently away from the car and thudded to the gravel driveway. Coleman instinctively crouched several inches lower and moved the binoculars toward the front door. For the briefest of moments, he saw Beth Jansen alive and staring, her mouth agape, at the limp body of her husband lying on the ground. Before she could overcome the shock of watching her husband struck down, a bullet hit her in the forehead and sent her into the bushes next to the porch steps.

15

Irene Kennedy greeted the start of the week with little enthusiasm. The Monday morning traffic was heavy, and so was her mood. Mitch Rapp was still missing, and the only two people other than Rapp who could tell her what had happened in Germany were dead. For someone who prided herself on being able to block out distractions and focus on the task at hand, she wasn't exactly measuring up to her expectations this morning. Sitting on her lap was a copy of the president's daily brief, or PDB. The document was a highly classified newspaper that was prepared by the CIA's Office of Current Production and Analytical Support. The PDB was prepared by a dozen officers and analysts who spent much of their evenings amassing the most current information that may affect the national security of the country. Every president since John F. Kennedy has handled the document differently. Some have read it religiously every morning, while others have directed their national security advisors to do so. President Hayes treated it with the zeal of a Calvinist. He read it every morning, asked his briefer pointed questions, and took notes. As deputy director of Counterterrorism,

Kennedy did not usually give President Hayes the daily briefing, but the attack on the White House had changed all of that. Combating terrorism had become Hayes's top priority. It worked out that she gave the briefing about once a week, sometimes more, sometimes less. President Hayes used the briefing as a cover so the two could discuss the activities of the Orion Team.

Kennedy closed the book and looked out the window. The government sedan she was traveling in had just turned off Constitution onto 17th Street. The Ellipse was to her right, and ahead was the White House. The entire mansion was covered in scaffolding as workers raced to mend the damage of the terrorist attack by Christmas. President Hayes had been adamant that repair of the old, glorious building be conducted with around-the-clock vigilance to help erase the scars from the American mind as quickly as possible. The entire building had been placed in a bubble of aluminum and plastic to keep the cameras away. Fortunately, severe damage had been avoided, thanks to the quick actions of the fire department. The buzz around town was that the general contractor that had been hired was ahead of schedule. If they finished by Christmas, they would get a twenty-percent bonus. The West Wing was already open for business, but there was much speculation and wagering on the street about whether or not the president and the first lady would be celebrating the birth of Christ in the Executive Mansion. For now, they were staying in Blair House across the street from the Old Executive Office Building.

The four-door sedan maneuvered its way through the barricades designed to thwart a truck bomb and stopped at the southwest gate of the White House grounds. Two uniformed Secret Service officers stepped out from the guardhouse and began checking IDs. It wasn't too long ago that they would simply have opened the gate and waved them through, but the attack had changed everything. Kennedy visited the White House frequently, and often with the same driver and bodyguard, but that didn't matter anymore. She rolled down her window and handed over her credentials. The officer looked at them briefly and then handed them back. A third Secret Service officer circled the sedan with a bomb-sniffing dog and checked the trunk. The whole exercise took less than a minute, and then the gate opened.

The driver pulled up to the long cream-colored awning that led to the ground floor of the West Wing. Kennedy thanked the two men and told them to wait in the car. Once through the doors, she held up a heavy blue pouch with a metallic lock across the top. The officer was used to seeing the arrival of the blue pouch, which contained the PDB. The Secret Service officer sitting behind the desk said good morning and spun a clipboard around so the doctor could sign in. With that done, Kennedy headed up the stairs to her left. One of the blue suits, an agent from the president's Personal Protection Detail, was standing at the top of the stairs. She knew this meant the president was in the West Wing. Kennedy checked her watch; at 7:12, he was probably eating breakfast and reading his morning papers.

Just before she reached the Oval Office, she stopped at a door on her right and held up the blue pouch. A towering Secret Service agent in a dark gray suit nodded and allowed admittance into the president's private dining room. Kennedy found the president sitting in his usual spot, with his four folded newspapers laid out in front of him.

A small Filipino man dressed in a white waistcoat and black pants approached and said, "Good morning, Dr. Kennedy."

"Good morning, Carl."

The man took the pouch from Kennedy and then her jacket. Kennedy sat at the circular oak table across from the president and unlocked the pouch.

The president glanced up and said, "Good morning, Irene."

"Good morning, sir."

"How was your weekend?"

"Just fine, sir, and yours?" Kennedy extracted a copy of the PDB and slid it across the table. She knew they would continue with the small talk until Carl left.

"It wasn't too bad. Camp David is really beautiful this time of the year." Hayes perused the headlines on the first page of the PDB and noted that they covered many of the same topics that were on the front page of the *Washington Post*. He knew the content would be a different matter.

Carl approached Kennedy and set down a mug of black coffee and a blueberry muffin. "The muffins are very good today. Low fat."

Kennedy smiled. "Thank you, Carl." The man always went out of his way to try to get her to eat.

"Mr. President, the pot on the table is full. If you need me, just buzz."

"Thank you, Carl." President Hayes was a huge coffee drinker. Eight to ten cups a day was his standard. He liked to point out to all who criticized his coffee consumption that Dwight D. Eisenhower drank twenty-some cups a day and smoked four packs of unfiltered cigarettes while he was the Supreme Allied Commander. After that, the man went on to serve as president for two terms and lived until he was seventy-nine. Hayes was very fond of telling overly concerned types the Eisenhower bio. His wife was equally fond of telling him, "You're no Dwight D. Eisenhower." It had now gotten to the point where Hayes told the story just so he could hear his wife utter her line. Hayes was the first to admit he was no Dwight D. Eisenhower. Very few people were. Hayes was a Democrat, but the more time he spent in the Oval Office, the more he grew to like Eisenhower, who was a Republican. Ike was Hayes's dark horse candidate for best president. Everybody always mentioned Washington, Jefferson, Lincoln, and FDR, but Ike was the only one of the group who came from abject poverty and rose to the most important office in the land. Add to that the fact that he whupped the Nazis, his trailblazing efforts to end segregation, the way he helped out the farmers, and the way he kept military spending at bay, and in Hayes's mind he had a real shot at being the best.

The outer door clicked shut while President Hayes was pouring another cup of coffee. Looking over the top of his reading glasses, he asked, "What in the hell happened in Germany? We have a meeting with their ambassador in forty minutes."

Kennedy didn't quite know how to answer the question since she herself was in the dark. "I'm trying to figure that out, sir. In a nutshell, we're short on specifics."

"Haven't you talked to Mitch?"

Kennedy shook her head. "No. Originally, we were told that he had been lost during the operation."

Hayes leaned forward, moving his bowl of cereal and newspapers out of his way. "Say again?"

"Some of the other assets that were involved in the operation reported that Mitch had been killed. We no longer believe that to be true."

Hayes frowned. "You'd better back up and give it to me from the start."

Kennedy began to do so but cautioned that her information was incomplete. She went on to explain the details they had learned from their counterparts in Germany. Hayes was particularly interested in the description of the suspect who had kidnapped a cab driver and taken him to Freiburg. For the most part, the president remained calm during her summation of the weekend's events.

When she was finished, Hayes asked, "Why haven't you debriefed the other two who were involved?"

Kennedy hesitated at first. One of her jobs, as she saw it, was to insulate the president from this type of mess. Plausible deniability could be a very important thing. Her decision to tell him was eventually based on fear, fear of what or who might be behind the death of the Jansens. "Sir, we sent a team to pick the Jansens up in Colorado. They were preparing to make contact when they witnessed a second team . . . a team we know nothing about, move in and eliminate the Jansens. Our team watched from a distance as the bodies were removed and the area sanitized."

The frown returned to the president's face. "Now I'm really confused."

"So are we, sir."

"Who would want to kill them?" Hayes's face twisted in a scowl. "Why?"

"We're looking into that, sir."

"Could the Germans move that fast?"

"I doubt it, sir."

"What about something completely unrelated? Is it possible this was about something else they were involved in?" President Hayes was grabbing for any reason other than the one he didn't want to hear. That they had been compromised, that there was a leak somewhere.

"Anything is possible, but for obvious reasons, I don't like the timing."

"What about Mitch? What are we doing to bring him in?"

"Nothing."

"What?"

"Sir, this is what Mitch does best. He's trained to disappear. If we start looking for him, it will only make things worse."

Hayes still didn't like the idea. "There has to be something we can do."

Kennedy shook her head. "Director Stansfield agrees with me."

"Then what's our plan of action?"

"The unknown team that hit the Jansens . . . we are in the process of tracking them down."

The president sat back and looked out the window at the Old Executive Office Building. For almost a minute, he didn't speak. His mind was filtering through all of the possibilities, none of which he particularly liked. It would be nice if these Jansen people were killed by a former employer, but Kennedy was right; given the timing, it was highly unlikely. For an operation that no one was supposed to know about, things didn't look good.

Finally, Hayes turned back to Kennedy and said, "Find out who got to the Jansens, and do it as quickly and quietly as possible."

"I will, sir."

"Now, about this meeting with the German ambassador, we need to get on the same page about a few things."

AT ELEVEN MINUTES after eight, President Hayes, Dr. Kennedy, and the president's national security advisor, Michael Haik, entered the Oval Office through the president's private study. Seated at the two long couches in front of the fireplace were some of the administration's biggest hitters. Robert Xavier Hayes didn't become president of the United States by missing out on the importance of showmanship. He had a rough plan for how this meeting would go, and the list of attendees was part of it.

Everyone stood when Hayes entered the room. The President walked over to the German ambassador, Gustav Koch, and shook his hand. He then grabbed one of the two chairs in front of the fireplace. Michael Haik took the other chair, and Kennedy sat on the couch next to General Flood, the chairman of the Joint Chiefs. Next to General Flood sat his boss, Secretary of Defense Rick Culbertson. Directly across from them sat Secretary of State Midleton and the German ambassador.

President Hayes sat back and crossed his legs. He had a deeply concerned look on his face as he glanced over at Ambassador Koch. Inside, he was relishing the thoughts that must have been going through his secretary of state's head as well as the German ambassador's. They were the ones who had called this meeting. It was unusual, to say the least, that the secretary of Defense and the chairman of the Joint Chiefs were asked to attend a meeting that clearly fell under the purview of Foggy Bottom.

Introductions were made for the benefit of the ambassador. Hayes clasped his hands over his knee and asked, "What can I do for you this morning, Mr. Ambassador?"

Ambassador Koch cleared his throat and glanced at the secretary of state before starting. Then, turning back to President Hayes, he said, "Chancellor Vogt asked that I speak to you about a very serious matter." Koch spoke perfect English, without the slightest trace of an accent. He was not a dumb man. A career politician for thirty-one of his sixty years, he understood the significance of the presence of the two men from the Pentagon. That was why he had immediately interjected the name of the leader of Germany into the conversation.

For Hayes's part, he wasn't going to make this easy for the ambassador and, more importantly, for the secretary of state. He made no effort to communicate that he knew what this meeting was about. Koch grew a little uncomfortable at the silence and looked to the secretary of state for assistance.

Finally, Midleton said, "Sir, I assume you've been briefed about what happened in Germany over the weekend." Midleton looked at Hayes for confirmation but got none. "Sir, I'm referring to the assassination of Count Hagenmiller and the fire that destroyed one of the finest homes in Europe and," Midleton added with an agonized tone, "a priceless art collection."

Hayes finally nodded. "I'm familiar with the situation." No words of sympathy were offered.

"Sir," Secretary Midleton continued. "Ambassador Koch knew Count Hagenmiller quite well, as did Chancellor Vogt."

Hayes nodded just once and again offered no words of condolence.

Koch was confused by President Hayes's lack of sensitivity, but since he had only dealt with the man on a limited basis, he ignored the strangeness and stated his case. "Chancellor Vogt is deeply concerned that the assassination of Count Hagenmiller may have been carried out by a foreign intelligence service."

"Really, and why does he think that?" The president kept his eyes focused on the ambassador's.

"We are privy to certain information that leads us to that conclusion."

"And what would that information be?"

Ambassador Koch sat rigid. "We have been told that the count was under surveillance during the days leading up to his death."

"By whom?"

Koch glanced at Irene Kennedy and then the president. "The CIA."

"And?"

"Can you confirm or deny that the CIA had Count Hagenmiller under surveillance?"

"I can confirm that the CIA had him under surveillance prior to his death."

The ambassador was happy that he had received an honest answer. He was, however, less than enthusiastic about where he had to take the conversation. Choosing his words carefully, he said, "We have been very good allies for a long time, Mr. President. Chancellor Vogt is deeply concerned that the relationship may be in jeopardy over this incident."

"Why is that?" Hayes knew what the ambassador was implying, but he wanted to hear him say it.

Koch looked down uncomfortably at his hands and then glanced at Kennedy before turning back to the president. "The chancellor is worried that . . . the CIA . . . may have acted without your authority and done something that would offend even the most ardent American supporters in my country."

In a way, Hayes felt sorry for the ambassador. It was highly probable that he had intentionally been kept in the dark about Count Hagenmiller's recent business dealings. He was advised by Kennedy that there was a good chance the German chancellor was also unaware of Hagenmiller's nefarious dealings. This was the only thing that was keeping Hayes from going ballistic.

"Mr. Ambassador, I, too, value our friendship. Germany is one of our greatest allies." The president leaned forward and rubbed his hands together. "How well do you know Count Hagenmiller? I mean, did you know?"

"Fairly well. His family is very well respected and very involved in the arts and a variety of philanthropic endeavors."

"Did you know that he has been selling highly sensitive equipment to Saddam Hussein? Equipment that is used to manufacture components for nuclear weapons?"

The bomb had been dropped. Secretary Midleton shifted uncomfortably, and his face turned a touch ashen. Ambassador Koch took a little more convincing. "I find that very hard to believe, Mr. President."

"Is that so?" Hayes stuck out his hand, and Kennedy handed him a file. The president opened it and held up a photograph. "The man on the left I'm sure you recognize. Do you know who the other man is?"

Koch shook his head. He had a sinking feeling that he didn't want to know either.

"He is none other than Abdullah Khatami. Does the name ring a bell?"

"No."

"He's a general in the Iraqi army." Hayes's voice was beginning to take on an edge. "He is in charge of rebuilding Saddam's nuclear weapons program. What you see happening here"—the president stuck out the photo so there could be no misinterpretation—"is Count Hagenmiller receiving a briefcase from Khatami containing five million dollars."

Ambassador Koch was disbelieving. "I knew Count Hagenmiller. I don't think he was capable of such a thing. He didn't need money. He was very wealthy. Are you sure the cash wasn't for artwork? The count was an avid collector."

Secretary of State Midleton managed to compose himself just long enough to add a pathetic nod for support.

Hayes let his anger build. It was all part of the plan. In a much louder voice, he said, "Count Hagenmiller was nowhere near as wealthy as you thought. Did you know that last night, the same night the count was killed, a break-in occurred at the Hagenmiller Engineering warehouse in Hanover?"

Kennedy corrected him. "It was Hamburg, sir."

"Hamburg. Thank you. This break-in was part of an elaborate plan by the count and Khatami to ensure that Khatami got what he needed for Saddam." Hayes shook his fist and added in an icy tone, "Before you come in here and start accusing me and my people of assassination, I think you should start looking for answers within your own government. And while you're at it, you might want to ask the Iraqis what they were up to last night." The president stood. "Now, I have a very busy schedule today, Mr. Ambassador, so if you'll excuse me, I have to get some work done."

The ambassador rose slowly and kept his eyes averted from the president's. "My apologies if I've upset you, sir. In my position I am not always given the full picture."

"I know you aren't, Gustav. Don't blame yourself. But do me a favor and tell the diplomats back in Berlin to do some checking with the BKA before they send you in here to toss wild accusations about."

"I will, Mr. President."

The two men shook hands, and then the German ambassador started for the door. Secretary Midleton rose to follow, but President Hayes cut him off. "Mr. Ambassador, I need a few minutes of Secretary Midleton's time. Would you please wait for him outside?" The ambassador left, and Hayes turned back to Midleton. "Sit."

Midleton reluctantly returned to his seat. The president took off his suit coat and threw it over the chair he had been sitting in. With his hands planted firmly on his hips, he studied his secretary of state. Hayes had known Midleton from his time in the Senate. He liked him well enough, but the man had not been his first choice for the top job at the State Department. In truth, Hayes found him to be a bit of an elitist snob. To make matters worse, there had been a recent spate of foreign policy statements released from the secretary's office that were not in line with the White House's official position.

"Chuck, whose side are you on?" Hayes intentionally called him Chuck instead of Charles.

Midleton rolled his eyes. "I won't dignify that question with an answer."

"Please," baited the president, "lower yourself to my level."

Midleton took the offense. "Count Hagenmiller was a good man. I don't buy this story the CIA has concocted. My people in Berlin are telling me this looks very bad for us."

"Concocted!" shouted Hayes. "You haven't seen one-tenth of what she has on him." The president pointed at Kennedy.

"Why was the CIA watching him?" snapped Midleton.

Hayes folded his arms across his chest. He had a temper but rarely let it be seen. If he had an issue with someone, he usually took them behind closed doors and had it out. This was now beyond that. Midleton's arrogance was insufferable. Hayes speculated that the man had never gotten it into his head that they were no longer equals. Hayes had been junior to him in the Senate, and now with Midleton holding the glamour post in the administration, it appeared the man thought he was untouchable. Hayes stared him down and thought, *You've challenged me in front of three other cabinet members. You've left me no choice.*

"Chuck, let me get a few things straight. First of all, it's none of your damn business why the CIA had Hagenmiller under surveillance, and, more importantly, I'd like to know how in the hell you ever found out about it."

Midleton hesitated. Hayes was as angry as he'd ever seen him. Sidestepping the question didn't appear to be an option. He looked across at General Flood and Secretary Culbertson. Neither looked as if he would intervene on his behalf. "Jonathan Brown told me, but," Midleton cautioned, "it was perfectly legitimate. I spoke with him on Saturday morning when I found out that the count had been assassinated."

Jonathan Brown was the deputy director of Central Intelligence, Thomas Stansfield's number two man. Hayes looked at Kennedy briefly and then went back to Midleton. "Let's get something straight, Chuck. In the future, if you would like to get any information from Langley, you are to go through this man right here." Hayes pointed to Michael Haik. "As national security advisor, that is Michael's job. And more importantly, the next time you feel like sharing sensitive intelligence information with a foreign diplomat . . . check with me first."

16

The large chateau-style home was located in the prestigious Wesley Heights neighborhood just off Foxhall Road. Ivy covered the entire front of the house with the exception of the windows and main entrance. Four chimneys jutted above the hipped slate roof, two at each end. The estate sat on three perfectly landscaped acres and was surrounded by an eight-foot black wrought-iron fence.

In the study, located in the southern wing of the house, Senator Hank Clark was relaxing in a well-worn leather chair, his shoes off, his necktie loosened, and a drink in his hand. In his other hand was the remote control for the TV. It was eight in the evening, and *Hardball* with Chris Matthews was about to start. Clark enjoyed watching the blond Irishman run at the mouth. He had a knack for pinning down people and making them take a position. Sitting on the floor next to Clark were Caesar and Brutus, the senator's golden retrievers. The names had raised more than a few of his colleagues' eyebrows over the years. Clark, of course, loved the names. The assassin and the assassinated. The dogs were a daily reminder of the importance of keeping tabs on friends and foes alike.

Clark's study was filled with expensive western art and antiques. Balanced on two pegs above the fireplace mantel was an 1886 Winchester .45–70 lever-action rifle with not a scratch or a smudge. It had been given to President Grover Cleveland as a wedding present. On top of the mantel were two Frederic Remington sculptures, the *Bronco Buster* on one side and the *Buffalo* on the other. And above it all was one of Albert Bierstadt's breathtaking originals depicting a group of Indians on horseback riding across the plain. Across the room, the top shelf of the glass bookcase contained a first edition of each of Ernest Hemingway's novels, all of them signed by the old salt himself. Clark admired Hemingway greatly. He lived life hard. He saw and did things that all but a few only dreamed about. Rather than live as a fallen angel, as a shadow of his former self, he decided to check out. Not a bad way to go when you considered his life in its entirety.

The room was Clark's favorite in the house. It was where he went at the end of each day to unwind. Wife number three was not allowed to enter before knocking, and even then, she was not encouraged to stay long. Clark loved to collect beautiful objects. He had grown up in trailer parks and slept in the same bed with his brother until the morning he left for college. He would never again be deprived of the finer things in life.

Over the intro music for *Hardball,* the senator heard the doorbell. Caesar and Brutus didn't even bat an eye. They had grown soft over the years and were no longer interested in finding out who was entering the castle. Clark, however, was. He turned down the volume and slid his feet back into his shoes. He was very interested in talking to his visitor. With more effort than he would have liked, he slid his aged athlete's body to the edge of the chair and pushed his two-hundred-sixty-pound frame up. One of the other things Clark liked was good food. He'd have to head down to his compound in the Bahamas and spend a week eating nothing but fresh fruit and fish. He'd take hikes, swim in the clear blue water, and do some deep-sea fishing, just like Papa. With any luck, he'd shed some weight.

The door to the study opened, and the butler showed Peter Cameron into the room. The senator met him halfway across the parquet wood floor. Sticking out his hand, he said, "Good evening, Professor. May I get you a drink?"

"Please."

Clark turned for the bar. He wished Cameron would shave his ridiculous-looking beard. It made him look unkempt.

Cameron walked over to the fireplace, and his eyes fell on the Winchester rifle as they did every time he entered the room. The gun was beautiful. A real piece of craftsmanship and, at the time, cutting-edge technology.

The senator returned with a drink in each hand. "Here you go."

"Thank you." Cameron grabbed the drink.

"I was expecting to hear from you this morning. What happened?"

"We had some problems." Cameron took a drink of his chilled vodka.

"How serious?"

Cameron rolled his eyes in an exaggerated gesture. "It could have been very serious, but I took care of things."

"Details, please." The senator placed one hand on the mantel.

"The Jansens screwed everything up. They missed Rapp. It appears he's alive, and I presume he's on his way back to the States."

Clark looked confused and displeased. "I don't understand. The message I received on Saturday said that everything had gone according to plan."

"That's what I thought. That's what they told me when I met them at the airstrip in Germany, but they were wrong. I don't know how Rapp survived, but he did."

Clark was enraged that Rapp was still alive, but he wasn't about to show it in front of Cameron. After taking a drink, he said, "The Jansens are a liability."

"Not anymore. That's where I've been the last few days. I grabbed Villaume and a few of his people and flew out to Colorado where the Jansens live . . . or I should say lived."

The senator nodded. "Details, please."

"It went very smoothly. I put a bullet in both their heads as they were leaving their house on Sunday morning. No witnesses. I went through the whole house and checked for anything that might link them to me and came up empty. It could be weeks before the cops suspect anything."

"You took the shot?" the senator asked, a little surprised.

"Yes. It was my mess to clean up." Cameron was very proud of himself.

"Did you collect their fee?"

Cameron had, in fact, retrieved the fifty thousand dollars in cash. He was hoping the senator wouldn't bring it up, but there was no such luck. Hank Clark was not a man to lie to. "I got the money back."

"Good. Use it to cover your other expenses, and pocket the rest."

"Yes, sir." Cameron couldn't have been more pleased.

"What did you do with their bodies?"

"I took them straight from Colorado down to the island on the plane, then loaded them onto the boat, brought them out about ten miles, and fed them to the sharks." Clark owned a compound on Williams Island in the Bahamas with its own lagoon and private marina.

"Did anyone see you on the island?"

"Yeah, but I had the bodies folded up in two large duffel bags. I made sure your caretaker wasn't around when I loaded them onto the boat. I went out early this morning like I was going fishing. Came back five hours later with a few catch-and-release stories. No one was wise to what I'd done."

"What about the pilots?"

"I loaded the cargo myself. They never saw it."

Clark thought it over for a second. It appeared the Professor had cleaned up after himself. The question of Irene Kennedy and her still intact reputation remained, though, and possibly the more serious issue of Mitch Rapp on the loose.

"Any chance you could be tied to the Jansens by Kennedy or Rapp?"

Cameron shook his head. "No."

"Peter, did you know that most criminals think they'll never get caught, right up to the moment that they get caught?"

Cameron tried not to be offended by the word *criminal*. He knew the senator didn't mean it in the common sense. "What would you like me to do, sir?"

"I'd like you to tie up this loose end. From everything I've heard, Mitch Rapp is not a man to be taken lightly. I would prefer it if he was out of the picture permanently."

"I'll take care of it," replied Cameron with confidence.

"Villaume and his people?"

"Yeah?"

The senator looked Cameron in the eyes. "They know too much."

Cameron nodded. "Okay, but that's going to take some money."

"Let me know how much, and I'll get it to you."

"What about Kennedy?"

The senator looked over at the TV for a moment. Chris Matthews was flirting with some attractive reporter. Looking back to Cameron, he said, "I'm going to have to think about that for a little bit. I'll let you know as soon as you take care of these other things."

Peter Cameron nodded and took a drink of his vodka. He strained to hide his smile of excitement. He would get his wish. He would lay a trap for Mitch Rapp, and then he would kill him.

* * *

ANNA RIELLY WASN'T doing so well. As NBC's
White House correspondent, she couldn't let her personal life get in the way of her duties. She had just finished giving her last live update during the nightly news
for the people on the West Coast. Israel's prime minister
was meeting with the president in the morning to discuss yet another impasse in the implementation of the
peace accords. Standing under the bright lights just outside the West Wing, she took off her earpiece and handed
it and her microphone to the cameraman who was packing the rest of the gear away. They would be back in the
morning to say virtually the same thing, first to the people in the East and Midwest, and then again to the
mountains and the West Coast.

Her mind was barely up to the task, and her heart was
elsewhere. Thank God Brokaw hadn't thrown any impromptu questions at her. Anna thanked the cameraman
and told him she'd see him in the morning. She couldn't
stop worrying about Mitch. They hadn't heard a word
from him since Saturday, and that had been nothing more
than a cryptic message. On top of that, she also felt horrible for putting the O'Rourkes in such a bad spot. Liz was
pregnant and deserved some peace. In a way, though,
worrying about Liz's pregnancy had helped her get control of herself after her Saturday evening meltdown. She
had apologized to Michael the next morning, and he had
apologized for his lack of sensitivity. Liz had given her
husband the cold shoulder for much of the day, until
Anna told her to knock it off. "None of this was Michael's
fault," Anna had explained, "and he shouldn't be the one

taking the heat." Anna had tried to leave and go to her apartment, not wanting the O'Rourkes to have to get any more involved in this than they already were. This was her problem, hers and Mitch's. Poor Mitch. She didn't know whether she should be worried about him or mad. It was about ninety percent the former and about ten percent the latter. She wanted him home safe, but there had been moments when through her tears she swore she was going to kill him for putting her through this.

Mitch was good at what he did. That much she knew. She had seen him in action during the White House hostage crisis. He was a one-man SWAT team, but in the end he was human. He bled like everyone else. Rielly's father was a cop, and so were two of her brothers. They all worked for the Chicago PD. Rielly had seen invincible men go down. They were all stubborn just like Mitch. If she was lucky enough to see Mitch again, she would show him what stubborn was all about. He would retire whether he liked it or not, and they would walk down the aisle together. She had come too far and gone through too much to lose him.

Rielly was still seething as she yanked open the door and entered the main-floor foyer of the West Wing. The Secret Service officer sitting behind the desk smiled at her, but she ignored him. She'd been faking her mood for the last two hours as she talked to the producers in New York, and enough was enough. As she turned to her right, she heard her name called from behind.

Jack Warch, the special agent in charge of the president's Secret Service detail, rounded the corner with a file in his hand. "How are you tonight, Anna?"

Rielly brushed a wayward strand of her auburn hair off her face and said, "Not so good, Jack. What are you still doing here?"

"The president is working late tonight."

Rielly paused and looked down the hall past Warch, in the direction of the Oval Office. There was a good chance the man behind that door knew where Mitch was. Whether he would admit to that was a whole other matter. After the terrorist attack on the White House had ended, President Hayes had personally pleaded with Rielly to remain silent about the identity of Mitch Rapp. The president didn't want the press, the politicians on the Hill, and the militia nuts to find out that a covert operative for the CIA had been the driving force behind the successful rescue of the hostages. In return for her cooperation, the president had agreed to grant her unusual access. As she and Mitch became close, he had made it very clear that she was never to use her access to the president to dig for information about what he did for the CIA. Considering what she'd gone through over the last two days, breaking that promise seemed minor.

"Who's he with?"

Warch smiled. "You know I can't tell you that."

There was no smile on Anna's face. "I need to see him."

The Secret Service agent could tell she was serious and looked back down the hall for a second. Looking back to Rielly, he said, "Stay right here. I'll see what I can do."

Rielly waited in the foyer and took off her black raincoat. She thought about calling the O'Rourkes. Michael had dropped her off at the White House this morning, and she had promised Liz that she would call when she was done with the nightly news so Michael could come pick her up. She was about to pick up the handset on one of the house phones when Warch came back around the corner.

"Come with me, Anna." The agent turned around and started back down the hallway, Rielly on his heels.

PRESIDENT HAYES WAS sitting behind his desk in the Oval Office when they entered the room. Jazz music was playing softly from a stereo that Rielly could not see. The president was sandwiched between two stacks of manila files, busily scanning documents and signing his name. As Warch and Rielly approached the desk, he grabbed a new file, read the note that was paper-clipped to the front, opened the file, and signed his name on four separate pages. The folder was closed and placed on top of the pile on his right. Hayes took off his reading glasses and stood, putting on his suit coat.

Walking around the desk, he said, "Good evening, Anna." Hayes extended his hand. He really liked Rielly. Like all reporters, she could be tough on him, but she had kept her word when he'd asked for it, and that was not something to be taken lightly, considering her profession.

"Good evening, Mr. President."

Hayes knew that Rielly had been seeing Rapp. How close they were he didn't know and wasn't about to ask. It had been a very long day, the first lady was out of the country, and he was bushed. He wanted to tune out, not to have to carefully measure every word that left his lips. The president looked at Warch and said, "Thank you, Jack." When Warch had left the room, Hayes brought Rielly over to the couches and sat next to her. He silently hoped this would be about anything other than Mitch Rapp. "What's on your mind, Anna?"

Rielly stared down at her fingers for a moment. "Sir." She hesitated, not knowing quite where to start. "This is all off the record. Very far off the record. It will never be on any record."

Hayes grinned. "All right."

"Where is Mitch, and what kind of trouble is he in?"

The grin on Hayes's face vanished. He began to cautiously consider his reply. "Anna, you already know more than you should. What Mitch does for—" The president paused. He was going to say "the government" but decided that would be too much of an admission. "What Mitch decides to do on his own is something that I am not at liberty to discuss."

"So you know where he is right now?" Rielly stared at the president with her green eyes, watching every little expression.

Having his law degree and working in Washington for several decades allowed Hayes to focus on the words *right now*. The president shook his head. "I have no idea where Mitch is."

"Do you know why he left the country on Thursday?"

Hayes blinked several times and said, "No . . . I don't."

Rielly studied him. "Sir, with all due respect, I don't think you are being entirely honest with me."

"Anna, I don't think we should be talking about this."

"Sir, I did you and your administration a huge favor by not going public with my story after the hostage crisis was ended."

"Yes, you did, but this has nothing to do with that."

Rielly's voice took on a more confrontational tone. "It has everything to do with it."

Hayes held up his hands. He didn't want this to get heated. "Anna, for your loyalty, you have been given phenomenal access. The fact that you were able to get in here to see me at this hour speaks volumes."

Rielly cut him off. "And that has been greatly appreciated, sir. But that was the deal you made so I would stay quiet."

"That's not the only reason you've stayed quiet."

"What do you mean?"

"Anna, Mitch saved your life. He saved mine. He saved a lot of people's. His wish to keep his life private deserves our respect and continued commitment."

"I owe Mitch my life. A day doesn't go by when I don't think about it." She frowned. "Please don't confuse the issue here. This is not about keeping Mitch's life private. I'm not going to tell anybody about what he does for the CIA. This is about me being worried sick that something has happened to Mitch. It's about me needing to know if he's all right."

Hayes sighed and looked up at the ceiling. He couldn't believe he was discussing something with a reporter that he wouldn't even discuss with his own national security advisor.

Rielly reached out and touched his arm. "Sir, all I want to know is if he's all right. As far as I'm concerned, we never had this conversation."

"As far as I know"—Hayes shook his head—"he's fine. But that's all I'm going to say."

Rielly's face lit up. She reached out and grabbed the president's hand. "Thank you, sir."

17

It was dark when American Airlines Flight 602 touched down on the runway at Baltimore Washington International Airport. The flight had just completed its 1,565-mile nonstop journey from San Juan, Puerto Rico. Mitch Rapp looked down at his watch as they taxied to the gate. It was twenty past nine on Monday evening. Once he was out of Germany, the journey back to America had been fairly simple. From Lyon, France, he had taken a Trans North Aviation flight to Fort de France, Martinique, in the Caribbean. The nonstop 4,440-mile flight allowed him to catch a full six hours of sleep as he stretched out in first class. On the tiny island, which was an overseas department of France, he had checked into a quaint family-run hotel up in the hills overlooking the blue waters of the eastern Caribbean Sea. Rapp paid for both Saturday and Sunday night in cash. Sunday was spent by the pool, relaxing, healing, staring out at the fishing village below, and planning his next step. That evening, he'd allowed himself a cold six-pack while he sat on his balcony and listened to the waves crash in on the rocky shoreline below. He'd allowed his imagination to roam as he thought about what he'd do to the Hoffmans when he got his hands on them.

That night he'd slept for almost eight hours. He awoke with a slight hangover, but after a jog down to the water and a one-mile swim, he felt invigorated and ready to face whatever awaited him back in the States. The two nights and one day spent on tranquil Martinique had brought his mind and body back into focus.

On Monday morning he caught an Air Guadeloupe flight to San Juan, where he cleared U.S. Customs. Monday afternoon was spent shopping for new clothes and eating, and then at 6:15 that evening, he boarded the flight for Maryland. Rapp stepped off the plane in Baltimore looking every bit the tourist who had just returned from a weekend in the sun. He was wearing a faded red baseball cap from Larry's Dive Shop in San Juan, a blue-and-white Hawaiian shirt, a pair of khakis, and blue boat shoes. His face and forearms were tanned.

Rapp was all but sure the folks at Langley had not been able to track him. He had traveled using two separate identities, identities the watchers at Langley had never been told of. If they got lucky and saw him on one of the airport's security tapes, that would be fine. He would be gone by then, having disappeared into a city that he knew intimately. There was a chance they might have people at the airport staking out the gates. If they were there, Rapp was confident he'd spot them. As he walked with the rest of the vacationers toward the baggage claim, Rapp stayed close to two women he had met at the airport in San Juan. He kept the brim of his hat down and his eyes alert. He'd stay with the crowd until he was sure he could make a safe break.

On Martinique, Rapp had devised three different plans. The first stage of each involved obtaining some protection. None of them involved going back to the house. At least not until he did a little digging and found out what in the hell had happened. Anna also would have to wait. He desperately wanted to talk to her but knew it was a bad idea, and for more than one reason. She would want him just to walk away and put the whole thing behind him. What she didn't understand was that in this line of work, loose ends had a way of coming back and biting you in the ass. He would get word to her that he was safe and back in the country, but that would be it.

When the herd of freshly tanned tourists neared the baggage claim, the two women from Bowie, Maryland, suggested to Rapp that they get together for drinks. Rapp smiled sheepishly and told them he didn't think his girlfriend would like the idea. With that, he took the escalator up and walked out the door onto the curb. There were three cabs within thirty feet in either direction. All three were dropping passengers off. The drivers were not allowed to pick up passengers on the departure level. They were supposed to go back downstairs and line up with everybody else. Rapp waited for one of the cabbies to get back in his vehicle and then darted into the back seat. Before the cabbie could protest, Rapp shoved a fifty-dollar bill in his face. The money did the trick. The cabbie looked around to see if anybody had noticed and then put the car in drive.

"The Hyatt Regency in Bethesda, please."

The man nodded and pushed the button to start the meter. Rapp turned sideways so he could glance out the back window to see if someone might be following. A few minutes later, they were on Interstate 95 headed south for Washington. The drive proved uneventful, at least as far as Rapp could tell. One never knew anymore, though. In this day of satellites and microtransmitters, eyes and ears could follow from hundreds of miles away, and you'd have no way of knowing.

When the cab pulled up to the Hyatt, Rapp gave the driver another fifty and then went through the revolving front door and into the lobby. After finding the payphones, he plugged in some change and dialed a number from memory. After six rings, an answering machine greeted him. Rapp took this as a good sign. The odds just went up that Marcus Dumond would be where he wanted him to be. Before leaving the lobby, Rapp grabbed a sweatshirt out of his backpack. It was a little cooler here than it had been in the Caribbean.

The coffee shop was six blocks away. It was the brainchild of Marcus Dumond. Mitch Rapp and his brother Steven had put up the money and were silent partners. The name of the place was Café Wired. It was one of the original Internet coffee shops, and Rapp was sure one of the only profitable ones. Rapp had met the incredibly unique Dumond while he was a graduate student at MIT with Rapp's brother. Dumond could be classified as one of those people who was smart in school and dumb on the bus.

Dumond was a twenty-seven-year-old computer genius and almost convicted felon. Rapp had brought Dumond into the fold at Langley three years earlier. The young cyber-genius had run into some trouble with the feds while he was earning his master's degree in computer science at MIT. He was alleged to have hacked into one of New York's largest banks and then transferred funds into several overseas accounts. The part that interested the CIA was that Dumond wasn't caught because he left a trail; he was caught because he got drunk one night and bragged about his financial plunders to the wrong person.

At the time of the alleged crime, Dumond was living with Steven Rapp. When the older Rapp heard about Dumond's problems with the FBI, he called Irene Kennedy and told her the hacker was worth a look. Langley doesn't like to admit the fact that they employ some of the world's best computer pirates, but these young cyber-geeks are encouraged to hack into any and every computer system they can. Most of these hacking raids are directed at foreign companies, banks, governments, and military computer systems. But just getting into a system isn't enough. The challenge is to hack in, get the information, and get out without leaving a trace that the system was ever compromised. Dumond was a natural at it, and his talents were put to good use in the Counterterrorism Center.

Rapp opened the door and stepped into a room filled with the aroma of fresh-ground coffee. There, sitting in the rear of the establishment, was Marcus Dumond, with his back to the door. Rapp frowned. Dumond's instincts were horrible. He would last about five minutes in the field. Rapp stopped at the counter and said hello to the young woman who was working. He was pleased to see that, unlike the last one, this employee didn't have any pierced body parts, at least none that he could see. Rapp tried to read the hodgepodge of flavors, blends, and specials scrawled across the grade-school chalkboard that hung on the wall above the espresso machines.

The number of choices was too great. "I'll just take a cup of your daily roast."

"Small, medium, or large?"

"Large, please."

Rapp continued to check the place out. There were fourteen customers at the moment. Most of them looked to be around twenty. The four computers on the back wall were all being used, one customer was reading a book, and two more were scribbling in spiral note-books. *Aspiring anarchists,* Rapp thought to himself. The rest of the customers were working on their own lap-tops.

Dumond was sitting at a table with two women surf-ing the Web and chatting. Dumond had heard the fa-miliar voice ask for a cup of coffee, and he fought the urge to turn around and look. It belonged to Mitch Rapp, a man he knew things about that he wasn't sup-posed to—that no one was supposed to. It wasn't un-usual for Rapp to stop by the café, but he usually did it on Sundays with his girlfriend. Dumond stood and grabbed his half-finished cup of coffee. As he walked up to the counter, he unconsciously licked his suddenly parched lips.

Rapp paid for his coffee and thanked the woman. As he turned, he faced Dumond and nodded toward the back. The two men picked their way through the tables and chairs and sat down in a booth next to the bathrooms. Rapp took the side facing the front door.

"Nice afro, Marcus."

Dumond instinctively reached up and touched his black hair. "They're coming back, you know."

"I'm sure Dr. J will be happy to hear that."

"Who?"

Mitch shook his head and grinned. Marcus had to be the only twenty-eight-year-old African American in D.C. who didn't know who Dr. J was. "Never mind."

"You look like you've been in the sun."

"I've been traveling."

"Business or pleasure?"

Rapp grabbed his cup of coffee with both hands and said, "Business."

"How did it go?" asked Dumond a little tentatively.

"Not so good." Rapp took a sip. "How have things been at the center?" He was referring to the Counterterrorism Center.

"Same old shit."

"Nothing unusual in the last three days?"

"No." Dumond frowned. "Nothing that came across my screen."

"How about Irene? How's she been acting?"

"Same as always. She's Irene."

"Nothing at all?"

"Mitch, the woman probably doesn't even moan

when she has an orgasm. Hell, she's probably never even had an orgasm."

Rapp frowned at Dumond, and before he could say anything, Dumond added, "I'm sorry. I like Irene, but you know what I mean. She's a cool customer. The building could be burning down, and she'd just keep on going like she always does."

Rapp knew what he meant. "You haven't noticed anything?"

Dumond leaned back. "Well, shit, Mitch, there's always something. Maybe if you told me what your business was about, I might be able to tell you more."

He thought about it for a moment. For now, he decided he would keep Dumond in the dark about Germany. "I assume you still have that case I gave you?"

"Yep. I haven't touched it just like you told me." Well, in truth, he'd touched it, he'd sat on it, and he'd looked at it. He'd wondered over and over what was inside the cold metal case. His mind almost always settled on a combination of guns and money. Mitch Rapp was a bad dude, and he wouldn't waste his time asking people to keep a locked metal case of clothes.

Rapp turned his wrist up and checked the time. "It's still at the four-plex?"

"Yeah, just around the corner."

"All right, let's go."

18

Mario Lukas awoke on Tuesday morning at five. He was not a good sleeper, hadn't been for as long as he could remember. He figured it was just one more thing in a long list of liabilities associated with his profession. It's not always easy for a hired killer to relax. And at Mario's level, it's not the feds you worry about, it's the other shooters. You spend a lot of time looking over your shoulder wondering if someone is going to come after you for revenge, or if you might get double-crossed by someone you thought was a friend, or if an employer has decided you are too big of a liability to let live.

When Mario rolled out of bed in the predawn hours, this was what was on his mind. The person he knew as the Professor was not to be trusted. Mario had watched the man closely while they were in Colorado. Villaume had told him to do so, and Mario didn't like what he saw.

Operations like the one they had just done in Colorado were never good. Mario thought they were kind of like screwing a married woman. If you ended up getting seriously involved with her, you shouldn't be surprised if you woke up one day and found out she was doing the same thing to you that she did to her first, second, or third husband. In essence, the Professor had hired the couple in Colorado to do a job, and then he had them killed. He had also hired Mario, Villaume, and Juarez to do a job, and now what was there to prevent him from hiring another set of killers to take them out? This was why he couldn't sleep.

Mario swung his feet onto the wood floor of his Spartan one-bedroom apartment. He sat there for a minute scratching himself and waiting for the light-headedness to fade. Then standing, he started for the bathroom, his back and legs stiff. The tiny apartment came furnished with only the necessities, which was fine for Mario. He didn't like collecting things. He'd been living in apartments like this for thirty of his fifty-some years. Even Mario wasn't sure how old he was. He'd had so many aliases over the years and lived in so many different places, he'd forgotten if he was fifty-five or fifty-six. Everything he owned could be placed in the trunk of his car. With what he did for a living, it made no sense to accumulate too many things. On a moment's notice you might have to pick up and disappear. He couldn't help but think that this was one of those times.

When he was done in the bathroom, he walked to the door and got his newspaper. He grabbed a jug of orange juice from the refrigerator and a glass from the cupboard. As he started to read the paper, he thought of an old associate who had tried to talk him into buying a house one time. The man had tried to sell him on the idea that they could use the tax write-off. Mario reminded him that since they were paid in cash, the write-off would do them no good. That acquaintance had disappeared, never to be found again.

Villaume was the only true friend Mario had ever had and the first person he had met in the business whom he could unquestioningly trust with his life. Villaume had helped him look toward retirement. Mario had always kept his money in a series of safe deposit boxes. Villaume had taken that money and put it into offshore bank accounts where it was now handled by a money manager. The return was so good that he could retire today if he wanted. In light of the job in Colorado, he thought it might be a good idea at least to take a little time off.

At 6:25, he got ready for his walk to the neighborhood bakery. Having lived in France for more than twenty years, Mario hated American coffee. It had taken him more than a week to find a place that served good cappuccino, but he had prevailed. It was a little bakery six blocks away. Before leaving, he stuck a 9-mm pistol in the front of his pants. Leaving his dark shirt untucked, he put on his jacket and hat and left.

JEFF DUSER WAS on speed. Sitting in the driver's seat of the gray Dodge Durango, he tapped out a tune on the steering wheel as his eyes darted back and forth between the two side mirrors and the rearview mirror. He was wearing a dark brown suit and a tan trench coat. In the breast pocket of his suit were credentials that identified him as Steven Metzger, a federal agent with the Bureau of Alcohol, Tobacco and Firearms. Duser still kept his hair short—buzzed and flat on top but not skinned on the sides like he'd had it when he was in the Marine Corps. He had joined the Marines when he was eighteen. It was either Parris Island or jail. The local cops in Toledo, Ohio, had his number. The police chief had personally driven him to the recruiting station on his eighteenth birthday.

Duser thought he'd found a home in the Marine Corps. That was until the Corps got soft on him. If the politically correct politicians thought they were going to force him to let faggots serve in his unit, they had another thing coming. He had openly encouraged and participated in the hazing of suspected homosexuals. A particularly green private right out of boot camp had taken the platoon's first sergeant's words a little too seriously. After an evening of beer and prodding, the private went back to the barracks and beat a fellow Marine to death. The subsequent investigation exposed Duser's role and many of his other shortcomings. He was court-martialed and run out of the Corps. From there he'd found his way into private security and then contract killing.

Wally McBride sat in the front passenger seat, a silenced Steyr TMP submachine gun on his lap. Duser and his people had a crate of the weapons stashed at a warehouse in Richmond. They had gotten them in one of the shipments they had hijacked from a gun dealer who was importing them from Austria. The weapon was compact. Even with the sound suppressor attached, it was easily concealable. They had meticulously filed the serial numbers off the weapons and then swabbed them with acid. Duser didn't have many rules, but there was one he was adamant about. If you used a weapon to kill someone, it was dumped in the ocean as soon as possible.

Peter Cameron was in the back seat watching the two men fidget. He had seen them take the speed but said nothing. He knew why they did it, and he himself was wondering why he didn't take one when they'd offered it to him. He had been up all night with Duser planning what they were going to do, and in an effort to stay awake, he drank a few too many cups of coffee. Now he had to go to the bathroom but didn't dare leave the vehicle. It was getting light out, and their target would be along shortly.

Before leaving Colorado on Sunday, Cameron had stepped away from Villaume and his people and made a phone call. It was to Duser. Cameron hadn't been given the order to take out Villaume and his people yet, but he thought he would be proactive. Cameron told him where and when they would be landing and whom he wanted followed. When they'd touched down at the Montgomery County Airpark, Duser and his people had been waiting. They'd placed transponders on eight different suspected cars in the parking lot. When Villaume, Juarez, and Lukas left the airport, Duser and his men followed. They stayed a good way back and let the transponders do the work. Juarez parked her car on the street right in front of her apartment, very stupid on her part. Lukas parked his eight blocks away, and they'd lost him. On Monday, one of Duser's people reestablished contact with the massive man, and now they knew where he lived. Villaume had vanished into thin air. The car he had taken from the airport was still under surveillance, and they were canvassing the neighborhood where it was parked but had yet to come up with anything.

This didn't really bother Cameron. He didn't think much of Villaume. Without Mario Lukas, the man was a bear without claws. Cameron was convinced that Villaume would run scared as soon as he found out his old friend was dead.

Duser heard the call come in over his earpiece and glanced over at Wally McBride. McBride nodded and got out of the car. Mario Lukas was headed in their direction. Duser had three vehicles and six people in the area. If they were lucky, he was on his way to the same bakery he had gone to the morning before. The plan was to distract Lukas and take him from behind. The job of distracting Lukas fell on the shoulders of Sandra Hickock, a former stripper and vivacious beauty whom Duser had personally recruited and trained.

THE STREETS WERE empty for the most part. The streetlights were still on but weren't needed. The sun would be up in another fifteen minutes. Mario recognized a neighbor who was out taking her poodle for a walk. As they neared, he touched the brim of his hat and nodded. Mario had learned long ago that his size was very intimidating to people. Sometimes this was a good thing, and sometimes it wasn't. The woman smiled back as they passed. A block later, Mario took a right. He never walked the same route to the bakery each morning.

An early-morning jogger was running toward him on the opposite side of the street. Mario thought he looked vaguely familiar. He continued on, looking at the parked cars and checking over his shoulder every half block or so. He made one last turn, and the bakery was just ahead on his right. When he was midway down the block, a woman rounded the corner up ahead and started toward him. She had her arms folded across her chest, and her hands were stuck under her armpits. She looked cold despite the fact that it was a relatively mild morning. Mario noted her clothes and her obvious beauty, even at this distance. This was a woman he would have remembered seeing. As they drew closer, the woman looked up, brushed some of her long black hair from her face, and smiled.

The warning bells went off immediately in Mario's large head. While looking quickly over his shoulder, he slid his right hand under his untucked shirt. There was a man rounding the corner behind him, and he was moving fast. Mario snapped his head back around, first checking if there was anything across the street and then looking back to the woman, who was still smiling. A blue U.S. Postal Service box was just up ahead. Mario picked up the pace and moved to his right while he drew the 9-mm Colt 2000. The smile on the woman's face vanished at the sight of the gun. She started to unfold her arms. Mario noticed a black object in her right hand, and before she could bring the weapon to bear, Mario had the Colt up and leveled. He squeezed the trigger once, the loud crack of the automatic pistol echoing off the walls of the brick apartment buildings.

The bullet struck the woman in the face. Mario went into a crouch and ducked between two parked cars. Before he could turn to search out the man, a hail of bullets sliced through the hood of the car just behind him. Keeping his head down, Mario lifted the gun up and fired three shots down the sidewalk. As he brought the gun back down, he heard an engine revving and tires squealing. Bullets continued to thump into the cars around him.

DUSER WAS PUSHING the gas pedal to the floor. He yelled into his lip mike, "Keep him pinned down, I'll be there in a second!" The Durango skidded around the corner. He rolled down the driver's-side window and got ready to shoot. Up ahead on his left he could see glass flying as bullets smashed into the windshield of a parked car. Duser stuck his compact Steyr submachine gun out the window and started firing. As he neared the spot, he slammed on the brakes and brought the truck to a stop. Dead in his sights, crouched down behind the trunk of the car, was Mario Lukas. Duser held the trigger down and emptied the remainder of the twenty-five-round magazine into the man's broad back. Lukas slumped over and fell facedown in the gutter.

19

Senator Clark's limousine pulled into the Congressional Country Club and started up the drive. The golf course, originally designed by Devereaux Emmett and later redesigned by Donald Ross, Robert Trent Jones, and, more recently, Rees Jones, was one of the finest courses in the country. The limo veered to the right and passed the starters' shack. Four golfers dressed in sweaters and wind shirts stood on the first tee. Clark frowned. He'd have to see if he could clear his schedule this afternoon and sneak in eighteen. It looked as if it was going to be a beautiful day. The car continued around the circle drive and stopped in front of the classic Mediterranean-style clubhouse. The senator thanked his driver and told him he'd be no more than an hour.

Once inside, Clark headed downstairs to a private meeting room he'd reserved. He was flanked, as he wove his way through the maze of hallways, by black-and-white photographs laying out the history of the club—President Calvin Coolidge on opening day in 1923, U.S. Open and Kemper Open photos, and Clark's favorite, a shot of the course during World War

II when it had been turned into a training camp for OSS spies.

Clark entered the windowless meeting room to find Congressman Rudin and Secretary of State Midleton in heated debate. Clark said hello and stopped at the side buffet to grab a bagel and a bowl of cereal. Before sitting down, he filled up a glass with cranberry juice and signed the ticket. Both Rudin and Midleton were members of the club, but in the twenty-some years that Clark had known them, he had yet to see either of them pick up the tab for anything. The two men were cheap in different ways. Rudin was a simple spendthrift, whereas Midleton was from *Mayflower* stock. He'd been raised in the way of the Daughters of the American Revolution. His family was royalty, and royalty didn't carry cash, nor did they pick up the tab. So once again, it fell on the shoulders of the boy who'd been raised by two alcoholics in a trailer.

Despite the huge social chasm that lay between them, Clark was by far the wealthiest of the three men. With a net worth in excess of one hundred million dollars, he was one of the top five wealthiest politicians in Washington. Midleton had his precious estate that had been passed down to him. It was worth eight million dollars, pitiable by today's new standards of wealth. Midleton was very proud of the fact that he'd never touched the principal in his inheritance. The money was handled by the same bank that had managed Midleton's great-great-grandfather's money. Clark had done some checking. The portfolio had shown a laughable return of eight percent over the last decade. It seemed the secretary of state invested his money the old-fashioned way. He paid huge fees to stodgy old bankers who put his money into tax-free municipal bonds and a few old stalwart utilities.

Congressman Rudin was somewhat better off. Having been in the House for thirty-four years, he could retire tomorrow at full pension and benefits, more than enough money to support his frugal lifestyle. He'd been squirreling his money away over the years. Two years ago, his IRA was worth almost eight hundred thousand dollars. That was when Clark had finally persuaded him to let his money managers take a whack at growing the account. It was like pulling teeth to get Rudin to turn over control. In just two years, Clark's people had turned the eight hundred thousand dollars into $1.7 million, and Rudin had yet to offer a thank you, let alone pick up a tab.

There had been a time when this would have bothered the senior senator from Arizona, but Clark had risen above his feelings. He pitied the way the two men nervously fretted every time a waiter delivered a check. It was truly pathetic. Today, as he sat at the table and spread cream cheese on his bagel, he tried to gauge just how far he could play these two before they figured out what he was up to.

Clark had no intention of asking the secretary of state why he had called this meeting. The senator knew why. His spies in the White House and over at Foggy Bottom had told him there had been an incident between the president and his top Cabinet member. An incident involving the German ambassador and one that had been extremely embarrassing to Secretary Midleton.

Rudin was perched over a bowl of Grape-nuts, shoveling the tiny rocks into his mouth. In between spoonfuls, he would lean even closer to Midleton and spew forth his own take on what was going on at the Central Intelligence Agency. When Clark appeared to be settled in, Rudin turned his attention away from the secretary of state.

"Hank, did you hear what happened at the White House yesterday?"

Clark played dumb and shook his head. For the next forty seconds, Rudin retold his inflamed version of what had taken place in the Oval Office. For Midleton's part, he sat there looking wounded in his gray suit and paisley bow tie. Clark was on tricky ground. As amateurish as Rudin and Midleton could seem at times, one could not forget the fact that they were two of the most influential and powerful politicians in town. They were Democrats, and he was the enemy. If they got even the slightest whiff that he was playing them, it would be over.

When Rudin was done rambling, Clark set his juice down and looked at the secretary of state. "I'm sorry you had to be embarrassed like that, Charles. It's inappropriate to take you to task in front of other Cabinet members. But it sounds like the president did have a point."

Before Midleton could respond, Rudin was lurching forward. His weather-beaten face twisted in a grimace of disbelief. "What point could you be talking about? Did you listen to a thing I said?"

"Al, this Hagenmiller guy was consorting with the wrong people."

"Wrong people. That's the CIA's side of the story, and we all know how much that's worth."

"We've discussed this before, Al. We differ on the value of Langley." Clark took a bite of his bagel and waited for the inevitable tirade.

"The wretched Central Intelligence Agency is the biggest waste of money this country has ever seen. The way they operate is unconstitutional, and they are a danger to the future of democracy not only in this country but around the world."

Clark pushed himself back and folded his arms across his chest. "I didn't come here to be preached to about something that we will never agree on. Now, if there is something constructive you two would like to discuss, let's get to it. Otherwise, I have other things to attend to."

Rudin shook his head in frustration. It drove him crazy that his friend from Arizona couldn't see the CIA for what it was.

Midleton, always the diplomat, stepped in. "Hank, what are you hearing about Thomas Stansfield's health?"

Clark stifled a grin. They had gone right where he wanted them to. "My sources tell me he could be gone in two weeks or two months but no longer than that."

Midleton nodded thoughtfully, as if he were actually mourning Stansfield's approaching demise. "Are you concerned over who will succeed him as director?"

"Of course I am."

"Have you heard any names?"

"No." Clark shook his head. "You're in the administration, not me."

"Well, as the chairman of the Senate Intelligence Committee, you're going to have a lot of say in the matter."

"In confirmation only. Your man is the one who gives us the name. All we do is ask a few questions and vote up or down."

"You are being far too modest," countered Midleton. Rudin was busy shaking his head and trying to pick something from his teeth. "Surely you must have heard a few names thrown about?"

"No, not really."

Rudin pulled a toothpick from his mouth and barked, "What about Irene Kennedy?"

"No, I haven't heard her name mentioned, but I think she would be a good nominee."

"Oh my God! You can't be serious!" Rudin was back out over the table.

Calmly, Clark replied, "And what may I ask is wrong with Dr. Kennedy?"

"Where do you want me to start?" asked an incredulous Rudin.

"Wherever you'd like."

"First off, she's an insider, and we sure as hell don't need another insider running that damn place. We need someone who will go in there and clean house. Someone who will pay the strictest attention to congressional oversight. Above and beyond that, she's not even qualified."

"She's done a very good job with the Counterterrorism Center," argued Clark.

"Bullshit, I don't believe a single briefing she gives my committee. That woman is a liar and a conniver, and I'll be damned if I'll allow her to take over as DCI."

"From what you just said, it sounds like she's the perfect person to run an intelligence agency." Clark couldn't help smiling just a little. This was going all too well.

"I'm glad you think this is funny, Hank. It's one thing to lie and connive when dealing with our enemies, but when they come before my committee, I want the truth, and the bottom line is that there is no way in hell that woman is going to give it to me."

Clark pointed at Rudin. "Did you ever stop and think that she doesn't tell you things because she knows you would like to cut funding for her agency in half?"

"That isn't her prerogative. She is bound by law to report the facts to my committee, and she doesn't, and it pisses me off."

"Then you should investigate her." Clark had just put Rudin in check. He knew Rudin was the ultimate party man. To investigate Kennedy would mean bringing down the heat on President Hayes, a fellow Democrat. Rudin retreated and crossed his arms, conflicted between his loyalty to his party and his hatred of the CIA.

"Let's all just calm down a bit," interjected Midleton. As unhappy as he was with the president at the moment, the last thing he wanted was Rudin going off on a witch-hunt. The Republicans would gain serious mileage out of a Democratic congressman going after a Democratic president, and as a member of that president's Cabinet, the last thing Midleton wanted to see were congressional hearings. They had a habit of expanding, and once the shooting started, no one knew who might get caught in the crossfire.

"I am calm." Clark took his napkin and set it on the table.

"Good." Midleton glanced over at Rudin as if to tell him to stay quiet for a few minutes. Looking back to Clark, he said, "Who would you like to see take over at Langley?"

This was far too easy. Clark cautioned himself not to overreach. He had his person and two more as backups, but now was far too early to throw a name out. "As I've already said, it's not my job to nominate. I only confirm."

"But if you could pick someone?"

Clark shrugged his shoulders. "I have no idea. I haven't put any thought into it." He added with a laugh, "Not that it would matter."

"It might," offered Midleton.

"What he's trying to say," interjected Rudin, "is that we don't like the idea of Kennedy taking over. And from what you're telling us, she's the president's choice. I am prepared to go to the president and tell him that I oppose Kennedy's nomination, but considering how vocal I've been on the issue, it will be no big surprise to him. He and I have been around and around on this issue, and we cannot see eye to eye."

"Why don't you threaten to cut funding?" It was a very subtle jibe. Clark knew Rudin didn't have the votes on his own committee to push such a policy.

"I'm a party man, and you know it, Hank." Rudin said this as if it was the most honorable thing that could be said of a person. "I can't go against my president on this."

"Well, I don't know what to tell you, gentlemen. If you don't like Kennedy as a nominee, then you'd better find a way to change Hayes's mind." It was a high lob back to their side of the net.

Midleton fidgeted in his chair before speaking. "If you were to come up with a nominee who was more palatable than Kennedy, we would be willing to take that name to the president and plead your case."

Clark tried to act surprised. "So you'd like me to play the bad guy."

Midleton didn't like the term but nodded.

"Please tell me why I'd want to do this?"

"Because," started Rudin, "there are a thousand people in this town alone who could do a better job of running that damn place."

Clark nodded slowly. "I'll think about it." Then, while checking his watch, he said, "I should get going. Is there anything else?"

Both men said no, and then Midleton added, "Just please be open-minded about this. We can help each other."

Clark said he would try and then left. As soon as he was gone, Rudin turned to Midleton and said, "He'll play ball. I know how to handle Hank."

"I hope you're right. I don't think our foreign policy could take much more of this cowboy mentality."

"Don't worry, I am."

Midleton wished he could feel more optimistic, but he was still smarting from his meeting the morning before. The president had turned into an absolute hawk. He needed someone to reel him in. Kennedy needed to be cut out of the inner circle. Midleton looked over at his fellow Democrat. "Maybe it would be a good idea to call Dr. Kennedy before your committee."

Rudin scowled. "Why would I want to give the Republicans a chance to make political hay out of this?"

"Think of it as taking the wind out of their sails before they can make an issue out of it on their own."

Rudin liked the idea. He'd love to take her to task and remind her whom she answered to. "I'll do it, but I don't want to hurt the president."

"Don't worry, it won't. I don't think she would ever expose him to that type of scandal."

While waiting for his limousine to pull around, Senator Clark could barely contain his glee over how the meeting had gone. Things had not turned out in Germany the way he had planned, but now, with these two buffoons offering their assistance, the end result would be the same. His backers for the Oval Office would be very happy. Very happy indeed.

20

The warehouse was located near the National Arboretum off Blandensburg. When the gray Dodge Durango came skidding around the corner, one of Duser's men was waiting with the garage door open. The truck disappeared into the old brick structure. The man standing watch looked up and down the street and then pulled the door down.

Duser stopped the vehicle but left it running. When he got out, a man was standing by with a trash bag. Duser dumped his submachine gun in the bag and went around to the rear of the Durango. Sandra Hickock was lying in back. The bullet had smashed her beautiful face. He looked down at her and shook his head. Part of him was glad she was dead. She'd started to get a little possessive. In the end, it was probably the best thing, but right now it was a pain in the ass. He stepped away from the tailgate and began shouting orders.

His men went to work immediately. New plates were put on the Durango while Hickock's lifeless body was stuffed into an oil drum. The drum was topped off with sand, sealed, and loaded onto the back of a flatbed with eight other drums just like it. In less than five minutes, the body and the guns were gone. As was the Durango, on its way to a chop shop.

Peter Cameron used the time to calm himself. He was an idiot for going along. This would be all over the news within the hour. Close to a hundred rounds had to have been fired. Almost all of them from silenced weapons, but that wouldn't matter much once the police and the media showed up. The two parked cars looked as if they'd been caught in the world's worst hailstorm, and the body of Mario Lukas was riddled with bullet holes. This was not the way he'd wanted things to go. Villaume had been right about Duser. The man was as subtle as a wrecking ball.

Duser approached Cameron with a new weapon in his hand. "Let's go get the girl."

"No." Cameron was appalled.

"Don't worry about the cops. They'll be busy enough with the first crime scene."

"No. We're done for the day." He rubbed his temples and muttered, "This is going to be all over the news."

"Big deal. Reporters don't catch criminals, cops do, and we have nothing to worry about. Any evidence that might tie us to that hit just exited the other end of this warehouse."

Cameron was tempted to ask where it was headed and then thought better of it. "Nope. We're done for the day."

"What in the hell is wrong with you?" Duser took a step forward. "We have to keep moving while we've got surprise on our side."

"No, we don't. For the last time . . . we're done for the day."

Duser looked as if he wanted to choke someone. "Bullshit! We move now, and we keep moving. I'm telling you, man, we're going to have to deal with them sooner or later, and we're better off doing it right now."

Cameron shook his head. He did not like the idea of further exposure. Duser sensed this might be the problem and said, "Listen, you stay here, and we'll take care of it. I want Villaume alone and on the run."

He thought about it for a second and said, "No. Change of plans. I want Villaume, too, and the girl will lead us to him as soon as she finds out about Lukas. We keep Juarez under surveillance, and then we take both of them."

Duser liked that idea. "Good plan. I'm sorry I got in your face. I'm just a little pumped up right now."

It's probably all that speed you took, Cameron thought to himself. "That's all right, just make sure you don't lose Juarez. She's our only link to the Frog."

A minute later, Cameron watched as Duser and McBride got into a Ford Taurus and left. Maybe he was having the wrong people killed. No, he thought to himself. Duser was unpolished and wild, but he could be controlled.

RAPP HAD SPENT the night on Marcus Dumond's couch with a 9-mm Beretta clutched firmly in his left hand. Any thoughts of keeping Dumond out of it were gone. Rapp had come to grips with the fact that he needed some help. One huge question remained. Did

Irene Kennedy send the Hoffmans to kill him? All his instincts told him no. He'd known Irene for more than a decade, and she was the most trustworthy person in his life. But in this paranoid business, how well did you ever really know someone? Rapp wanted to believe that Kennedy had nothing to do with the mess, but it was a hard one to swallow. She was not only the most logical choice but really the only choice. She was *the* link between the Hoffmans and him.

The two men were sitting at Dumond's kitchen table. The apartment was a good-sized one-bedroom. The kitchen had a small breakfast nook, and the dining room had been converted into Dumond's office. An eight-foot solid oak door laid across stacked cinder blocks served as a desk. The surface was covered with three computer monitors, mouses, keyboards, scanners, and a few things Rapp had never seen. Framed posters of several X-Men Marvel comic book heroes adorned the walls. Rapp was only four years older than Dumond, but it was as if the two had been born in different centuries. Dumond was out there on the edge, riding the wild waves of cyberspace.

Dumond was shoveling Cap'n Crunch cereal into his mouth while Rapp gave him instructions. "Make sure you don't set off any alarms while you're digging around."

Dumond looked up, a drop of milk running down his chin. "Relax, Mitch, it's what I do for a living." Dumond's job was a fantasy come true. He was both sanctioned and paid by the United States government to spend his days hacking.

"Yeah, but this is different. This time you'll be hacking into files at Langley and the Pentagon."

Dumond grinned, his mouth full of golden Cap'n Crunch. After he had enough of it swallowed, he said, "There ain't nothing different about that."

Rapp eyed him for a moment. Dumond had a smartass streak in him a mile wide. "Don't jerk my chain, Marcus."

"I'm not. I'm usually in the Pentagon's system at least once a day."

"And Langley's?"

"I'm on the system."

"But what about areas where you're not supposed to be?"

"Not every day, but I've been known to look around from time to time."

"How often?"

"Every day." Dumond shoved another spoonful in his mouth.

"Does Irene know that you do this?"

"No . . . not always."

Rapp shook his head like a troubled father. "Marcus, I'm telling you for your own good, you'd better watch what you're doing. You open up the wrong person's file, and you might suddenly disappear." Rapp snapped his fingers.

"How are they going to catch me when they don't even know I've been there? Hmm?"

"Marcus, I know you're good, but no one's perfect. You keep screwing around like this, and you're gonna get caught." Dumond smiled and shook his head in disagreement. Rapp pointed his finger at the younger man and said, "Marcus, I'm not fucking around on this! You're playing a very dangerous game, and sooner or later someone is going to be on to you. And when that happens, you can kiss your ass goodbye, and I don't mean your job . . . I mean your life." Rapp turned his finger on himself. "The CIA and the Pentagon, they have dozens of guys just like me. They don't know dick about computers, but they know a lot about killing people."

Dumond heeded the warning. "All right . . . all right." He got up and dumped the rest of his cereal down the garbage disposal. His appetite was suddenly gone.

A few minutes later, they left the four-plex, Dumond out the front and on his way to Langley, Rapp out the back and on his way to a storage shed in the sticks. Rapp walked eight blocks to Wisconsin Avenue and went underground, where he caught the Metro going north. He was wearing the same clothes from the night before— his baseball cap, a sweatshirt, his khakis, and blue tennis shoes. The outfit would be fine until he got to the storage locker. The train was relatively empty since most of the people were headed into the city to work, and he was headed out. Rapp's backpack was on the empty seat next to him, his arm resting on top of it. The train gently rocked as it rolled through the tunnel, and a short while later it was above ground, the bright sunlight spilling through the windows.

The only other person in the car pulled out a cell phone and started talking. Rapp's hand slid over to one of the outer pockets on the backpack and patted it. Dumond had given him a digitally encrypted phone. He told Rapp it was safe to use whenever he wanted and for as long as he wanted. But Rapp, always the skeptic, planned to use it sparingly and only for a few minutes at a time.

The desire to see Anna was overwhelming. He looked out the window as the train rolled north. He knew he shouldn't do it, but he had to. At the very least, he had to hear her voice. Rapp pulled out the phone and turned it on. He quickly punched in her work number and nervously counted the seconds. After three rings her voice mail picked up. Mitch listened to her voice and then, at the beep, he punched the end button on the phone. His spirits plummeted. It wasn't just about not finding Anna. For the first time in his life, Rapp was filled with doubt. Doubt over whether or not he should just walk away. Whether they would even let him walk away. He was so close to where he wanted to be. Why did he have to take that last mission? Why couldn't he just have called it quits? He took his baseball cap off and ran a hand over his short, bristly black hair. He knew the answer to all of those questions, but at this moment he didn't feel like admitting it. All he wanted was Anna. To put all of this behind him and live a normal life.

IRENE KENNEDY ENTERED the conference room on the seventh floor of the CIA's headquarters in Langley, Virginia, and set her notepad on the table. Lunch would have to wait. This meeting had been sprung on her. The rectangular room was adjacent to the director's office. Bland and functional, it contained a long mahogany table and a dozen leather chairs. The room was swept every morning by the Administration Director- ate's Office of Security—the CIA's Gestapo, as it was affectionately referred to by some of the Agency's more than twenty thousand employees. Hidden behind the curtains were small devices that caused the windows to vibrate, making penetration by a parabolic microphone impossible. For obvious reasons, the CIA took its secu- rity seriously, and in very few places was it taken more seriously than the executive suite of the seventh floor.

There were five other individuals at the conference table, and none of them spoke to each other. Max Sal- men, the oldest of the group, didn't care for the others, with the exception of Irene Kennedy. They were, to him, dangerous mongrels—each a mix of bureaucrat, politician, and lawyer and each nearly incapable of mak- ing the correct decision for the right reason. They headed three of the Agency's directorates, and Salmen headed the fourth. As deputy director of Operations, Salmen was in charge of the spies. It was his people who ran the black ops, recruited agents from both friend and foe, kept tabs on counterespionage, and tracked the ter- rorists. His people were the front-line troops, the case officers, the people out in the field getting their hands dirty and taking the real risks. Salmen had cut his teeth with Stansfield in Europe, and then, as Stansfield had risen through the ranks, the crusty Salmen had come with him. Salmen was Kennedy's immediate boss, al- though she often reported directly to Stansfield.

The other three people at the table were also deputy directors. Charles Workman ran Intelligence. His people were the bookworms, the Mensa geeks who pored over reams of information day in and day out. Rachel Mann ran Science and Technology, and Stephen Bauman was in charge of Administration.

Of the three, Salmen disliked Workman the most, but Bauman was a close second. To say that he hated Mann would be unfair. Under different circumstances, Bauman thought he would probably like her. She was very bright and for the most part tried to avoid the political backstabbing that Workman and Bauman thrived on, but in the end there was only so much money to go around, and everyone wanted to take it from Operations. If it wasn't for the recent spate of terrorism, Salmen knew his budget would be in serious trouble.

Salmen folded his nicotine-stained hands across his bulging belly and wondered how much longer he could hold on. His days were numbered. He'd been at the Agency since 1964, stationed first in Cambodia and then in Laos, doing things for his government that were still classified. After Vietnam, he moved on to Europe, where he worked in various embassies before becoming the station chief in Berlin. When Stansfield became director, he recalled Salmen and brought him into his inner circle. Now, with Stansfield on his deathbed, things looked bleak. The only reason Salmen put up with all of the bullshit was out of a sense of duty to the people in the field. He needed to protect them. He needed to keep these desk jockeys off their backs. And there was one other reason. Stansfield had asked him to stay and keep an eye on things, and, more explicitly, he had asked his old friend to watch Irene Kennedy's back.

The door to the director's office opened, and Jonathan Brown entered. The deputy director of Central Intelligence, or DDCI as he was known, was the second in charge at the Agency. In theory, the four deputy directors reported to him, and he reported to the director himself, but Salmen had never played that game. He went right to the director when there was a problem. Brown had shown some irritation with this, and Salmen knew the second Stansfield was gone, his ass was grass. Until then, he would try to keep the bureaucrats' attention focused on him and off Kennedy.

Brown sat at the head of the table and looked over the attendees with his usual dramatic flair. Because of the sensitivity of most of the things Kennedy worked on, she rarely reported to the DDCI. Kennedy did not have a problem with Brown. The man was more than talented enough to handle his job. Under different circumstances, he might even have made a good director of Central Intelligence. But in the end he was an outsider, a former federal prosecutor and judge. He owed his job at the CIA to a handful of politicians on the Hill who lobbied for him. His loyalty was to them and not to the Agency.

Kennedy was invited to these types of meetings more than she would have liked. Within the four directorates were thirty-plus offices or groups. Of those, Counterterrorism was the one that garnered the most attention. Kennedy had a pretty good idea why she had been yanked out of the CTC on such short notice to attend this meeting on high, and she wasn't happy about it. The CIA was supposed to be about compartmentalization, not openness. If Brown wanted to talk about Germany, he didn't need to bring Science and Technology and Administration in on the meeting.

Brown cleared his throat and appeared to be choosing his words carefully. "I just received a call from Chairman Rudin." Brown looked genuinely troubled. "He wants everything we have on what transpired in Germany this past weekend."

The assassination of Count Heinrich Hagenmiller had taken on mythic proportions in just a few days. Even within the secretive bubble of Langley, it was being discussed by almost everyone. The three top suspects were the United States, Israel, and Iraq. But as of yesterday, the British, the French, and even the Germans were added to the list. The British were added because they were the British, and they'd been doing just this type of thing better and longer than anyone else. The French were added to the list because it was said Hagenmiller had cut them out of the deal. And the Germans, it was being said, killed the count because he was an embarrassment. Kennedy didn't mind any of this. The more speculation, the better. This was, after all, the intent of the operation, to send a message to all who dealt with Saddam. The more governments to be suspicious of, the better.

Brown looked in the direction of Kennedy and said, "And he would like to see you in front of his committee first thing in the morning, Irene."

Salmen let out a moan, and Kennedy said, "All right. Would he like anything specific?"

"He didn't say. He just asked me to remind you that

you'd be under oath." Brown said this with all of the reverence of a former federal judge.

Salmen scoffed at the comment and said, "What a joke!"

Brown did not like dissension. "Is there a problem, Max?"

"Yeah. Rudin is the problem."

"Pardon me?" Brown seemed to be in an even more serious mood than normal.

"Chairman Rudin is a frustrated little man who's had a bug up his ass since day one about this Agency."

Deputy Director Brown did not think the comment was funny, and two of the other deputy directors were forced to stifle their reactions to Salmen's candid and accurate analysis. Kennedy, as always, kept a neutral expression on her face.

"I would appreciate it if you'd show the congressman from Connecticut a little more respect."

This caused Salmen to laugh out loud. "The congressman and I have had a hate-hate relationship for years. If I started to respect him at this stage of the game, he'd be very upset."

Brown decided to move on. Looking to Charles Workman, the deputy director of Intelligence, he said, "I want a report on my desk by five. Anything and everything you have on what went down in Germany." Workman dutifully replied that he would personally take care of it. Brown turned back to Salmen. "Is it true that we had Hagenmiller under surveillance?"

Salmen stuffed his hands under his armpits and shrugged. "That's on a strictly need-to-know basis."

Brown's face became flushed over Salmen's blatant disrespect. "I am in the *need to know,* and I expect a report from you on my desk by five."

Salmen remained defiant. "I will give you no such report until Director Stansfield tells me to do so."

"Listen, Max, I have done nothing to deserve this from you. I am the DDI, and for all intents and purposes the acting DCI. When I tell you I want something on my desk by five, I mean it."

Salmen appeared to back off just a touch. "Jonathan, I mean no disrespect, but I've been doing this a hell of a lot longer than you. The bedrock of this agency is the philosophy of 'need to know.' When Director Stansfield tells me you need to know, I'll tell you."

"Max, Director Stansfield isn't going to be around to protect you forever. And when he's gone, I'm going to relish putting you out to pasture."

Salmen stood. "Yeah, well, until then, Your Honor . . . you can kiss my big white ass." The deputy director of Operations turned and left the conference room with a broad smile across his face.

After a period of uncomfortable silence, Kennedy looked to the DDI and said, "Sir, I would like to apologize for Max. He has been under a lot of stress lately. As you know, he and Director Stansfield are very close. I don't think Max is taking his poor health very well."

"You don't need to apologize for him." Brown appreciated Kennedy's comments. She was one of the most competent and professional people he had ever worked with. It was too bad she was going to end up being a casualty of this whole mess.

"I know I don't, sir, but please don't take it personally. Max is just very cranky, and on top of that, he
doesn't care much for Congressman Rudin."

"Yes, I know. I can assure you that the congressman
feels the same way about Max." Brown looked at his
notes for a second and then said, "I want you to be
completely forthright when you go before the committee tomorrow. The last thing we want is to have Director Stansfield's career end in disgrace."

Kennedy nodded in agreement, but internally she
was deciphering Brown's real intent. Stansfield had let
it leak that he would last six months to a year. Kennedy
knew he'd be lucky to last a month. Brown's concern
had nothing to do with Thomas Stansfield's reputation.
It had everything to do with his own career. Scandals in
Washington were a media and political feast to be sa-
vored, death by a thousand cuts to be drawn out over a
period of years not months. Brown, not Stansfield,
would be the one in the hot seat if a congressional investigation were launched. And it was extremely rare for
someone's career to survive such a bloodletting.

21

Rapp drove west on Georgetown Pike in a black 1994 Volkswagen Jetta. It was dark out, and rush-hour traffic was starting to dwindle. The car was registered under the name of Charlie Smith. Rapp had a Maryland driver's license in his pocket with the same name. The CIA had taught Rapp many things over the years, but two of the most important were to be thorough and paranoid. A shrink had once told him to use the word *cautious* because of the negative connotations associated with the word *paranoid,* but Rapp had only laughed. He had always been cautious, it was second nature to him, but *paranoid* described his current mental state perfectly. When you were on your own, up against the world's largest and best-funded intelligence agency, there was no more appropriate word.

Rapp had an advantage over most, though. He was an insider. He knew how the Agency operated, and despite all of their technological advancements, they were still limited. If a person was proactive and paranoid enough, disappearing was easy. And Rapp was both. That was why three years ago, he had set up the Charlie Smith alias and paid eight-thousand dollars cash for the Jetta. That was why he kept it in a storage yard up in Rockville along with a few other items that might come in handy. Rapp had been the hunter long enough to understand that someday he might become the hunted. And when that happened, it was best not to waste time trying to buy weapons and steal vehicles.

As they passed under Interstate 495, Shirley let out a yawn. Rapp looked over his shoulder to see how she was doing. She looked back at him with her big brown eyes and licked her lips. Rapp had picked her up at 7319 Georgia Avenue NW. For a mutt, she was a good looker. The people at the Washington Humane Society had been very helpful. He'd asked for a medium-sized dog that was mellow and, if possible, didn't bark too much. They had brought him back to the kennels and showed him Shirley. She was part collie, part Labrador, and part something else. She'd been with them for three weeks, and no one had claimed her, which surprised the woman who was showing Rapp around. It appeared Shirley had been very well trained. When Rapp asked the woman how they had come up with the dog's name, she told him they went down a list of names until she responded to one. "It could be Curly, Burley, Hurly, or anything that sounds like Shirley, but I picked Shirley. She looks like a Shirley." Rapp didn't argue. Shirley was fine with him. After picking her up, he stopped at a pet store and got a leash, some dog food, and a few treats to help woo her.

At Linganore Drive, he took a right off the pike and then took his first left onto Linganore Court. Rapp drove the car to the end of the street, turned it around, and parked. He grabbed Shirley from the back seat and went over to the walking path. It ran between two houses and into the Scotts Run Nature Preserve. The preserve consisted of three hundred eighty-four acres of wooded land overlooking the Potomac River in McLean, Virginia. The hiking trails were well used during the day and especially the weekends, but on a Tuesday night they would be empty. Rapp and Shirley disappeared into the darkness and broke into a jog.

IRENE KENNEDY ARRIVED at 7:20. She had left Langley at six and stopped at home just long enough to make Tommy a bowl of macaroni and cheese and eat a salad for herself. After spending exactly forty-three minutes with her son, she handed him off to Heather, the teenager who lived next door. There was no need to brief Heather on the rules and numbers to call if anything scared her. They had run through the routine at least a dozen times. Kennedy set the security system and left, getting in back of the government sedan with her protector behind the wheel. The ride to Stansfield's house was filled with guilt and doubt. More and more, Kennedy was feeling like a bad mom. When she wasn't at Langley working, she was at home working. Tommy was spending a frightening amount of time glued to the TV.

The demands put on her time were growing with fewer respites between the flare-ups. The life of a single parent was hard enough, but with her job, it was nearly impossible. She didn't blame her ex, though. It was better that they had parted when Tommy was little. The man was out west and out of their lives. At least he would never get close enough to disappoint his son the way he had disappointed her.

Kennedy felt torn between her obligation to her son and her obligation to a very serious job. A job that saved lives. But something was going to have to give. She couldn't go on like this. Her work would suffer, and so would her relationship with her son. As they turned into Stansfield's driveway, Kennedy forced the thoughts from her mind. She needed to focus. The last thing her mentor needed right now was to worry about her.

The car stopped in front of the garage, and Kennedy got out. She walked up to the front door, where she was met by one of Stansfield's bodyguards. Kennedy went down the hall and entered the study, where she found Thomas Stansfield sitting in his leather chair, his feet up on the ottoman and an afghan on his lap. She walked over and kissed him on the forehead. All things considered, he looked good.

Leaving her hand on his shoulder, she asked, "How are you feeling today?"

"Just fine, thank you. Would you like anything to drink?"

Kennedy knew he wasn't fine. He couldn't be. The doctors had told her the cancer was very painful. But that was Thomas Stansfield. He wasn't about to feel sorry for himself, and he didn't want anyone else to, either. Kennedy declined the offer of a beverage and sat on the sofa across from her mentor. "Congressman Rudin wants me on the Hill first thing in the morning."

"I've heard."

Kennedy didn't bother to ask how. She'd stopped wondering years ago how the man got his information. "What else have you heard?"

"He wants to know if we were in Germany and, if so, if we had a hand in the Hagenmiller business."

"And how would you advise me to answer that question?"

"Very carefully," replied the older man.

"At the very least, I was planning on doing that."

"I'm sure you were." Stansfield thought about Rudin for a second and then said, "If he is so bold as to hold the committee in open session, you should answer nothing and politely refer him to me." Stansfield frowned. "As much as he hates us, I don't think he would be so brash."

"Neither do I."

Stansfield pondered the question further and finally said, "You have to tell him that we had the count and his corporation under surveillance. Lay out the same case that the president did to the German ambassador yesterday. Despite Rudin's deep hatred of us, we have enough allies on the committee to block him. Once they find out what Hagenmiller was up to, any interest in pursuing the matter further will die."

Kennedy wasn't so sure. "Maybe we could have the president call him? Rudin is a party man through and through. He'll do whatever President Hayes asks of him."

Stansfield shook his head. "No. I want the president kept out of this. It's become far too murky. We can handle it on our own."

Kennedy reluctantly agreed and then said, "We're missing something here."

"In regard to Rudin?"

"In regard to the whole thing." Kennedy stared out the window. "I don't know . . . there are leaks we haven't identified. Someone is out there working against us, and for what reason I still haven't figured out."

"I'm working on that."

"Do you have any ideas?"

"It's all a question of motive, Irene."

"Motive for what?"

"Did you know that Rudin and Midleton met with Senator Clark at Congressional Country Club this morning?"

"No." Once again, he amazed her with his network of informants.

"They had breakfast together."

"What did they discuss?"

"I don't know, but I do know their motives. Rudin despises me personally and would like nothing more than to see me take my last breath. Midleton and I are cordial, but he would like to have more of a say in what the CIA is up to."

"What about Clark?"

Stansfield adjusted the afghan on his lap and thought about the question. "I'm not sure about Senator Clark. For the most part, he has always been good to us, but I sense no loyalty in the man. In the end, I think he is looking to serve only himself."

"What are they after?"

Stansfield looked at Kennedy and decided it was time. "We need to discuss something."

Kennedy tensed a bit. "All right."

"I've spoken to the president, and he has agreed that you will be his nominee to succeed me as DCI."

Kennedy had not seen this coming. She had wondered who would succeed Stansfield but had honestly never thought of herself as a candidate. "I'm very flattered, but I don't think I'm qualified."

In a rare show of emotion, Stansfield grinned. "You are more than qualified."

"But what about all of the other people . . ."

"You are the best candidate for the job."

"I disagree." Kennedy slowly shook her head. "I can barely keep up with things as it is. It's to the point where I'm lucky if I spend an hour with Tommy a day, and then I have to try to tear him away from the TV."

"Right now you have the hardest job at the Agency. Things will get easier when you become director."

"How?" asked an incredulous Kennedy.

"You surround yourself with good people, and you delegate."

Kennedy was still filled with disbelief. How could a job with more responsibility translate into fewer hours? It didn't compute.

"Irene, how many Sundays have you seen me work since you've known me?"

Kennedy thought about it for a second. "Not very many."

"Correct."

The more she thought about it, the more she knew he

was right. The CTC was a pressure cooker. "I'm not qualified."

"You are more than qualified."

"I'm too young."

"You're a little young for the job, but that is balanced out by your success with the CTC."

"I don't know, Thomas. I don't know if I want your job, and that's assuming they'll confirm me."

"Oh, they'll confirm you. The Republicans love your hard stance on terrorism, and they won't want to look like sexists. The Democrats . . . well, they'll follow the president. He might have to grant a few favors, but that's nothing unusual."

Kennedy took a deep breath. This was a little too much of a surprise. "I'll have to think about all of this."

Stansfield smiled. "Of course you will, but keep in mind that the Agency needs you. It needs someone like you to protect it from the likes of Chairman Rudin and Secretary Midleton."

Kennedy frowned as a piece of the puzzle fell into place. "Is that what this meeting tomorrow is really about?"

"I don't know for certain, but I think so." Stansfield looked at Kennedy with steely gray eyes. "They fear you, Irene, just like they fear me. They fear us because they can't control us."

IT TOOK RAPP and his new four-legged friend eight minutes to reach the far side of the preserve. After that, it took several more to find the house he was looking for. Rapp had been to the house before, but he had been invited and had arrived by car—not on foot through the woods. He almost mistook the neighbor's house for Stansfield's. They were similar—both colonials. The neighbor had a small storage shed in the back corner of his lot that was adjacent to Stansfield's. Rapp and Shirley walked through the tall grass and took up a position behind it.

The complete lack of security that was placed around high-ranking U.S. officials here in America never failed to amaze Rapp. With the exception of the president, the vice president, and the first family, protection was a joke. When officials were out of the country, it was much better, but here at home, they usually had no more than a glorified home security system and a chauffeur who doubled as a bodyguard. He expected Stansfield's to be a little better than most, but still nothing he couldn't overcome.

Rapp pulled a small pair of field binoculars out of his jacket and started checking the windows. All of the lights were off on the second floor. On the first floor was a woman in the kitchen who appeared to be washing some dishes. Rapp wondered about the woman briefly and then decided she must be domestic help. There was a car in the driveway. Rapp focused the lenses on it and saw a driver sitting behind the wheel of a government sedan. Something looked vaguely familiar about the man, but the top half of his face was obscured by the visor. Taking Shirley, he went back into the tall grass and worked his way down toward the river. Midway down the property line, he found something interesting. Set up to look like landscaping lights next to a flower bed were two laser tripwires. Rapp grabbed his night-vision pocket scope and held it to his eye. The red beams invisible to the naked eye popped to life on the small scope. Rapp followed them around the perimeter. They wouldn't be a problem.

He and Shirley continued around the back of the property line until they had a view of the other wing of the house. Rapp had a pretty good idea that this was where Stansfield would be. He wanted to talk to the man. He wanted to find out the truth. And for Thomas Stansfield's sake, Rapp hoped he had some answers. After that, he would go to Kennedy's to see if her story could withstand some intense scrutiny. He'd labored over the decision for several days, but he had decided it was the quickest and most effective way to get to the bottom of what had happened in Germany.

When Rapp reached the far end of the lot, he brought the binoculars up and found Stansfield sitting in his study. He looked frail, a good ten pounds lighter. He was talking to someone, but Rapp couldn't see who, so he moved to a different spot. When he focused in on the woman sitting across from Stansfield, his throat became dry. Rapp brought the binoculars down and stood motionless. His paranoia had just gone into overdrive.

As he worked his way back to the neighbor's storage shed, he began to cling to the hope that neither of them had anything to do with it, but a sickening feeling in his gut told him otherwise. As Rapp prepared to make his move, a pair of headlights flashed across the front lawn. A car was coming down the driveway. Rapp put his plan on hold for a second and kneeled down next to Shirley. She hadn't made a peep so far, and he hoped her good behavior would continue. The car was actually a four-door SUV. Rapp watched with increasing interest as the driver got out. As the man walked across the driveway toward the front door, he knew instantly who it was. The sight of him sent Rapp's pulse racing and his mind scrambling to come up with a reason for this person from his past to be here on this night. The man was like him. He was a killer, but one whom, until now, he thought he could trust.

Fear suddenly gripped Rapp. It was not a fear of the man but fear of something that he may have done. He looked at his watch. It was almost seven-thirty. Before he went forward with his plan, he needed to make a call. All of his discipline told him he shouldn't do it, but he had to. He had to know. Rapp retreated into the woods with Shirley and turned on his digital phone.

22

J ust outside the main entrance to the West Wing, an almost nightly occurrence was taking place. Reporters from all the major networks and cable news stations were positioned in front of their cameras, loaded up with makeup and hair spray. They were waiting to tell the people in the mountains and on the West Coast what they had already said to the people in the eastern and central time zones an hour earlier.

Anna Rielly was in her usual spot or, as her smartass cameraman Pete liked to remind her, "NBC's spot." Pete kept things interesting; he was a little immature, but in a good way. Rarely serious, Pete loved to give people a hard time. Normally, Rielly was more than willing to play along, but today she hadn't been. The last several nights of sleep hadn't gone so well. She was worried sick about Mitch. He wasn't okay, she was convinced of that. If he were okay, he'd pick up the phone and call her. She had spent every spare minute of the day looking at the newswire, paying particular attention to the Middle East. That was where Mitch was trained to operate. Since the Israeli prime minister was in town for meetings with President Hayes, she had a tailor-made excuse for her interest in the region.

During lunch she broke down, and she'd been cursing herself ever since. She couldn't believe she had cried in front of two other reporters and a producer from CBS. Over a mediocre Caesar salad, Pete started razzing her about Mitch. He began with his usual, "Where's Don Juan? I haven't seen him in a while." This led to more questions by the others, which gave Pete more material and an audience to entertain. Rielly tried to smile and roll with the punches, but it proved too difficult. The vision of Mitch lying dead in some faraway city was too much, and the tears came. They were there before she knew it. Embarrassed, she got up and abruptly left the restaurant. Pete showed up a short while later in Rielly's closet-sized office in the basement of the West Wing and apologized. Rielly tried her best to act as if it was no big deal, but it didn't work. Pete could see something serious was bothering her, but after already stepping all over it, he dared not delve into the matter.

Pete's camera was set up on a tripod, and he was standing behind it with his hands in his pockets. Underneath his headset was an Atlanta Braves baseball cap. Pete was chewing gum and in general looked very bored. He was still uncomfortable over having made Rielly cry at lunch. The control room in New York called out the time to Brokaw's intro, and Pete held up his left hand with two fingers extended. "Two minutes to Marble Mouth."

Rielly smiled under the bright lights and nodded. She took this as a good sign. "Marble Mouth" was Pete's nickname for the network's top anchor. Rielly knew

Pete felt bad and was about to tell him once again not to worry about it when she felt her cell phone vibrate. She checked the caller ID, but the number came up as unavailable. Her thumb sat poised over the talk button. Normally, this close to the broadcast she'd let it roll into her voice mail, but she decided to answer it with the hope that it was her significant other.

She pressed the button and held the phone to her ear. "Anna Rielly here."

Rapp's heart melted at the sound of her voice. "Honey, it's me. Are you all right?"

Rielly was speechless for a second, and then she managed to say, "Mitchell."

"Honey, it's me, but I can't talk long. Are you okay?"

Rielly turned her back to the camera. "No, I'm not okay. I've been worried sick for the last four days."

"I'm sorry about that, but it couldn't be helped. You're fine, though . . . right? I mean, other than being worried."

"I think I'm the one who should be concerned about you."

"I'm fine." Rapp sounded rushed. "Are you staying with our friends?"

"Yes. Where are you?"

"I can't answer that. Have you noticed anyone following you?"

"No. When can I see you?"

"I'm not sure. Maybe a few days, maybe a week."

Rielly didn't like his answer. "Mitchell, I don't care what kind of errands you're running for you know who, I want you home immediately."

"I can't. Not for a few days."

"You said you were going to quit, and right now seems like a very good time to me."

"I am going to quit, but I have to tie up a few loose ends first."

"Mitch, honey, please. I can't take this anymore. Just please come home."

"Honey, I'm safe . . . I'm here in town, and when I finish what I'm doing, I'm going to quit and we are going to spend the rest of our lives together. But you have to trust me on this. I have to take care of a few things before I can do that." Rapp paused. "I love you, Anna. Will you please just trust me?"

"Yes, but . . ."

Rapp cut her off, "No buts, honey. You have to believe me."

"All right, but please be careful and hurry up."

"I will, but I have one more question for you. Has our friend talked to Scott C., or have you seen him?"

Anna had to think for a moment. "I don't think he's talked to Scott, and no, I haven't seen him. What is his involvement in all of this?"

"Nothing. I have to go now. Keep staying where you have been until I tell you different, okay?"

Rielly hesitated briefly. "All right."

"I love you, Anna."

"I love you, too." Rielly listened for a second, and then the line went dead.

RAPP TURNED OFF his phone, relieved that Anna was safe. Now it was time to get some answers. With

Shirley in tow, he headed back to the small shed. Rapp had to do some guessing. He knew that Stansfield liked to keep a low profile. Hence no fence or gated driveway. No guards patrolling the grounds with dogs to provide good perimeter deterrence and early detection. Rapp could recite a long list of Stansfield's counterparts in Europe and the Middle East, intelligence chiefs from state-run and terrorist groups, who had five times the protection Stansfield did. In America it was a different story.

The director's only security would be his house itself. At first glance, it looked like any other dwelling on the quiet street, but Rapp suspected it was anything but. Just kicking the door in wasn't going to work. He would have to get them to open the door, and that was where Shirley would come in. Somewhere inside the house was a man from the Agency's Office of Security. The man was bored stiff, probably reading a novel, or, if Stansfield allowed it, he might even be watching TV. He was at, or near, a console that monitored the home's security through a web of cameras, laser tripwires, and probably a few more high-tech gadgets.

Rapp had an idea that might work. If it didn't, he was reasonably confident that he could abort without Stansfield or Kennedy ever knowing that he had been there. He checked the windows again and tried to get a feel for how many individuals might be in the house and where. There were at least five: Stansfield, Kennedy, Coleman, the housekeeper, and one bodyguard. There was a chance there might be two bodyguards, but Rapp doubted it. Congress liked to count every penny in the CIA's budget. They would pay close attention to how much money the director was spending for his own protection.

Rapp grabbed the bag of dog treats from his pocket and held it in front of Shirley, who got excited at the sight and smell of the large rolled-up tubes of faux bacon. Still holding on to her leash, Rapp took out one of the pieces, made sure that Shirley saw it, and then tossed it into Stansfield's backyard. The piece landed midway between where they were hiding and the door by the kitchen. Shirley tried to go after it, but Rapp held on to the leash. She whimpered a little bit until Rapp pulled out another piece. He tossed this one a little farther, and again Shirley tried to bolt. Rapp continued until he had launched five of the treats onto the property, the last one coming to rest a few feet from the back door.

The dog kept looking toward the treats and then back at Rapp. Each time, she would strain a little harder on the leash. Rapp grabbed her collar and took off the leash. Releasing her, he stepped back and watched her fly across the yard. As expected, she skidded to a stop at the first treat and snapped it up in her mouth. At the same time, several powerful floodlights came on and lit up the backyard.

Rapp retrieved his Beretta from his shoulder holster and screwed a silencer onto the end. He didn't bother to check if there was a round in the chamber. He knew there was, and there were fifteen more in the magazine. With the silencer, the gun was too long to put back in the holster, so he shoved it into the back of his pants and let his jacket fall down over it.

Shirley moved from one treat to the next, working her way closer and closer to the door. Rapp patiently waited behind the shed for his opportunity. A moment later, he saw a man appear at the back door. He looked out the door at Shirley. Rapp prepared to move. If the man was smart, if he was really good, he'd stay behind the locked door. Rapp was banking on the fact that, like bodyguards all over the world, the man would be bored and let his guard down. A dulling of one's senses and enthusiasm was inevitable in the job. That was why organizations like the Secret Service hammered procedure into their agents, but it didn't always work.

When the door started to open, Rapp forced himself to wait for another second. He watched the man poke his head outside and look around the backyard. It appeared he was less concerned with Shirley than with who her owner might be. Rapp was tempted to move but told himself to wait just a second longer. Finally, when the man stepped onto the patio, Rapp moved casually from behind the shed. He didn't walk directly at the house. He walked parallel to it and yelled, "Here, Nimitz! Here, Nimitz!" Rapp intentionally used the name of the dog he'd had as a boy, hoping that Shirley would stay where she was. He continued walking casually along the back edge of Stansfield's yard with Shirley's leash in his right hand.

"Is this your dog, Mister?"

Rapp stopped and turned toward the house. "Oh, I'm sorry. Is that you up there, Nimitz?" He started walking toward the house. "Leave that man alone, and get over here," he added in a lighthearted voice. "I'm sorry about this. She's usually pretty good." He continued to close in on the man, hoping that Shirley would stay right where she was. The dog finally looked up, and the bodyguard appeared as if he was about to retreat, so Rapp blurted out, "Hi, my name is Dave. My wife and I just moved in over on Linganore Court." Smiling, he stuck out his hand and said, "She must have smelled food. I apologize." The bodyguard was standing with his right side turned away from Rapp, and his hand was hanging loosely at his side instead of up at his hip where it should be. *Hell,* Rapp thought to himself, *he shouldn't even be out here.* The guy looked very young. Rapp guessed he was still in his twenties.

Then the guard actually extended his hand. "Hi, I'm Trevor."

Rapp smiled and took it, thinking to himself, *You stupid son of a bitch.* "Nice to meet you." Rapp pumped the bodyguard's hand and pointed to Shirley with his free hand. As soon as Trevor looked at the dog, Rapp unleashed a vicious left hook that caught the bodyguard square on the jaw. The man's knees crumpled, and he began to sink. Rapp caught him before he could hit the ground and carried him straight back into the house, where he deposited him on the floor of the mud room. Moving quickly, he closed the door, leaving Shirley outside, and pulled out a pair of plastic flex cuffs. He bound the man's wrists behind his back and checked his body for any backup weapons. There were none. Rapp took the man's gun from his holster and stuck it in his coat pocket, just as he began to show signs of coming to. Rapp quickly undid the bodyguard's pants and started to stand him up. The dress slacks fell to Trevor's knees. With his Beretta drawn, Rapp grabbed the bodyguard by the hair and began pushing him down the hall toward Stansfield's study.

Rapp's right hand had a firm grip of the hair on the back of the bodyguard's head, and his silenced pistol was pressed into the center of his back. The man shuffled as Rapp pushed him forward, his pants now down around his knees. They were at the study door in seconds. Rapp didn't know if it was locked, so he knocked just in case and heard Stansfield say "Enter" a moment later. He kept the gun pressed against the bodyguard's back and let go of his hair. Reaching around his prisoner, Rapp turned the knob and thrust the door open. Taking half a step back, he placed his boot on the man's butt and pushed. The man tumbled into the room, falling to the floor with his pants around his ankles.

Rapp followed right behind him, searching for Coleman with his gun leveled. Stansfield and Kennedy weren't a threat. He found Coleman sitting on the couch next to Kennedy. Rapp shut the door with his free hand. Coleman started to move, but Rapp was quicker. He fired one shot as he crossed the room. Coleman stopped, frozen in complete shock, his eyes fixed on the bullet hole in the cushion of the couch he was sitting on.

In a flat voice, Rapp said, "The next one goes in your kneecap. Sit on your hands, Scott, and don't move."

Coleman looked back down at the bullet hole. It was less than two inches from his groin. As calmly as possible, he slid his hands under his butt and nodded to Rapp, letting him know that he had the upper hand.

23

Rielly's spirits were soaring. Just hearing Mitch's voice, knowing that he was alive, seemed to make all of the pain and worry vanish. He would be safe now that he was back in America. And she didn't doubt for a second that this would be it. Mitch wanted to put it all behind him every bit as much as she did. She still wished she could see him, but when she stepped back and really looked at it, she could understand what must be happening. He was probably going through some type of a postmission briefing. She was, after all, a reporter, and she doubted that Mitch's handlers at Langley looked very favorably on their relationship.

Rielly was covering the tripod and some other equipment with a tarp while Pete, squatting on one knee, packed up the camera. Looking up, he said, "What's got you in such a good mood all of a sudden?"

Rielly smiled. "I got some good news before we went on the air."

"You didn't act like it when you were on the phone. You seemed pretty upset."

"I was kind of caught off-guard."

"Was it Mitch?"

"Yes."

"So everything is okay between you two?"

Rielly hesitated. "Things were never bad between us. We just had a little problem over the weekend."

"Great," replied Pete with sarcasm. "You guys had a little problem, I make a little comment at lunch, and then you make me feel bad about myself for the rest of the day."

Rielly smiled. "I'm sorry, Pete, it was just bad timing. I was a little sensitive today."

"That's fine," he continued in his sarcastic tone. "I'm a big target. I can take it. Whatever you need to do to make yourself feel better . . . go right ahead."

Rielly laughed. "I see the little baby has his sense of humor back." She punched him in the arm. "You are so full of it."

Pete stood up with a weepy expression on his face. "You know, I have feelings, too."

"Yeah, I know you do, big shooter. I'll make it up to you and buy you a beer."

"Really?" The pained look vanished.

"Yeah, but not tonight, maybe tomorrow." Rielly wanted to get home and give Liz the update.

"If you really cared, you'd take me out right now. I'm feeling very vulnerable tonight."

Rielly just shook her head. "Oh, please. I'll see you tomorrow." She turned and walked away toward the northwest gate. On her way, she called Liz. After four rings, her friend answered.

"Liz, I'm leaving work. I'm going to grab a cab."

"No you're not! Michael's right here. I'm kicking him out the door as we speak. He'll be there in five minutes."

"No. I'm fine. Don't worry, I can catch a cab."

"Anna, don't argue with me. Michael is on his way."

"Liz, everything is fine. I talked to Mitch. I'll tell you about it when I get there." Her friend tried to protest again, but Rielly cut her off. "Don't bother sending Michael. I'll be there in less than ten minutes."

Rielly hung up the phone without giving Liz a chance to argue further. She passed through the gate, waving good night to the uniformed Secret Service officers behind the bulletproof windows. Walking west down Pennsylvania, she lifted her face to the sky and grinned with relief. The night's fall air felt crisp and clean. One block over, in front of the Renwick Gallery on the corner of 17th, she caught a cab and told the driver the address in Georgetown. The cab pulled out into traffic, and Rielly sank down in the back seat. Her energy was gone—her mind was set on a big glass of merlot and a good night's sleep.

A DARK BLUE Crown Victoria was parked on 17th Street facing south. It had U.S. government plates and two antennas affixed to the back window. Dave Polk sat behind the wheel and watched the cab pull away with his surveillance target in the back seat. Polk started the car and pulled out into traffic. In the trunk of the car was a suitcase. It looked ordinary, but inside was a sophisticated piece of equipment designed to intercept analog and digital phone calls. It was made in Taiwan and was most effective at picking up analog calls, but if the user were in possession of the specific digital number they were monitoring, it was no problem. Two cables ran out the back of the suitcase. One was attached to the antenna on the back window, and the other one was strung under the back seat, under the carpeting, and came up between the front seats. It was attached to a small earpiece that Polk was wearing.

He had been on post since three P.M. Most of his shift had been uneventful, with the exception of the last fifteen minutes. This was the first day they'd had her under surveillance. Polk hadn't been told why, and he didn't ask. He was a good soldier that way. He followed orders. That didn't mean he was a robot, though. He kept up on current events, and he had a healthy libido. The two together made it impossible for Anna Rielly to stay off his radar screen. She was the hottest reporter in Washington, and she'd been involved in the hostage standoff at the White House the year before. Polk remembered reading an article about how her colleagues admired her for not trying to capitalize on her personal involvement in the tragedy. Polk had a sneaky suspicion that there was more to the story.

When you were on surveillance, there was a lot of extra time. He had already read the *Washington Post* and the *Washington Times* cover to cover. Polk liked to compare the papers and how they spun stories, one liberal and one conservative. They were a daily lesson in how biased the press was.

Polk continued following the cab west down G Street. He was careful to stay far enough back. One of the few things they had told him to look out for was any communication between Rielly and a man named Mitch Rapp. From what Polk had heard earlier, he could safely assume this Mitch Rapp was Rielly's boyfriend. Polk had originally thought that this assignment was about Rielly. Probably something to do with a story she was digging into. But now, after hearing her conversation with Rapp, he was beginning to wonder if it wasn't about him.

RAPP TOLD KENNEDY and Stansfield to leave their hands on their laps where he could see them. Both did as they were told. They were well aware of Rapp's capabilities. Rapp moved behind Stansfield and positioned himself so his back was against the wall and not one of the windows. He rested the butt of the pistol on the back of the leather chair and kept the long black silencer aimed at Coleman. His dark eyes were trained on Kennedy. They were searching for the slightest sign of guilt. There was nothing, exactly what he had been afraid of. The woman was utterly unflappable.

Kennedy was momentarily caught off-guard. It was now evident that she had missed something. She had been so worried about Rapp the last several days that it had never occurred to her that he might think he had been set up by her and Stansfield. She told herself to stay calm and said, "Mitch, I know what you're thinking, but I could never do that to you."

"Oh, really. And how is it that you know what I'm thinking?"

"Why else would you come in here like this?"

Rapp ignored the question and asked, "Why did you send those two to kill me?"

"Is that what they tried?" Kennedy glanced at Stansfield. At least they had been right about that. "Mitch, I gave them no such order. I'm afraid we were compromised. By whom we do not know."

Rapp wanted to believe her, but he needed some proof. "The way I see it, Irene, there were only three people who were in a position to set me up. Director Stansfield, you, and the president. Now, which one of you was it?"

"Mitch, I would never do that to you . . . nor would Thomas or the president."

"Why were you acting so strange when I talked to you about it being my last job? Was it because you didn't want me walking around with all of your dirty little secrets? Did you want to end it nice and clean?" Rapp raised an eyebrow.

Kennedy shook her head sadly. She looked offended by the accusation. "You know me better than that. I would never harm you. I was acting strange when we last talked because of Thomas." Kennedy gestured to the director. "He's dying of cancer. You didn't know that, did you?"

"No." Rapp looked down at Stansfield. Come to think of it, he did look frail.

"All of the vultures are circling, and they're getting ready for their next meal. There's pressure coming from all sides." Kennedy paused and then added, "Look me in the eye, Mitch, and tell me you really think I could have done such a thing."

If Rapp had learned one thing in the last ten years, it was that people were capable of almost anything. Despite all of that, though, Kennedy had always been the one person he could depend on. The person who was supposed to watch his back. "If it wasn't you, then who was it?"

"That's what we've been trying to figure out."

"Just put me in a room alone with the team you sent to Germany, and I'll take care of it."

Kennedy blinked. "That's going to be a problem."

"Oh, let me guess," said Rapp with feigned surprise. "They've disappeared."

"No, worse."

"They're dead."

"Yes."

"How convenient."

"Believe me, no one wanted to talk to them more than me."

Rapp grunted. "Actually, I'm at the top of that list." He aimed the gun at Kennedy. "She didn't try to pump two rounds into your chest."

"What exactly happened in Germany?"

"I have a few more questions before we get to that. How is it that you happen to know they're dead?"

Kennedy looked at Coleman. The former SEAL Team commander said, "I witnessed it."

"You saw it, or you pulled the trigger?"

Coleman shook his head. "I didn't kill them."

"Scott, no offense, but what in the hell are you doing in the middle of this?"

Stansfield coughed and raised his right hand. "That

would be my doing, Mitchell. We received one communi-
qué from the Jansens—you knew them as the Hoffmans—after the mission. They stated that the count had
been eliminated, but you'd been lost in the process. As we
followed developments, it became apparent that the Jansens may have been wrong. There were reports that someone fitting your description was seen leaving the count's
estate five to ten minutes after the Jansens left. Then there
was the fire. The Jansens had said nothing about that. We
became suspicious, and I asked Scott to go to Colorado
and bring the Jansens back for a thorough debriefing."

Kennedy inched forward. "Mitch, what happened in
Germany?"

"In a minute." Looking to Coleman, he asked, "Tell
me about Colorado."

"I went out there with a few men to retrieve them."

"When was this?"

"Saturday night. The Jansens had a place west of
Denver in a little town called Evergreen. We put them
under surveillance and were getting ready to move in
on Sunday morning when another group showed up
and took them out."

Rapp studied him for a moment, trying to detect a
lie. "Who was this other group?"

"I don't know." Coleman shook his head. "There
were four of them. Three men and a woman. They
were very professional. Quick and thorough."

"You honestly have no idea who they were?"

"No."

"That's bullshit, Scott." Rapp raised his voice. He
looked to Kennedy. "And you?"

"We were discussing this very matter when you burst in here," Kennedy said a little testily.

"Well, excuse me if I forgot to knock, but I hope you understand if I'm just a little pissed off. You send me on a mission that only a handful of people are supposed to know about, and right after I take care of the count, I turn around and that bitch you sent to assist me pumps two rounds into my chest." Rapp pointed at himself. "From where I'm sitting, it's pretty clear that someone set me up. You"—Rapp pointed the gun at Kennedy— "had the method and the means, and now I'm trying to figure out what your motivation was."

Kennedy stood abruptly. "If you think . . ."

"Sit back down!" shouted Rapp.

"No, I'm not going to sit back down! And stop pointing that gun at me!"

"Sit back down, Irene, or I swear I'll . . ."

"What? Shoot me?" Kennedy said defiantly as she took a step closer to him. "I know you well enough, Mitch, to know that you would never do such a thing. Not to me, and you know damn well I would never give an order to have you killed." She took a deep breath and stared at him.

Rapp studied her. Her face was flushed, and her fists were clenched tight. He had never seen Kennedy raise her voice, let alone yell. In the end, he believed her because, more than anything, it was what he wanted to believe. Slowly, he retracted the pistol and pointed it at the ground. Nodding to Kennedy, he said, "Okay. So let's try to figure out who did."

24

The colonial grandfather clock in the corner announced the arrival of the day's twenty-second hour. Senator Clark was sitting behind an expansive hand-carved oak executive desk in his study. A glass of cabernet sauvignon was in his left hand. It was the last of a sixty-dollar bottle from McLaren Vale, Australia. Clark never bought French wine. It was overpriced and, more importantly, was made by a bunch of snobs. The man who had literally come from the wrong side of the tracks was a little sensitive when it came to elitists. For the most part, Clark kept these opinions to himself. No sense in announcing your hot buttons to a potential adversary. Secretary of State Midleton was a perfect example. The man was a full-blown cultural elitist. As a senator, he had voted for every liberal pet project that came down the aisle, just so long as it didn't affect the gentry in his blue-blood neighborhood. Midleton didn't know it, but Hank Clark wasn't his friend. Clark not only didn't like his former colleague in the Senate, he could barely tolerate the man, but he was willing to put up a front until the time was right.

Clark studied a memo that one of his senior staffers

had prepared at the senator's request. It summarized the lack of affordable housing for military personnel. It was a sad state of affairs. The men and women in the military were getting the short end of the stick, living in conditions comparable to those of people on welfare. As could be predicted, morale was suffering, and readiness was way down. The cuts in military spending had gone too deep. This was going to be his issue. The issue he would run on. A newly commissioned officer in the armed forces made less than a new city bus driver in Washington. He made less than your average federal government administrative assistant, and he made far less than a teacher. That was another thing the senator was planning to exploit. He was sick of hearing the NEA gripe about teachers' salaries. When you factored in their personal days, sick days, workshops, holidays, and summers off, they barely worked two-thirds of the year. The men and women of the armed services were getting screwed.

The NEA was in bed with the Democrats; there was nothing he or any other Republican could do about that. He wasn't going to get their votes regardless of what he did, so he might as well make hay of it. The plan was to go into California, Texas, and Florida—all states with huge blocs of electoral votes and loaded with military bases. He would run on a ten-percent pay increase for all military personnel. The states would salivate over the potential boost to their economies. In addition to that, he'd demand that the brave men and women of the armed services be given the same health benefits as all other federal employees. The HMOs, pharmaceuticals, medical device manufacturers, and insurance companies would throw cash at his campaign. They would line up to get a piece of the action. That combined with the other backers he already had would give him a substantial war chest.

The sound of the doorbell made him turn his attention to some more immediate issues. A lot of different factors were involved in getting elected president. But no two were more important than money and name recognition. No one was going to vote for you if they didn't know who you were. Hell, right now he'd be hard pressed to get his own party's nomination. Outside his home state, Clark was relatively unknown. Most people knew him only as "that big senator." At six foot five, he was a full head taller than most of his colleagues. Clark was hoping to change all of that. There was nothing in Washington like a few months of televised Senate hearings to raise one's profile.

There was a knock on the study door, and the senator said, "Come in."

Peter Cameron entered the office scratching his black beard. Clark made no effort to get up. Instead, he gestured to the chair sitting in front of the desk. Normally, Clark would have offered him a drink, but from the tone Cameron had used on the phone earlier, Clark was waiting until he heard why his minion was rattled. Clark took a sip of his wine and leaned back in his chair.

"Did you watch the news tonight?"

"I caught a bit of it earlier."

"Did you happen to see the local story about the man gunned down in College Park?"

Clark leaned forward and set down the wine glass. The murder in College Park had been the lead news story on every local station and appeared to be headed for the front page of the *Post* in the morning. More than fifty rounds had been fired. Most of them from silenced weapons, and most directed at the lone fatality. There were several eye-witness reports that a woman also had been shot, but the police had yet to confirm her existence. They were monitoring local hospitals for gunshot victims.

"I saw the story."

Cameron shifted uncomfortably in his chair and finally said, "I was there."

"Why?"

"I was keeping an eye on things."

Clark said nothing for a moment. He just stared at Cameron and his unkempt beard. Finally, he asked, "Why don't you tell me what happened?"

Cameron started with an apology for not doing a better job of controlling Duser and his people. From there, Cameron went into the play-by-play of events. He verified that the woman mentioned in the story had been shot—killed, as a matter of fact—and that her body had been disposed of, as well as all of the weapons and vehicles that had been used. On a positive note, the muscle behind Gus Villaume, namely Mario Lukas, was no longer a threat.

Clark managed to stay calm and listen without interruption, despite the fact that he desperately wanted to ask Cameron one blindingly obvious question. When Cameron finally finished, Clark got his chance. "What were you doing there?"

"I'm not sure I follow."

"What were you doing in the car? Why would you expose yourself like that?"

Cameron was slightly embarrassed. Clark had preached to him about keeping a low profile. "I knew this was going to be complicated, and I wanted to make sure Duser didn't screw things up."

Clark felt the need to take a sip of wine. He reflected on the possibility that Cameron was not telling the truth. The man was a voyeur, that was obvious enough. His sudden desire to be so hands-on was dangerous. Cameron was the one and only person who could tie the senator to the events of the last five days. He took a second sip, and while the expensive red liquid slid down his throat, he decided Cameron would have to go. Clark didn't know where he would find a replacement, but he would. The man had become too big a liability. The senator would have to make arrangements for his disappearance, but until then he would keep Cameron close and happy.

"Peter, you've done very good work for me. I want you alive and out of jail." The senator frowned. "No more field trips with the boys. You're too valuable for that. Let them do the dirty work, and concentrate on keeping your hands clean."

"Yes, sir." Cameron let out a sigh of relief and said, "There has been another development."

"Good or bad?"

"Oh, I think you'll like this one," replied Cameron with a smile. He retrieved a small tape recorder from his pocket. Holding it up, he said, "Earlier this evening, one of my people intercepted this conversation." Cameron turned up the volume and pressed play.

"Anna Rielly here."

"Honey, it's me. Are you all right?"

The quality of the tape was good. Clark leaned forward, resting his forearms on his desk. "Is that who I think it is?" Cameron nodded.

"Mitchell."

"Honey, it's me, but I can't talk long. Are you okay?"

A slow chill of excitement ran down Clark's back. This was the first time he had heard Mitch Rapp's voice. After carefully studying him for months, this was the first time he had felt the man's presence. The voice was deep and a little scratchy, just as the senator had expected. Clark listened to the rest of the tape intently and then had Cameron play it back for him two more times. Clark memorized every word of the tape. He was beginning to see a path. A way to complete his plans. After a long moment of reflection, he looked up at Cameron and said, "I want you to get into the girl's apartment. See if she keeps a journal. If she does, copy it. If there are any computer disks, copy them also. Find out what type of books she reads, what magazines she subscribes to, if she takes any medication." Clark paused. "See if you can get her medical history. I want to know as much about her as possible, and I want it by tomorrow night."

"That might be a little difficult."

That was not what Clark wanted to hear. Not with Rapp so close. Things were reaching critical mass. "Peter, I pay you well. No excuses. I want that information by tomorrow evening." Always aware of the need to keep both friend and foe close, he added with a warm grin, "When this is all over, I will make sure you are very well compensated, Peter. To the extent that you just might choose to retire." Clark held up his wine glass in a toast to the future.

Cameron nodded. "I'll get it done."

With a smile still on his face, Clark decided to go ahead and hire the person who would get rid of Cameron. There was no telling when he might have to have him taken out.

THE CLUB WAS located off 695 in Dundalk. Downtown Baltimore was four miles due west. It was a Bally's Total Fitness club, one of hundreds nationwide. That's why Gus Villaume had joined. Flexibility and anonymity. At Bally's he was just one of millions trying to fight the never-ending battle. Villaume was in the twenty-sixth minute of his workout, and he was sweating profusely. Four more minutes on the stationary bike, and he was done. There were eight televisions mounted on the wall in front of him. They carried the signals of MTV, VH-1, ESPN, CNN, ABC, CBS, NBC, and FOX. Most of Villaume's attention, however, was focused on the issue of *Condé Nast Traveler* that was sitting in the bike's magazine stand. Villaume's real job—or fake job, depending on how you looked at it—was travel writing. He was published under the name Marc Gieser, and his two areas of expertise were southern France and French Polynesia. The job provided him with a great cover for international travel and a good thirty to fifty grand a year in legitimate income. The other benefits were obvious: he could stay at some of the world's finest hotels for next to nothing, just so long as he continued to write nice things.

The club was pretty calm. Villaume refused to enter the place between the hours of eleven A.M. and nine P.M. This evening, there was one guy running on a treadmill and two women talking to each other on the stair steppers. Villaume had chosen Baltimore as his home because it kept him close enough to Washington to be readily available but far enough away to keep him from bumping into the wrong people when he was out and about. He had been thinking a lot about Peter Cameron since returning from Colorado. There was something unsettling about the man. In a nutshell, he couldn't be trusted.

Villaume and his people were not usually hired to kill someone. More often his work involved simple intelligence gathering: rifling through an office in the middle of the night, copying a computer hard drive, tapping phones, and planting bugs. Attorneys and businessmen were his two biggest clients. He knew who they were, but very few of them knew who he was. The rules were simple. Villaume had a network of overseas accounts that he used to collect fees. He would receive a name and summary of the information desired. Villaume would then quote a price to the client. If the client agreed, he or she would transfer half of the fee into one of the accounts. When Villaume handed over the desired information, they would wire the other half. It was usually very simple.

That was, until Peter Cameron had shown up. The

man had been insistent on meeting face-to-face. To help assuage Villaume's fears, Cameron offered to double his fees. At the relatively young age of fifty-two, Villaume was looking to retire. There was, however, a catch. He wanted to make sure he was absolutely set—no financial worries. The lifestyle he had in mind required at least two million dollars. When Cameron waved the prospect of double fees in his face, the temptation was too much to resist.

Now he wondered if it might not be a good idea to take what he had and disappear, at least for a while. He would have to alert the others. Tell them to cool it for a while and lie low. Maybe take a long trip. He'd already warned Lukas and Juarez to be careful. With Cameron associating with the likes of Duser, things could get ugly.

The thirty minutes was up. Villaume stopped pedaling and closed his magazine. He had made up his mind. Lukas and Juarez needed a vacation. There were two others on the team, but, fortunately for them, Cameron didn't even know they existed. As Villaume stepped from the bike, he looked up at the array of televisions above the running track. The local news was starting. It appeared all three stations were leading with the same story. Villaume froze upon seeing the words "College Park" flash across the screen directly in front of him. The volume was off, but subtitles were running across the bottom of the picture. A reporter was standing in front of a yellow maze of crime scene tape. She pointed over her shoulder at two parked cars. Villaume scrambled to read the white-on-black words as they were typed in from left to right. There was something about one hundred shots being fired . . . one dead for sure, maybe two. The police were looking for a silver SUV. A Maryland driver's license appeared on the screen. The station reported that the victim's name was Todd Sherman. Gus Villaume knew better. He turned and started walking for the exit. The face on the driver's license belonged to Mario Lukas.

Villaume forced a smile and said good night to the attendant behind the front desk. Inside he was burning up. Mario Lukas had been his friend for a long time. He had taken care of Mario, and Mario had taken care of him. Mario was the muscle, and Gus was the brains. Alone they were adequate, together they were the best. Villaume thought of running. They had made arrangements years ago that if one of them died, the other would get all the money. With Mario's passing, Villaume's retirement account had just effectively passed the two-million mark. He could disappear and never look back. But that meant allowing that smug prick Cameron off the hook. Villaume crossed the parking lot to his car. At the very least, he had to alert Juarez. After that, he could decide what to do with Cameron. As Villaume opened his car door, he was overcome with grief for the loss of his friend and hatred for a man he barely knew.

25

In any other city, in any other walk of life, Donatella Rahn would have been seen for exactly what she was—a ravishing beauty—but in Milan, Italy, she was over the hill. At thirty-eight, the former model was washed up. Donatella was two inches short of six feet, and with a good diet, a daily walking regimen, and the help of a skilled plastic surgeon, she had maintained her gorgeous body. It was amazing enough that in her late thirties she looked as good as, or better than, she had when she was prancing across the runways of Milan, Paris, and New York, but it was even more amazing considering what she had been through. Donatella Rahn was a unique and complicated person.

It was a nice fall morning in Milan as Donatella walked to work. Every spring the people of Milan eagerly awaited summer. It meant trips to some of the world's most beautiful lakes. But by the time August rolled around, they were once again ready for fall. The warm, humid air of summer brought smog and choking pollution to the city. The crisp cool air of autumn helped clean things up.

Donatella took her time walking this morning, which

probably had something to do with the boots she was wearing. They had a four-inch heel on them, and as was the case with most of the fashion she helped sell, they were not very practical. She passed the House of Gucci on Via Monte Napoleone and resisted the urge to spit on the display window. She took a right onto Via Sant' Andrea and crossed the street. Up ahead was the House of Armani, her home for almost fifteen years. Donatella was fiercely loyal. It was, in fact, probably the only thing she had inherited from her mother other than her looks. She was the byproduct of an Austrian father and an Italian mother. Her mother was a Jew from Torino, Italy, and her father was a Lutheran from Dornbirn, Austria; it was no surprise that their marriage had failed.

Italy was, after all, the Vatican's backyard. The country had a not so illustrious record of crushing religious dissent. The marriage lasted three short years, and then she and her mother returned to Torino, where they lived with Donatella's Orthodox Jewish grandparents. At sixteen she ran away to Milan. She wanted to model, and she didn't want any more religion. She got her way on both counts, and it was the start of a very bumpy road.

Now, all of these years later, Donatella Rahn entered the House of Armani knowing that her colleagues hadn't the slightest idea of her full range of talents. She eschewed the elevator, as always, and climbed the stairs to the fourth floor. As usual, she was one of the first to arrive. She entered her sanctum and closed the door for privacy. Her office was modern industrial, a miniaturized version of an airplane hangar. Sketches of clothes cluttered every available inch of the two couches and four chairs. Her coworkers liked to complain that there was nowhere to sit in her office. Donatella wondered if they would ever take the hint that she wanted it that way.

The only thing in the office that wasn't covered with sketches was a large glass desk. Donatella sat down behind it and turned on her computer. Her sleek flat Viewsonic screen came to life a moment later. She checked her work e-mail and then her personal e-mail. After wading through seventeen messages, she checked a third on-line mailbox. This mailbox, she had been assured, could not be traced back to her. There were only three people in the world who knew about it. One in Tel Aviv, one in Paris, and one in Washington. Almost all of the messages came from the person in Tel Aviv.

This morning was no different. Donatella clicked on the message, and the decryption software on her computer went to work. When it was done, she began to read. She was being offered a job in Washington. It was rated at a quarter of a million dollars, which meant the individual was not high profile. If he were, the rate would be a half million or more. On this she had to trust her handler. He had only screwed up once. It had almost cost her her life, but in his defense, it had been an honest mistake. She read a brief profile of the target and then checked her electronic organizer. There was a show in New York this coming weekend. It wasn't a big one, but then again, part of her job was to find undiscovered talent.

She thought it over for a minute and then decided to accept. She typed in her reply and logged off. She would receive a more thorough dossier within several hours. The next call was to her travel agent to book a ticket and check the availability of the company's apartment in Manhattan. With that accomplished, she set about clearing her schedule for the remainder of the week. Donatella Rahn was indeed a very complicated woman.

IT WAS RAINING, and the Wednesday morning temperature was a chilly fifty-two degrees. Kennedy's sedan drove east on Independence Avenue. Traffic was thick, as the deluge of government employees scrambled to make it to their desks by nine. The sedan rolled past the Air and Space Museum and then crossed 4th Street. Kennedy looked out the window at the throngs of people huddled under umbrellas waiting for the light to change. Normally, she would have brought something to work on during the ride from Langley to the Hill, but she had forced herself not to. She needed to straighten some things out in her head.

The only good piece of news since Saturday was that Mitch was alive. She could have done without his dramatic reappearance and his skepticism in regard to her loyalty, but, as he had pointed out, she wasn't the one who had been shot. Mitch was a different breed, and Kennedy had always respected that. He operated much closer to the edge than she ever would or could. He had once again proven that his level of skill was bewildering. With no help whatsoever, he had made it out of Germany and back to the United States, where he then broke into the CIA director's house and in the process also broke the jaw of the CIA employee who was there to make sure such a thing never happened.

When Rapp finally settled down, they filled him in on what little they knew. He in turn had asked a lot of questions for which they had almost no answers. The situation was dismal, Rapp was disgusted, and Kennedy was embarrassed. Rapp, never one to pull a punch, had placed the blame squarely on the shoulders of the director of the Counterterrorism Center and Stansfield, telling them, "You've got a leak, and if you don't find it, I'll find it for you."

Kennedy already knew she had a leak, but in the current political climate, the last thing she needed was Mitch Rapp running around Washington banging people's heads together. To Kennedy's consternation, Stansfield had actually encouraged Rapp to find the leak, but in her opinion, it was time to let Mitch take a long vacation. With the chairman watching like a hawk, she didn't need Rapp drawing unneeded attention to himself, and ultimately her—no matter how good he was.

What Stansfield had neglected to tell Kennedy was his real reason for wanting to turn their bull loose in the china shop. His doctor had told him the day before that the cancer was progressing much faster than anticipated. And indeed, he could feel it eating away at his insides. Each day was a little worse. It was no longer an issue of months but weeks. He needed to put things in order before he passed. He needed to find out who was behind the recent events. Rapp had been the target in Germany, but something told the old director that whoever was behind this move had a much bigger target in mind than Rapp. There wasn't enough time left for subtlety, only results, and if there was one thing Rapp was exceptional at, it was getting results.

The government sedan passed the Sam Rayburn House Office Building. The four-story behemoth was named in honor of Samuel Taliaferro Rayburn, the congressman from Texas who had served in the U.S. House of Representatives from 1912 to 1961. The people of Texas had sent Rayburn to Washington a staggering twenty-five times. From 1940 until his death in 1961, Rayburn served as speaker of the house seventeen times. During that time, very little happened in Washington without Sam Rayburn's approval. Chairman Rudin had an office inside the Rayburn Building, but he spent most of his time in a second office on the top floor of the Capitol. He liked to refer to it as his eagle's nest. Max Salmen, the CIA's deputy director of Operations, called it the vulture's lair. Rudin didn't like this one bit, but that, of course, was Salmen's intent. In recent years, Salmen had stated that his sole mission before retirement was to drive Rudin insane. At first, Kennedy wondered why Stansfield tolerated this, and then it dawned on her that the more Rudin focused his hatred on Salmen, the less he would have left over for the rest of the Agency. She wished that were the case this morning.

The sedan pulled up to a checkpoint manned by the Capitol Hill police. After a brief inspection, they were waved through. Kennedy was dropped off near the ground-floor entrance on the southeast side of the building. She stepped from the car and opened her umbrella. With her leather organizer in her other hand, she walked through the rain and entered the huge neoclassical building, where she lined up to go through the metal detectors. Most of the ground floor of the Capitol was occupied by committee rooms and offices and was not accessible to the general public without a pass. The areas that were accessible tended to be located in the middle of the building and included the Hall of Columns, the Old Supreme Court Chamber, and the Brumidi Corridors. The south wing of the building held the House of Representatives, and the north wing held the Senate. On the second floor were the chambers for both the House and the Senate, along with offices for leadership of both bodies. The Capitol's most identifiable feature, its rotunda, was also on the second floor. The third floor had more committee rooms and offices and the galleries from which visitors could watch the House and the Senate in action. All three of these floors were immaculately maintained.

Kennedy was headed to the fourth floor, which she often thought of as the neglected child of the Capitol. The offices there were far less glamorous, the paint was chipping in places, and water stains on the ceiling were not uncommon. Visitors rarely glimpsed the fourth floor, which was one of the reasons it was chosen as the location for the House Permanent Select Committee on Intelligence. Kennedy walked past Office H-405, which housed the committee's staffers. She opened a door a little farther down and stepped into a tiny waiting area.

There were two people in the room: a staffer sitting behind a reception desk and a Capitol Hill Police officer. The staffer greeted her and told her to take a seat.

He picked up the phone and told someone on the other end that Dr. Kennedy had arrived. The man listened for a few seconds and then hung up. Looking at Kennedy, he said, "It'll be a few minutes."

Kennedy nodded and thought to herself, *I'm sure it will.* Chairman Rudin was notorious for making CIA employees wait. Kennedy checked her watch. It was 8:56. They'd told her to be there by nine. She would be shocked if she was called in before a quarter past nine. She was right. At 9:24, she was summoned to the inner chamber. The committee room was the smallest in Washington. There was no gallery—no room for reporters to sit and listen. The sixteen members— eight Democrats, seven Republicans, and one independent—sat ten feet in front of the witness table in two rows. There were chairs for staffers behind the top row, and on the wall were the thirteen seals of the government agencies that made up the intelligence community, or IC.

Like the committee room for the Senate, this was also a room within a room. Highly secure, it was swept by technicians from the National Security Agency on a weekly and sometimes daily basis, depending on the business that was being conducted.

Kennedy set her organizer on the table and looked up to see Michael O'Rourke coming toward her. The congressman from Minnesota was the lone independent on the committee. O'Rourke said hello and asked Kennedy how her son was doing. After their pleasantries were concluded, O'Rourke said, "Irene, I need you to be honest with me about something."

Kennedy studied the young congressman for a second and said, "I'll try my best. What is it?"

"Does the name Mitch Rapp mean anything to you?"

Kennedy studied O'Rourke before answering. Looking over his shoulder at the other committee members, she said, "Maybe you should come out to Langley, and we can talk about this." Kennedy was fully aware that Anna Rielly and Congressman O'Rourke's wife were best friends. Rapp had kept her in the loop.

"So you know him?"

"I never said that." Kennedy reached out and touched his arm. "Come see me at Langley, and we'll talk about it."

O'Rourke nodded. "I'll be out this afternoon, then."

"That's fine. Call my office and see what time works best."

O'Rourke agreed and went back to his seat. *One more thing to worry about,* Kennedy thought to herself. She looked up and saw Chairman Rudin scowling at a piece of paper. From his perch, he looked down his beaklike nose at Kennedy and said, "You may be seated."

Congressman Zebarth, the ranking Republican on the committee who sat immediately to Rudin's right, leaned forward and said, "Good morning, Dr. Kennedy. Thank you for coming to see us on such short notice." Zebarth winked and leaned back in his chair. Zebarth was the only other member on the committee who had been in Washington as long as Rudin. Very few politicians, let alone Republicans, got along with Rudin, but Zebarth was a throwback to the old days when politicians could agree to disagree and then go have a Manhattan. Keenly aware of the rules of debate and decorum, the silver-tongued Virginian could slice an adversary to pieces without a single angry word. The Republican leadership had placed him on the Intelligence Committee because they thought he was the only man who could handle Rudin's crotchety attitude.

Rudin shuffled some papers around and cleared his throat a few times. When he was done, he took a drink of water and removed his glasses. Looking down at Kennedy, he said, "I have been hearing some very upsetting things about your organization lately."

Kennedy looked back impassively, waiting for Rudin to elaborate.

The chairman continued to stare at her, but Kennedy's composure was sending his blood pressure north. It infuriated him that these professional liars from Langley kept coming before his committee and trying to play him for a moron. "Ms. Kennedy, would you mind telling me just what in the hell happened in Germany last weekend?"

Before Kennedy could answer, Congressman Zebarth said, "I am progressing in years, but if my memory serves me right, it's Dr. Kennedy, not Ms. Kennedy."

Rudin mumbled something under his breath and then said, "Dr. Kennedy, what happened in Germany last weekend?"

"Could you be more specific, Mr. Chairman?"

"I could, but I won't, because you know damn well what I'm talking about."

"Excuse me, Mr. Chairman," interjected Zebarth

with a confused look on his face, "I don't know whether or not the good doctor knows what you're talking about, but I'm a tad bit embarrassed to admit that I certainly don't. Not that I claim to *understand* you in the most esoteric sense of the word, but in regard to the CIA, I can usually extrapolate some type of a read on your position."

Rudin refused to look at Zebarth, who was sitting only four feet to his right. He hated the old windbag. Staring straight ahead, he said, "She knows what I'm talking about, and you will soon enough. Just conserve your oxygen for the next couple of minutes. It should help clear the fog."

Zebarth snickered. Imitation was the greatest form of flattery, and Rudin had just stolen a line right out of Zebarth's playbook.

"Now, Dr. Kennedy, let's get back to my question. What happened in Germany this past Saturday, and what was the involvement of your agency?"

"Are you referring to the events surrounding Hagenmiller Engineering?"

"I'm referring to the assassination of Count Hagenmiller," replied a stern Rudin.

"There isn't much that I can add that you don't already know, Mr. Chairman."

Rudin had his hands folded in front of him. He kept his eyes on Kennedy. "I don't believe you." A chorus of rumbles erupted from the Republican side of the committee. Rudin ignored them and pressed the point. "I want you to tell this committee, *in detail,* what role the CIA had in the assassination of Count Hagenmiller.

And I would like to remind you, if you lie to my committee, you will be prosecuted."

This time, Democrats and Republicans alike turned around to look at the chairman. An accusation as blatant as this was a rare event in the tiny committee room.

"Well, well, well . . ." interjected Zebarth. "Given the fact that Dr. Kennedy has been very cooperative with this body in the past, I am assuming that the exuberant chairman has some information that he would like to share with the rest of us before we continue down this possibly reckless line of inquiry."

Rudin snatched his wooden gavel and gave it several whacks. "Order. The chair has not yielded. When I have, I will let you know." From the righthand side of the bench came a chorus of questions. Each time Rudin tried to get back to Kennedy, a Republican would ask loudly, "Will the chair yield, please? Point of order, Mr. Chairman." This unruly behavior smacked of the antics displayed on the Judiciary Committee, but it was very unusual for the Intelligence Committee. Even the Democrats seemed a bit miffed by Rudin's aggressiveness.

Kennedy kept her mouth shut and watched. Rudin's blunt question had her concerned, but she didn't show it. The Orion Team didn't exist, and she had nothing to do with the death of Hagenmiller. She would utter those falsities until she was dead. She could never admit any of it no matter how bad it got. The big question was whether or not Rudin was bluffing, or if he had been given some information. A week ago, she would have bet the farm that he was bluffing, but today, with the unknown leak lurking out there somewhere, she couldn't be sure.

With a red face, Rudin yelled over the din of protests, "Dr. Kennedy, answer my question! Did the CIA have anything to do with the assassination of Count Hagenmiller?"

Kennedy calmly looked up at the angry chairman and said, "To the very best of my knowledge, the CIA had no involvement whatsoever in the death of Count Hagenmiller." Kennedy did not blink; she did not waver. She had just committed a felony. It wasn't the first time, and it wouldn't be the last.

26

The face looked familiar. It was hard to be sure because the subject's eyes were closed, but it definitely resembled one of the men he'd seen in Colorado. Scott Coleman looked at the computer screen and squinted. It was mid-morning, and they were in Marcus Dumond's apartment in Bethesda. With Kennedy's approval, the reigning computer expert from the Counterterrorism Center had called in sick. His orders from Kennedy were to assist Rapp and make sure that whatever he did, he didn't get caught.

It was not unusual for a person to die a violent death in Washington, D.C. It happened all the time. What was unusual about the homicide was the number of bullets fired and the fact that most of them were from silenced weapons. Dumond had caught the story on the nightly news. The D.C. police were handling the homicide, and they had sent information to the CTC on the off chance that there might be a terrorist connection.

Coleman leaned over Dumond's shoulder. "Are there any other photos?"

"Let me check." Dumond maneuvered his mouse and clicked on an icon. With his high-speed connection, it took less than a second to download the second photograph. It was of the body lying on the street between two parked cars. "He looks like a pretty big guy."

"Yeah, this guy out in Colorado was a house." Coleman squinted. "I think this is him. Do they have a vitals sheet on him?"

"Let me check." Dumond went to work. A short while later, he asked, "Will the autopsy report do?"

"Very nicely." Coleman read from the new screen. It listed the deceased's name as Todd Sherman and said that he was six five and weighed two hundred eighty-six pounds. "I think this is the guy."

Rapp came in from the kitchen. "You think who is the guy?"

"This guy who was killed in College Park yesterday . . . I think he's one of the people who was involved in the hit out in Colorado."

"Let me see." Coleman moved out of the way, and Rapp bent over Dumond's shoulder. "Todd Sherman. Can you show me what he looks like?"

"Yep."

The screen changed, and Rapp looked at the second photo, the one of the victim lying in the street. "How about a face shot?" The screens changed, and the first photo appeared. Rapp tilted his head and studied the photo for a second. "Can you access the Seven Dwarves from here?" Rapp was referring to the seven Cray supercomputers in the basement at Langley.

Dumond smiled. "I can access anything from anywhere."

"Great. Get me in there."

Dumond slid over to a second computer and began typing. Rapp turned to Coleman. "I think I might know this guy."

"From where?"

"It was an operation we ran in France. I received some logistical support from a guy who used to work for the Agency. He had this big fella working for him . . . he was massive. Big huge hands and a head you wouldn't believe. We called his boss the Frog."

"I'm in," said Dumond. "Do you want me to look up Todd Sherman?"

"Was that the name on the autopsy?"

"Yeah."

Rapp thought about it for a second. "I doubt it's his real name, but we might as well give it a try."

Dumond went to work. The computer came up with thirty-one Todd Shermans. "Do you want me to narrow the search?"

"Yeah."

Dumond typed in a range for age and a brief physical description. The list was narrowed to eleven. Rapp and Coleman pulled up chairs, and Dumond began scrolling through the files. All but two of them had photographs attached, and the two that didn't were for a man in his sixties and another in his seventies.

"Try Kyle," said Rapp. "That was one of his contact names."

"First or last name?"

"I don't know. Put it in as an alias, and let's see what you come up with."

Dumond did as he was told and said, "You're not

going to like what we get back." Surprisingly, the search came back with a matching request of 1,462 files.

"Shit." Rapp leaned back and clasped his hands behind his neck.

"I bet there are more than a billion dossiers in this system."

"Are you serious?"

"Oh, yeah."

"How can that be?" asked Coleman.

"Easy. They have individuals from all over the globe in this thing, and it goes back at least a hundred years."

"Let's work on the search criteria and see if we can narrow this thing down." Rapp leaned in to study the screen and began telling Dumond what to type.

THE EXPRESS CARPET cleaner van drove up Garfield and passed the Washington Cathedral. After crossing Massachusetts Avenue and then Wisconsin half a block later, it started down the hill. Four blocks later, it took a right onto New Mexico and stopped in front of a large brick apartment building. Two men got out, and the third stayed behind the wheel. They were wearing leather gloves and light blue coveralls with the company logo embroidered over the left breast. Both men also wore baseball caps, sunglasses, and fanny packs. The shorter man carried a clipboard.

The two men stepped into the foyer of the apartment building, and the taller one picked up the security phone and began looking over the list of tenants. When he found the woman's name, he punched in the number for her unit and counted the rings. He didn't expect anyone to answer. The other man casually pulled a device from his pocket that looked like a cross between a gun and a fancy wine bottle opener. It was, in fact, a lock-pick gun. He put the pick into the lock and shielded his movements with the clipboard. In less than five seconds, he had the door open. The other man hung up the phone, and they entered the lobby. They walked past the elevators and took the stairs up to the fourth floor.

Before leaving the stairwell, they cracked the door and looked down the hallway. The only thing that could stop them at this point was a nosy neighbor. They had no idea who had hired them. It had been handled by a simple phone call and some directions on where to pick up the package. It was a dead drop out at the Tyson's Corner shopping mall. The manila envelope contained a brief bio of the target and a laundry list of things their unknown employer would like to know. It also contained ten thousand dollars in crisp one-hundred-dollar bills. Twice their normal rate, and considering who the target was, they felt they deserved every penny of it. They knew who the woman was. They had all seen her on TV. She was beautiful. In light of her job, they had decided someone with deep pockets wasn't too happy about a story she was working on and was probably looking for a little insurance policy. They had done this type of job before. Almost everyone had things they would like kept a secret.

The chances of her coming home were slim, and if she did, there were people near the White House watching her who would alert them. They emerged from the stairwell and walked softly down the hall. When they reached her door, the short man went to work again. This time, it took him eight seconds to break in. Both men stepped into the apartment and closed the door. The tall one latched the security chain and looked through the peephole to see if they had aroused anyone's curiosity. After ten seconds, he gave up the vigil and went to work. Pulling out a small radio, he told the man down on the street that they were in. The driver moved the van to a parking spot, where he could watch the street and the entrance to the apartment building.

Methodically, starting with the bedroom, the two men began an inventory of everything in the apartment. A journal was found on the bedside nightstand, and every page was photographed. Bugs were planted in each room, and their location was noted on a quick sketch. They were required to present their employer with a floor plan of the apartment marking the exact location of each device and the frequency.

A small desk in the living room contained much of the information they needed: bills, correspondence, an appointment book, and, most importantly, her laptop computer. It took less than five minutes to get past the password and copy all of her files. Her e-mail accounts were noted, as well as the passwords. Every aspect of Anna Rielly's life would be monitored, though to what end they would never know. They didn't care, either. Their jobs, their lives really, depended on asking few questions. They would hand the information over and disappear. In less than an hour and a half, they had it all and were on their way out, leaving no sign that they had ever been in the apartment.

★ ★ ★

CAMERON BACKED HIS shiny Lexus SC 400 out of the narrow garage down the street from his Georgetown apartment. The car was Cameron's treat to himself. It had a 4.0-liter, 290-horsepower, four-cam, thirty-two-valve V8 engine and could fly like the wind. It came with leather interior, genuine bird's eye maple trim and a seven-speaker, 215-watt stereo that would make a sixteen-year-old heavy metal fan wet his pants. All of it, plus a couple of free racing mats, had cost him fifty thousand dollars. The price didn't bother Cameron. He was finally making good money.

The Professor was in no hurry this morning. He had to teach a class at eleven, but other than that, he had no official duties. Cameron hadn't slept well. He had been too excited after his meeting with Senator Clark. The man was amazing; the way he cultivated loyalty, it was easy to see why he had done so well in life. The sky was the limit. Cameron had hitched his wagon to a rising star, and he was going right to the top. Hank Clark was going to be the next president of the United States, and Cameron was going to help make sure it happened. The senator hadn't filled him in on all of the specifics, but he had once again promised that there would be a place for someone as talented as Peter Cameron.

For Cameron this was all new. At Langley no one had appreciated his skills. Occasionally, a superior would have a nice thing to say during a review, but that was about it. The place was known for turning out acolytes, not handing out accolades. And to make matters worse, the pay was substandard. Cameron had busted his ass for years, giving service to his country, and he had little to show for it. Hank Clark changed all of that. He had shown Cameron the light. How to work half as hard and make five times the money. And not simply five times the normal money but the bulk of it in wire transfers into an extremely discreet bank in the Bahamas. Money that would never be taxed.

Cameron was living the life he had dreamed of for years. He was helping manipulate the outcome of events by using his tradecraft, and he was getting compensated properly. His life had never been so exciting. Mario Lukas was dead, Gus Villaume was on the run, and Mitch Rapp was about to walk right into his crosshairs. The thrill of it all caused him to smile broadly as his car maneuvered through the mid-morning Georgetown traffic.

The last year had been a great learning experience for Cameron. Away from the constraints of Langley, his skills had expanded exponentially. Watching Clark had taught him to keep his enemies close and keep them off-balance. Cameron grabbed his phone from the center console. That's what this call would be about. Cameron was confident that the death of Lukas would have Villaume scared. The trick now was to keep him guessing—to make him think that someone else was after him. That Cameron had no involvement in the hit on Lukas. And if he was really lucky, get Villaume to trust him enough to meet.

There was one thing about the previous evening's meeting that Cameron was unhappy about. It was the way Clark had second-guessed him on his direct involvement with the hit on Lukas. The senator had a good point in theory, but in practicality Cameron disagreed. You needed to be in the field to really see what was going on. Cameron felt the freelancers, with their lack of loyalty, were prone to understate their screw-ups and overstate their accomplishments. They needed to be watched. The senator could criticize all he wanted from the comfort of his study, but Cameron knew better. He was going to have to see this thing through up close and personal. There was too much riding on it.

As Cameron rounded Washington Circle, he punched in the number and listened to the rings.

"Hello." The voice was Villaume's, and it betrayed no emotion.

"What in the hell happened?" asked an eager Cameron.

There was a pause. "You need to be a little more specific."

"Don't jerk me around, Gus. You know exactly what I'm talking about. I watch the news. What in the hell have you two gotten yourselves into?"

Gus Villaume was sitting in a Starbucks just off Dupont Circle, a cup of French roast in one hand and his mobile phone in the other. He had left Baltimore as a precaution. He doubted this fool on the other end of the phone could track him, but he had found Mario Lukas, so until he knew more, he would stay away from his apartment. Villaume had little doubt that the Professor knew exactly why Lukas was dead. He didn't buy into his feigned outrage for a second. "I assume you're talking about Mario."

"You're damn right I am."

Villaume watched a cop walk in front of the window. "How much did you pay Duser to kill him?" It was a shot in the dark but a well-aimed one.

The response was instantaneous. "What are you talking about? I didn't pay anyone to kill Mario."

"That's not what I've heard." Villaume counted the seconds, waiting for the reaction from the Professor.

"I swear to you, I didn't have anything to do with Mario's death."

The Professor actually sounded sincere, but Villaume had drawn his conclusions in the predawn hours and wasn't about to be swayed. "Listen to me, Professor." Villaume drew the name out with disdain. "I don't know what your real name is, but my guess is you're ex-CIA or NSA. You're too soft to have been in the military. I shouldn't have too much difficulty in finding out who you really are." Villaume was overstating his contacts, but he doubted the Professor knew that.

Cameron laughed. It sounded a little forced. "Don't bother wasting your time. I'm a black hole."

"No one is a black hole. You have a history just like everyone else. And more importantly, you have to be working for someone . . . you're not smart enough to be on your own."

The comment offended Cameron. "Keep talking like this, Gus, and I will put a price on your head. I'm trying to help you. I don't like the fact that someone killed Mario. It makes me very nervous when business associates of mine start dying."

"You must think I'm really stupid. I know who killed Mario, and I know who gave the order."

Cameron's hands were sweaty. "Gus, I think you should take a few days to calm down, and then we can talk. I want to know who killed Mario as much as you do. I have to go now." He ended the call just before he pulled into the parking ramp at George Washington University. Cameron hadn't expected the call to be cordial, but he definitely didn't think Villaume would be so aggressive. Cameron concluded that he may have underestimated him. He would have to put a call in to Duser and take his leash off. Villaume could not be allowed to go digging around. Cameron could not afford to have the attention of his former employer brought to bear on his recent dealings.

27

The Ritz-Carlton on Massachusetts Avenue NW was one of the nicest hotels in Washington. Foreign dignitaries from almost every country had stayed there, as had many of America's greatest industrialists. Mitch Rapp and Scott Coleman were parked across the street in a loading zone. Rapp was in the passenger seat of Coleman's Ford Explorer, eyeing the front entrance to the hotel. He was looking for Michael Gould, the hotel's concierge. They had found his name in Gus Villaume's file. Gould was the contact Villaume used to talk to his employers. Rapp had done his homework on Gould. He was French and had dual citizenship. He was fluent in four languages, which helped greatly with his job. The CIA's file on the man said that he had no official affiliation with any intelligence services, but Rapp was skeptical. He had dealt with these types often. They were sellers of information. They respected money, and they feared brute force. If enough money was waved in front of their faces, there was little they wouldn't tell. Rapp hadn't yet decided if he would use money or his fists to get the information he needed.

He had spoken to Gould more than an hour ago. His message to the Frenchman was simple: "I need to speak to Monsieur Villaume, and I need to speak to him immediately." Rapp had given Gould the number to his mobile phone, and he and Coleman had driven to the hotel on the off chance that Villaume might show his face. That was, if he was still alive. With Mario Lukas dead, it wasn't hard to imagine the same fate befalling Villaume. Rapp desperately wanted Villaume breathing. He was the only link to the person who had ordered the hit in Colorado and, Rapp assumed, the same person who had ordered the hit on him in Germany. If Villaume was dead, Rapp was skeptical that he would ever find out who was behind it all.

Neither Rapp nor Coleman was big on conversation, so the stakeout had proceeded in near silence. The rain had subsided just after lunch, but the sky was still gray. Rapp had decided they would wait, keep an eye on the hotel for another hour, and after that they would go take a look at Gould's apartment. At a bare minimum, the man had to have a way to contact Villaume and a way to receive payments. The longer Rapp waited to hear back from Gould, the more he was leaning toward getting the information out of the little Frenchman through less than pleasant means.

It was almost two in the afternoon when Rapp's phone finally rang. Rapp pressed the talk button.

"Hello."

"Is this the Man of Iron?"

"It is. Is this the Frog?"

"I'm afraid it is."

Rapp wasn't sure how to play it. He had worked with Villaume and Lukas on three separate occasions, all of them in France, and he had been impressed by both men. They were proficient and dependable. They had helped Rapp hunt Rafique Aziz, a Palestinian terrorist who was one of the men responsible for the downing of Pan Am Flight 103 over Lockerbie, Scotland. Villaume and Lukas had been there on a night when Rapp had come within inches of losing his life. In fact, if Lukas hadn't arrived when he had, Rapp probably would be dead.

"I'm sorry to hear about Mario. He was a good man."

"I appreciate that." There was a pause. "Mario liked you. He believed you were honest."

"He was, too. Very dependable."

Slightly overcome with emotion at the loss of his old friend, Villaume said nothing for a while. "I hope you will forgive me, but in light of Mario's incident the other day, I'm a little skittish."

"I don't blame you, but we need to talk."

"In person?"

"That would help."

"I'm afraid that's out of the question."

Villaume's position did not surprise Rapp. He would do the same. "That's too bad, but I understand."

The NSA captured literally every cellular and digital call made in the metro area. The cellular calls were analyzed almost instantly. The digital calls took more time because they had to be deciphered. The massive computers out at Fort Meade sifted through them searching for key words such as *gun, bomb, assassinate,* and thousands more. If the computers came across a word that was flagged, they would kick the call up to the next level of programmed analysis. If a call contained enough flagged words, it eventually garnered the attention of a real person. Conversations that took place in Arabic, Chinese, or Russian received extra attention. The easiest way to defeat the system was to talk like a normal businessperson.

Rapp formulated his next sentence carefully. "I think we might have a common problem."

"What would that be?"

"I was across the pond on business last week, with your friends from Colorado. Do you know the ones I'm talking about?"

"I think so."

"They screwed me on a deal."

"How do you mean?"

"They were supposed to be working with me, and they ended up working for someone else."

"I'm not sure I follow."

Rapp's voice took on an angry tone. "They double-crossed me and tried to send me into permanent retirement."

"Oh . . . I see. Were they following company orders?"

"I can assure you they were not. I went to the top to find out, and they were in the dark as much as me."

"I'm not sure where I fit into all of this."

"Someone hired you to make that trip to Colorado. I have a pretty strong idea that same person interfered with my business deal across the pond." Rapp waited for a second and added, "I would also bet that same person had something to do with Mario's accident the other day."

There was a long pause, and then Villaume asked, "How did you know I had business in Colorado?"

Rapp looked at Coleman. "There were some people there watching you."

"Were they with the company?"

"No . . . but they were sent by the company."

"I'm not sure I believe you."

Rapp switched the phone from his left ear to his right. "Listen, I know you're in a tough spot. I was there just a few days ago myself. If you can't meet, I understand. But I need to know who hired you." Rapp sat there and waited for a response. He knew how Villaume felt. He could trust no one. After five seconds of tense silence, Rapp added, "Mario saved my life. I owe him. Give me the goods on whoever hired you, and I'll make sure the guy pays for what he did to Mario."

Villaume was tempted. Iron Man would be a powerful ally. The Professor would shit his pants if someone like Iron Man was onto him. It would be the easiest form of revenge he could dream up. Maybe too easy. The timing was a little too convenient. Villaume needed to think about it.

"We've been on the line too long. Let me think about this and get back to you."

"Hey . . . I understand your reluctance. If I were in your shoes, I wouldn't want to meet, either. All I need is for you to point me in the right direction."

"I'll think about it."

Rapp started to speak, but the line went dead. Looking over at Coleman, he said, "Fuck! I sure hope he stays alive long enough to tell us what he knows."

KENNEDY WAS ALONE in her office, thinking about Rapp and the traitor in their midst who had almost gotten him killed. Marcus Dumond was keeping her informed on the progress he was making with Rapp and Coleman. The deputy director of Central Intelligence had stopped by to pepper her with questions about her testimony to the House Intelligence Committee. It was surprisingly easy to lie to Jonathan Brown, despite the fact that he was a former federal judge. Stansfield had taught her well. Once you learned to control your emotions, it was nearly impossible for an adversary to discern if you were telling the truth. As with a great poker player, the name of the game was to keep a straight face whether you were holding a royal flush or a pair of twos. Under Stansfield's tutelage, Kennedy had mastered the skill. The only person in the world who could consistently get a reaction out of her was her son, Tommy. Not even her ex-husband had been able to do it. He sure as hell had tried, but he had failed miserably. Kennedy didn't harbor any ill will toward him. When she looked back on the marriage, it was easy to see it was destined for failure from the moment she took the job as the director of the Counterterrorism Center. There weren't enough hours left over after running the CTC to be both a good mother and a good wife.

The phone on her desk emitted a soft tone, and then a voice came over the intercom. "Irene, Congressman O'Rourke is here to see you."

Without looking up, Kennedy said, "Show him in, please."

O'Rourke entered Kennedy's office with a slightly troubled look on his face.

"Hello, Irene." O'Rourke sat down in one of two chairs across from Kennedy's desk. He was wearing a three-button brown suit with a white shirt and tie.

"Good afternoon, Michael."

Never one to waste time or words, O'Rourke said, "I'm sorry about this morning. Chairman Rudin is a real ass."

"I hope you'll forgive me if I don't expand on that."

"No . . . I understand." O'Rourke crossed and then uncrossed his legs. "About that name I brought up this morning?"

Kennedy wasn't going to make this easy. She stared back at O'Rourke with her brown eyes, waiting for him to expand.

"You do remember the name I mentioned?"

"Yes."

"Well, what can you tell me about him?"

"Absolutely nothing."

O'Rourke leaned forward. "Come on, Irene. I deserve an answer." Kennedy continued to sit calmly behind her desk. "Can you at least tell me if you know him?"

Kennedy had thought this through thoroughly. "Michael, let me ask you something. If someone, let's say one of your colleagues, were to come to me and ask if I knew your grandfather, how would you want me to answer them?"

O'Rourke began fidgeting with his wedding ring. He knew Kennedy would bring this up, and that was why he had dreaded coming here. He had hoped to get a quick answer from her while they were on his home turf, but he should have known better. The story was long, twisted, and bloody. When O'Rourke left the Marine Corps, he went to work for Senator Erik Olson. His best friend, roommate, and fellow staffer during those wild years had been Mark Coleman, the younger brother of Scott Coleman. Mark had been tragically killed just two blocks from the Capitol one night on his way home from work. His assailant was a strung-out crack addict who had been released from the D.C. jail because of overcrowding. The effect it had on O'Rourke was devastating. It was during this time of grieving that O'Rourke had learned of a cover-up involving a prominent senator and a blown covert operation that had cost a dozen SEALs their lives. The commander of those SEALs was none other than Scott Coleman, the older brother of Mark. Michael had labored over telling Coleman that it was Senator Fitzgerald who had blown his operation in northern Libya. It was O'Rourke's grandfather Seamus who had convinced him he should tell Coleman. The reasoning was simple: if Michael were still in the Corps, and it was his men who had been killed, he would want to know.

O'Rourke rated his decision to tell Coleman the identity of his betrayer as one of the worst in his life. Roughly a year after telling him about Senator Fitzgerald's role in the disaster, O'Rourke awoke to the startling news that Fitzgerald had been assassinated along with two other prominent Washington politicians. In the bloodbath that played itself out over the next week, more people were killed, including Senator Olson and the president's national security advisor. The most damaging piece of information was that O'Rourke's grandfather had been directly involved with Coleman and his team of disgruntled former Navy SEALs. He had funded their mini-revolution and helped them plan it.

Congressman O'Rourke had been assured by Director Stansfield that the involvement of Scott Coleman and Seamus O'Rourke would never be made public. Not even President Hayes or his predecessor, President Stevens, knew the whole story.

O'Rourke decided that the best way to handle Kennedy's question was to ignore it and try a different approach. "Do you know who Anna Rielly is?"

"Of course."

"Do you know that she dates Mitch Rapp?"

"If you say so."

"Come on, Irene. Don't play these games with me. I need an answer."

"I'm not playing games with you, Michael. You refused to answer my question."

"What question?" asked O'Rourke with a frown.

Calmly, Kennedy asked it again. "If someone came to me and asked if I knew your grandfather, how would you want me to answer them?"

"I don't see what Mitch Rapp has to do with my grandfather."

Kennedy looked him straight in the eye and replied, "Yes, you do. I know you are fully capable of grasping the principle at hand. It's a very important one in this line of work, in fact it is our cornerstone. It's called secrecy."

"Yeah . . . yeah . . . I know. I've heard it all before, but this is different. You can trust me."

"Can I?" asked Kennedy with a raised eyebrow.

"You know you can. You have a gun to my head. If you wanted to, you could end my career tomorrow."

"Something tells me you wouldn't mind that, Michael."

"Yeah, well, you might be right, but you're still the one holding the gun. Maybe you should put me out of my misery. It'd give me a good excuse to get out of this town."

"Don't say that. I have no desire to cause you any harm. We need more people like you on the Hill."

O'Rourke ignored the compliment, not sure if it was sincere or self-serving. "Here's my problem, Irene. My wife's best friend is Anna Rielly. They went to the University of Michigan together. Anna is in head over heels with this Mitch Rapp fellow. My wife tells me they are going to get married. I like the guy. We spend a fair amount of time with them going out to dinner, taking in an occasional ball game, stuff like that. We've even been to his house on the bay. I've noticed some things about him." O'Rourke stopped to get a read from Kennedy, but she gave him nothing. "I'd swear the guy has had some military training at some point. You can see it in the way he carries himself, except he's a little more refined, not . . ." O'Rourke searched for the right word. "Not as mechanical. I could give you a list a mile long on little stuff that I've noticed. Last Saturday, my wife gets an e-mail from this guy. He wants us to do him a favor. Go out to his house and pick up Anna. In the e-mail he assures us that he is all right but that he wants us to take care of Anna until he tells us things have settled down." O'Rourke paused a little, still unnerved by the next piece of information. "At the end of the note, he wrote, *I know all about Seamus, Michael, and Scott C.* Now, as far as I'm concerned, that entitles me to know just who in the hell this Mitch Rapp is." O'Rourke sat back and folded his arms across his chest, waiting for a reply.

Kennedy was surprised, but she didn't show it. Rapp had said nothing about sending Liz O'Rourke an e-mail, but it was obvious by the congressman's tone that he wasn't making it up. Even with this new information, Kennedy was not inclined to tell O'Rourke anything about Rapp. As far as she was concerned, Rapp, his identity, and what he had done for the CIA were the Holy Grail of secrets.

"Michael, all I can tell you is that your secret is safe with me."

"The hell it is," replied O'Rourke with a bit of an edge to his voice. "How did Mitch Rapp find out about it, then?"

"I can look into that if you'd like."

"Come on, Irene." O'Rourke was mad. "You can do better than that, and if you can't, you're not going to like my next move."

"And what would that be?"

"I'll call my contacts at the FBI, the NSA, and the Pentagon, and I'll have them do a little digging. I'll call your deputy director of Admin and have him rattle some cages. Hell, I might even call a very unconventional asset in Israel and ask him to see what he can come up with."

Kennedy didn't like the sound of any of this. The last thing she needed right now was to draw an ounce more attention to Rapp and possibly herself. She carefully considered how much to reveal and then said, "The only thing I can tell you about the person in question is that he is extremely good at what he does, and he's on our side."

"That's not good enough."

"I'm afraid it's going to have to be."

"No, it isn't." O'Rourke leaned forward. "I want to know how in the hell he knows about Seamus, Scott, and myself."

Kennedy eyed him coolly, and after a long moment of thoughtful calculation, she told him the truth. "I told him."

28

It took Gus Villaume less than two hours to decide on a course of action. Despite Mario's death, he felt almost himself again. There was a chance that Iron Man was working for the Professor, but Villaume doubted it. The assassin he had seen operate in Paris could not tolerate a man as amateurish as the Professor. No, Villaume had decided, Iron Man wanted the Professor as much as or even more than he did.

And what sweet justice it would be to point Iron Man in the direction of that phony, smug double-crosser. If the man was as connected as he liked to claim, he would wet himself when he found out that Iron Man was onto him.

Villaume caught the city bus on New York Avenue and 11th Street near the convention center and found a seat near the back. He counted seven other riders. Rush hour wouldn't start for another hour. When the bus started moving, Villaume punched in the number. After three rings, a deep voice said hello.

"Iron Man?"

"Yes."

"Do you have something to write with?"

"Yes."

Villaume hunched over and spoke in a soft tone. "The man's called the Professor. He's about five eleven, and I'd guess he weighs around two thirty. Hazel eyes, black hair and beard . . . probably around fifty, give or take a couple of years. I'd guess from his accent that he grew up around D.C. Probably on the Virginia side but definitely not as far south as Richmond."

"What else?"

"I've got a number." Villaume gave Rapp the number he used to contact the Professor.

"Anything else?"

Villaume thought about it for a second. "Up until Colorado, I would have guessed that he had never got his hands dirty before, but he insisted on taking them out himself."

There was a moment of hesitation on the other end. "From how far?"

"About two hundred meters. He had a really unique piece of hardware."

"What was it?"

Villaume looked up. No one was paying any attention to him. "A Stoner SR-25."

"Anything else?"

"Unfortunately, no."

"Come on. You can do better than this!"

"I'm sorry, but it's all I've got for you. Believe me, I wish I knew more."

"How am I going to get hold of you?"

"You aren't going to."

"Come on, Gus, I need your help."

"I'm sorry, but I need to disappear for a while."

"You can trust me. We both want the same thing now." Rapp was pleading.

"That's the problem with this job, my friend. Everybody tells you to trust them right up to the moment they put a bullet in your head."

There was a long period of silence while Rapp thought of the position Villaume was in. He knew if he were in his shoes, he would run. He would trust no one, and he would live to fight another day. Finally, he said, "Gus, I understand. You take care of yourself, and call me if you think of anything else."

"I will. And good luck. I hope you get him." Villaume turned off his phone and closed it. As he looked out the window, the bus rumbled over a decaying bridge, the National Arboretum off to the right. He felt like a coward, but he knew he was doing the right thing. If Iron Man was sincere, Villaume had no doubt the Professor would be joining Mario in the afterlife in the not so distant future.

THE OTHER TWO men watched Rapp and waited for him to speak. He left his phone on and set it in the charger stand, then handed Scott Coleman the notepad with the information Villaume had given him. After a second, Rapp looked at Marcus Dumond, who was sitting in front of his desk. The surface was covered with mouses, keyboards, and three computer screens.

"Can you track him the next time he calls?"

"Villaume?"

"Yeah."

Dumond grimaced. "I don't think so. I can maybe get you in the right area of the city, but that's about it." Dumond paused and thought of something. "How cautious do you think he is?"

"Right now, I'd say very."

"Do you think you could keep him on the line for ten minutes?"

Rapp tried to think what in the world he could say to get Villaume to take such a risk. "No way. I'd be lucky to get him to stay on for five."

"Then I can't track him."

"Can you at least get me the number he's calling from?"

"That's going to be tough. I'll see what I can do, but I'm not going to make any promises."

Coleman handed the notepad back to Rapp and said, "It sounds like the guy I saw out in Colorado. What else did Villaume tell you?"

Rapp gave a brief summary of the discussion, making special mention of the fact that the Professor was the man who had taken the shot in Evergreen. While he did so, Dumond looked over the notes and began typing away at one of his keyboards. "This Professor has to have a past," started Rapp. "You don't just fall into this line of work. He either works in the intelligence community or used to. Marcus, can you take that description and see how many matches you get for current and former Agency people?"

"Yeah, but I'm afraid it's going to be a big number."

"That's fine. Just pull all the photos so Scott can see if he recognizes anybody. If we come up blank at the Agency,

we'll move on to the NSA and from there to the DIA."
While Dumond worked, Rapp thought of something Villaume had said. "If we could get a voice print on this guy, would it help?"

"It might. The NSA keeps some pretty intense files on that stuff."

Rapp pointed to the number he had written down. "What about getting a line on that?"

Dumond slid his chair over to a second computer and accessed a reverse listing service. He punched in the phone number, and the computer went to work. Five seconds later, it came back with bad news. The number was not in the system.

"What does that mean?" asked Rapp. "Is it a bogus number?"

"No. Not necessarily. The directory is constantly changing. It's impossible to keep up with."

"So what do we do?"

Dumond leaned back in his chair and chewed on the end of a Bic pen. "It's got to be a mobile number, right?"

"I'd be shocked if it wasn't." Rapp looked at Coleman. "Scott?"

"Yeah. It has to be."

Dumond continued chewing. "If we call this number, I can figure out who the provider is, and I might be able to get you pretty close to him."

Rapp and Coleman looked at each other. "How?" asked Rapp.

"Once I find out who his carrier is, I can get into their records and track his tower usage."

"What do you mean, tower usage?"

"The call has to be relayed by a tower. We track the towers that his phone is using."

"How close can you get us?"

"Usually within a zip code or two."

"Can you do any better than that?" asked Coleman.

"Yeah, but I'd need to get one of the special vans from the Agency, and you'd have to keep him on the phone."

"For how long?" asked Rapp.

"If we got lucky and were close when he took our call, we could have it narrowed down to the right structure within a minute or two. If not, it might take several calls."

"What if he's on the move?"

Dumond shook his head. "Not good for us."

"Why can't you do this with Villaume?"

"I'd have to get his number first. He calls us, and it's blocked, and then he only stays on for a minute or two. That's not enough time to crack it."

"But you might be able to with the Professor?"

"Might be able to."

Rapp rubbed his chin for a second while he thought about making the call. "So what do you suggest we do?"

"I think we should call this number and see what we can find out." Dumond looked eager.

"Any chance it can be traced back here from the other end?"

Dumond scoffed at such an idea. "Not with my gear. I'll have this baby bounced off six different satellites and twice as many ground stations before I'm done with it."

"What about the NSA picking it up?"

"Big Brother." Dumond shrugged. "It's hard to say. Sometimes I think they are all-knowing, and other times I think they know nothing. I always recommend keeping it short and staying away from details."

Rapp and Coleman both nodded. They had lived by the exact same philosophy for years. Rapp glanced over at the former SEAL. "What do you think?"

Coleman looked down at the notepad, and he thought about the man he'd seen in Colorado. The man they now knew as the Professor. He didn't strike him as a killer. He also didn't strike him as a leader. He was working for someone, and if Coleman had to guess, that someone was a big hitter.

Coleman tossed the notepad back on the desk and said, "We need some backup. In fact, I'd recommend we move this whole operation to a safe house."

"Marcus says this place is fine. What's bothering you?"

"This Professor is working for someone. And whoever that person is, he or she has the type of pull that put them in the know about that little op you were running over in Germany." Coleman raised an eyebrow. "That worries me."

Rapp hadn't spent a lot of time dwelling on this obvious fact. He was leaving that up to Kennedy and Stansfield. He could tell by the look on Coleman's face that he suspected someone at the NSA. He could very well be right, but the last thing they could afford right now was to become incapacitated by fear. "I trust Marcus on this one. If he says they can't trace us, I believe him."

Coleman looked over at Dumond. "This is no time

to be cocky. Give me the straight poop. Can Big Brother track this call or not?"

Dumond thought for a moment. Finally, he answered, "I don't think they can trace it, but just to be safe, we should keep it under two minutes."

"You're sure?"

"At two minutes or less, I'm positive."

"Are you satisfied?" asked Rapp of Coleman.

Coleman nodded slowly. "Yes, but I think it would be a good idea if we brought some more people to the party."

"Who do you have in mind?"

"A couple of my men. You've worked with them before."

"All right."

"What are you two talking about?" asked Dumond.

"We're going to get a few more guns over here just in case," answered Rapp.

Dumond's expression soured in an effort to show he didn't like the idea.

"Take it easy, Marcus. It's for your own good." Rapp pointed to the computers. "Do you have everything ready to make this call?"

"Give me a minute."

"All right." Rapp turned to Coleman. "What's bothering you?"

"I don't know if I like letting him know we're onto him just yet. I'd like to get some more info."

"I'd like to spook him into doing something stupid. Besides, there's a chance I might know this guy. Get a hold of your guys and make the arrangements. Then we'll make the call."

29

Peter Cameron was in his small office at George Washington University reading a paper one of his students had written. Cameron taught a special topics course on the CIA for GW's Elliot School of International Affairs. The course was nothing earth-shattering, rather a mundane look at how the bureaucracy of the CIA functioned with its counterparts in the intelligence community. One section met on Mondays, Wednesdays, and Thursdays at eleven in the morning for one hour, and the second class met at six in the evening for two hours on Mondays and Thursdays. The day class was made up of fourteen professional students who thought they were smarter than everyone, including their professor. The evening class, however, was far more interesting. At least half of his students were military officers or other intelligence types who had a little better grasp of reality and the practical side of the business. The professional students in his night class tended to listen more and pontificate less, which he rather enjoyed.

Cameron's mind tended to wander when he was reading, and right now he was wondering why he hadn't gotten into teaching earlier. He worked an average of about ten hours a week, had ample vacation time, and was paid forty thousand dollars a year. The job was a complete boondoggle. The respect he was given when introduced as a professor at GW was amazing. And he could actually talk about this job. When he was at Langley, about all he could say was that he worked there. Cameron had decided he could easily teach into his seventies. It might be the perfect position to have when President Clark called on him to help out with his new administration.

Cameron set the paper down and stared aimlessly at his wall. Would national security advisor be too lofty a post? Maybe not. He had the practical experience and now the academic title. If anyone could make it happen, it would be Clark. His pie-in-the-sky daydream was rudely interrupted by the ringing of one of his phones. He knew it wasn't his office phone—that had an entirely different ring. But he could never tell his two cell phones apart. One was legitimate, meaning it was purchased under his real name. The second phone was purchased using a bogus name. He had paid for a year's worth of service using a money order. One thousand minutes a month, anywhere, any time.

The phones were in his leather briefcase. Cameron reached in with two hands and grabbed both phones. The Motorola was the one ringing. No number came up on the caller ID, but that wasn't unusual.

He pressed the send button and said, "Hello." There was no immediate response, so Cameron repeated himself.

"Professor, how are you doing?" came the slightly menacing voice.

Cameron leaped from his chair—the voice on the phone caused the hair on his neck to stand on end. He knew instantly who was on the line. He had listened to that voice in Germany. Attempting to sound unfazed, Cameron replied, "Ahhh . . . fine. And you?"

"I would say I'm doing very well." Rapp offered nothing further, intentionally letting the tension build.

Cameron went over to the window and looked down on the street to see if anyone was watching him. Silently, he cursed himself for not preparing for this contingency. "I'm sorry, but you're going to have to help me out. I have no idea who this is." He did not sound convincing.

"Oh, I think you do." Rapp's voice was steady and direct.

"No . . . I really don't."

"Come on, Professor. We have mutual friends, or should I say *had* mutual friends?"

"I don't follow."

"The Jansens of Evergreen, Colorado, or should I say the Hoffmans of Germany?"

Cameron was shaking. How in the hell had Rapp found him? Grasping for words, he finally managed to say, "I have no idea what you're talking about."

"Oh, I think you do."

"Who is this?"

"I told you . . . I'm an old friend of the Jansens. In fact, I think we almost bumped into each other in the woods once."

Cameron grabbed his forehead with his free hand and squeezed. How in the hell did Rapp know he'd been in the woods that night? He hadn't even told the Jansens. "Listen, I don't know who you are or what you're talking about."

"Why don't you drop the act, Professor? We need to negotiate."

"Negotiate?" asked an incredulous Cameron. "For what?"

"Your life."

"My *life*." Cameron's voice cracked under the strain. "Just what in the hell are you talking about?"

"Cut the bullshit." Rapp's voice took on a harder edge. "I'm going to call you back in one hour. In the meantime, I suggest you calm down and gather your thoughts. My offer is simple. You tell me what I want to know, specifically who hired you, and I'll let you live. And if you have half a brain, you won't tell your employer about this call." Rapp paused, giving Cameron a second to think about things, then added, "If you screw with me in the slightest way, I'm going to do to you what you did to the Jansens. Except I'll be much closer than you were. I promise you, the last thing you'll feel before you die is my warm breath on the back of your neck."

The line went dead. Cameron was left standing in the middle of his office staring at his phone—shaking. "How in the hell did he find me?" Cameron felt the urge to run. He needed to get out of his cramped office. He shoved the phones back in his briefcase and grabbed his laptop. He left everything else where it was and locked the door behind him. He needed to find some-place safe. A place where he could think things through and figure out what he was going to tell Clark.

30

It had been more than an hour. Eighty-seven minutes, to be exact. Rapp paced in frustration from Dumond's kitchen through the dining room and into the living room. He stepped over a lime-green Nintendo Game Boy that was on the floor in front of the fifty-two-inch TV and looked out the window. Rapp's new companion, Shirley, came up beside him and rubbed her neck against his leg. Rapp scratched the top of her head. Kevin Hackett and Dan Stroble, two of Coleman's men, were supposed to be arriving any minute. They were bringing more firepower in case they needed it. That had been Coleman's idea, and Rapp didn't argue. Rapp felt more than secure with his 9-mm Beretta. Anyone who was foolish enough to try to take them down would lose a lot of men.

Rapp checked his watch. It was twenty past four in the afternoon. The rain had started to fall again in a slow, steady trickle. He had tried the Professor's phone five times, and each time he had received a recorded message telling him the customer was not available. Something was wrong. Coleman had listened to the first call on another extension and had agreed with

Rapp. The Professor sounded scared, and he was lying. He knew exactly who Rapp was and what had happened in Germany and Colorado.

Now Rapp feared they may have lost the man. They may have spooked him into disappearing entirely. Rapp worried about how long this would take to tie up. He was going to see it through to the end, no matter how long it took, but if this Professor decided to disappear, it could be years, and it would mean using the Agency's legitimate assets, something Rapp was loath to do.

Coleman approached Rapp at the window and said, "I hope he didn't decide to tell his employer about the call."

"Yeah, I know." Rapp watched the drops falling in a puddle that had formed between two heaved sections of sidewalk. "They need to know what we know."

"How do you mean?"

"If he's with his employer right now, they're trying to figure out just how much we know."

"Well, based on the conversation you had with him, he should be able to figure out that you don't know who he's working for."

"And we have to hope that he doesn't pass that on to his boss, or he's going to end up just like the Jansens."

"Yeah," Coleman agreed. "You know, there's something we haven't discussed enough."

"What's that?"

"Motive. Who and why? You have a lot of enemies, Mitch."

"Most of my enemies are the same as yours. They live in the Middle East, and they don't have the type of clout to penetrate that operation I was running in Germany."

"So who is it?"

"I'm not sure, but I'm leaning toward someone here in D.C."

"What about the Israelis?"

Rapp shrugged. "I don't know. I don't think so. As I look back on what happened in Germany, I'm starting to think that I wasn't the target."

"That doesn't make any sense."

"Think about it. The Jansens had ample opportunity to kill me. Why did they wait and shoot me after I had killed the count?"

"I don't know. Why?"

"Because they wanted me to be fingered for the hit."

Coleman thought it over for a second. "Then why are you ruling Israelis out? They get you to do their dirty work and make sure none of the heat comes down on them."

"No." Rapp shook his head. "The Israelis are never afraid to take a little heat. Especially if they can prove the person they killed was in bed with Saddam."

"Yeah . . . I suppose you're right."

"Whoever did it wanted me exposed. They didn't want personal vengeance."

"How can you be sure? You've been involved in some pretty serious shit over the years. You probably couldn't begin to count the enemies you've made."

"No, I couldn't, but you're missing the point. Someone had the clout to penetrate that operation in Germany. That is no easy thing. It would take a person in a pretty powerful position to have accessed that information." Rapp pointed at himself. "If I was the target, why dust me in Germany? Why not have the Jansens kill me here in town, out at my house? Why not have this Professor put a bullet in my head from two hundred meters like he did to the Jansens?"

Coleman slowly nodded. Rapp was right. It didn't make sense. "So, if you weren't the ultimate target, then who is?"

"I don't know, but if their intent was to have me found at the scene and identified . . ." Rapp paused and thought about the ramifications. "That would have spelled trouble for a lot of people."

"Namely the president."

"Yep, and the Agency."

Coleman thought about it for a moment and added, "That still doesn't rule out foreign involvement."

"No, it doesn't. But my gut tells me it's someone here in town."

Dumond called from the other room. Rapp and Coleman went back into the dining room and found a grinning Marcus Dumond leaning back in his chair.

"I've got some info on your man." Dumond pointed to the computer screen in the middle. "His mobile phone account is through Sprint, and it's registered under the name of Tom Jones. It was purchased at a Radio Shack in Alexandria five months ago. It looks like he paid for a full year of service in advance."

"What did he use?" asked Rapp.

"A Mastercard. I already checked into the credit card account. It was opened and closed a month later. The billing address is for an apartment in Falls Church. We can look into it, but my guess is it's a dead end."

Rapp agreed. "What else do you have?"

"Something you're going to find interesting." Dumond pointed at the screen to his left. "This is a map of downtown from the Hill to the Potomac. All of these little red dots you see are towers that Sprint owns and operates." Dumond scrolled down the screen. "This is a list of all the calls that have been made to this phone in the last thirty days."

Rapp looked at the list. "What about calls he has made?"

"There aren't any. He's smart. He knows someone could do exactly what I'm doing right now. The trail ends here."

"Shit."

"Don't distress just yet. I do have one piece of information that might be useful." Dumond scrolled back up to the map of the city. "Almost half of the calls he has received have been handled by this one tower right here." Dumond pointed to a spot four blocks west of the White House. "After this tower there's another one in Georgetown that pops up a lot, and then one more on the Hill. Other than that, the rest appear to be random."

Rapp knelt down and looked at the screen. "Can you sort these calls by the time of day they were received?"

"I'm already on it for you. I'm going back to the start of the service and plotting them by tower, day of the week, and time."

"How long until you have something you can show me?"

"An hour or two, and I should have it pretty well nailed."

"Good work, Marcus." Rapp looked over his shoulder at Coleman and pointed at the screen. "Look at what's just two blocks away from this tower."

Coleman squinted. "George Washington University."

"No." Rapp moved his finger a couple of inches down. "The State Department." He tapped the spot with his index finger and said, "I'll bet my left nut this guy works for State."

Frowning, Coleman looked at the screen. "Why State? He could just as easily work at the White House or . . ." Coleman looked at some of the other buildings. "The World Bank or maybe the Federal Reserve. Hell, the United Nations has even got an office there."

"It's State. I know it is. Remember what Irene told us about Secretary Midleton calling her Saturday morning to find out if the Agency had anything to do with Hagenmiller's death?"

Coleman thought about what Kennedy had said. It was true that Midleton had seemed to be in on the action a little too quickly. Coleman felt his chest tighten just a notch. If this thing was connected to the State Department, things could get really ugly. "I think you might have something, but we need to talk to Irene about it immediately." As an afterthought, Coleman added, "And I don't think we should do it over the phone."

SENATOR CLARK HAD all of the players gathered. They were in one of the Senate Intelligence Committee's soundproof briefing rooms on the second floor of the Hart Building. Clark sat at the head of the long black table with a glass of scotch in his hand. It was a few minutes before five in the evening. He usually waited until after five to pour his first drink, but tonight he had made an exception. He was trying to get the others to relax, especially Congressman Rudin. He was sitting to Clark's left, looking as ornery as ever. Midleton was next to Rudin, and across from them, on the other side of the table, was their guest of honor—Jonathan Brown, the deputy director of the Central Intelligence Agency.

Congressman Rudin had demanded that something be done. Kennedy's bald-faced lies to his committee could not go unpunished. Clark, always willing to play the role of problem solver, suggested they hold a very discreet meeting. Rudin liked the idea. In his current state of rage, anything other than doing nothing sounded good. Clark had personally made the phone calls. He first called DDCI Brown and asked if he could come to the Hill on an informal visit. *Informal* was code for *off the record*. Brown, always willing to keep the chairman of the Senate Intelligence Committee happy, readily agreed to the meeting. He had arrived in an unmarked car and entered the building through the underground parking garage. Secretary of State Midleton had done the same. It wouldn't do to have him parading across town in his armor-plated limousine, so he came in a government sedan with blacked-out windows.

Senator Clark leaned back in his chair and crossed his long legs. Looking at the number two man at the CIA, Clark said, "Jonathan, my colleague from the

House is a little concerned over who is running the show at your place."

"I'm more than a little concerned," snapped Rudin. "I'm fucking irate. I'm so irate, I'm thinking about holding hearings."

Clark reached out and placed a hand on Rudin's bony forearm. *Not yet, my friend,* he thought to himself. *I'll let you know when it's time for that.* Clark patted Rudin's arm. "Let's try and stay civil. I don't think Jonathan is the problem."

"Well, I'll tell you who the problem is. It's that bitch Irene Kennedy."

Secretary of State Midleton frowned. "I don't think that kind of language is necessary."

Rudin, never one to be concerned with decorum, scoffed at the secretary's concern. "Get off your high horse, Charles. This is no time to worry about etiquette. This is serious shit. I think the CIA killed Count Hagenmiller, and I think that *bitch* Irene Kennedy came before my committee this morning and lied about it."

Jonathan Brown's face was as white as a sheet, and Midleton was busy pursing his lips and shaking his head in disgust. Clark sat back and enjoyed. It was Brown who spoke first. His voice was a little shaky.

"I can assure you that the CIA has taken no such action."

"Oh, can you?" Rudin's voice was filled with doubt. "You're not going to like this, Mr. Brown, but I don't think you have the faintest idea what Thomas Stansfield does and doesn't do. He runs that agency like a dictator-ship."

Brown was on the defensive. "I have found Director Stansfield to be honest and fair."

"That's because you haven't bothered to dig too deep."

"Listen." Brown stuck his hands out in an attempt to slow Rudin down. "If you have evidence of such illegal action by either Director Stansfield or Dr. Kennedy, bring it to me, and I will make sure explanations are given."

"Bring it to you! Do you think I'm an idiot? If I had any evidence, I'd haul their asses before my committee, and I'd sic the Justice Department on them."

Clark could tell Brown was about to snap. As a former federal judge, he was not used to being addressed in such a manner. Clark grabbed Rudin's arm again and said, "Take it easy, Albert."

"Yes, please do," added Midleton. "Your behavior is embarrassing."

"Oh, don't give me that horse shit, Charles." Rudin wheeled around and faced the secretary of state. "You wipe your ass just like the *rest of us.* Just because you're not on the Hill anymore doesn't mean you're any better than the *rest of us.*"

Rudin had overstepped his bounds. Midleton hadn't become secretary of state by letting people run him over. He spun his chair around and faced Rudin. "I have always been better than you, you emotional little hack, and I always will be better than you. Now, I suggest you keep your tongue in check, or I will have a little meeting with the party leadership and demand that you be stripped of your pathetic little committee."

This was almost too good to be true, Clark thought. If only his colleagues could see it. It was time to settle things down, though, and get back to the plan. Clark grabbed Rudin's shoulder with one beefy hand and pulled him away from Midleton before he could do any more damage. "Albert, calm down and shut your mouth for a minute." Rudin tried to speak, but Clark stopped him. "This is coming from one of your best friends. Just shut your mouth. I understand why you're upset. So does Charles, and I think Jonathan does, too, but you're not doing anybody any good by taking this out on the wrong people."

Again, Rudin tried to speak, but Clark held up a finger and silenced him.

"If you are right about Kennedy and Stansfield, and I'm not so sure you are, then we need to work with Jonathan to try and get to the bottom of this. We don't need to beat him up over something he had no control over."

"If I may," Midleton interjected. "I see some potential conflicts over separation of powers."

"Listen." Clark sighed as if he wanted nothing to do with any of this. "My position has always been clear on this issue. I think the CIA is a very important part of this nation's national security. My friend and I disagree on this." Clark gestured to Rudin. "The last thing I want to see is the CIA weakened by hearings." Clark looked Midleton in the eye and prepared to address his real concern. "I like President Hayes. He's a good man. I mean no harm to his administration, and I think you know that, Charles. You and I sat across the aisle from each other for years. Have you ever known me to put party politics before national security?"

Midleton shook his head. "No. You were always very honorable, Hank."

"Thank you. And so were you, Charles." Clark took a drink of scotch and shifted gears. "I don't think we can go back and change the past, gentlemen. We need to look to the future. Director Stansfield is dying. I've heard he has about six months left." The men nodded. "Our job, as I see it, is to help the president pick someone who can bring the Agency into the twenty-first century. Someone who will be respectful of the concerns of the Congress." As Clark looked at the other men, he couldn't help but feel a sense of accomplishment that he had almost perfectly maneuvered all of the pieces of the puzzle into place. Just as he was about to put one more very important piece into play, the phone next to him buzzed and stopped him short.

Clark snatched the phone from its cradle. "Hello."

"Sir, I need to speak with you immediately."

It was Peter Cameron. Clark remained calm, even though the man's timing couldn't have been worse. "I'm in the middle of something."

"This is really important. I'm in the briefing room across the hall from you."

Clark thought about it for a second. Cameron sounded very serious. "Give me a minute. I'll be right over."

31

Cameron scratched his beard and tried to figure out what to do. He was standing in the parking ramp at George Washington University. After hanging up on Rapp, Cameron was forced to make a practical decision: use his own car, or find other transportation. As he huddled behind a concrete pillar in the ramp, he went over the phone conversation, trying to figure out how Rapp had found him. Something occurred to him. Rapp had never used his real name. He only called him Professor. Cameron put himself in Rapp's shoes. If he were the one doing the confronting, he would use the person's real name, not an alias. Hell, he wouldn't even call them, he'd show up on the person's doorstep with a little muscle and beat the truth out of them.

Cameron had decided it was Villaume. That slimy little frog had gotten hold of Rapp and given him the phone number. That was the only thing that made sense; otherwise, Rapp would be all over him. Cameron checked the underside of his car for tracking devices and left the ramp. He took his time driving to the Hill. The normal ten-minute drive took forty-five as Cameron zigzagged his way across the city. When he finally pulled into the underground garage of the Hart Senate Office Building, he was pretty confident that he had not been followed.

Senator Clark entered the small room and shut the airtight, soundproof door. He was in a light blue shirt with a white collar and an expensive gold silk tie. He had left his suit coat across the hall in the larger conference room. He was far from enthused about the interruption, but he didn't show it.

Clark remained standing. "What's wrong, Peter?"

"Nothing we can't handle," answered Cameron with reserved confidence.

The senator eyed him cautiously. "Elaborate, please."

"I received a phone call this afternoon from Mitch Rapp."

Clark's eyes opened wider. "Really?"

"Yes, but I don't want you to be too alarmed. He doesn't know my real name."

Clark wasn't sure if he believed Cameron. "How did he find you?"

Cameron held up his mobile phone. "He called me on this."

"How did he get the number?"

"Villaume gave it to him." Cameron neglected to tell Clark that this was an educated guess.

The senator took a deep breath and glanced over at the blank wall. "I thought you said Villaume wasn't going to be a problem now that his large friend is gone."

"I don't think he will be," Cameron lied, again ne-

glecting to mention the conversation he'd had with Villaume earlier in the day.

"Well, I think him giving Rapp your number would
fall into the creating problems category."

"It's not what you think." Cameron held the phone
up again. "There is no way they can use this to find
me. It was purchased under a false name and was paid
for with a credit card that can't be traced to me. Villaume doesn't know my real name; he knows nothing
about me."

Clark strained to keep his demeanor calm. None of
this was good news. "You don't feel the slightest bit
threatened by Rapp?"

"No," Cameron lied. "I can handle him."

"I'm not so sure." The senator looked away and said,
"Maybe I should bring in someone else to take care of
things?"

"No. I can handle it."

"You're sure?" The senator studied him.

"Yes."

"How are things proceeding with the girl?"

"We have all of the information you requested."

"All right." Clark sat at the small table, and Cameron
did the same. "Grab the girl, and be very discreet about
it. Has Rapp shown up at his house yet?"

"No, and I don't think he will until this thing blows
over."

Clark sat in silence for a while, concentrating on how
to proceed. After several minutes, he began to tell Cameron what to do. His attention to detail was amazing. So
much so that Cameron felt the need to take notes, but he

knew better than to ask. After ten minutes of Clark talking and Cameron listening, the meeting was over. Clark had sent his minion on his way with very specific orders on how to proceed.

Clark stayed in the small room by himself for several minutes, taking the time to gather his wits before he went back into the other meeting. As he sat there, he thought of one thing he'd forgotten. This would be the end of his relationship with Cameron. Whether the man succeeded in taking care of Rapp or not, he had become too big a liability.

He had received confirmation that a man called the Colonel had accepted the contract on Cameron and was on his way to Washington. When Clark got home, he would have to put the Colonel in a holding pattern until this business with the reporter was taken care of. He absolutely could not allow Rapp to get his hands on Cameron.

ANNA RIELLY WAS tired. She'd just finished giving her last nightly news update and was packing up to head home. The rain had finally stopped. She did her first two stories standing under an umbrella on the north grounds of the White House. The dreary weather was affecting people's moods, including hers. It had been a long week, and it was only Wednesday. All she wanted to do was go home, curl up in her own bed, and go to sleep. It would be nice if Mitch was there, but she doubted she would be that lucky.

She had told Liz all about her conversation with Mitch. She had yet to tell Liz who Mitch worked for or what he did, and Liz had been a good enough friend not to force the issue. Although Liz O'Rourke seemed to be relieved by the news that Mitch had contacted Anna, the same couldn't really be said for Liz's husband. Michael was not happy about the events of the last week, and Anna was still worried that he might use his contacts to start digging around.

As Rielly walked toward the northwest gate, she made the decision that she would stay at her apartment tonight. She had imposed enough on the O'Rourkes. They didn't need this kind of stress in their lives, especially with the baby on the way. Mitch had called and said everything was fine. If he wasn't worried, then she could relax a little.

As she approached the first gate, Rielly stuck her access badge under a sensor, and the lock on the gate released. She pushed the gate open and waved good night to the uniformed Secret Service officers as she walked past the guardhouse. At the next gate, she repeated the process and then stepped out onto the sidewalk bordering Pennsylvania Avenue. As she turned west, her thoughts settled on taking a nice, long, hot bath when she got home. Then maybe she would put a call in to her parents in Chicago and see how things were going.

There were always plenty of good stories about her nieces and nephews. The count was even right now. Three boys and three girls with two unknowns on the way. Rielly and her mother were hoping for girls. Anna had grown up with four very protective older brothers. Three of the four were married, and one was currently unmarried and looking for number two. Rielly needed to get home and see them. It had been almost three months. That was too long. Maybe when Mitch came out of his debriefing or whatever it was that he was doing, they could book a trip. The family had met Mitch the previous summer, and they had all gotten along wonderfully.

Rielly didn't even notice the two men at first. She was a thousand miles away, skinny-dipping in the water of Lake Poygan with her future husband, reliving the pleasant memories of last summer's trip. She stopped abruptly and looked up at the two serious-looking individuals.

"Ms. Rielly, I'm Special Agent Pelachuk with the FBI." The man gestured to his right. "And this is Special Agent Salem. We need to ask you a few questions."

Rielly took half a step back and glanced over her shoulder. The White House was only a block away. She was not nervous; rather, she was checking to make sure none of her fellow reporters was witnessing the exchange. "May I see your badges, please?"

Without hesitation, both men produced their identification. Rielly studied them, not really knowing what an FBI badge looked like, other than what she'd seen on TV. The pictures matched, and they looked fancy enough. Rielly handed them back and asked, "What is it that you would like to talk to me about?"

"I'd rather not say, right here." The man looked uncomfortable as he glanced over his shoulder and then across the street at the Old Executive Office Building.

"I'd rather you did." Rielly folded her arms across

her chest as if to say she wasn't moving until she got some answers.

The man slowly leaned forward and whispered, "This has something to do with your boyfriend."

Rielly took half a step back. "Excuse me?"

The man waved his hands back and forth in an attempt to rid Rielly of her fears. "It's not what you think. It's a good thing." He smiled.

"What?"

"I can't really talk about it out here on the street." Rielly still looked concerned, so the man again leaned in and whispered, "He wants to see you."

"Where is he?"

"I can't say. All I can tell you is that he is safe, and he would like to see you."

"And if I say no?"

"If you say no, we will walk away and report back that we tried and you rejected us. It's not a big deal. He should be done in about two weeks, and you can see him then."

Two weeks was out of the question. Rielly didn't know if she could wait two days. "All right. I'll come with you, but I need to make a phone call. Someone is expecting me."

"That's fine, but we'd ask that you not mention his name on a nonsecure line."

"That's not a problem."

"Good. Our car is right here."

Rielly walked with them to a sedan that was parked only a few feet away. Always the reporter, Rielly checked the plates and was relieved to see they were government issue. She got into the back seat and pulled out her cell phone. After a few rings, Liz O'Rourke answered.

"Hello."

"Liz, it's me. I think everything is back to normal."

"Are you sure?"

"Yeah. Don't worry."

"So you talked to him again."

Rielly watched through the front window as the car pulled out into traffic. "No . . . not really." She wasn't sure how much she could say. "I'm on my way to meet him right now."

"Is that good?" Liz asked.

"Yes. I'll call you in the morning."

"All right. Let me know if you need anything."

"I will, Liz, and thanks for everything. Apologize to Michael for me, please."

"Don't worry about him. You don't need to apologize for anything. He'll just be happy he gets to sleep in our bed again."

Anna laughed. "Liz, you're the best. I love you."

32

He'd taken his last shot of morphine some-where between five and six P.M. Now, some three hours later, the pain was hitting him in waves—deep, stabbing discomfort in the pit of his stom-ach. Thomas Stansfield wanted to be lucid for this meet-ing. It was probably the last time he would see the president. He did not want to be remembered as a glassy-eyed morphine addict, and, more importantly, he needed to have a firm grip on his faculties.

Many would think Stansfield's way of thinking was antiquated, but it had served him well during his years in Washington. His duty was to his country and then his president, in that order. Not all of those presidents had been good, and Stansfield had worked hard to limit the damage the bad ones could do to his beloved Agency through their whimsical or ill-conceived proposals. President Hayes was different in this regard. The man was about as whimsical as a CPA. Hayes was not the brightest president to occupy the Oval Office, but in Stansfield's mind he was one of the best. Unlike some of his predecessors, Hayes disdained polls. He instead chose to surround himself with talented individuals. He would heed their counsel, and when the time was right, he would act decisively.

Stansfield allowed his bodyguard to help him from the back of the limo. It would take all of the strength he could muster to make it to the Situation Room under his own power. He was, as always, in a suit and tie. He had never gone to the White House in anything other than business or formal attire. There were no casual days for Thomas Stansfield.

It was approaching nine P.M., and the West Wing of the White House was relatively calm. The president was still on-site, working late in the Oval Office and waiting for his guest to arrive. That meant the Secret Service was there in full force, but most of the support staff was gone. Stansfield used a cane for balance as he walked to the door. The man looked as if he had aged ten years in the last month. They entered the building through the ground-floor entrance on West Executive Avenue, and Stansfield was escorted to the secure conference room within the Situation Room.

Stansfield was a little surprised to find President Hayes waiting for him. Hayes was sitting in his usual spot at the head of the table reading a report. His suit coat was draped over the back of the chair, and his tie was loosened several inches.

Hayes stood and snatched his reading glasses from his face. The first thing he noticed about Stansfield was how thin he looked. The president took his hand and said, "Thank you for coming, Thomas. I wish you would have let me come to you."

"Nonsense, sir. I needed to get out of the house. Besides, it is I who serve you."

Hayes laughed softly. "Sometimes I'm not so sure about that." The president pulled out a chair for Stansfield. "Here, Thomas. Have a seat." Stansfield sank into the plush leather chair, and the president asked, "Can I get you anything?"

"No thank you, sir."

As the president took his seat, Stansfield's bodyguard retreated and closed the door. In the still silence of the room, the president studied Stansfield, and after a long reflective moment, he asked, "How are you doing?"

"Between you and me?" Stansfield asked. The president nodded. "It won't be long now."

"What are the doctors telling you?"

"Not much. I've stopped talking to them."

Hayes looked confused. "Why?"

"I'm eighty years old, sir. I have lived a very full life. I see no sense in torturing myself for another six months of questionable living."

The president had tried to get Stansfield to call him by his first name when they were alone, but the director of the CIA had resisted. "Do you miss your wife?" Mrs. Stansfield had passed away just a few years before.

"Every day, sir."

The president smiled sadly and said, "I respect your decision, Thomas. You have lived an incredible life and have given immeasurable service to this country."

"That is kind of you to say, sir."

President Hayes brought his hands together and said, "I heard Irene had some trouble on the Hill this morning."

"Where did you hear that?" Stansfield always wanted to know where people got their information before responding.

"I received a call from one of the committee members."

"Chairman Rudin?"

"No." The president laughed slightly. "Chairman Rudin and I aren't exactly on speaking terms."

"If you don't mind me asking, sir, why can't you get the party leadership to reel him in?"

President Hayes thought about the question for a moment and said, "Chairman Rudin is a strange duck. Between you and me, I've never liked the man. He is filled with irrational hatred which tends to cloud his judgment. He has his place in the party, however." Hayes shook his head. "Unfortunately for you and me, the party put him where they thought he could do the least damage. I suppose I could make a few calls, but it might only serve to enrage him further."

"Well, do what you think is best. I might be able to do some things to help, but my real concern is where he's getting his information."

"He could just be guessing." The president looked at Stansfield for a response.

"He could, but given the fact that Mitch's mission was compromised, I'm inclined to believe we have a leak."

President Hayes didn't like hearing this. He exhaled a slow, painful breath. "What in the hell have I gotten myself into, Thomas?" The president put his elbows on the table and cupped his face with his hands.

"What do you mean, sir?"

"If it gets out that I ordered the assassination of one of Germany's leading citizens, it will be devastating."

"Sir, in your position, you have three options to deal with this growing threat. The first, diplomacy, has had very poor results; the second, military action, is ill suited to combat the small force we are up against; and the third option, sir, the one you have chosen, is the best option. We take the battle to them with small covert units. You made the right decision, sir."

"If this thing blows up in my face, it will not have been the right decision."

"I will not let that happen, sir."

"How?" The president sounded skeptical.

"We are making some progress in finding the leak."

"Really?"

"Yes."

"What have you found?"

"We think it might be someone at the State Department."

"How high up?"

Instead of answering the question, Stansfield said, "Irene told me about the meeting you had the other day with the German ambassador."

Hayes leaned back in his chair. "And?"

"How have things been between you and Secretary Midleton?"

After thinking about it for a moment, the president replied, "I don't think he ever got it in his head that I'm the boss."

"He thinks you're both still colleagues back in the Senate."

"Yes. You've seen it before?"

"Many times. It's strange that it always seems to be that position more than the others."

"Secretary of state?"

"Yes. For some reason they tend to think of themselves as the most important person in each administration."

"I should have known better. Charles has always fancied himself as American royalty. When I won the election, I owed him. He had raised a lot of money for the campaign, and I knew he would be an easy confirmation. He was my first nominee, and I wanted to get it right."

"You're not the first, sir."

"And I'm sure I won't be the last."

"No, you won't."

"What have you found out?" asked the president.

Stansfield had thought this next part through and was determined to get his way. He had the gift of all great tacticians. He could focus on the smallest detail and never lose sight of the overall picture. Over the last few days, he had seen a pattern developing. Like reconnaissance photos before a battle, he was beginning to see what the enemies' objectives were.

"Sir, I have decided that for your own good, I am going to keep you in the dark about what I know so far and what I think is going to happen over the next week or so."

President Hayes looked miffed. "I'm not so sure I like that idea."

"I knew you wouldn't, sir, but it's for your own

good. If things go wrong, I want you to have complete deniability."

"I'm afraid that will be impossible."

"No it won't, sir. You will be able to blame the whole thing on me. I will have the documents prepared, and I will leave them in Irene's care."

President Hayes was more than surprised. After staring at Stansfield for a while, he asked, "Why would you do that?"

"I am about to die, sir. It was I who counseled you to use the third option, and it is I who will take the blame if things don't work out."

"I'm not so sure about this, Thomas."

"I am, sir. I think things are going to get very ugly."

"How ugly?"

Stansfield thought about his answer for a second. "Mitch has made some progress in finding who it was that set him up in Germany."

"And?"

"And I've given him orders to follow that trail as high as it goes."

The president cleared his throat. "What are his orders once he finds them?"

"Deniability, Mr. President. You don't want me to answer that."

Hayes leaned forward and in a whisper said, "Thomas, if this thing ends up at the feet of Charles Midleton, you can't just simply have Rapp kill him."

"Sir, it is my sincere hope that this trail does not go that far."

★　★　★

NINE BLOCKS AWAY from the White House, a taxi pulled into the drive of the Four Seasons Hotel on Pennsylvania Avenue and 28th Street. A doorman dressed in black from head to toe opened the back door of the cab and extended a gloved white hand for the passenger. A woman with shimmering auburn hair emerged from the cab, and heads turned. It was difficult for Donatella Rahn to hide her beauty. She was wearing a simple black Armani pants suit. Nothing fancy, nothing too sexy; it was perfect for thirteen and a half hours of transatlantic travel. Donatella had left Milan shortly after noon. The eight-hour flight to New York's JFK landed at 2:34 in the afternoon, local time. It took about an hour to clear customs and then another hour to get into the city. Donatella stopped in Manhattan just long enough to say hello to a few of her fashion contacts and grab some things, and then it was off to Penn Station. It was 8:30 in the evening by the time her train pulled into Union Station just two long blocks north of the United States Capitol.

Donatella was tired, but she could handle it. She'd been through a hell of a lot in her life. She didn't let simple things like fatigue get to her. She walked casually across the expansive lobby of the Four Seasons Hotel and ignored the looks she was receiving from men and women alike. She had stopped noticing them years ago. She approached the front desk, where an Asian woman was standing ready to punch the new arrival's information into the hotel's computer.

"Hello." Donatella spoke perfect English.

"Good evening, ma'am. Are you checking in?"

"Yes. The name is Mary Jones." Donatella extracted a credit card from her purse and slid it across the counter. She also had a California driver's license with the same name. She had picked them up in Manhattan at a safe deposit box she kept.

"You'll be with us for four nights, Ms. Jones."

"That's right." Donatella signed the charge slip with her own pen and took the room key. The woman pointed to the elevators and informed the guest that a bellhop would be up with her luggage in a moment. Donatella thanked the woman and took the elevator to the fifth floor. Once in her room, she grabbed a sunglasses case from her purse and opened it. Inside was a small countermeasure device designed to detect RF transmitters, tape recorders, and AC line carrier transmitters. Donatella swept the entire room. She didn't bother checking the phone, though. She would not be using it.

When the bellhop arrived, she gave him a five-dollar bill and then locked and chained the door. The clock next to the king-size bed told her it was 9:41, which meant it was almost three in the morning in Milan. Sleep would have to wait. Donatella took off her Armani suit and hung it in the closet. From her suitcase, she grabbed a pair of jeans, brown boots, and a large wool sweater. She dressed quickly and put a faded red Eddie Bauer baseball cap on her head, pulling her ponytail out the back. From her purse, she grabbed a pair of small binoculars, her StarTAC Trimode phone, and her Heckler & Koch HK4 pistol. The compact gun carried eight .32-caliber rounds and was easily concealable under her bulky sweater.

Donatella left the hotel, heading west on M Street for several blocks and then taking a right onto 30th Street. The evening air was chilly but pleasant. It felt great after spending most of the day on a plane and a train. On the flight over from Milan, she had carefully studied the dossier of her target. The choice of the Four Seasons Hotel was an easy one. It was centrally located between the man's home and office. Donatella took her time walking up the steep hill. She was canvassing the neighborhood as she had been taught by the Mossad.

Donatella Rahn was not a very conflicted woman, at least not when compared to the person she had been in her twenties. At thirty-eight, she had learned to let certain things go. The Mossad, however, was a different story. They had turned her into something she had never been and in all likelihood would never have become. The vaunted Israeli intelligence service had turned her into a spy and an assassin, and it had not been of her free will.

As Donatella's modeling career had taken off, so had her drug use. By the age of twenty-one, she was a full-fledged coke fiend. On a modeling job in Tel Aviv, she had been busted trying to bring an ounce of coke into the country. She was in a jail cell, strung-out and freaking out, when a man named Ben Freidman came to her and offered her a way to avoid going to prison. The man told her he would help her kick her drug habit, and after a period of time she could return to Milan. He also assured her that her release had nothing to do with sex.

Not exactly being of sound mind and desperately wanting to avoid jail, Donatella agreed. The next day, she found herself strapped to a bed in a medical facility shaking and sweating from withdrawal. By the time the first week was over, they had helped her shake the habit. It would not be the last time they would do so. They indoctrinated her slowly at first, teaching her information-gathering techniques and then self-defense. She was sent away after that first month feeling grateful and, for the first time in her life, as if she had a real purpose. They had helped her understand her Jewish roots, helped her understand the plight of her people and their need to defend themselves against those who had sworn to rid all Jews from the face of the earth.

This was just the beginning. At first, her assignments were simple, nothing more than observing a certain individual or passing on information as she jetted around the world, but as the years passed, things got more serious. She had four more relapses into drug use, and with each one they drew her in a little more. The training changed. At first, it was done under the guise of self-defense, but it slowly became apparent that something else was going on.

Colonel Ben Freidman of the feared Mossad had become her teacher and her protector. He was one of the two men she had ever met in her life whom she could trust completely. The other hurt too much to think about.

Donatella had to be honest with herself, though. From the beginning, she had enjoyed it immensely. The thrill of stalking another human being and killing them was like nothing she had ever experienced. It was better than any drug, even better than sex. Donatella Rahn had an addictive personality, and she couldn't stop. She enjoyed her work, and she was paid extremely well.

As Donatella hiked up the heaved cobblestone sidewalk, she did so knowing who she was. She knew it might seem like a small thing to most people but not to her. She had spent her entire life confused, searching for a father she never knew, and eventually hoping she would never find him. And now, she had finally figured out who she was and where she was headed. To her, that was a very big thing.

THE CROWN VICTORIA rocked gently as it rolled down the old country road in rural Maryland. The familiar landmarks gave Rielly some comfort. They had just spent more than an hour driving all around the city. At one point, Rielly thought she might get carsick. She didn't know her way around the city that well and had been lost five minutes after they'd picked her up. There were a couple of times where she thought things looked familiar, but she couldn't be sure. The experience was very disorienting, and after a while she found it best to sit back, crack her window, and close her eyes.

The two agents seemed competent enough. Special Agent Pelachuk had told her when they got into the car that they were going to have to take some standard precautions to make sure they weren't being followed. Special Agent Salem, the blond one, was doing the driving. He didn't say much. Early on, she had asked them where they were taking her. She was happy to find out that they were going to Mitch's house. Rielly asked if

Mitch was already there, and Pelachuk told her he didn't know.

Rielly grew eager with anticipation as they turned off the country road and onto the street that would take them to Mitch's. There were no streetlights this far from the city. The communities around the Chesapeake Bay had a tendency to want things to stay as they were a hundred years ago. Building permits had to be paraded past one inspector after another, and variances were rarely granted. Something as modern as a street lamp would be a blight on the landscape. Rielly knew this was one of the reasons Mitch had moved this far out. He loved his alone time, and out here he could get it. As Rielly looked out the window, the only things she could make out were the lights of several farmhouses off in the distance.

A few minutes later, the car slowed to ten miles an hour, and the two agents stuck their chins over the dashboard in an effort to find the right address.

From the back seat, Rielly said, "It's the third one on the left." As they got a little closer, she added, "That one right there by the white mailbox."

The car turned and started down the long driveway. Rielly immediately noticed that all the lights were off in the house, and her heart sank. Mitch wasn't there yet. Salem turned the car around, driving on the lawn in the process, and parked in front of the garage facing the street.

Neither agent made an effort to get out of the car, so Rielly asked, "What are we doing?"

"We're waiting," answered Pelachuk.

"For what?"

As innocently as possible, he said, "I don't have a key."

"Well, I do."

Pelachuk looked at his partner. "What do you think?"

"How long are we going to be waiting?"

"I don't know. An hour . . . maybe two."

"I say we wait inside if she has a key."

Pelachuk looked back at Rielly. "Would you like to go inside?"

"Yes." Rielly reached for the door handle.

"Hold on a minute. Let me go check things out first, and then we'll go in." Turning back to his partner, he said, "Anything funny happens, get her out of here and don't worry about me."

Special Agent Pelachuk got out of the sedan and closed the door. Standing next to the car, in plain view of Rielly, he drew his weapon and disappeared around the side of the house. When he reached the deck in back, he looked down at the dock briefly and then put his gun away. The man knew no one was there. They'd had the house under surveillance since Monday. Grabbing his digital phone, he punched in a number and held the tiny encrypted phone to his ear.

After three rings, a voice said, "Hello."

"We have the girl, and we're at the rendezvous point."

"Does she suspect anything?"

"No. She even offered to let us in. Just like you thought."

"Good. Don't touch anything when you get inside.

We have no idea what kind of surprises he might have."

"All right. Anything else?"

"What are you doing about her phone?"

"We're jamming it from the mobile unit in the trunk."

"Good. Keep me informed if anything changes."

"All right." The man posing as a federal agent ended the call and put the phone away. After they took care of this reporter, and whoever her boyfriend was, he would have to convince the Professor to let him go after Gus Villaume again. Jeff Duser looked out at the blackness on the other side of the deck railing and thought about how profitable things had gotten since they started working for the Professor. He decided he would kill Villaume for free. It would be fun.

33

Peter Cameron was sitting on the long brown leather couch in Senator Clark's study. He closed his flip phone and set it on the coffee table in front of him. With a huge grin spreading across his bearded face, he leaned back and clasped his hands behind his head. "They have Rielly, and she suspects nothing."

Clark took a moment to look up and acknowledge Cameron. The senator was sitting at his desk, wearing his reading glasses and a pair of latex gloves. Resting on the surface before him was Anna Rielly's journal. A few days ago, Clark had begun to wonder if divine intervention were responsible for allowing Rapp to escape his executioner in Germany. Now things were falling into place more perfectly than he ever could have dreamed. Far better even than his original plan.

"Are they at Rapp's house?"

"Yes, and she's going to let them in just like you thought."

"Good."

"Are you going to tell me the rest of your plan?"

Clark closed the journal and placed it back in the

bag. He took off the gloves and set them on his desk. With drink in hand, he walked over and sat in the leather chair across from Cameron. "What does Mitch Rapp want more than anything in the world right now?"

"Anna Rielly."

"Wrong. He doesn't know we have her yet."

Cameron thought about the question and shook his head. "I don't know."

Clark pointed at the Professor with his drink. "He wants you, Peter."

Cameron licked his lips. "So what's your plan?"

"It's simple. You are both the bait and the trap. Rapp wants to meet you, right?"

"Yeah, but that's because he wants to get to you."

"That's what he said, but believe me, he wants to kill you as bad as or worse than me."

"That's only because he doesn't know who you are. If he knew it was you . . . Senator . . . the chairman of the Senate Intelligence Committee . . ." Cameron rolled his eyes. "You'd be at the top of his list."

"He's never going to find out that I am behind all of this, is he, Peter?"

"No . . . no, sir, he isn't."

"And why not?"

Cameron wasn't sure how to answer the question. "Ah . . . because I'd never tell him."

"And because you're going to kill him, Peter. You are going to use yourself as bait, and you are going to, as deftly as possible, get him to meet you at his house. If you can do that tonight, it would be perfect, but if come tomorrow morning he isn't responding, I want you to use the girl. Tell him he has thirty minutes to meet you at his house, and if he doesn't come alone, the girl dies." Clark looked at Cameron sternly. "Under no circumstances are you to set foot in that house. I don't want you anywhere near it. Let Duser and his men handle it. I want them to make it look like Rapp killed Rielly and then blew his own brains out. A murder-suicide."

Clark raised his glass and took a drink. The plan was perfect. NBC's White House correspondent found dead in the home of suspected CIA operative. The investigations would start in both the House and the Senate. Clark would take the high road and remain dignified during the televised hearings, and then, when the timing was absolutely perfect, he would produce Rielly's doctored journal. The journal would be filled with facts that would bring President Hayes to his knees and disgrace the Democratic Party. By the time the next election rolled around, Senator Hank Clark would be the GOP's lead horse. The plan was perfect.

THEY HAD GATHERED in Stansfield's study. It was a quarter past ten in the evening. The director had just returned from the White House and looked tired. At Rapp's urging, Stansfield had requested extra protection. No one in the CIA's Office of Security had asked any questions. They didn't even bat an eye at the request. They were used to such things. Within thirty minutes of Stansfield making the call, a mobile command post and a Chevy Suburban arrived at the director's house. The mobile command post came with two men to monitor the CP's communication and surveillance equipment and two more heavily armed men to provide security. The Suburban had brought two German shepherds. The dogs and their machine-gun-toting handlers now patrolled the perimeter.

Inside the study, seated around the fireplace, were Rapp, Coleman, Kennedy, and Stansfield. Rapp looked at Stansfield and said, "I think it's someone at the State Department."

"It could be, but I'm not so sure." Stansfield was speaking with a slight lisp. He was back on the morphine.

"Secretary Midleton has never been a big fan of the Agency," added Kennedy.

Stansfield looked over at Coleman. "What do you think, Scott?"

The former Navy SEAL thought it over and then said, "We don't have enough information."

"We rarely do in this business," said Rapp.

"I've gone back and looked at the map of that area where the cell tower is located." Coleman shook his head. "The State Department isn't the only organization around there that has a beef with the CIA."

"True, but they are the strongest candidate," Stansfield said.

"We need to find out who this Professor is." Coleman looked from Stansfield to Rapp. "He is the key to this whole thing."

"I agree, but he's not answering his phone, and right now that's the only link we have to him."

"How is Marcus coming along with the search

through the State Department files?" Kennedy asked.

"We looked at photos for almost three hours tonight," said Coleman. "And we came up blank. When we're finished here, I'm going to go back to look at more."

"This is the key," said Stansfield. "You have to keep looking for this Professor. He has to have a past. People don't just fall into this line of work with no prior experience." Everyone nodded in agreement.

"What about Secretary Midleton?" asked Rapp. "From the get-go, he was sticking his nose in this thing." Rapp looked at Kennedy. "He called you the very next day after I hit Hagenmiller and wanted to know if the CIA had any involvement. Isn't that jumping the gun just a bit?"

"That's why I don't think it's him," Stansfield said.

"Why?"

"Because it's too obvious. Charles Midleton is a very subtle person. If he knew the real facts behind what had happened in Germany, he would not have been so eager to call Irene."

"I don't know. There's something about the man I don't trust."

A rare smile creased Stansfield's face. It must have been the morphine. "Mitchell, how many people *do* you trust?"

Rapp smiled. "Not many."

"Exactly. That is why you are still alive, despite multiple attempts on your life." Stansfield paused for a moment, then looked at Coleman and back to Rapp. "I want you two to do whatever it takes to find out who this Professor is, and then you must take him alive. If need be, we'll have Dr. Hornig go to work on him."

Rapp grimaced at the thought of getting Dr. Hornig involved. The woman was a complete sadist, skilled in the art of physical and mental torture. "You're setting no boundaries for us."

"There are always boundaries, Mitchell. Just use your best judgment, get results, and don't get caught."

"I might have to turn Marcus loose inside the NSA's computer system." Rapp checked to see how Kennedy was reacting to this piece of news.

Kennedy looked less than pleased, but before she could respond, Stansfield said, "Just make sure he doesn't get caught. There is more at stake here than I fear any of you realize. No offense, Mitchell, but you were not their end game. Whoever is behind all of this has much bigger plans."

"What do you think they're after?"

Stansfield looked into the fire. "I'm not sure yet, but I'm beginning to see a few things . . . a few possibilities." Looking back to Rapp, he said, "You two need to get moving, but before you go, there is one more thing we need to discuss. I want both of you to go pay Congressman O'Rourke a visit. It appears that you sent him an e-mail, Mitchell, that has him a little upset." Stansfield looked at Kennedy.

The director of the Counterterrorism Center turned to Rapp. "Why didn't you tell me about the e-mail?"

Rapp shrugged. "I didn't think it was important."

"Congressman O'Rourke is very important to me," Stansfield said. "And it is my hope that in my absence, he will be very useful to Irene."

"I don't see what the problem is."

"Like all of us," started Kennedy, "he doesn't like too many people knowing certain things about his past. He came to my office today, very upset. He wanted to know who you were and how you knew about the relationship among himself, his grandfather, and Scott."

"That e-mail might not have been the best idea, but at the time I didn't know what I was up against. I wanted him to take me seriously and keep his mouth shut."

"Well, you don't know Congressman O'Rourke very well," Kennedy stated evenly. "I think I repaired the damage that you caused, but I want both of you to go over to his house and explain to him that his secret is safe."

"When do you want us to take care of it?"

"Tonight. The sooner you can calm him down, the better. Call him first, and see if you can stop by on your way back into the city."

34

They began cruising the Georgetown neighborhood at 10:56 P.M., the standard routine. Starting four blocks out, they worked their way toward the O'Rourkes' house in a box pattern. Coleman was driving his Ford Explorer and was responsible for the left side while Rapp checked the right. They noted several vans parked within the four-block perimeter, but that was it. No individuals sitting behind the wheel of a parked sedan. Rapp felt confident enough to make the call. Besides, any idiot who tried to take on Coleman and him would be in for a very short fight.

Rapp wasn't overly concerned about his diplomatic mission to appease Congressman O'Rourke. Yes, it was a good idea to calm the man down before he started asking too many questions, but Rapp was confident that O'Rourke would have never gone that far. Rapp liked Michael O'Rourke. He was a good man and a good husband. With hindsight, Rapp had to admit it might not have been fair to get him involved in this mess, but no harm, no foul.

Rapp would have liked to put the meeting off until morning, but the truth was, it gave him an excuse to see

Anna. His stomach was doing flips over the thought of holding her. He had never felt like this in his entire life. Rapp grabbed his phone and dialed the O'Rourkes' number. After just one ring, Michael answered.

"Michael, it's me. I'm sorry I'm calling so late, but I need to talk to you."

"I'm listening." The voice was detached and cool.

"Not on the phone."

"When?"

"Right now. I'm only seconds away. It won't take long. I just have to explain a couple of things to you."

"All right, but be quiet. Liz is asleep."

A minute later, Coleman backed the Explorer into the brownstone's small driveway. Michael O'Rourke was waiting for them at the door with his yellow Lab at his side. Rapp and Coleman bounded up the steps, both men checking the street as they went. They quickly ducked inside the house. O'Rourke held his index finger to his lips and then closed and locked the door. He gestured for the men to follow, and they went down the hall to the kitchen.

Rapp went straight to the back door and pulled back the curtain. After he was satisfied that no one was in the backyard, he sat at the kitchen table. Duke immediately came up and dropped his snout on Rapp's knee. The two had met before, and Duke liked him. O'Rourke asked if they wanted anything to drink. Both men declined. O'Rourke grabbed a beer from the fridge and twisted off the top. He chose to remain standing at the kitchen counter.

"I'm sorry about the e-mail," started Rapp. "I didn't

do it in an effort to blackmail you, I did it so you would take me seriously."

O'Rourke studied Rapp. "Who do you work for, Mitch?"

"I didn't come here to get into all of that, Michael. I came here to tell you that your secret is safe with me. There is no reason I would tell anybody about your grandfather and Scott."

O'Rourke looked over at Coleman and shook his head. "Well, I'll tell you what, your secret is safe with me, too. So fill in the blanks for me, and we'll be even."

"Michael, I'm not going to tell you what I do. Just trust me on this one. Your wife and the woman I'm going to marry are best friends. I like you, I like Liz, there is no reason in the world for me to do anything that would harm you or your family."

He took another drink of beer and seemed to think long and hard about what Rapp had said. "You know, I like you, too, Mitch, but I'll be honest. If you're involved in the type of stuff that I think you might be, I'm not exactly crazy about having you around my family."

The words hurt. Rapp didn't let it show, but they hurt. He didn't want this life anymore. He wanted out. He wanted a normal life with a wife and some kids. "I respect that, and if you don't want me around, I'll do my best to stay away. Just know that your secret will always be safe with me."

"If you really mean that, then tell me who you work for."

"Michael, you are a congressman. There are certain things you don't want to know."

"Try me." O'Rourke folded his arms across his chest. "I did a little digging into your past. There is no record of you serving in the armed forces, yet something tells me you have formal paramilitary training."

"How is this information going to help you?"

"I want to know who I'm dealing with. Don't worry about the committee. I'd just as soon stick a hot poker up my ass than tell Rudin something like this."

The comment brought a smile to Rapp's face. "All right, Michael, I'll tell you what I do, but it goes no further. Not even Liz. I've known about your grandfather and Scott for some time, and I've never breathed a word of it to Anna."

"Whatever you say is between us and no one else."

Rapp tried to think of the best way to say it, and in the process he was reminded of something he'd said to the previous attorney general. It was at a meeting during the White House hostage crisis. Rapp had overstepped his bounds and allowed his temper to get the best of him. But it was worth it. In the end, he got his way, and a terrorist he had hunted for the better part of a decade was dead.

Rapp looked at Coleman briefly and then said, "I work for no government agency. I want to be very clear about that. I'm what you might call a counterterrorism specialist."

"Okay . . . and what, may I ask, does a counterterrorism specialist do?"

Rapp was not well versed in trying to spin what he did, so he just blurted out the hard, cold truth. "I kill terrorists."

"Say again?"

"I hunt them down, and I kill them."

The congressman set his beer down. He was expecting something along this line, but he didn't expect to hear it in such a blunt way. After he had rebounded from Rapp's confession, something fell into place for O'Rourke. "Is that how you met Anna? During the hostage crisis?"

"Yep."

"Were you involved in the takedown?"

"Yep."

Coleman laughed. "Shit, he *was* the takedown."

"What do you mean?" asked O'Rourke.

"He means we'll have to tell you that story a different time." Rapp looked at Coleman and shook his head. Then, standing, he approached O'Rourke and stuck out his hand. "Michael, I'm sorry about all of this. Maybe someday after you leave office, I can tell you more, but until then, I'm sorry."

O'Rourke took his hand and looked into Rapp's eyes, not sure what to make of the whole thing. "I'd like that."

"Just remember we're on the same team."

"Yeah."

Coleman looked at his watch and said, "Hurry up and kiss your girlfriend. We have to get back to the ranch and check on the boys."

Rapp grinned with a mix of embarrassment and anticipation. "Where's Anna, upstairs?"

"No." O'Rourke shook his head. "She called just after eight and told Liz she was going to meet you. I thought that was why you were here. I thought she made you come over."

35

Peter Cameron flew down Maryland Highway 214 in his silver metallic Lexus coupe with Rimsky-Korsakov's *Scheherazade* blaring out of the car's seven speakers. He had bought the car under one of his assumed names. Cameron was in the process of disobeying Senator Clark's orders. He simply could not resist going to the house. It was too tempting. The home of Mitch Rapp. He had to see what it was like. He had to be involved in the hit. Senator Clark would not be happy, but if Cameron was careful, his boss would never know. He had called ahead and warned Duser of his arrival. The last thing he needed right now was the former Marine or one of his trigger-happy cronies shooting him by mistake. That was the other reason he needed to visit the house. If this plan was going to work, he couldn't have those clowns showering the target with bullets.

As Cameron turned off of 214, he looked at his mobile phone and wondered when Rapp would call again. Rapp had called every hour since they had talked this afternoon, and he had intentionally neglected to answer the phone. The last call had been around nine P.M., almost two hours ago. Cameron hadn't thought of this, but if Rapp didn't call back, they would have a problem. He decided not to worry about it. Rapp would call him again. If not tonight, he would do it in the morning.

He ran his car through its paces as he zipped down the dark country road. The senator's plan was great, but there were some areas where it needed work. Multiple contingencies had to be put into place in case something went wrong, and the odds were good that something would. Cameron had envisioned for months finding Rapp's head perfectly centered in the crosshairs of one of his high-powered rifle scopes. That dream had been destroyed by the senator. Clark didn't give him any specifics beyond ruling out a long-distance shot, only that he was adamant that it must look like a murder-suicide. The girl would be easy, but Rapp might pose a problem. He was not a man to be underestimated, and the trick here would be to get close enough to shoot him in the head. With the way forensic science was today, they would have to be very careful how they left the crime scene.

They would have to keep the girl alive and take Rapp first. Cameron had decided on the weapon. He would use a .22-caliber pistol. That way, there would be no exit wound and no blood splatter. They would get Rapp to enter the house alone, hold the girl at gunpoint, and shoot him in the side of the head before he had a chance to do anything. Then they would shoot the girl with the same gun and leave. An anonymous call would be made to the local sheriff and then several more to the TV stations just to make sure the CIA didn't try to cover it up.

Cameron knew there was one weakness in his plan. It was not going to be easy to get close enough to Rapp to kill him, and do it with only one shot. That would have to be his responsibility. He would have to stay cool right up until the last moment.

Cameron pulled into Rapp's driveway and parked in front of a sedan. One of Duser's men was standing on the small front porch. Cameron approached the man and told him to go get his boss. The sky was still overcast, the moon nowhere in sight. Duser came outside a minute later and offered Cameron a cigarette. He declined and watched Duser light up.

"How is she?"

Duser pulled the cigarette from his mouth. "She's all right. A little nervous, but nothing I wouldn't expect."

"What's she doing?"

"Watching the nightly news."

"Did you disable her cell phone?"

"Yep." Duser took another drag from his cigarette. "What's the skinny on her boyfriend?"

"What do you mean?"

"What's his story? Is there anything I should know about him?"

Cameron looked out across the lawn. The neighbors were about fifty feet away on both sides, and there was a lot of vegetation dividing the property lines. "There's a chance he might be armed, but I wouldn't worry. He won't do anything as long as we have the girl."

"You sure?"

"How many men do you have?"

"Six, counting me."

Cameron smiled. "He's no match for you and your boys." Duser was cocky and more than willing to believe the shit Cameron was shoveling at him. After checking his watch, Cameron said, "It's getting late. I doubt it's going to happen tonight. I want to talk to her, and then I should head back into town and grab a few things."

"Why don't we just tie her up and wait for him to show?"

"I don't want to leave any marks on her unless we have to." Cameron opened the door and walked into the house. Two of Duser's bruisers were sitting at the kitchen table playing cards. Their suit coats were off, and their weapons were clearly visible in their shoulder holsters. Cameron nodded to the two men and continued into the living area.

"Hello, Ms. Rielly, my name is Barry Lenzner." Cameron stuck out his hand.

Rielly was sitting in the oversized chair with her legs crossed. She grabbed the stranger's hand and said, "Hello."

Cameron sat on the couch. The first thing he noticed about Rielly was her stunning green eyes. "I work for the Agency." He gestured to the men in the kitchen. "I hope none of this has alarmed you?"

"No . . . not too much." Rielly brushed some of her hair back behind her ears.

"Good, because I don't want you to get upset over nothing. There is a small chance Mitch might make it by tonight, but I doubt it." Cameron saw the look of despair on Rielly's face. "Don't worry. Nothing bad has happened. It's just that a few things came up."

"What?"

With a grin, Cameron said, "You know I can't get into that, Ms. Rielly."

"I know what Mitch does for a living."

"I know that you know certain things, probably far more than you should, but it's not my place to discuss these issues with you. Mitch is in the middle of something very important, something with huge national security implications."

"Is he safe?"

"Yes, he's safe." Cameron smiled. "It's the other guys I'd worry about."

"What other guys?"

"The bad guys."

"Oh."

"Listen, I don't want you to worry. I'm pretty sure Mitch will be here in the morning. If you want, we can take you back into the city and then bring you back out here bright and early, or you can spend the night here. We will, of course, stay out of your way."

"Is there a chance he still might come tonight?"

"Yeah, but I don't want to get your hopes up."

"Then I'll stay here."

"Okay." One of Cameron's phones started to ring. He looked to see which one it was and said, "If you'll excuse me, I need to get this."

WITHIN SECONDS OF the words leaving Michael O'Rourke's lips, Rapp knew Anna was in trouble. He asked O'Rourke if he was sure Anna had told Liz she was going to meet him. O'Rourke said he was sitting right next to his wife when she took the call. Rapp was tempted to go upstairs and wake Liz, but after weighing what could be learned, he thought better of it. The last thing he needed right now was an emotional pregnant reporter on his hands. Rapp tried Rielly's apartment first. The answering machine picked up after four rings, and he hung up. When he tried her cell phone, a recorded voice told him the customer he was trying to reach was not available. Anna always answered her cell phone unless she was on the air. Something was wrong. Rapp strained to remain calm in front of O'Rourke. The ante had just been upped, and whoever these fuckers were, they were going to pay.

Before leaving, Rapp told O'Rourke not to say a word to his wife. O'Rourke was a bit reluctant at first until Rapp assured him that he could do a better job of finding Anna than the feds. Rapp promised to call, and then he and Coleman disappeared into the night.

He gave Coleman the address for Anna's apartment and told him to step on it. On the way, he dialed Stansfield's secure home number. When Kennedy answered, Rapp asked, "How's he doing?"

"He's asleep."

"I think they have Anna."

There was a moment of silence and then, "Are you sure?"

"Unfortunately, yes."

"What do you want me to do?"

"I want you to get a team over to Anna's apartment right now." Rapp gave her the address. "We should be there in two minutes."

"What else?"

"Put one of the SOG teams on alert. I might need them for backup."

Kennedy was wondering how to handle the request for one of Langley's Special Operations groups. They were the CIA's equivalent of a SWAT team. She had the authority to make the request, but it would probably be better if Stansfield did it.

"I'll take care of it. Anything else?"

"This changes everything."

Kennedy didn't like the detached calmness she heard in his voice. "How so?"

"I don't care how high this goes, I'm going to kill every last one of them." Rapp ended the call and stared out the window as the truck raced up Wisconsin Avenue.

THEY CIRCLED THE apartment building twice, checking for surveillance, and then parked in front of a fire hydrant. Rapp and Coleman entered the building with their heads down, not wanting to give the surveillance camera a shot of their faces. Rapp used his set of keys to gain access. Once in the stairwell, they both drew their weapons and attached silencers. Rapp was carrying a 9-mm Beretta and Coleman a H&K USP .45 ACP. He took ten seconds to give Coleman the basic layout of the apartment. Coleman was used to working in pairs. It was a cornerstone of SEAL training. Rapp, on the other hand, was a lone wolf. Coleman took a couple of seconds to make sure they were on the same page, and then they started up the stairs.

When they reached the fourth floor, Rapp gave the hallway a quick check and then left the stairwell. They were not pausing for anything. If someone was waiting for them, the best way to handle it was to move fast and hit hard. Rapp took up a position on the right side of Rielly's door and Coleman on the left. Rapp quietly inserted the key and opened the door. Coleman entered the apartment right on Rapp's heels. He closed and locked the door behind them. They checked the front hall closet first and then the kitchen and the living room. Neither man spoke. They moved from room to room, Rapp taking the lead, Coleman watching his back. Every door was opened and then closed. In less than thirty seconds, they had checked the entire place. Thirty seconds after that, they found the first listening device. They left it undisturbed and retreated from the apartment, leaving the door unlocked.

Back in the truck, Rapp called Kennedy.

"The apartment was wired. Put your best people on it. Tell them to find the transponder and sit on it. If someone shows up to check on it, I want them followed. We're on our way to Marcus's. I'll call you when we get there."

Coleman gunned the engine as they turned off New Mexico and onto Nebraska. Two blocks to the northeast, they hit a traffic circle. Coleman took it two-thirds of the way around and shot onto Massachusetts Avenue. As they cut through the swank Spring Valley neighborhood, Coleman asked, "What's our next move?"

Rapp couldn't get the bad images out of his mind. He could tolerate astronomical amounts of pain. He'd been shot and stabbed, he'd broken a dozen bones and pushed his body to the point where the only thing that kept him going was the will to live, but this was different. He was close to crying. The idea of someone hurting Anna was the most agonizing thing he had ever felt. Rapp shook the images from his mind and turned to look out his window. He wiped some of the moisture from his eyes. He didn't want Coleman to see him like this. "We'll find out if Marcus has made any progress, and then we'll try the Professor again."

36

Rapp had regained his composure by the time they reached Dumond's. Kennedy had already called Dumond and told him that Rielly had been taken. Dumond, never quite knowing how to deal with Rapp, decided not to attempt any words of comfort. Instead, he explained how the search for the Professor was going. Unfortunately, it wasn't going so well. Coleman's two men, Kevin Hackett and Dan Stroble, had been looking over thousands of photos of current and former State Department employees, and they had yet to come up with a solid match.

This was not what Rapp wanted to hear, and he could barely contain his anger. Dumond, however, had an idea that he thought might help. "When was the last time you tried this guy?"

"Around nine this evening."

"And he hasn't answered since the first time you talked?"

"Yep."

"Well, he's going to have to, isn't he?"

"Why?"

"If he's the one who took Anna, he's going to want to talk to you."

"Yeah, you're right, but I don't see where you're going with this."

"Well, he has no way of getting ahold of you. You never left him a number."

"And?"

"He's waiting for you to call him."

Rapp was a little irritated with Dumond for stating the obvious. "That's what I'm planning on doing once you have everything set to track the call."

Dumond held up a finger. "I have a plan. I have a Smart Van on the way over. Irene authorized it." Dumond was referring to a fourth-generation mobile digital surveillance unit that was made by Audio Intelligence Devices, a division of Westinghouse. The CIA's Science and Technology directorate customized the vehicles upon delivery.

"Marcus, you know how I hate all of this technical shit, so just give it to me in a language I can understand."

Dumond started and stopped himself twice as he tried to state in the simplest terms what he wanted to do. Finally, he said, "If we have the van in the right position prior to the call, and you keep him on the phone long enough, I think I can track him."

"You're sure?"

"No, I'm not sure, but if we get lucky and are in the right neighborhood when he takes the call, I can at the very least get us to within a few blocks." Dumond cautioned, "That's assuming he's stationary."

"How long until we can make the call?"

"The van should be here within five minutes." Dumond pointed to a map on the kitchen counter. As he walked over to it, he said, "We really don't have any hits on his cell phone at this time of the day, so I can't guarantee we'll be in the right area when he takes the call."

"What are you talking about, Marcus?" Rapp's voice was tinged with irritation.

"I pulled up his cell tower usage for the last three months and plotted it on the map. These bright yellow pieces of paper mark the top ten towers he has most frequently used." Dumond grabbed a piece of paper lying on the map. "This lists the calls, what time of the day they were made, for how long, and what tower they were routed through."

"Get to the point, Marcus."

"The point is, I don't have him making too many calls after eleven in the evening, so it's going to be hard to predict what area of town he'll be in."

"Shit."

"In the morning we'll have a better chance."

Coleman placed his hand on Rapp's shoulder and nodded toward Dumond's bedroom. Rapp followed him into the room and closed the door.

"What's up?"

"Are you sure you're up for this?" asked Coleman.

"What kind of a question is that?"

"It's a damn good one."

"Have you ever known me not to be up for something?"

"I've never seen you in love."

"What in the hell does that have to do with this?" snapped Rapp.

"It has everything to do with this. They have Anna, and it's affecting your judgment. You're too emotional."

"Don't worry about me, Scott."

"I am going to worry about you. You're out there snapping at Marcus like he's your little brother."

"He is like a little brother to me."

Coleman took a step back. "This isn't good, man."

"What isn't good?"

"I'm telling you, you're too emotional. I think you should turn this over to someone else."

"Who? The fucking feds? Yeah . . . let's get the HRT in here. That would go over really well, right up to the point where Anna gets killed and they start asking who I am."

"I'm not talking about the feds, Mitch. Just calm down for a second. You need to know when to let go. This thing is going to get worse before it gets better, and you can't let your emotions get in the way of making the right call."

Rapp was going to argue but thought better of it. "If at any time you think I'm blowing this thing, you let me know. I respect your judgment, and I'll listen." He paused for a second and added, "With one exception. Every last one of these motherfuckers is dead, and don't try to talk me out of it."

THE CATERING VAN pulled up in front of Marcus Dumond's four-plex. It was white with a large black chef's hat on both sides and the back cargo doors. Above the hat was the name of a catering outfit, Kip's, and beneath it was a phone number. The catering outfit was legitimate, run by a former Agency employee and his wife. The Agency had arranged some very favorable financing for the couple, and in return they had a legitimate cover for some of their surveillance vans.

Dumond climbed into the back of the van with two laptops and a bag of equipment. Rapp and Coleman joined him in the van, and Kevin Hackett and Dan Stroble followed in Coleman's Explorer. Dumond told the driver to take them to Washington Circle and closed the door. Dumond went to work immediately, getting his laptops set up and bringing the rest of the equipment on-line. One side of the van contained three pizza racks stuffed with high-tech surveillance equipment. In the middle were two color active-matrix flat panel displays. The top one was touch-sensitive and used to control a vast array of technology, and the bottom one was for video feed. Dumond sat in a captain's chair that was bolted to the floor. There was a small space under the monitors for Dumond's legs. Rapp and Coleman watched him work from a bench seat in the back.

It took almost fifteen minutes for them to reach Washington Circle. There was a luggage rack on the roof of the van. It was never used. Instead, it housed a myriad of antennas, video cameras, directional microphones, and a direction finder. After Dumond had hacked his way into the Sprint network, he got the direction finder ready and told Rapp it was a go.

Rapp and Coleman had been discussing how to

handle the call. They both agreed that, to start with, it was best if Rapp acted as if he knew nothing about Rielly's disappearance.

Dumond had rigged the cell phone so both he and Coleman could listen in on the call. He was also recording the conversation on a DAT. Rapp punched in the number and counted the rings. When he hit four, his heart sank for fear that the call would once again go unanswered, but then, after the sixth ring, someone picked up. Rapp said, "Professor, how are you doing?"

PETER CAMERON HAD left Rielly sitting in the living room and walked toward the front of the house when his phone started ringing. When he reached the foyer, he answered it and heard the familiar voice of Mitch Rapp. Cameron left the house and went to stand in the driveway next to his car. He didn't want Duser or his men to hear him talking.

"I'm sorry I haven't taken your calls, but a few things came up."

"Like what?"

"I'd rather not talk about it over the phone."

"Does that mean you'd like to meet in person?"

"Maybe." Cameron hesitated. "If you can guarantee my safety."

"That all depends on what you have to tell me."

"Listen, when I was hired to do this, I had no idea who you were, and if I had, I would have never taken the job."

"That makes me feel much better," Rapp responded with sarcasm. "Who hired you?"

"I don't want to talk about it over the phone."

"Then let's meet."

Cameron leaned against his passenger door. "I would, but something tells me I might not leave that meeting alive."

"That depends on what you have for me and how honest you are."

"What I have for you is big! Really big! But you need to give me some assurances."

"Like what?"

"That I'll live, and you'll leave me alone. That no one from the Agency ever knows who I am."

"That might be a tough one."

"Then you can forget it. I'll just disappear and take my chances that you'll never be able to track me down."

"If I were you, I wouldn't feel so confident about that."

Cameron looked up at the night sky and grinned. *If only this fool knew who he was dealing with.* "Listen, can't you see the position I'm in? I want some guarantees from you, or I'm better off on the run."

There was a long pause, and then Rapp said, "All right, what is it that you need?"

"First thing . . . I meet you and only you. If I see anyone else around, I'm outta here. Second, I want your word that you will never reveal to anyone who I am."

"That's going to depend on how good your info is."

"It's good. It's going to blow you away."

"Give me a hint."

"The person who hired me is someone big here in town. Someone you'd never suspect."

"If he's as big as you say he is, I'll get you a new name and a new face."

"I can take care of that on my own. I just want your word that you'll keep my identity to yourself and you won't try to kill me."

"You have my word."

Cameron checked his watch. He'd been on the line long enough. "Give me a number where I can reach you."

Rapp hesitated for a second and then gave him the number to his mobile phone. "When are we going to meet?"

"Tomorrow morning around sunup. I'll call and give you instructions. I'm going to run you through some paces, and if I see anyone following you, I'm gone." Cameron pressed the red button on his phone and laughed. It was too easy. Rapp was going to walk right into the trap. The man had no idea they had Rielly.

THE VAN WAS stopped. They had pulled over on 23rd Street between the State Department and the Navy Bureau of Medicine. Dumond worked the keyboard of the laptop on his right while Rapp and Coleman watched. After a few seconds, the boyish Dumond looked at Rapp and said, "We weren't even close."

"What do you mean?"

"He's not even in the city. Hell, he's not even in the county."

"Where is he?"

"He's out by the bay. South of Annapolis."

Rapp jumped up from the bench seat and looked over Dumond's shoulder. "Show me where the tower is."

Dumond pointed to the screen. "Right here. By Mount Zion."

Rapp squinted at the screen, trying to decide if this was a coincidence or not. Keeping his eyes on the map, Rapp asked, "You said you've got a log of calls he made for the last four months."

"Yep."

"Has he ever used this tower before?"

Dumond grabbed the printout and flipped through the pages. It took him twenty seconds to scan the entire list. When he was done, he looked up at Rapp and said, "This is the first time this tower has handled a call for him."

Noticing that something was bothering Rapp, Coleman asked, "What are you seeing that I'm not?"

"My house is about two miles from there." Rapp pointed to the screen.

"Hmmm." Coleman scratched his chin and looked at the map. "They could have taken Anna to a safe house out there."

"Yeah, they could have." Rapp opened the small door leading to the driver and said, "Take us out to two-fourteen. Let me know as soon as we cross three-oh-one." Rapp closed the door and looked at Coleman. "Tell the boys we're going out to Maryland." He quickly punched Stansfield's number into his phone. When Kennedy answered, he said, "How quickly can you get a surveillance chopper to take a look at my house?"

"I can scramble one out of Andrews. I'd say they could be there within ten or twenty minutes."

"Good. Get them airborne on the double."

"Mitch, what's going on?"

"I can't get into it right now. Get the chopper moving, and call me back."

37

The small hangar sat on a secluded portion of the massive Andrews Air Force Base, just south and east of Washington, D.C. It was manned twenty-four hours a day, seven days a week, by a rotating set of pilots, technicians, and mechanics. When the call came in to scramble, the pilots were off the couch and strapped into the cockpit of the advanced Bell 430 helicopter within seconds. With the help of the chopper's Full Authority Digital Electronic Control system, the bird was started and ready for takeoff in thirty seconds. The Bell 430's normal civilian configuration was for two pilots and seven passengers. This bird had room for only four passengers. The rest of the room was taken up by surveillance equipment. A lone technician sat in back to monitor it.

As the four-bladed chopper began to roll away from the hangar, the copilot asked the control tower for permission to take off and gave them his desired heading. The request was granted almost instantly. No flight plan would be filed. No record would be kept of the helicopter's departure.

The pilots were both alumni of the Army's famous

160th Special Operations Aviation Regiment, based out of Fort Campbell, Kentucky. The group was known as the Night Stalkers. Both men had flown together in the dangerous skies over Somalia back in 1993. They considered themselves lucky to be alive. Several of their closest friends didn't make it back from that deployment.

The power was increased to the twin-turbine Allison 250-C40B engines. The helicopter lifted gracefully from the tarmac, its three landing wheels instantly retracting into the smooth underbelly of the machine. Heading due east, to avoid the main north-south runways of the base, the helicopter reached an altitude of three hundred feet and leveled off. They quickly reached a cruising speed of one hundred forty miles an hour on a loose easterly heading. One minute into the flight, the technician in back gave the copilot the exact location of their target. The copilot punched the numbers into his navigational computer, and a second later the computer gave him an ETA of nine minutes and thirty-four seconds.

The fast and quiet helicopter sliced through the cool fall air. Most pilots would be nervous flying at three hundred feet during the day, let alone a dark overcast evening, but these pilots were different. They had been trained by the U.S. Army to fly in the worst weather conditions possible, and in helicopters that were far less responsive than the Bell 430. To them, going from the noisy drab green choppers of the Army to the sleek, shiny, and quiet Bell 430 was like going from a Ford Taurus to a Jaguar.

As they neared the bay and the bright lights of the

city faded behind them, the pilots donned their night-vision goggles in staggered intervals, making sure to give each other time to adjust. They looped in south of the target, turned off their navigation lights, and swung out over the bay to a distance of three miles. Less than twelve minutes had elapsed from the time they had received the phone call to the time they were on station.

The pilots put the bird into a hover fifty feet above the dark water of the Chesapeake, and the technician in back went to work. Using an array of high-resolution and IR thermal imaging cameras, he began to survey the target.

PETER CAMERON WALKED back into the house and sat down on the couch near Rielly. With phone in hand and a genuine grin on his bearded face, he said, "I've got some good news and some bad news. Which one do you want first?"

"The bad."

"Mitch isn't going to make it tonight, but he will be here bright and early in the morning."

"What time?"

"Around seven."

Rielly seemed a little dejected. She picked up the remote control and turned off the TV. It was approaching midnight, and she was tired. "I'm going to bed, then." Rielly stood. "I assume none of your men is upstairs."

"No. They're all down here. You will have complete privacy."

"Thank you." Rielly left the room, and Cameron followed her to the foot of the stairs.

"I'm going to have to leave for a little bit, but I'll be back before you get up."

"All right." Rielly said good night and went upstairs.

Cameron watched her ascend the staircase and admired her figure. Duser approached and did the same. When Rielly closed the door to the bedroom, Duser said, "She's got a nice ass."

Cameron frowned and jerked his head for Duser to follow him. The two men stepped out onto the front porch. In a hushed voice, Cameron said, "Keep your head in the game, and don't even think about touching her."

"Relax. She's going to be dead in the morning. What do you care?"

"Just keep your fucking hands off her, all right? Her boyfriend is going to be out here early, and I need you to concentrate on matters at hand." Pointing to the vehicles in the driveway, he said, "The cars have to be moved."

"Where?"

"I don't know, but they can't be here when he arrives."

Duser nodded. "I'll figure something out. I need to send someone on a coffee and food run."

Cameron wasn't sure what coffee and food had to do with moving the cars, so he ignored the comment and said, "I have to go back into the city to grab a few things. It should only take me a couple hours." He checked his watch. "I'll be back around two. Three at the latest, all right?"

"Yeah."

"If anything unusual happens, call me."

"Will do."

"I HAVE ONE individual. He looks to be standing post at the rear of the house on the bay side."

Rapp, Coleman, and Dumond had all donned headsets equipped with lip mikes. Using the van's secure communications equipment, Dumond had uplinked to a satellite so they could communicate with the chopper and see what they were viewing in real time.

Rapp listened intently as the faceless voice described the situation at his house, the van rocking slightly as they drove east on Highway 214. The lower screen in front of Dumond showed a picture that looked like a film negative—black and white with varying shades of gray in between. The shots were being taken by an IR thermal imaging camera. The picture on the screen changed to one filled with mostly black and areas of red, yellow, white, and blue. Rapp stared at an area he knew to be his kitchen and listened to the technician say, "The curtains are drawn, but I'm getting two . . . maybe three more heat signatures on the inside . . . that's on the first floor of the house . . . and possibly one more upstairs on the second floor."

Rapp lifted his eyes to the area above the kitchen. He eagerly asked, "Can you tell if any of them are female?"

"The guy in back is definitely male. The people inside are sitting down, so I can't tell."

"What about the one upstairs?"

There was about five seconds of silence and then, "It could be male or female, it could be a dog. I can't tell. I'm only getting a small heat signature."

"Are you getting any audio?" asked Rapp.

"A little background noise, but that's it. I think they might have the TV on."

"Can you get me an idea of what's happening on the other side of the house?"

"Affirmative. Give us a minute to relocate."

Rapp pushed the lip mike on his headset up and said to Dumond, "Get Irene on the horn, and tell her to get the Special Operations group airborne and en route to my house immediately." While Dumond was making the call, Rapp looked at Coleman and asked, "What in the hell is going on?"

"It looks like someone is having a party at your house."

Rapp actually smiled. This was good news. He finally had an enemy he could engage. "What do you think the chances are that the Professor is in there?"

"Based on his cell tower usage, I'd say it's a pretty good bet that he's sitting at your kitchen table as we speak."

Rapp looked at his cell phone. "We could confirm that pretty easily."

"How?"

"Call him right now. The bird should be able to pick up the noise of his phone ringing."

Coleman thought about it for a second and said, "Wait until the time is right. Let's get out there and get the SOG in place. We don't want to spook him."

"All right."

"Do you think that's Anna upstairs?"

"I hope so."

The faceless voice came back over their headsets. "We have a couple of cars in the driveway." Rapp, Coleman, and Dumond looked up at the screen and watched. "We also have one individual standing near the front door. He appears to be carrying a weapon. Let me see if I can get a little closer." The picture zoomed in on the warm body standing on the front porch. The man's body was mostly red with a yellow glow around the edges. Near his waist was an elongated area of blue.

Coleman spoke before the technician did. "It looks like a machine pistol with a suppressor attached to the end."

"Either that or an assault rifle." Rapp squinted at the image.

A second red figure appeared on the front porch and then a third. Rapp's immediate fear was that they had somehow sighted the chopper. Using their call sign, Rapp asked, "Libra Three, have you been discovered?"

"That's a negative." It was a different voice this time. "We're two miles out and obscured by a tree line."

One of the men left the porch and walked over to one of the cars. He climbed in, and a moment later the car started moving. The technician announced, "One of the cars is leaving."

"We see it." Rapp flipped up his lip mike, looked at Marcus, and snapped, "Find out where we are, and tell him to step on it!" Pulling the lip mike back down, he asked, "Libra Three, can you keep contact with both targets?"

There was no response at first, and then, "That depends on how big the separation gets between the two."

"Keep an eye on both for as long as you can."

Dumond left the small door to the front of the van open and sat back down at his console. "He said we just passed Queen Anne Road."

"That means we should be at the Muddy Creek exit in five minutes." Looking at Coleman, Rapp pointed behind them with his thumb and said, "Tell the boys to be ready for some action." Rapp watched the screen and listened to the technician call out the car's maneuvers. Rapp's thoughts kept going back to Anna. He was going to have to decide pretty quickly if the chopper was going to keep an eye on the house or follow the car.

Coleman knew what Rapp was thinking and said, "The house isn't going anywhere." Rapp didn't say anything, he just kept staring at the screen. Coleman said, "Did you hear me? I said the . . ."

"I heard you."

The secure phone on Dumond's console started ringing. Dumond grabbed it and then turned to Rapp. "It's Irene. She wants to know what's going on."

Coleman persisted. "Mitch, the Professor could be in that car."

"I know, I know." He looked at Dumond and said, "I can't talk to her right now."

The pilot of the chopper came over the headset. "You're going to have to make a decision between the car and the house."

"We can't afford to lose contact with the car," Coleman persisted.

Dumond held out the phone a second time. "She says she wants to talk to you."

Rapp felt like ripping the phone from the console and throwing it out the door. It wasn't what he wanted to do, but he knew what was right. Rapp lowered his lip mike and said, "Libra Three, stay with the car." Then, tearing the headset off, he grabbed the phone and growled, "What?"

38

Rapp was at his core a lone wolf. He was not a team player unless he was the leader, and he expected others to support him and follow without question. In a business that was filled with huge egos, he often found it easiest to work on his own. Rapp never apologized for this behavior. He let his results do the talking. His government had sent him on dozens of nasty missions, and he had achieved the primary goal in almost every single one of them.

Clutching the phone firmly in his left hand, he said, "Irene, I am really busy right now."

"I know you are, but I need to be kept in the loop."

"We have at least four individuals in my house," snapped Rapp, "that I obviously didn't invite over. I think Anna might be there, but I can't be sure. A car just left the house with one occupant that we think might be the Professor. These are all things that Marcus could have told you. I've got my hands full right now, Irene. I will call you when I need something." He leaned forward and slammed the phone down.

He turned to Dumond, his face red with anger. "We are in the field, not back at Langley! I am calling the shots, and I expect my orders to be followed to the letter." Rapp turned his glare on Coleman. "I expect and want your input, but when it's time to take action, the debating is over. Are we all clear on this?"

Coleman and Dumond both nodded—Coleman out of respect for the need of a chain of command and Dumond out of fear. A moment later, Dumond touched his headset and said, "The car is stopping."

Rapp's head snapped around and looked at the monitor. The sedan was pulling into a gas station. Rapp tried to figure out which one it was. He yelled to the driver up front, "How far until the Solomons Island Road?"

"We're coming up on it right now."

"Take it south, get over in the left lane immediately, and be ready to turn into the Exxon station." Rapp turned to Dumond. "Turn some of these lights off."

"Scott, tell the boys there's a Standard station on our right when we get off the exit. Tell them to pull into the lot and wait to back us up if we need it." The van started to slow, and Rapp stuck his head into the driver's compartment. As they took a right onto Solomons Island Road, Rapp looked across the street at the parking lot of the Exxon station. He sighted the dark blue sedan parked right in front of the store. He had to think quickly. Rapp noted that the driver of their van was wearing black pants and a white shirt with a black bow tie. He looked like he should—a caterer. "How much gas do we have?"

"Three-quarters of a tank."

"Do you have a credit card on you?"

The man hesitated momentarily. It was a strange

question coming from a man he'd never met. "Yeah."

"Are you wired?"

The driver tapped his left ear. "Yeah, your man's got my channel."

Extending his arm and pointing at the station, Rapp said, "Pull up to those pumps right there. Right behind that Crown Victoria. Get out of the car, and start to put gas in. I'll tell you what to do over the radio."

Rapp went back to Dumond and pointed at the screen. "Can you get me a shot of the store on this?"

Dumond nodded and went to work. Four seconds later, they were staring at an image of the store. Rapp patted him on the shoulder and put his headset back on. "Libra Three, we have the car. Please go back to the house and keep us informed of any changes."

"Roger that, Virgo One. We're heading back to the house."

Rapp closed the door to the driver's compartment, and the three of them huddled around the screen. "Marcus, you're recording all of this, right?"

"Yeah."

The driver of the car was not visible inside the store, so Rapp said, "Get us a quick shot of the car, and run the plate."

When the camera focused in on the rear plate of the sedan, Coleman let out a groan and said, "Shit."

Rapp added a second expletive, and Dumond asked, "What's wrong?"

"The car's got government plates."

"Run them anyway," Rapp said.

"Mitch, this complicates things."

"Maybe, maybe not."

"What do you mean, maybe? There's no maybe about it. If this guy is a fed, we've got problems."

"We'll see. Marcus, get us a shot of the store again." A man in a suit with sandy blond hair was at the counter checking out.

Coleman said, "That's not the Professor."

"Is there anyone else in the store?"

Dumond moved the joystick around in an attempt to peer into the far corners of the store. After a second, he brought the focus back to the man at the counter. "It looks like he's the only one in there."

Rapp watched him pull out his wallet and hand the cashier some money. Grabbing Dumond's shoulder, Rapp said, "Tell our driver to get back in the van." Dumond repeated the command, and a few seconds later they heard the driver's door close. Their eyes were glued to the screen as they watched the man in the store pick up a cardboard tray filled with four towering Styrofoam cups. A white plastic bag was also hooked to one of his hands.

Rapp spoke quietly. "Tell the driver to pull into the spot on the left of the sedan and park."

While Dumond was repeating the order, Rapp took his headset off and pulled out his silenced Beretta. Coleman did the same. As they moved forward, Dumond manipulated the camera atop the van to keep the target in view. They came to a stop just as the man was setting the tray of drinks on top of the roof of his sedan.

Rapp opened the door quickly and stepped to the asphalt. The man had his back turned to him. Just as he was starting to look over his shoulder, Rapp raised his left hand and brought the butt end of his pistol grip crashing down. The hard blunt steel of the Beretta smacked the back of the man's head and immediately buckled his knees. Rapp grabbed him under one arm while Coleman grabbed the other. They dragged him the few feet to the van and dropped him onto the floor. While Rapp swung the man's legs into the vehicle, he checked for an ankle holster and a potential backup weapon. Coleman snatched the man's automatic from his shoulder holster and grabbed his car keys.

He held the car keys in front of Rapp. "What do you want me to do with the car?"

"Follow us in it. There's an industrial park just down the road."

THE INDUSTRIAL PARK was a mix of two-story office buildings and warehouse space. The van and the sedan pulled around to the back of one building. Across the street was a strip mall with a bar at one end. Hackett and Stroble parked near the bar and kept an eye on the street. When Coleman opened the side cargo door of the van, he was greeted by the sight of Mitch Rapp sitting on top of the man they had just grabbed. Rapp's knees were on the man's arms, and the tip of his silenced Beretta was pressed firmly into the man's right eye socket.

With a clenched jaw, Rapp asked, "Give me one good reason why I shouldn't kill you."

Coleman stepped into the van and closed the door. "What does his ID say?"

"I haven't had a chance to check it yet. We've been too busy talking, right?" Rapp stuck the tip of his silencer a little further into the man's eye.

Coleman reached down and pulled open the man's suit coat. He snatched a leather case out of the breast pocket and opened it. Instead of saying anything, he held the document in front of Rapp's face.

"Special Agent Salem of the FBI." Rapp looked down at the man. "Would you mind telling me what in the hell you were doing in my house?"

"I don't know what you're talking about."

Rapp looked at Coleman and jerked his head toward Dumond. "Give him the ID and have him run it."

"I'm not going to ask you this again. What were you doing at my house? The one on the bay that you just came from five minutes ago?"

The man's lone eye darted back and forth. "I'm telling you I don't know what you're talking about."

"Last chance. Tell me why you were at my house and what you're doing with Anna Rielly."

"I told you I don't have any idea what you're talking about. Do you know how much trouble you can get in for kidnapping a federal . . ."

Before he could finish, Rapp reached down with his left hand and grabbed the man's right index finger. At the same time, he increased the pressure on the man's eye socket and slid his knee down to his forearm. With a quick yank, Rapp snapped the man's finger. He let out an agonizing scream. Rapp took the opportunity to move the silencer from the man's eye and stick it deep into his mouth. When the tip of the silencer reached his throat, he started to gag.

Looking for recognition in the man's eyes, Rapp asked, "Do you know my friend Mario Lukas? The big fella you gunned down in College Park the other day?" Rapp saw the sign, a flicker of fear. Over his shoulder, Rapp asked, "Anything on that plate?"

"Nothing. It came up blank. I'm checking the name now."

Looking over at Coleman, Rapp said, "This guy isn't a fucking fed. If he was, he'd tell us something."

"Yeah, I think you're right." Coleman looked down at the man and said, "Don't make us torture you."

Rapp withdrew his gun, and the man spat, "You two can go fuck yourselves. You are in deep trouble."

Coleman smiled. "That was very original." Reaching down, he grabbed the finger that Rapp had already broken and gave it a yank. The man started screaming again. Rapp took the opportunity to shove the silencer back in his mouth.

Dumond announced, "This guy is no fed. He's nowhere in the database."

Rapp removed the gun and asked, "What do you have to say for yourself now?"

The man gasped for air and said, "I'm undercover."

"Yeah, right, dumb shit. You're an undercover FBI agent posing as an FBI agent." Rapp switched the Beretta from his right hand to his left and grabbed the man's good index finger. Rapp didn't even bother to ask a question this time. He just took the finger and snapped it like a twig.

The man screamed, "All right . . . all right! What do you want to know?"

"Is Anna Rielly in that house?"

"Yes."

"Where?"

"She's upstairs."

"Is she all right?"

"Yeah."

"Don't fucking lie to me. Have you guys laid a hand on her?"

"No, I swear we haven't."

"Why is she there?"

"I don't know." Rapp didn't like the answer, so he started for the finger. Before he got to it, he yelled, "We told her we were bringing her there to meet you."

"Whose idea was that?"

"I don't know. I'm just a foot soldier. They tell me what to do, and I do it."

Coleman leaned in. "Did the Professor give the order?"

"Yeah, I think so."

"Is he at the house?"

The man shook his head with a pained face. "He was earlier, but he left."

"How many people are in there?" Rapp asked.

"Ah . . . I don't know."

Rapp grabbed a finger and twisted for five full seconds. He screamed and tried to buck Rapp off, but Rapp was too strong. When the man stopped gasping, Rapp repeated the question. "How many people are with you, both inside and outside the house?"

"Two more."

"I know that's a lie, and I'm getting really sick of this

game." Rapp looked up at Coleman. "Let's waste him. We don't need him anymore."

"There's four more."

"You'd better not be lying to me, or I'll put you out of your misery right now."

"I swear I'm telling you the truth. Just don't kill me."

Rapp studied the man for a long moment. He thought he was telling the truth, but one could never be sure with something like this. Looking at Coleman, Rapp said, "Get the boys over here. I have an idea."

39

I don't know, Mitch. I think the smart play might be to let the SOG handle it." They were standing outside the van; their prisoner was inside tied up on the floor with Dumond keeping an eye on him. Dan Stroble and Kevin Hackett were listening to their former SEAL team commander and Rapp talk.

"No." Rapp shook his head. "They are expecting this guy back any minute. We can't wait."

"I think you're too close to this, Mitch. Let's get an ETA on the SOG and then decide."

"Forget it." Rapp threw his arms up in disgust. "I'll handle it myself." Rapp started toward the van, both sincere about what he'd said and completely aware of what made Scott Coleman tick.

Coleman reached out and said, "Hey, wait a minute."

"We don't have a minute, Scott." Rapp yanked his arm away. "Have you gotten soft? You think a Special Operations group from Langley can do a better job than us? They're good, but there isn't a single one of them that's a better shooter than you guys. I'm going with or without you guys." Rapp understood the SEAL psyche as well as anyone. He possessed the same attributes.

Stubborn, supremely confident, driven to win at almost any cost, and never afraid to take a challenge.

"What's your plan?" asked Coleman.

"I'm going to wire numbnuts with a camera and a mike and send him in first."

"How do you know he's not going to give you up, once he's inside?"

"I've got a plan for that." Rapp pointed to Hackett. "You take the guy on the back deck, and the three of us come through the front door. Are you guys in or out?"

Hackett nodded, and Stroble and Coleman followed suit.

"Good. Grab your demolition gear from the back of your truck."

THE MAN WAS standing next to the van with his pants down around his ankles. Dumond had his suit coat in the van and was rigging it with a microphone and fiber-optic camera. Stroble had a hold of one arm, and Hackett had the other. Rapp stood in front of him and asked, "What's your first name?"

"Dave."

"All right, Dave, here's the deal. I don't like you. You took my girlfriend, and you and your pals are in my house. Do you think you'd like it if I took someone you loved and then invited myself into your house?" Dave shook his head. "I didn't think so. My friends here would prefer it if I put a bullet in your head and threw your ass in that Dumpster over there, but I'm not going to do that. At least not yet. I'm going to give you one chance to live, but if you fuck up, even just a little bit, you're gone. Are we clear on that?"

"Yes."

"Good. Here's the deal. We're going to send you back to the house like nothing happened, with one exception. You're going to have a sheet of C4 strapped to your groin, and I'm going to have the detonator. If at any moment I think you're giving us up, I'll blow your balls off and leave you there on the floor to bleed to death. Any questions?"

The man swallowed hard and shook his head.

"Good." Rapp turned to Coleman. "Put the sheet in his underwear and secure it. Marcus, is the jacket ready?"

"In a second."

Rapp looked Dave in the eye and said, "You have my word. If you cooperate, I'll let you live."

It took Coleman a little more than a minute to rig the plastic explosives. Rapp took a second to go over the layout of his house and then told the men in detail how they would proceed. After a quick communications check, they piled into the Crown Victoria and were off. Rapp, Coleman, and Stroble were in the back seat, and Hackett was in the front. The van followed behind at a discreet distance. Coleman and his men all carried suppressed MP-5 submachine guns. Rapp had only his trusted Beretta 92F with three extra fifteen-round clips. On the way to the house, they received status reports from the helicopter. Everything was as expected. One man standing post on the front porch, a second on the back deck, and two more inside, presumably at the kitchen table.

As they turned off the county road and onto the street that would take them to the house, Rapp told the driver to douse the lights and stop. Next, he yanked the plastic cover off the dome light and pulled the bulb. Turning to Stroble, he said, "Once he turns into the driveway, stay low in the back seat. I'll tell you when to move." Rapp tapped the driver on the shoulder with the tip of his silencer. "If they ask what took so long, tell them they had to make a fresh pot of coffee for you. And then ask them immediately where the girl is."

Rapp nodded for Coleman to get out of the car. As the door opened, the driver asked, "Are you going in shooting?"

"If they reach for their weapons, they're as good as dead. It's up to them. Just drop your ass to the floor as soon as it starts, and you'll be fine." The driver shook his head, and Rapp asked, "What?"

"They'll reach for their weapons."

"Then they're dead." With that Rapp, Coleman, and Hackett got out of the car and began jogging down the road. Rapp led the way. The lots in the neighborhood were all similar. They were pretty narrow with one hundred to two hundred feet of shoreline, and they ran around five hundred feet deep. Each lot was separated by a line of trees and bushes for extra privacy. Two houses before his, Rapp turned off the road and cut through his neighbor's yard. Without the moon, it was extremely dark. When they reached the line of trees, Rapp found a small footpath and crossed into the next yard. The men ran in a crouch now. When they reached the next line of trees, they dropped to a knee. Rapp pulled down the lip mike on his headset and asked for one more status report from the chopper. They reported that the situation was unchanged.

Rapp grabbed Hackett around the neck and pulled him close. Pointing toward the water and whispering in his ear, he said, "About twenty feet before the cliff, there's a path that leads from Harry's yard to mine."

"Who's Harry?"

"He's my neighbor. Don't worry about him. He's eighty-one and as deaf as a door. Now, listen. These two guys standing post are dead. We don't have time to dick around with them. We don't have cuffs, and we don't have enough people to cover our asses. When I give the word, I want you to pop your man in the head. You got any problems with that?"

Hackett was unfazed by the question. It would not be the first time he had taken a man's life. He didn't blink or show the slightest sign of tension. He uttered his simple one-word reply. "No."

"Good." Rapp slapped his arm. "Get moving."

Hackett moved silently into the darkness. Rapp spoke to Stroble over the radio. "Dan, get him moving." He waited a second and said, "Marcus, I want continuous updates once he's inside the house."

CONAN O'BRIEN WAS on the tube. Jeff Duser stretched his arms above his head and let out a long yawn. He hadn't had enough sleep as of late. Too much work and no play. When he brought his hands down, he said, "Where the fuck is Polk?" The other man sitting at Rapp's kitchen table didn't bother to answer his boss's question. Duser stood and looked out the window onto the back deck. One of his men was pacing back and forth trying to stay warm. Looking around the kitchen, he said, "I can't believe this guy doesn't even have a bag of chips around here."

The man at the table looked up from his game of solitaire. "Maybe he's healthy."

"What in the fuck is that supposed to mean?" snarled Duser.

The man shrugged his shoulders. "Chips are full of bad stuff."

"Pedro, I've been eating chips my whole life. I'm thirty-five years old, and I've got a washboard stomach."

"Yeah, but what do your arteries look like?"

"My arteries are fine." Duser wasn't in the mood for one of Pedro's health lectures. He walked to the front of the house and checked the porch. His man was out there, but there was no sign of Polk. Mumbling to himself, Duser asked, "How long does it take to get coffee and sandwiches?"

Turning, he looked up the stairs and thought about the fine-looking piece of ass who was sleeping in one of the rooms. Duser thought about what the Professor had said to him about the girl. It didn't make any sense, but he didn't know if it was worth the risk of pissing the man off. He had paid them a lot of money in the last few months, and Duser was sure there would be more to come.

Duser's cell phone rang, and he grabbed it from the case on his hip. "Hello."

"It's me. How is everything?"

"Fine. We're just waiting for Polk to get back with some coffee and food."

"How long has he been gone?"

Duser noticed the concern in the Professor's voice. "Don't worry. It's late. I'm sure he had to drive farther than we thought."

"Is he carrying a phone?"

"Yes."

"Well, call him on it."

"Don't worry, I'll handle it."

"How's the girl?"

"She's fine. She's upstairs asleep." A pair of headlights cut through the front windows. "Hold on a second. I think Polk is back."

RAPP AND COLEMAN watched through the bushes as the car came down the driveway. It stopped in front of the other sedan, front bumper to front bumper. As soon as the headlights were doused, Rapp and Coleman moved. They stayed in a crouch and picked their way through the narrow path, stopping just short of Rapp's side yard. Each dropping to a knee, they watched their Trojan horse grab the tray of coffee and bag of sandwiches and walk between the two sedans. A voice from the porch asked, "Where the hell have you been?"

"I got hung up. They had to brew a fresh pot of coffee."

Dumond's voice came over their headsets. *"We have one person on the front porch. Make that two. Another guy just came out."*

Rapp whispered into his mike, "Let me know the second they start to enter the house."

"They're going in right now."

Rapp and Coleman dropped to their bellies and crawled across the grass, keeping the sedan that was closest to the garage between them and the front porch. They stopped near the trunk of the car and waited. They could now hear the audio from inside the house. *"Where's the girl?"*

"Upstairs asleep. What the fuck took you so long?"

Dumond's voice came over the line. *"We have two guys inside. One's standing near our man in the kitchen. His gun is holstered, but he's holding something in his hand. The second man is at the kitchen table."*

Rapp whispered, "Hackett, are you ready?"

"Roger."

"Wait for my word." Rapp looked at Coleman and nodded. Coleman gave him a thumbs-up. Rapp sprang from behind the car and began sprinting across the driveway toward the front porch. The man was standing with his back toward the door facing the street. Rapp was coming at him from the man's right side. He had his Beretta in his left hand and leveled it at the man's head. The entire scene unfolded in slow motion for Rapp. As the man started to move, Rapp said, "Take him."

The man sensed movement and started to turn toward Rapp. He had a machine pistol slung over his shoulder with one hand on the grip. He started to reach for the weapon with his other hand as his eyes made contact with Rapp. Rapp fired his weapon twice. Two bullets spat from the end of the silencer. The first bullet struck the sentry in the right eye and tore through his head. The second one hit him in the cheekbone an inch below the first shot. The sentry's body was propelled backward, sending him over the railing and into a bush.

"Tango one down." Rapp reached the porch just seconds later and put his hand on the doorknob. Coleman was there a step behind him. Over their headsets, Hackett's voice said, "Tango two down."

Rapp looked up to see Stroble coming across the lawn, and then he heard from inside the house, *"What in the hell was that?"* Rapp knew the noise they had just heard was the body of their comrade falling outside on the wood deck. Into his lip mike, he said, "Marcus, tell Dave to get down." He didn't do it out of concern for the man's life. It was a matter of practicality. He wanted him out of his field of fire. Rapp twisted the knob and shoved the front door. He was in the house, moving to his left toward the kitchen, his gun extended. There would be no shouts or warnings. Rapp wasn't a cop, he was a trained assassin. As he entered the kitchen, Dumond was saying something over the radio, but Rapp didn't register it. All of his senses were focused on a man holding a cell phone in one hand and drawing his gun with the other.

Jeff Duser heard the noise outside and instinctively reached for his gun. A second later, he thought he heard the front door opening. He turned to look and grabbed for his Glock. As he was pulling the weapon from its holster, a dark-featured man came around the corner with a gun in his hand. Duser freed his weapon from the holster and frantically tried to bring it to bear on the stranger. As he did so, he muttered, "Who the fuck are you?"

Rapp fired once and kept moving. The bullet hit exactly where he intended it to—dead center, right between the man's eyebrows. As he crossed the kitchen, he kept his gun aimed at the second man, who was standing by the back door. The guy made no effort to reach for his weapon as Rapp closed on him. He slowly brought his hands up. Rapp brought a finger to his lips and gestured with his gun for him to lie down on the floor. Rapp turned to Coleman and said, "Take care of him. I'm going upstairs."

PETER CAMERON WAS sitting in the living room of his Georgetown apartment, eyes wide, clutching his digital phone to his ear. Something was wrong. He had been talking to Duser. Everything seemed fine, and then there were Duser's first words of alarm, followed just a few seconds later by Duser saying, "Who the fuck are you?" Then came the loud crash that Cameron guessed was the phone on the other end dropping to the floor. Cameron squeezed his phone tightly as he strained to listen to what was going on.

There was some background noise, and then came an unmistakable voice. Upon hearing Rapp speak, Cameron became so unsettled he almost threw the phone across the room.

In a hushed and panicked voice, Cameron asked, "Jeff, are you there? For Christ's sake, answer me." Cameron listened for a while. He heard some other voices now, voices he didn't recognize, and then some breathing. "Jeff, is that you? Answer me, dammit." A moment after that, the line went dead.

Cameron stood and began frantically pacing his apartment. He scrambled to piece together what had just happened. How had it happened? How in the hell had Rapp figured out what was going on? Was it just luck? Did he just happen to go by his house to fetch something, or was he on to him? He couldn't begin to think of what he would tell Clark. Was there any way Rapp could learn his real identity from Duser? Cameron felt confident there wasn't, but then again, he had felt he had the upper hand against Rapp every step of the way, and the man kept proving him wrong. Cameron remembered the feeling of true fear he had had in the woods in Germany when he had attempted to follow Rapp. Cameron suddenly felt very unsafe in his apartment.

It might be time to lie low for a while, he thought. Cameron had a prearranged plan for this. He went into his bedroom and grabbed a suitcase from his closet. He tossed it onto the bed and started to fill it with essentials. His heart almost leaped from his chest when he heard his phone ring. Cameron raced from the bedroom and grabbed his mobile phone from the coffee table. He checked the readout before answering. It was Duser.

Cameron pushed the send button and said, "What in the hell happened?"

There was no reply for several seconds, and then, "I'm going to give you one more chance to live. Tell me who you work for right now, or I will hunt your fat, bearded ass down, and I will make sure you suffer a very slow and painful death. And don't think for a minute that you can run from me. Wherever you go, I will find you."

Cameron's free hand touched his beard while he looked in the mirror above his fireplace. Rapp knew what he looked like. Not knowing what to say, Cameron did the only thing he could think of. He ended the call and stood staring at himself in the mirror. With a chill creeping over every inch of his skin, he went into the bathroom and began to shave.

40

The sun was up but not out. Thick gray clouds once again blanketed the skies above Washington like a dirty circus tent. Rapp was tired but nowhere near exhaustion. Knowing that Anna was safe had given him back the sense that he could maneuver without fear, that his rear and flanks were secure. He had just left her with some people he could trust—the United States Secret Service. They owed Rapp in the biggest possible way and were more than willing to help. She was safely tucked away at Blair House with the president, the first lady, and several dozen Secret Service agents. She would go to work today like any other day, and then Rapp would have to decide what to do. His worst fears had been borne out the night before when they had taken her, and no matter how many favors he had to call in, he wasn't going to let it happen again.

Rapp had considered arranging protection through Kennedy and the Agency, but until they knew who in the hell they were dealing with, he decided the best thing was to keep her near the president while he sorted things out. For having been awakened in the middle of the night, Rielly took the news fairly well that the men who had picked her up just blocks from the White House were, in fact, not FBI agents. When she asked who they were, Rapp didn't quite know how to answer the question. When she found out that some of them had been killed, downstairs while she slept, in the kitchen of a home that she was beginning to think of as her own, she was less than enthused. When she asked who killed them and Mitch refused to answer, she got very upset. Rapp eventually told her. That was usually the case with Anna. She possessed a challenging combination of temper and determination.

Rielly had seen him kill before. He had done so to save her life and the lives of others. It helped that, in the most basic terms, her boyfriend was a good guy, and the people he killed were not, and it also helped that she had grown up in a house filled with cops. But, like ice on a broken wrist, though knowing these things made the pain better, it didn't solve the problem. What Rapp did for a living bothered her. It bothered her in a very real way, and Rapp knew if he didn't put his killing behind him, he would lose her. She was too special to let that happen. This would be the end of his days with the CIA. It was time to get out.

As he pulled off the Georgetown Pike, he checked the clock on the dash of his car. It was approaching seven in the morning. A short while later, he pulled up to the gate at the end of Director Stansfield's driveway. The ninja-clad machine-gun-toting security officers let him through without checking his ID. Rapp had called ahead and told Kennedy he was coming. Rapp parked and walked up to the house. Normally, Rapp didn't obsess about his appearance, but there were a few people he felt deserved the respect of a clean-shaven face and some decent clothes, preferably a suit. Director Stansfield was one of those people, and Rapp felt slightly embarrassed that he had a day's worth of thick black stubble on his face and was wearing jeans and a baseball cap.

He knocked on the front door, and a second later it was opened by a man with a large bruise on his jaw. The CIA security officer looked less than enthused to see his midnight assailant. Rapp eyed the man and asked, "How's your jaw?"

"Sore."

"Good." Rapp walked past him. "Maybe it'll teach you to be a little more careful next time." He continued down the hall and into the study. He didn't care if the man liked him. This business wasn't about popularity. Rapp only hoped he would learn from his mistake.

Kennedy was standing next to her boss reading him something from a piece of paper. When she saw Rapp, she held up the sheets of fax paper and said, "We have some info on one of the men from last night."

"From Hornig?" Rapp was referring to Dr. Jane Hornig. The woman specialized in getting information out of people who didn't want to talk. Rapp had sent the two men they had taken alive to Hornig for interrogation.

"No. We ID'd one of the men you shot. His name is Jeff Duser. A former Marine, thirty-five years old, was court-martialed and thrown out of the Corps for what appears to be a quite extensive list of infractions."

"Who does he work for?"

"We don't have that, but I've got some people looking into it."

Rapp looked at Stansfield. "I'm sorry for my appearance, sir. I didn't have time to get cleaned up."

"No apology needed." Stansfield was speaking with a slight slur. "Where is Commander Coleman?"

Kennedy answered for Rapp. "He's at Langley with Marcus and several of his men, reviewing files."

"State Department?"

"No," answered Rapp. "They came up empty on State, so I told them to check Langley's files."

"How is Ms. Rielly?"

Rapp was a little surprised by Stansfield's question. Neither man had ever acknowledged the relationship before. "She's doing all right."

"Do you need me to ask the president to have a talk with her?"

"No . . . I don't think so." Rapp stood near the fireplace, looking back and forth between Stansfield and Kennedy, nervously shifting his weight from one foot to the other. He wanted to get this over with. It was the reason he was here during this short respite in the action. With some awkwardness, he said, "As long as I have the two of you alone, I'd like to discuss something." True to form, Stansfield and Kennedy returned his look with stoic, expressionless faces. "When this is over . . . as soon as we find out who this Professor is . . . I'm done."

Neither of them spoke. They recognized his comment in no observable way. No head shaking, nodding, shrugging, raising of an eyebrow, nothing. They just stared back at him with their all-knowing eyes. "I'm serious," said Rapp. "And there's nothing you can do to talk me out of it. I'll take care of the Professor, and then I'm done."

Finally, Stansfield said, "I'm sorry to hear that, Mitchell. Your talents will be irreplaceable."

"There were talented people before me, and there will be people after me."

"The ones who came before you were not your equals, and I fear the ones who come after you will fall far short of filling your shoes."

"Langley will be fine."

"No. The truth is, Langley will not be fine. If the president can pull it off, Irene will succeed me, and if we are that fortunate, she will need you."

"Well, I'm not available." Rapp folded his arms stubbornly across his chest. "I've given enough."

"Yes, you have, but I'd like you to consider giving more."

"No." Rapp couldn't look at them anymore. He just wanted them to accept his wishes and move on without him.

"Mitchell, I can understand why you want out. Irene has told me that you plan to ask Ms. Rielly to marry you. I could not have stayed in the field and been a good husband and father. The two do not mix. But we could bring you inside. There is plenty of work for someone with your skills."

Oh God, Rapp thought to himself. *They're doing it to me.* "Sir, you possess many skills that I do not."

"I don't believe that."

"Well, it's true. I could never last at headquarters. I don't have the patience to put up with all the crap."

"It's not as bad as you think, and besides, you'll adapt. You always have."

"I don't want to learn. I'm a field man, sir."

Stansfield held his hands up in a temporary show of surrender. "We don't need to discuss this right now. All I ask is that before you make a final decision, you give me a chance to talk to you about a few things."

Rapp wanted to be firm. He wanted to say no. He desperately wanted to tell them there was no way in hell he would go to work at Langley, but looking at the old man, a man he had idolized for a decade, he couldn't do it. He couldn't tell the old spymaster no.

"Will you please promise me that you will give me one last audience? There are things we need to discuss before you make your final decision."

Slowly, Rapp let out a deep, pained breath and gave in. Stansfield returned Rapp's acceptance with a rare smile just as Rapp's phone started to ring. He checked the caller ID and then answered the phone. "What's up?"

"I think we have him." It was Scott Coleman.

Rapp looked up, his eyes wide. "Talk to me."

"His name is Peter Cameron. I'm not positive, but I think it's him. When we saw him in Colorado, he had a beard, and he didn't have one in any of the photos we've seen."

"Who is he?"

"He worked for the Agency from 'seventy-four to 'ninety-eight in the Office of Security. He did it all. He administered polygraphs, personal protection, debugging offices, you name it. His last couple of years he ran the show."

"He watched the watchers."

"Yep."

Rapp cringed at the thought of how much information someone in that position had access to. "Where can we find him?"

"He has an apartment in Georgetown."

"Where?" Coleman gave Rapp the address, and Rapp asked, "How quickly can you guys be there?"

"Twenty minutes."

"All right. Fax me a photo, and then meet me at the Safeway on Wisconsin. And bring the van and Marcus, and tell Marcus to keep this quiet. I don't want anyone at Langley to know what we're up to."

"I'll see you in twenty."

Putting his phone away, Rapp looked at Kennedy and Stansfield. "Scott thinks they might have found the Professor, and you're not going to like what he did for the last twenty-plus years."

"What?" asked Kennedy.

"He worked in Langley's Office of Security."

"What's his name?" asked Stansfield.

"Peter Cameron."

Stansfield shook his head. This was not good news. The director knew exactly who Peter Cameron was. The man had been in charge of the CIA's Office of Security from 1996 to 1998. During his tenure as the head of Langley's Gestapo, his access to sensitive information would have been almost limitless.

SENATOR CLARK GOT out of bed at seven A.M. It made no difference if he was in Washington or Arizona. Clark was a bit of a night owl, usually staying up until one in the morning. On this particular Thursday morning, the senator was sitting in the sun room just off the kitchen of his Washington, D.C., estate. Clark was in his white robe and a pair of slippers. He was alone. Wife number three was already off to the club for a morning aerobics class of some sort. It wasn't stepping or spinning, he knew that. She'd moved on to the newest fad and swore it was the best yet. Clark didn't care what it was called just so long as it worked.

He munched on a piece of toast and perused the front page of the *Wall Street Journal*. The help didn't arrive until eight. Clark always made his own breakfast, which was no great feat considering the fact that it consisted of black coffee and two slices of toast covered with butter and jelly. He rather enjoyed this time of the day. He was alone in his castle with no one there to intrude. It was usually the one and only time of the day that he devoted to his investments. Clark would peruse the *Journal* and then give marching orders to his various brokers, advisors, and money managers. Then he was done with it for the day. He refused to become a slave to the emerging trend of constant on-line market updates.

A buzzer sounded from the kitchen, and Clark leaned back in his chair to look at the TV mounted above the microwave. The estate's security cameras could be viewed by any TV in the house. The TV showed the senator a picture of a cleanly shaven Peter Cameron sitting behind the wheel of his car, waiting at the gate. Clark walked into the kitchen and pressed the intercom button.

"Good morning, Peter."

"Good morning, sir."

"I'll buzz you in. There's coffee in the kitchen if you'd like, and then show yourself into my study. I'll be down in a few minutes." Clark cinched the belt on his robe and headed upstairs. He had a good feeling about this unannounced visit by Cameron. If the news was as good as he hoped, he just might call off the hit. Cameron was a valuable tool. Too valuable to waste unless it was absolutely necessary.

PETER CAMERON PARKED his car and headed straight into the study. He didn't need any coffee. He was already edgy enough without it. The thought of the ensuing conversation with Senator Clark had his stomach acid acting up. Cameron felt the senator was a fair man, though. He took care of people who were loyal to him, and Cameron had been extremely loyal.

Cameron approached the fireplace and studied the beautiful 1886 Winchester .45-70 lever-action rifle. It was perfect. A weapon years ahead of its time. A magnificent piece of craftsmanship. He had secretly hoped that the senator would be so pleased with his recent work that he would give Cameron the rifle as a gift. That no longer seemed to be a possibility.

It was almost twenty minutes before Senator Clark

came down. He was dressed in an expensive suit and carried a cup of coffee. Clark crossed the room to his desk and set the mug down. Remaining on his feet, he said, "Peter, you shaved your beard. It looks much better."

"Thank you, sir." Cameron did not know what to say.

"You look ten pounds lighter already."

"Thank you." Cameron reluctantly crossed the large study and stood across from Clark.

Clark was about to sit, and then he noticed the less than confident expression on Cameron's face. "Please, sit. Can I get you anything to drink?"

"No, thank you." Cameron reluctantly sat in one of the two end chairs.

The senator slowly eased into his plush leather desk chair and looked over the top of his mug. He could see it in Cameron's slouched shoulders: things had not gone as planned. "I trust Rapp and his girlfriend have been dealt with?"

"Ah . . ." Cameron searched for the most delicate way to put it. "Things didn't go so well."

"Really?"

"Yes. In fact, I fear Rapp may have grabbed the upper hand."

Clark did not like what he was hearing. Setting his mug down, he said, "Tell me what happened."

"I left Rapp's house after midnight to head back into the city. I needed to get a few things set up for the rendezvous this morning. When I left, everything was fine." Cameron desperately wanted to stress this point. "Rielly was convinced that we were legit. Before leaving my place to head back out to Rapp's, I called Duser to see how things were going . . . and . . ." Cameron started to fidget. "That's when things started to go bad."

"How so?"

"I'm not exactly sure. While I was talking to Duser, there was a bit of commotion, and then the line went dead." With a pained look on his face, Cameron said, "And then a few minutes later, I received a phone call from Duser."

"And?"

"It wasn't Duser. The call was from his phone, but it wasn't him."

"Who was it?"

"It was . . . ah . . . Rapp."

Clark set his mug down, his mind rapidly filling in the blanks of what must have happened. "And what did he have to say?"

"Same stuff as last time. That he's going to kill me."

Clark didn't buy Cameron's story. Rapp was too smart for that. He'd want to know who was the real power behind Cameron. But now wasn't the time to push him. "Is Duser dead?"

"I assume he is."

"Or he's being interrogated."

Cameron was ready for this one. "There's nothing he can tell them. He doesn't know anything about me."

Clark wished he shared his minion's confidence, but the fact was he didn't. "What do you propose we do?" The question was asked not out of sincerity but in an effort to make Cameron think his opinion was valued.

"I think it is time to lie low for a while. Let the trail die with Duser."

"Retreat now so we can fight under more favorable circumstances."

"Exactly."

"You don't think there is any way Duser can lead Rapp back to you?"

"No." Cameron shook his head. "That's assuming he's alive, which I very much doubt. I was very careful in dealing with him."

"Good." Again, Clark did not share Cameron's confidence, but he didn't let on. "Are you sure you don't want to take one more shot at Rapp?"

Cameron thought about it for a moment. "I would . . . I really would, but I think things are a little too hot right now. If we just let things cool down a bit, it will be considerably easier to deal with him."

"I think you're right, my friend." Clark thought to himself, *It's too bad you won't be around to see it.* "How would you like to proceed?"

"I think I should leave the country for a few weeks."

Clark nodded. "I agree. Do you have any place in mind?"

"A few."

"How about my island?"

Cameron was hoping the senator would offer his private retreat in the Bahamas, but after the recent debacle he didn't dare ask for it. "The island would be perfect. I could avoid customs."

"Good. I will leave it up to you to handle the details.

You've been very valuable to me, Peter. I can't afford to lose you right now."

Cameron smiled. He was relieved that Clark had taken the news so well. "You're not going to, sir. I'll personally take care of Rapp when I get back."

"Good. When will you leave?"

"Later this morning. I have to stop by my office at GW and take care of a couple of things, and then I'm off."

"You're not going home at all?"

"No. I already have everything I need."

"Good." Clark stood and walked Cameron to the door. "Call me when you leave the office and then again when you've made it safely to the island."

"I will, sir."

At the door, Clark placed a hand on Cameron's shoulder. "Peter, I want you to be really careful."

"Thank you, sir. Don't worry about me. I can take care of myself."

"I know you can." The two men exchanged handshakes, and then Cameron was gone. Clark immediately closed the door and went back into his study, where he turned on his computer. After it warmed up, he went on-line and sent a message to the Colonel, giving him very specific instructions on how to proceed. At the end, he decided to throw in one more sentence of incentive. When Clark was done, he sent the message and logged off. With any luck, he would be rid of Cameron before the morning was over.

41

Donatella Rahn was sitting on the floor of her hotel room in the lotus position. Her breathing was rhythmic and effortless, like gentle waves rolling onto a quiet beach. She had slept well. For years the simple act of sleeping had been her own personal Holy Grail. No matter what she tried, or how hard she tried, the quest remained elusive. It was either the killing or the demons of her drug addictions, or probably both. The faces of her victims haunted her during the lonely dark hours from midnight to sunrise. At first she tried drugs, and with predictable results: she became addicted and strung-out. After a month of treatment at a private facility in the hills north of Milan, she was off the sleeping pills.

After that it was men, but not just any man. With Donatella's beauty, she could afford to be picky. This brought a new set of problems, and she eventually had to abandon that life raft in search of another. From men she moved on to hypnosis, massage therapy, acupuncture, aromatherapy, herbs, almost anything that was suggested to her. None of it worked for longer than a month or two. After years of struggling, she had finally discovered yoga. That had been six years ago, and ever since then, sleep had ceased to be a worry. She was at peace with herself for maybe the first time in her life. Yoga had taken her to levels of relaxation that she didn't know existed. It had allowed her to stop running from her past and start hoping for the future.

Rahn sat on a towel. She was naked. Her legs crossed, her hands resting gently on her knees, open and facing up. Her posture was straight but not rigid, and her chin was tilted up just slightly. Her eyes were closed, her breathing was even, and her heart was pumping in a slow, restful beat. Donatella imagined herself sitting on the terrace of a beautiful villa overlooking the breathtaking waters of Lake Como. This was often where she went, both in her mind and in reality. The long, smooth water of Lake Como was tucked in the Alps of northern Italy just south of Switzerland. It was, in her mind and the minds of most of her countrymen, one of the most beautiful places in the world. A place of sheer relaxation, where no one was in a rush and wristwatches were frowned on. Rahn had a small place there with a meager fifty feet of lakeshore. For now it was good enough, but she had hopes for an even more serene setting. She was saving, putting away the money so she could buy the place of her dreams. One of the old stone villas with several hundred feet of lakeshore and at least ten wooded acres to waste away the lazy afternoons. It was a dream that would one day come true.

The sun was bathing her smooth, naked body in warmth when her phone started to beep. The beauty of Lake Como vanished as Rahn opened her eyes. Slowly, she unfolded her long legs and stood. Her Motorola StarTAC phone was sitting on the desk. Donatella flipped it open, and the screen told her she had a text message. Rahn pressed the envelope button on the bottom row, and the phone automatically retrieved her e-mail. She concentrated on the tiny letters as the message scrolled across the screen.

YOUR SUBJECT WILL BE AT HIS OFFICE IN FUNGER HALL AT GW FROM APROXIMATELY 8:15 TO 8:30, AND THEN HE WILL BE LEAVING THE COUNTRY FOR A WHILE. IF YOU CAN MEET HIM AT OR NEAR HIS OFFICE IT WOULD BE PREFERRED. HIS DESTINATION IS THE CARIBBEAN. IF YOU CAN'T MEET HIM THIS MORNING YOU WILL HAVE TO MAKE ARRANGEMENTS TO MEET HIM THERE. IT IS PREFERRED THAT YOU TAKE CARE OF THIS THIS MORNING. OUR CLIENT IS OFFERING ANOTHER 25K IF YOU CAN CONCLUDE THE DEAL BEFORE HE LEAVES.

Rahn glanced over at the clock next to the bed. It would take her fifteen minutes to get ready and approximately nine minutes to leave her hotel and walk to Cameron's office. She had timed it last night when she had been out scouting the neighborhood. It took Rahn only seconds to decide. She could get there with just enough time to check things out and then abort or proceed. Moving with speed, she went into the bathroom and pinned her luscious auburn hair up on her head. She applied a base to her face and hands, changing her natural olive skin to a lighter shade. Next, she put on some underwear, a pair of black leggings that went down just below the knee, and a long-sleeved white T-shirt. Over that she put on a shapeless, beige, full-length linen tank dress. To top off the disguise, she carefully pinned a sandy blond shoulder-length wig to her head.

All of the makeup and toiletries were swept off the vanity into one of the hotel's plastic bags, and the whole thing was thrown in her suitcase. Donatella slipped into a pair of white J. Crew tennis shoes and stood in front of the full-length mirror. The outfit could not have complemented her figure less, but that was the point. It was standard East Coast yuppie. Donatella liked to think of it as suburban housewife camouflage. She could go to virtually any city in America and blend in perfectly.

She closed her suitcase, locked it, and left it by the door. On her way to the school, she would call the front desk and ask them to have a bellhop bring it down. She left the room with only her oversized shoulder bag and took the elevator to the lobby.

RAPP MADE IT to the Safeway a few minutes before the others. He studied the black-and-white photo and brief dossier that had been faxed to the director's house. He was ninety-nine percent sure he had never laid eyes on Peter Cameron. That probably ruled out any personal grudges. Cameron had to be working for someone else. The drive in from McLean had given Rapp time to think of the larger ramifications. He had been focused on himself and how the events of the last week had affected him personally; now he was beginning to see the big picture.

He had never seen Stansfield or Kennedy as worried as this, and the more he thought about it, the more he understood why. If Cameron worked for a foreign intelligence agency, the real question would be how long had he been doing so, and how much information had he passed along? To make matters worse, the man was a consultant with the intelligence committees, and that meant he still had access to sensitive information. The damage would make the Aldrich Ames scandal look like child's play.

Before leaving the director's house, Stansfield had impressed upon Rapp the magnitude of the situation. Cameron was to be taken alive, and it was to be done as quietly as possible. No scenes, nothing that would garner the attention of law enforcement, the media, and even anyone at the Agency. Stansfield was adamant that the Agency was to be kept out of it. He placed the entire matter on Rapp's shoulders. He could use Irene and the Counterterrorism Center in a very limited support role, but that was it. The Cameron matter was to be kept quiet.

When the van arrived, Rapp abandoned his car and climbed in. Dumond and Coleman were waiting for him in the back. Hackett and Stroble were parked on Wisconsin in the Ford Explorer. When the van pulled out of the lot, it took a left and headed south on Wisconsin. Cameron's apartment was less than half a mile away. At the top of the hill, they took a left onto R Street and slowed to a crawl. The Dumbarton Oaks Research Library was on the left. The old Federal-style mansion was located on one of the most expensive pieces of property in Georgetown.

Rapp grabbed a secure Motorola radio from the rack

and said, "Guys, I want you to hang back. Go down to Q Street and park. We'll go in and check things out first."

Dumond said to Rapp, "We'll do a slow drive-by. I'll scan the building with the directional mikes and see if I can find out who's home."

"Good." Rapp looked at Coleman. "We need to take him alive."

"I can't make any promises."

"I know you can't, but we have to try."

"All right."

"You and I are going in alone," Rapp said to Coleman. Then to Dumond he said, "Marcus, what else have you found out about this guy?"

"He teaches at George Washington University."

"When do they meet?"

"I'm trying to find that out. I've already checked customs, and there is no record of him leaving or reentering the country in the last six months."

"What about wheels?"

Dumond shook his head. "I checked DMV and came up blank."

"Finances?"

"I haven't gotten around to that yet."

"All right. Get me that class schedule first."

Dumond held up one hand to silence Rapp and pulled the arm of his lip mike down with the other. "Stop at the next corner and give me a second to get things ready." Looking over at Rapp, he said, "We're one block away. Are you guys ready?"

"Yes."

They cruised by once very slowly and then turned

around for another pass. There were no alleys in this neighborhood, so trying to get a look at the house from behind would not work. Both times Dumond manipulated the tiny directional microphones atop the van to try and pick up noises within the three-story brownstone. On the second pass, Dumond told the driver to stop briefly in front of the house. Using a joystick on his control panel, he zoomed the camera in on the mailboxes to the right of the front door. When he got the image he wanted, he told the driver to go to the end of the block and park. Dumond showed Rapp and Coleman the shot of the mailboxes. It appeared there were four units, one on the first, second, and third floors, and another one in the basement.

"It looks like Cameron has the third floor."

"Yeah." Rapp looked over Dumond's shoulder at the screen and then checked his watch. It wasn't yet eight. "What did you pick up on the mike?"

"Nothing on the third floor, but I got a TV on the second and some water running on the first."

"Nothing on the garden level?"

"No."

Rapp looked to Coleman. "What do you think?"

"I don't think he's there. Would you be if you were in his shoes?"

"Probably not. Let's go take a look." Rapp grabbed the radio. "Guys, we're going in. Bring it over to Twenty-ninth and sit tight."

"What's our cover?" asked Coleman.

They were woefully unprepared for this. Both were wearing jeans, jackets, and baseball caps, and both needed a shave. If the neighbors saw them snooping around, they were apt to call the cops. Rapp looked around the van and said, "Marcus, hand me that clipboard." Rapp took it and asked, "Can you find out who owns this place?"

"Yeah. All I have to do is access the city's tax records."

"Do it."

"What do you have in mind?" asked Coleman.

"We work for Metropolitan Roofing. The owner asked us to come out and get him a bid for some work he wants done."

"What if the owner lives here?"

"That's why I've got Marcus running the check."

On cue, Dumond announced, "You're clear. The guy listed on the title doesn't show up on any of the mailboxes."

"Good." To Coleman, Rapp said, "You got your tools?"

Coleman nodded and patted the breast pocket of his jacket.

"Marcus, give us a thirty-second head start, and then move the van in closer and give us audio surveillance. And while we're in there, keep digging. We need to know as much about this guy as possible, and we need it quick."

Rapp and Coleman left the van and started down the heaved cobblestone sidewalk. There was a small wrought-iron gate between the sidewalk and the tiny front yard. Rapp paused at the gate, as if not quite certain where he was. He looked at the clipboard and then the address on the house. He and Coleman continued through the gate and walked up onto the porch. Rapp stood between the bay window of the first-floor unit and the door while Coleman went to work on the lock. Rapp had his radio hooked to the top of the clipboard.

He brought it up to his mouth and said, "Marcus, bring the van around, and let me know what you can pick up from the third floor."

Coleman twisted the lock gun, and the old, heavy door swung in. They stepped into the small foyer and looked up the staircase. They waited there listening for almost thirty seconds. When Dumond told them he was on station, they continued slowly up the stairs. They kept their weapons holstered but had their hands under their jackets ready to draw at the first sign of trouble. They made it to the second landing without incident and continued to the third. Once past the other tenants' doorways, they pulled headsets from their jackets and plugged them into their radios so they could communicate with their hands free. The door to Cameron's apartment had three separate locks on it. While Coleman went to work, Rapp set the clipboard down and drew his gun, which he kept in his left hand.

"Marcus," Rapp whispered. "Are you picking anything up?"

"Nothing, just the hum of the refrigerator."

"Let me know the second you hear something. Guys, how does the street look?"

It was Stroble who answered. "Everything's quiet."

Coleman was working on the third and final lock. It was giving him the most trouble. After several frustrating minutes, he finally got it. Standing up, he put the lock pick away and grabbed his gun. He pointed to himself and then Rapp. Rapp shook his head stubbornly. This was his problem more than it was Coleman's. He would go through the door first.

"Marcus, we're going in." Rapp was slightly crouched with his silenced Beretta extended. He nodded to Coleman, who had a hand on the doorknob. Coleman twisted the knob, opened the door, and stepped out of Rapp's way. Rapp charged through the door, his heart beating a little faster than normal but not much. He heard the beep of an alarm but ignored it. It would have to wait. He moved quickly, sweeping his weapon from left to right and back again, searching for motion. Reminding himself with every step that he had to take Cameron alive, that he had to fight his training and aim for the shoulder and not the head.

Coleman entered the apartment right behind Rapp and closed the door. He also heard the alarm but ignored it. He looked to the far corners. When Rapp moved to the right, he moved to the left. The living room and kitchen were secure within seconds, and they continued down the hallway to what they assumed were the bedroom, a den, and a bathroom. They moved quietly. Rapp checked the bathroom quickly and then went straight for the bedroom. Coleman followed behind, closing the bathroom door and moving on to cover Rapp. The bedroom door was open. Rapp paused for just a second to allow Coleman to catch up, and then he came into the room in a low crouch. There was movement to his right, and he spun quickly to bring his Beretta to bear. Rapp had started to depress the trigger and then held off when he realized it was a cat leaping from the dresser to the floor. He looked around the room quickly. The bed was made and had several stacks of clothes lying on top of it. On the floor next to the bed was a suitcase. Rapp noted the suitcase and then moved on to the last room.

The study was also empty. It was not unexpected that Cameron was gone, but it was still disappointing. Rapp had just started to look at the desk when Dumond started chirping in his ear. "Is that beeping noise coming from a security system?"

"Yes," replied Rapp.

"You'd better hurry up and tell me which service it is, or we're going to have some unwanted company."

Rapp walked quickly back to the living room and approached the keypad next to the door. Rapp flipped open the panel and read the tiny writing. "It's Omega Security. Can you stop it?"

"No problem. Give me two minutes."

Rapp turned around and grabbed his phone. Coleman, always thorough, was busy checking the closets. A second later, Rapp had Kennedy on the line. "He's not here. We set off his security alarm, but Marcus is going into the firm's system to deal with it."

"Do you want me to send a team over?"

"Yeah, but be careful who you pick."

"I will. Anything else?"

Rapp thought about the suitcase in the bedroom. "We might want to think about alerting the airports. I think he's getting ready to run."

"That could be tricky."

"I know, but it's better than letting him get away."

42

The George Washington University garage was located on the corner of H and 22nd. Like most parking garages, it was a large, blocky, nondescript mass of concrete. As Cameron pulled into the structure, he was busy thinking about how he would make it to the island. The easiest way would be to catch a flight to Miami and then, under an assumed name, fly into Nassau or Grand Bahama. From either place, he would have to catch a puddle jumper to the island. The last leg was a part of the journey he did not look forward to. He could also take a day and drive down to Florida. The time alone in the car might do him some good. It would help him to sort things out.

Cameron found a spot on the sixth floor and parked. As he got out of the car, he decided against driving to Florida. Too many things could go wrong. It was best to get out of the country. He had pushed it far enough. He could take all the time he wanted on the island to decide upon a course of action. Rapp would have to be dealt with sooner or later, and although he didn't know everything about Senator Clark, he doubted the man had the connections to do it himself. That was Cameron's job. That was why he had been hired.

The Professor took the elevator down to the ground floor and headed west on H Street. Something bothered him about the senator this morning. He seemed to take the news about Rapp awfully well. Almost too well. There was more to Clark than he would ever have the time to figure out. The man seemed very simple and straightforward on the surface, but as Cameron had seen firsthand, he was a very cunning individual. Cameron admired people who were capable of taking decisive action and who were not afraid to use power to get what they wanted.

If they had succeeded in Germany, none of this would be happening. If only Rapp had just died. His body found dead next to Count Hagenmiller's would have been perfect. The outrage would have torn the CIA asunder and allowed Clark to take the high road. Hearings would have been launched by both the House and the Senate. Rudin would have come off looking like a rabid dog, and in the Senate, Clark would have played the perfect role of wise statesman. His stature would have increased tenfold.

Rapp had refused to cooperate, however. Cameron didn't like to admit it, but the man was a worthy adversary. He had misjudged him, and now he would have to retreat to fight another day. Next time, there would be no elaborate plans. Nothing but a simple, well-aimed shot from his Stoner. Rapp would never know what hit him.

* * *

RAPP AND COLEMAN were back down in the van. Dumond had accessed the George Washington University Web site and was showing Rapp and Coleman a map of the campus. He had tracked down Cameron's office. It was on the fifth floor of Funger Hall on the corner of G and 23rd.

Rapp keyed his radio and said, "Guys, bring the Explorer around." Looking at Coleman, Rapp said, "You and I will go check out the office while Kevin and Dan keep an eye on the apartment."

Hackett and Stroble were there in seconds. They got out of the Explorer and climbed into the van. Coleman got behind the wheel of his SUV, and he and Rapp were off. They took a right on 28th and headed down the steep hill toward M Street and the Potomac. Rapp called Kennedy and told her they were on their way over to the university. When they reached M, Coleman cut all the way across and turned left onto Pennsylvania.

Rapp checked the face of every pedestrian. Three blocks later, they hit Washington Circle and shot to the right. At the southern end of the traffic circle, they turned onto 23rd and entered the beginning of the George Washington campus. Coleman slowed; the sidewalks were crowded with students walking to class and workers heading into the GW Medical Center. Funger Hall was up on the left across the street from St. Mary's Episcopal Church, a Washington landmark. There were no spots on the street, so they took a right down a narrow alley next to the church and found a spot in back.

Before getting out of the car, Rapp looked at Coleman and said, "I want this guy alive, but if things get tight, I don't want you to hesitate." Rapp tapped himself on the forehead. "Put a bullet right in the center of his head."

DONATELLA CIRCLED THE building once, looking for any signs of surveillance, and then entered the lobby of Funger Hall. She was slightly surprised to see the lobby teeming with students, most standing in groups talking and others heading off in earnest. Then Donatella remembered that there was a class due to start in five minutes. She approached the bulletin board and acted as if she were searching for something. It was a good excuse to stop and see if anyone was watching her. The night before, after she had scouted out Cameron's apartment, she had walked to the university. She timed everything, checked out every alley and walkway. She had thoroughly checked Funger Hall, noting all of the exits and memorizing where the security cameras were. On her way back to the hotel, she picked up a schedule at the Foggy Bottom Metro stop. The underground station was only two blocks from Cameron's office. If something went wrong, that would be her best bet.

As the crowd of students started to thin, she walked to the south staircase. Funger Hall had six stories above ground. Cameron's office was on the fifth floor. Donatella went up to the second floor and exited the staircase. She walked casually down the hall, passing two students who paid her no attention. When she reached the north staircase, she paused and looked down and up, checking for anyone who didn't fit in. There were five students coming up the stairs. They left the stairwell on the second floor and Donatella continued up. She knew from her visit the night before that the fifth and sixth floors were occupied chiefly by offices. Donatella hoped that would mean fewer people.

She stopped on both the third and fourth floors and checked the hallways. She saw nothing unusual and continued to the fifth floor. Donatella was not nervous. Compared to many of her assignments, this was easy. Whether or not it remained that way would be learned in the next few minutes.

RAPP AND COLEMAN ran across 23rd Street, drawing the finger and a horn from an irate cab driver. They ignored the man and continued into Funger Hall, where they walked right past a security guard who was more concerned with his cup of coffee and newspaper than he was with the two highly trained killers who had just passed within feet of his post.

"Stairs or elevator?" Coleman asked.

"Elevator. Cameron doesn't look like he uses the stairs."

They continued across the lobby to the elevators and waited. Coleman looked around and said, "It would have been nice if we could have brought Kevin and Dan to keep an eye on the exits."

Rapp was also taking in the surroundings. "Yeah, I know, but I'm not comfortable leaving Marcus alone to watch the apartment."

"Yeah, you're right. We need more people."

A moment later, the elevator arrived, and they stepped in with six backpack-toting students.

* * *

BEFORE LEAVING THE stairwell, Donatella checked the items in her purse to make sure they were exactly where she wanted them. Her pistol with its silencer attached was in the right spot, but she was hoping she wouldn't need it. Her teacher, Colonel Freidman, had made sure that Donatella was schooled in the most subtle of assassination techniques. Freidman had always said that anyone could use a gun to kill, even a child. She had instead been trained to use everything from a shoelace to a pencil. Donatella knew all of the vulnerable points of the human body. Given the right tools, she could kill someone and barely leave a mark. And, more important, she could do it quietly and quickly.

She checked the position of two other weapons in her bag and then entered the long hallway. Donatella immediately noticed two people at the far end. Her right hand slid into her purse to touch the cold steel of her pistol. She watched the man and woman carefully. Both fit the profile of an academic type. The man had a beard and was wearing jeans with a plaid shirt and loosely knotted tie. The woman was in a dress and a pair of Birkenstock sandals. She relaxed a touch and continued down the hall.

Cameron's door was closed. Donatella approached and listened for a second. She heard the squeaking of a chair and decided to knock. There was no answer at first, so she knocked again and said, "Professor Cameron, my name is Amy Vertine. Dean Malavich sent me over to get a signature so I can register for one of your grad school classes next semester."

"I'm in the middle of something right now. Could you come back later?"

"Actually, I can't." Donatella placed a hand on the knob while she continued to talk. "I'm on my way to work. I really want to take this class." The door was locked. "I've heard you're a great teacher. It'll only take a second, I promise." Donatella looked down the hall and was relieved to see that the two teachers were no longer there. She began weighing the risk of shooting through the lock, and then the door opened.

Peter Cameron waved her in and closed the door. "I'm sorry, I have to keep this door closed or another one of my students will drop in, and I'll never get out of here."

Donatella stuck out her right hand. "My name is Amy. It's nice to meet you, Professor Cameron."

Cameron smiled at the pretty woman and took her hand. "Please call me Peter."

Donatella returned the smile and turned her head to the left, knowing full well that her target would do the same. Pointing at a plaque on the wall, she asked, "Is that from the CIA?"

Cameron turned to look at the award he had been given by some friends at the Agency. It commemorated his twenty-four years of service. As he proudly began to answer the question, Donatella's right hand slid into a pocket in her purse. Her hand wrapped around the rubber handle of a four-inch steel pick that had been sharpened to a fine point. She slowly slid the weapon out, keeping it close to her body. Pointing to a photograph next to the plaque, she asked, "Who is that?"

As Cameron's head started to turn, Donatella brought the pick up and moved with lightning speed. Her aim was perfect as she jammed the sharp, thin object into Cameron's left ear. Before he could scream, Donatella was on him, clamping her left hand down on his mouth and twisting the pick with amazing force. His body began to crumple as the four inches of steel slashed through his brain. Donatella lowered him to the floor and twisted the pick around one more time to make sure he was dead. Then she slowly extracted the weapon, and, lifting Cameron's arm, she wiped the pick against the fabric of the armpit to remove what little blood there was on it. Donatella put the pick back in her purse, and then, as if nothing had happened, she opened the office door, locked it, and closed it behind her.

THE ELEVATOR DOORS opened, and Rapp and Coleman stepped out. Coleman looked to the left, Rapp to the right. Both men had their hands in close proximity to their guns. There was one person in the hallway. A woman with blond hair was walking away from them toward the far end of the hall. Rapp studied her for a second. There was something strangely familiar about the way she moved. When she reached the door to the stairwell, she turned and looked in their direction for a brief second. Rapp got only a glimpse of her, and then she was gone. He tilted his head to the side and squinted in thought. There was something about her, something he couldn't put his finger on.

Coleman tapped him on the shoulder and looked

down the hall. They began to walk quietly toward the office. When they reached the right door, they stood one on each side and listened. Rapp placed one hand on the doorknob and his other on the hilt of his Beretta. Coleman kept an eye on the hall. When the doorknob didn't turn, Rapp stepped back and motioned for Coleman to knock on the door. Coleman tried three times and then pulled out his lock-pick gun. He placed the proper bit in the tip of the gun, and then, as quietly as possible, he threaded it into the lock and pulled the trigger.

Rapp pulled his silenced Beretta out of its holster but kept it under his jacket. When Coleman finally turned the knob, he stepped back and out of Rapp's way as he pushed the door in. Rapp hugged the metal door frame, shielding all but a fraction of his body from harm. His left arm shot out, the silenced Beretta swept the room. He saw the body on the floor immediately but continued past it to complete the search of the small office. Rapp stepped into the room, and Coleman followed him, closing and locking the door.

Both men knelt over the body. "Is it him?" Rapp asked.

"I think so."

Rapp reached out and touched his neck. The skin was still warm—very warm. They did a quick search of the body for a cause of death. It was Rapp who found the puncture wound inside the man's left ear. Rapp looked toward the door. He thought of the woman he saw in the hall. He looked back at Cameron, at the mark of death in his ear. Rapp knew someone who had killed like this before. He knew her very well. Rapp stood and for a moment thought of running after her. She was long gone, though. Besides, he knew where he could find her.

As Rapp looked down at the dead body of Cameron, he was not saddened in the least. The man's death was inevitable; it just would have been nice if he could have talked to him first. Rapp swore as he pulled out his phone and punched in the number. When Kennedy answered, he said, "We found him."

"Where?"

"In his office. He's dead."

"Did you do it?"

"No, we found him."

"Any idea who did do it?"

"No," Rapp lied.

There was a long pause, and then Kennedy said, "I'll send a team over to get the body."

"We'll wait for them." Rapp closed his phone and looked at Coleman. "Why do I get the feeling this trail is going to stop right here?" he said, pointing down at the lifeless body of Peter Cameron.

43

President Hayes studied Thomas Stansfield from across the smooth conference table of the White House Situation Room. The director of the Central Intelligence Agency was literally a shadow of his former self. He was rail thin, his face completely emaciated from the ravages of cancer. Neither of them had called this meeting. Someone else had. Someone who shared their secrets. Someone who sounded very concerned. While they waited for him to arrive, Stansfield took the opportunity to discuss a few things with the president. It was seven in the evening on Thursday, and it had been a very long day for the director. Since finding out that Peter Cameron was dead, Stansfield had struggled to find a link beyond the deceased man to the person or people who had employed him. Stansfield filled the president in on what had happened earlier in the day. He told him that Kennedy, Rapp, and several others were working feverishly to find out who the power was behind Cameron.

Stansfield had his enemies, certainly not the ones in Washington, but he had them. The ones he knew he did not fear. It was the ones he did not know who worried him. They all, though, had one thing in common. They wanted to succeed, and not just in small ways but by obtaining real power, the type of power wielded by the elite of Washington. For politicians, it meant chairing one of the more powerful committees or being the next secretary of state or defense, or even the presidency—the ultimate exclusive club. For bureaucrats, it was a job as an undersecretary in one of the big departments or a senior aide to the president—maybe even chief of staff. For the military officers, it could range from any one of a dozen prestigious commands, to being placed in charge of one of the branches of the armed forces, to taking the top spot of chairman of the Joint Chiefs.

These men and women roamed the back passages of Washington, and most of them were no more dangerous than their peers in corporate America. They were what he would call fairly harmless plotters, groups of people working together to further their careers. Experience had taught Stansfield, though, that there were always a few willing to use extraordinary measures to achieve their goals, a few who were willing to kill if need be.

One of these groups was obviously on the move, and their target appeared to be the CIA. Stansfield had yet to share these thoughts with anyone. He would wait to hear what their visitor had to say before he would draw any further conclusions. It was disheartening for him to have worked so tirelessly to ensure the neutrality and stability of his beloved Agency and then now, when he barely had the strength to fight, to find out that he was under an assault by a group that he could not identify.

He could not allow the CIA to fall into the hands of someone who might use its vast resources for political or personal gain. He had to make sure that Irene Kennedy succeeded him and that she was armed with the knowledge to defend herself.

The CIA was too powerful a weapon to let fall into the wrong hands. The president would nominate Irene Kennedy, and he would use all of his political skill and clout to make sure she was confirmed. Hayes had many reasons for agreeing to this, despite the missteps of the last week. First off, Kennedy was more than qualified, and secondly he trusted her. This led to the third and maybe most important reason as far as the president was concerned. He needed his flank protected. With Kennedy at the helm of the CIA, he wouldn't have to worry about any aggression coming from that direction.

As much as both men wanted Kennedy to be the next director of the Central Intelligence Agency, the man they were about to meet with had as much or even more say in whether or not that happened. The fact that he had asked to see them during the middle of this Peter Cameron problem was slightly unsettling.

Senator Hank Clark entered the Situation Room, and the president stood to shake his hand. When Stansfield tried to stand, Clark put a firm but comforting hand on his shoulder and said, "Now, Thomas, you just stay right there. A living legend like yourself doesn't need to get up for me."

The president smiled and winked at Clark, approving of his gesture. "Would you like anything to drink, Hank?"

"No thanks, Robert." Clark and Hayes had served in the Senate together for two full terms. Hayes was on the Intelligence Committee when Clark was named chairman. Hayes preferred to be called by his first name when they were alone like this.

"Are you sure? It's no trouble at all."

"No, I'm fine. I might need one when we're done, but until then, I think I'll lay off the stuff."

"All right." The president gestured to a chair on the other side of the table from Stansfield.

Clark walked slowly around the table and unbuttoned his suit coat before he sat. Looking across the table, he asked, "Thomas, how are you doing?"

"I'm dying."

Clark grinned. "We're all dying, Thomas." Clark glanced at the president. "Aren't we, Robert?"

"That's right. But not all of us have led a life like Thomas's."

"No. In fact, I would say that very few have led a life like Thomas's. This country owes you a great debt."

Stansfield seemed to soak the words in for a second and then said, "Thank you, Senator Clark."

Clark laughed at the formal use of his name. "Will I ever hear you call me Hank before you leave this world?"

The corners of Stansfield's mouth turned up ever so slightly. "No."

"I didn't think so." Clark clasped his hands together, and his mood seemed to darken.

The president noticed this and asked, "What's bothering you, Hank?"

Clark didn't respond at first, and then, glancing sideways at the president, he said, "Robert, we've always been able to cut through the crap and talk straight to each other." The president nodded. "We served on the Intelligence Committee together for years, and I always respected the fact that you put national security issues above party politics."

"And I've always respected you for doing the same."

"Thank you. I would like your word that you will handle what I'm about to tell you with discretion. Especially with reference to where you heard it."

The president's curiosity had been piqued by the request. "You have my word."

"I am very concerned about what is going to happen with the CIA when Thomas leaves us." Clark looked at Stansfield. "I think I know who you have chosen as your successor, and I approve. I think Dr. Kennedy is one of the best candidates for the job. And more importantly, if Thomas thinks she's the best person, you will have my full support during her confirmation hearing."

Stansfield was relieved. Clark's support of a Kennedy nomination was crucial. As chairman of the Senate Select Committee on Intelligence, he was the key to getting someone through the confirmation process.

"I am very pleased to hear this," said the president. No amateur in the art of politics, Hayes was waiting for the standard tit-for-tat request. "What is it that you seek for this cooperation?"

Clark acted slightly offended. "Robert, I took the chairmanship of the Intelligence Committee because I didn't want someone politicizing the oversight process for their own gains. I'm offering my cooperation because I think Dr. Kennedy will do a good job, but even more importantly, I want her to succeed Thomas because I don't think she's corruptible."

"Fair enough. I'm sorry if I offended you."

Clark waved his hand as if he were shooing a fly from in front of his face. "You know it takes a lot more than something like this to offend me."

"Yes," the president smiled, "it does."

"My real concern in coming here tonight is twofold. When we were in the Senate together, Robert, there was a select group of us who felt our government wasn't doing enough to battle terrorism. We took the very unusual and risky step of approaching the deputy director of Operations for the CIA." Clark looked at Stansfield. It was he who had been in charge of Operations for the CIA at the time. "We thought it was time to take the battle to the terrorists. Diplomacy was getting us nowhere, military intervention was disastrous and it was time to use the third option. We placed our confidence in Thomas and gave him a blank check to launch covert operations against terrorist groups across the Middle East. You were one of those original senators, Robert. Unlike the others who were involved in that decision, you and I are the only ones who know exactly how successful Thomas's group has been. Even with our success, however, it is paramount that the existence of that group remain a secret." Clark looked at the two men while they nodded in agreement. "Well, I don't know if it's dumb luck, intuition, or if we have a leak, but we have a problem, or I should say you have a problem, Robert."

President Hayes did not like the sound of this. Clark was referring to the Orion Team, of course, and the thought of its existence being made public caused a wave of nausea to wash over the president. "And what is that?"

"I met with two individuals from your party the other day. I informed Thomas of this meeting." Clark looked at the director of the CIA. "For reasons that are not known to me, these two individuals are working feverishly to make sure that Dr. Kennedy does not become the next director of the Central Intelligence Agency."

President Hayes's face was turning red. "And who are these two individuals?"

"Secretary Midleton and Chairman Rudin."

President Hayes's struggled to keep his composure. He bit his bottom lip and looked over at Stansfield.

"What troubles me even more is that they think Kennedy had a hand in the assassination of Count Hagenmiller. I don't want to get involved in how they know this, but I think it is paramount that you find out how they know and stop them from talking about it."

IT WAS APPROACHING midnight on Thursday. It had been an incredibly long day. None of them had slept. Rapp, Coleman, Dumond, and Kennedy all had heavy eyelids as they sat around Stansfield's kitchen table. The director was asleep. After returning from the White House, he'd met with Kennedy in private. He filled her in on what he'd learned from Senator Clark, and she in turn explained what Rapp, Coleman, and

Dumond had learned from picking through Peter Cameron's life. Stansfield gave Kennedy her marching orders, and then he was out. He had to return to the White House in the morning for some very important meetings.

As they sat around the table, it was Dumond who did most of the talking. He had recovered mounds of information from the PC in Cameron's apartment and the laptop they'd found in his office at George Washington University. As for Cameron's body, it was currently en route to an incinerator outside Baltimore. It had been taken from his office in a large cardboard box on a two-wheeler by a man in a brown UPS uniform. No one batted an eye. As an extra precaution, a man roughly fitting Cameron's description would board a flight in the morning to Bogota, Colombia. He would use Cameron's passport for the journey.

"A lot of this information doesn't mean a thing to me," said Dumond. "If he has any classified material on these hard drives, I wouldn't know it."

"Is there any mention of Midleton or Rudin?" Kennedy asked.

"Yeah, but his database reads like a Who's Who of Washington. He advised both intelligence committees and an unknown number of other politicians on national security issues. I mean, you could look through this thing, Irene, but you'd better plan on blocking out a week. Either that, or you're going to have to let me get some help from the CTC. There's just too much information."

Kennedy had already thought about bringing in some

of her people from the Counterterrorism Center, but she didn't like the downside. They had to find out if there were any leaks first. "We can't ask for any help from the CTC, at least not yet."

"Well, I don't know how you expect me to handle this. It's going to take me a long time, and to be honest, this isn't my specialty. I'm not an analyst. I don't know these names like you do, I don't see the issues or understand the agendas. I don't have the foggiest idea who's important and who isn't. I've got the financial stuff nailed, but the rest of it is a mystery to me."

"For now, concentrate on anything that might link him to the secretary of state or Congressman Rudin."

"What about the money?" asked Rapp.

Dumond had discovered two offshore accounts in the Bahamas totaling almost half a million dollars. "I spent more than an hour today trying to track where those payments came from, and I came up with zip."

"Should we let someone else take a crack at it?"

Dumond was offended by Rapp's question. "Listen, if I can't find out where that money came from, no one is going to."

"I'm just asking."

"His body was still warm when you arrived." Kennedy looked at Rapp and Coleman. "Did you see anyone leaving the building?"

Coleman thought about it and said, "There was one woman entering the staircase when we got off the elevator." He shrugged. "Didn't get much of a look at her."

"Mitch?"

Rapp thought of the woman he'd seen. The more he

replayed the scene, the more he believed it was Donatella Rahn. The way she moved and the way Peter
Cameron had been killed both pointed to the Italian
beauty. Rapp knew he couldn't tell Kennedy of his suspicions, at least not in front of the others. He owed too
much to Donatella. He would have to arrange a trip to
Italy and talk to her alone. No bosses, no official intelligence business, just two old lovers who owed each
other their lives.

Rapp shook his head and looked at Kennedy. "I
didn't see anything unusual."

"Well, I've sent someone over to grab the security
tapes. We'll have to sit down tomorrow and go over
them."

"Good thinking." One of the reasons Rapp liked
working for Kennedy was that she was so thorough.
Cameron's sudden disappearance would eventually garner the attention of the police, and through some very
simple detective work, they would discover that he had
entered Funger Hall on the last day anyone had ever seen
him but had never left. Not only was the killer probably
on that tape, but so were Rapp and Coleman. They had
been wearing hats and knew how to tilt their heads in
such a way as to prevent the camera from getting a good
shot of their faces, but still, they would prefer it if the
authorities never had the chance to get that far.

"So where do we go from here?" asked Coleman.

"We all go home and get some sleep, and then we plow
ahead in the morning." Kennedy looked at Dumond, remembering there was one more thing she was supposed
to take care of. "Marcus, Director Stansfield was wonder-

ing if you could create an offshore account in the name of Congressman Rudin and transfer the money from Cameron's account into it?"

Dumond rolled his eyes at the request. "Yeah, I can do it. No problem." It was obvious that Dumond was less than enthused about the idea.

"What's wrong?"

"We've put in a lot of hours on this." Dumond waved his arm around the table to include everyone. "I was hoping we could get a little bonus out of the deal."

Kennedy thought about it for a second. "I'll check with the director and see what he thinks. But you don't think it will be a problem to create the account and move the money?"

"No. I can have it done within an hour."

Kennedy had aroused Rapp's curiosity. "How does Congressman Rudin fit into this?"

"We're not sure. The director and the president are going to have a chat with him in the morning, but it never hurts to overdetermine your outcome."

44

It was Friday morning, and the West Wing of the White House was bustling with activity. Word had quickly swept through the halls that the president was on the warpath. This didn't happen often with President Hayes, but when it did, the members of his administration usually knew enough to stay away. Today, things had been complicated by two additional pieces of information. The first was that upon entering the Oval Office at 7:54, the president had called his chief of staff, Valerie Jones, and demanded that Secretary of State Midleton be tracked down and told, not asked, to get to the White House immediately. The second was that a very frail-looking Thomas Stansfield had arrived and was now in the Oval Office with the president. The president's surly mood, his rather forceful request for the secretary of state, and the appearance of the director of the CIA had created an uneasy mood in the West Wing.

White House staffers prided themselves on being in the know, but on this particular Friday morning, they found themselves in the unnerving position of not knowing a thing about what was afoot. As the word spread that something big was going down, the phones began to buzz. Valerie Jones, the president's chief of staff, was being bombarded with questions from other important members of the administration. She also received a call from an old friend at the State Department, who wanted to know what was up. Jones answered honestly that she was out of the loop on this one, but she suggested to her friend that he make sure Secretary Midleton didn't keep the president waiting. Jones received her first call from a reporter before Midleton had even arrived. The word was out.

Inside the Oval Office, the president had calmed a touch. Seeing Stansfield in such obvious pain made him forget about his troubles for the moment. Hayes, like almost all of his predecessors, understood the importance of good theater. There were far more subtle ways to confront this problem, but that was not what Hayes wanted. He wanted to send a message. He wanted to make an example of the pompous Charles Midleton and put him in his place. Hayes knew full well that by the end of the day, anyone who mattered in Washington would know that the president of the United States had handed the secretary of state his ass, and it would be done without a single word being printed.

Stansfield hadn't been so sure about the president's plan. There were many ways to handle such a meeting without anyone being the wiser. Both Stansfield and Senator Clark had entered the West Wing the night before without anyone other than the Secret Service knowing they were there. President Hayes explained to Stansfield that Midleton had already been warned to mind his own shop. His unusual cooperation with the German ambassador after the Hagenmiller assassination was bad enough, but his meddling in the nomination of the next DCI was indefensible.

There was also a second meeting planned for this morning. The wheels for that gathering had been set in motion the night before. The president had called on two old and very close friends to make it happen. It would be held in private with far less fanfare than the first. The attendees were already downstairs waiting in the Situation Room.

SECRETARY OF STATE Midleton was not a stupid man. He had tried to make several calls to find out what was going on, but since everyone else was in the dark, he got nowhere. He had managed to learn one thing from Michael Haik, the president's national security advisor, and that was that the president was in as bad a mood as he'd seen him in for some time. Armed with this limited amount of information, Midleton decided to make the trip to the White House without the accompaniment of any of his aides. Midleton entered the Oval Office by himself, his chin held high, trying to exude an air of confidence.

President Hayes wasn't about to stand to greet his guest, and Director Stansfield didn't have the strength or desire to do so.

"Mr. President, I came as soon as I could. What is wrong?"

"Sit" was the single biting word that left the president's mouth.

The president and Stansfield were sitting in separate chairs in front of the fireplace. Midleton crossed the room and sat on a couch that was closer to Stansfield. "What's wrong, Robert?"

Hayes let the tension grow for a moment before speaking. Staring at Midleton with a look that would be impossible to mistake for anything other than disdain, Hayes said, "I think I should be the one asking you what's wrong."

Midleton had racked his brain on the way over trying to figure out what he could have done to so anger the president, and he had only come up with one answer. It must have been his meeting with Congressman Rudin and Senator Clark. Until he knew for sure, though, he would keep his mouth shut. There was no sense in taking the heat for two wrongs. Using a more formal tone, Midleton said, "Sir, I honestly don't know what you are talking about."

"Charles, I worked with you in the Senate for more than a decade. I know when you're lying." Hayes stared at him. "What did I tell you before you left the White House earlier this week?"

Midleton didn't want to answer the question, and gave his standard evasive answer. "I don't recall."

"You don't recall." The president's fists were clenched as he mimicked Midleton. "Let's cut through the bullshit, Chuck. I told you to mind your own damn shop and keep your nose out of the CIA's business. Does that ring a bell?"

Midleton swallowed hard and said, "Yes."

"Then would you like to tell me what in the hell you

were doing the very next morning when you met Hank Clark and Al Rudin at the Congressional Country Club for breakfast?"

"They wanted to talk to me about some recent security breaches at the State Department."

"Bullshit!"

Midleton looked away from the president and shook his head. "This is really no way to be running an administration."

"Oh, I suppose you think it would be better if I scheduled secret breakfast meetings and plotted to stab you in the back."

"You know, I really don't think I . . ."

Before Midleton could finish, Hayes cut him off sharply. "Shut your damn mouth, Chuck. You never got it through that pompous head of yours that I won the presidency, not you. When you quit after New Hampshire and agreed to throw your support behind me in exchange for a spot in the administration, that's when you lost, *Chuck*. The people didn't want you, and then, in exchange for your support, I made what is starting to look like the worst decision of my political career. But I can live with that because I can be rid of you by this afternoon and do so with a clear conscience." Midleton's eyes grew large in disbelief. "Oh, I'm not kidding. Have you seen my approval numbers lately? They're over seventy percent. I can demand your resignation, and a week from now you'll be history."

Midleton sniffed disdainfully. This couldn't be happening to him. He wouldn't dare.

"You don't think I'm serious? You don't think there

aren't a hundred guys on the Hill who wouldn't jump at the chance to take over at State? I could even get the Republicans on board . . . you're not exactly their favorite character."

Midleton straightened himself and said, "Are you done threatening me?"

"No, I haven't even started. You have about one minute"—Hayes held up his index finger—"to explain to me what you were doing the other morning at Congressional, and you'd better do so with some sincere remorse."

Midleton's mind scrambled to find some cover. "As secretary of state, I need to be concerned about the national security issues that affect this country."

President Hayes stood abruptly. "As secretary of state," he shouted, "you need to be concerned with what I tell you to be concerned with. I specifically told you earlier this week that if you had any questions regarding the CIA, you were to go through my national security advisor. Whom I choose to succeed Thomas"— Hayes pointed to the silent Stansfield—"is none of your damn business, and believe me, you will get no sympathy from the party when they find out you were conspiring with a Republican to thwart my nominee."

"I would hardly use the word *conspire* to describe a harmless breakfast meeting, and I don't think the party will be all that thrilled when they find out you've been spying on a senator, a congressman, and your secretary of state."

Midleton had taken it one step too far. Hayes yelled, "I didn't have to spy, you idiot. People came to us with the information." The president didn't want it to come to this. He honestly thought Midleton would see the error of his ways and admit fault, but the man was apparently incapable of such an act. The president marched across the room to his desk and grabbed a leather folder. He came back and tossed it onto Midleton's lap. "Open it and read. It's your resignation. I typed it myself, Chuck. I didn't want to use it, but since you have proven beyond a shadow of a doubt that I can't trust you, I see no other choice."

Midleton tried to speak, but Hayes didn't allow it. "I'm done listening. You had your chance to fess up, and you blew it. Just consider yourself lucky that I'm not firing you. If you sign that resignation, we can do this the easy way. I will let you announce that you are resigning for health issues. You go ahead and pick the ailment. If you don't sign it, I'll walk out of here and go down to the press room and fire your ass on national television."

Midleton was in shock. His face was ashen as he stared at a very angry and serious president. In his wildest imagination, he never thought it would come to this. He was Charles Midleton. He was one of the most loved politicians in Washington. Midleton imagined Hayes marching down the hall to the press room to tell the world that he was firing his secretary of state. The embarrassment would be too much to handle. Midleton would have no platform from which to launch a counterattack. Hayes was too popular to confront. He had once again misjudged Robert Hayes. There was no way out. With great reluctance, Charles Midleton began to sign his name. He knew at that moment he would never recover from the embarrassment. His whole life, everything he had worked for in politics, was over.

CONGRESSMAN RUDIN WAS not amused by the skulduggery that had been used to get him to this meeting. He had received a call from the speaker of the House the previous evening requesting that he meet him in his office the next morning. Rudin had arrived on time and was forced to wait fifteen minutes. When Speaker Kaiser emerged from his spacious office in the Capitol he told the chairman of the House Intelligence Committee that they were going for a ride. Rudin, never one to shy away from confrontation, demanded to know where they were going. Kaiser told him in very clear terms that if he had any hopes of keeping his chairmanship of the Intelligence Committee, he'd better change his attitude and keep his mouth shut.

Kaiser was a former offensive lineman from the University of Alabama and still looked as if he could rumble through the Cloak Room knocking fellow representatives from their feet. His stern rebuke left Rudin scrambling to try to figure out what he'd done wrong. When the speaker's limousine pulled through the Secret Service checkpoint at the south end of West Executive Avenue, Rudin was still unsure of what he'd done to offend the gods of politics. The two congressmen were escorted to the White House Situation Room—a further sign that things were serious. In Rudin's thirty-four years in Washington, he'd never seen the inside of the Situation Room. Matt Rohrig, the chairman of the Democratic National

Committee, was waiting for them in the room. This was another bad sign. Rohrig was the party's money man.

When Rudin attempted to ask Rohrig what was wrong, Kaiser took the opportunity to tell Rudin one last time to sit quietly until the president arrived. Rudin racked his brain trying to figure out what he'd done wrong. At one point, he thought of the breakfast he'd had with Secretary Midleton and his friend Senator Clark earlier in the week, but he ruled it out as the source of the problem. It was no secret what Rudin thought of the CIA, and the president had yet to nominate anyone as Stansfield's successor. All he was trying to do was head the president off from making a horrible mistake.

Finally, the president entered the room with Thomas Stansfield. Albert Rudin literally recoiled with revulsion at the sight of the CIA's director. There was no one the congressman hated more, no one in the history of the Republic who had so brutally abused and ignored the authority of Congress. The only thing that pleased Rudin about the appearance of Stansfield was that the man looked as if he might drop dead at any moment.

President Hayes helped Stansfield into his chair and then sat in his spot at the head of the table. He placed a leather folder in front of him and leaned back. With his hands folded, he looked around the table. Kaiser and Rudin were sitting to the president's right, and Stansfield and Rohrig were on his left. The president was more than willing to play the heavy again, but Kaiser had asked for the honor. The speaker of the House believed that the president should stay above the fray.

Hayes opened the leatherbound folder and pulled out a sheet of paper. "I have some unfortunate news." Hayes held the sheet between his thumb and index finger and let it hang. "The secretary of state has just resigned." The president looked to Rudin for a reaction.

With a sour, confused look on his face, Rudin asked, "Why?"

"There's a long version, which I don't have the patience to give to you, so I'll give you the short version. Secretary Midleton is a pompous, arrogant man who doesn't know how to follow a simple order from his boss." Hayes pointed to himself. "That would be me, Al, in case you're wondering. I am the president of the United States. I run the executive branch of the government."

Rudin was thrown by the remedial lesson in civics. Looking to Kaiser, he shook his head and said, "What do I have to do with this?"

Kaiser didn't hesitate for a second. "Did you have breakfast the other day with Charles Midleton and Hank Clark?"

Rudin shrugged his shoulders. "Yeah. It is not unusual for me to have breakfast with colleagues."

"Who requested that meeting?"

"I don't know."

"Don't bullshit me, Albert. You're on very thin ice right now." Kaiser stared at the rail-thin Rudin.

"I think it was Hank Clark's idea."

The president scoffed at the accusation, and Kaiser rumbled, "You don't honestly expect us to believe that, do you?"

"What is this all about? I don't know where you're getting your information, but I wouldn't be surprised to find out it came from a lying, senile, corrupt old man." Rudin pointed his beaklike nose at Stansfield.

The president beat the speaker to the punch this time. Hayes slammed his clenched fists down on the table, creating a dull thud that caused Rudin to blink. "Albert, if you so much as utter one more offensive word toward Director Stansfield, I will crush you."

Kaiser jumped in. "What in the hell were you doing meeting with Midleton and Clark?"

"Nothing. We were talking about intelligence issues."

Kaiser looked to Rohrig. "What's the name of that young hotshot who wants to challenge Albert for his seat?"

"Sam Ballucci. He's going to make a very good congressman someday."

"Mr. President, would you be willing to raise some money to help Sam Ballucci win the party's nomination?"

"How does twenty million sound, and I'll throw in half a dozen appearances with the young man. Maybe I could even speak to the delegates at the state convention?"

"I think that would be a good idea," answered Rohrig.

Rudin's crinkled face had taken on an angry red sheen. "I can't believe you are doing this to me. After all I have done for this party."

"All you've done for this party?" challenged Kaiser. "In my opinion, you've been nothing other than a major pain in the ass. Would you mind telling me what in the hell you were doing when you called Dr. Kennedy before your committee this week?"

"I would say I was doing my job."

"You now consider throwing wild, unfounded accusations at the director of the CIA's Counterterrorism Center your job? Accusations that do nothing more than harm our president, a fellow Democrat?"

"I take oversight of the intelligence community very seriously," snapped Rudin.

"Albert, so help me God, if you don't lose that irritating tone of yours and start showing some remorse for your stupidity, I will leave this meeting, and before noon I will have you stripped of your chairmanship."

Rudin pushed his chair away from the speaker and blinked. This was so unfair. All of this anger should be directed at Stansfield, not him. He was the one trying to protect Congress.

"For the last time, Albert, what did you talk about with Hank Clark?"

Rudin licked his dry lips and looked down at the shiny table. "We discussed the need to find a suitable candidate to run the CIA after Director Stansfield leaves."

"Did Dr. Kennedy's name come up?"

Rudin reluctantly answered. "Yes."

"How so?"

"We didn't feel that she was the right person for the job."

Kaiser shook his head in disgust. "There are two things about this, Albert, that really chafe my ass. The first is that it is not your job to find a suitable appointee to head the CIA. That's the president's job. The second thing that really, and I mean *really* chafes my ass is that you and that windbag Charles Midleton decided to recruit a Republican to help conspire against the president's nominee. Do you know what that makes you, Albert?" Kaiser didn't give him a chance to answer. "It makes you a goddamned Judas, that's what it makes you."

45

I t was after nine when Rapp showed up. The streetlights were on, and there were plenty of open meters. He eased his black Volvo S80 into a spot on F
Street. Before getting out of the car, he checked all of
his mirrors. Then, when he stepped onto the asphalt, he
casually scanned the street, first to the west and then the
east. If the last week had taught him anything, it was
that he needed to be paranoid, especially here in Washington. He had sensed that something wasn't right in
Germany, and he'd been careless enough to ignore those
instincts. It was a valuable lesson, one he hoped he'd
never have to learn again.

Rapp started walking toward 17th Street and the
looming Old Executive Office Building. He had to
admit he lived a strange life. Here it was, a Friday night,
he'd been sitting on the couch with Anna and their new
dog Shirley, and he had gotten a call telling him that the
president would like to see him. Rapp actually had the
nerve to ask Kennedy if it could wait until the morning.
Kennedy told him to get over to the White House and
hung up. They were all tired and frustrated. Peter Cameron was turning into a dead end, and Rapp knew that it

would only get worse with each passing day. He didn't know if he had it anymore—the energy to keep this frantic and dangerous lifestyle going. And there was the bigger question of Anna. She wouldn't tolerate it. She'd said so, and the recent week's events would only solidify her opinion.

It didn't bother Rapp in the least that he was wearing a pair of jeans and a black leather jacket. If the president couldn't wait until morning, this was what he'd get. As Rapp dragged his tired bones across 17th Street, he couldn't help but wonder what the president wanted from him at this hour. Rapp feared he knew the answer. It wasn't as if he were being called on to receive a commendation or medal. They didn't hand those out for what he did. Rapp was one of the dark weapons in the national security arsenal. People didn't even talk about what he did, let alone acknowledge it either privately or publicly. There was only one thing the president could want from Rapp, and he wasn't so sure he would accept it. He was an assassin, and he was sick of killing. It was time for them to find someone else. With more than 250 million people in the country, there was surely some other poor bastard whose life they could ruin.

Rapp walked up to the Secret Service checkpoint on the west side of the EOB. There were several men standing watch. "I'm here to see Jack Warch."

One of the men from the Secret Service's Uniformed Division eyed him suspiciously, while the other one called the special agent in charge of the presidential detail. "There's a man here to see you." The officer lowered the phone. "What's your name?"

"Mitch Kruse," Rapp threw out one of his aliases.

The officer spoke into the phone. "Mitch Kruse . . . yep . . . okay." The officer hung up the phone and opened the gate. He pointed up a drive that led to a courtyard in the center of the building. "Head through there. Special Agent Warch will meet you in the court-yard."

Rapp said nothing and walked up the narrow drive. When he reached the courtyard, he saw Warch approaching from the other side. Warch had a big grin on his face as he saw Rapp. Warch owed his life to the man.

"Good to see you, Mitch." The agent stuck out his hand. "You look like shit."

"Thank you. I feel like shit." Rapp grabbed his hand and gave it a firm squeeze.

"How's Anna doing?"

"Good. Thank you for your help, by the way."

"Don't worry. I figure we owe you a lot more than that." Warch started walking and Rapp followed. "How have you been?"

"You want the long version or the short one?"

"I don't think I'm cleared for the long one. Hell, I'm probably not even cleared for the short one."

Rapp laughed as they entered the EOB. "Come on, Jack, you guys are the eunuchs of the twenty-first century."

Warch placed a hand over his groin. "Tell me about it. Sometimes I feel like one."

The two continued to talk as they left the EOB and crossed over to the White House. They entered through the ground floor and continued straight down the hall and to the right. This was Rapp's first trip back to the White House since the terrorist attack had partially destroyed the building the previous spring. He was amazed at how quickly they had got the West Wing back up and running. It looked exactly as it had before the bombs had ripped her apart.

Warch knew what Rapp was thinking and said, "It's pretty amazing, isn't it?"

Rapp looked down the hallway toward the White House mess. "Yeah, it really is."

"The building wasn't as bad as you might have thought. The fire department was here so fast they got the flames put out before they did too much damage."

"Yeah, but still. This is amazing."

The two men stopped in front of the door that led to the Situation Room. Warch asked, "Mitch, are you carrying?"

"What do you think?"

"I know you are, but I'm trying to be polite."

Rapp was tempted to make a smart-ass comment, but he knew this was a subject that the Secret Service found little humor in. "Would you like to hold on to my gun for me?"

"Very much so."

Rapp took his Beretta out of his shoulder holster and checked to make sure the manual safety catch was in the up position. Warch took the weapon and then punched a code into the cipher lock. The door clicked, and the Secret Service agent opened it. Immediately to the left was the door to the conference room. Warch knocked twice and then opened the door. Staying in the hallway, he ushered Rapp into the room and closed the door.

Rapp stood awkwardly for a moment, slightly surprised to see Kennedy and Director Stansfield. For some reason, Kennedy had given him the impression that he would be meeting alone with the president. President Hayes spun around in his large leather chair.

"Thank you for coming, Mitch. Could you please take a seat?"

Rapp said nothing as he took the first available chair, which was next to Stansfield. He sat and looked briefly at Kennedy, who was on the other side of the table.

"How is Anna?" asked the president.

Rapp didn't answer at first. He looked at Hayes and wondered where to start. Anna was doing well in the sense that she was alive and apparently out of harm's way, but other than that, he wasn't sure she was doing all that well. Rapp decided it was best not to open up that can of worms in front of the president. "She's fine, sir. A little concerned, but essentially she's all right."

"She's a tough woman. I'm sorry she got caught up in this mess."

"It's not your fault, sir."

Hayes wasn't so sure. The president leaned forward, placing his elbows on the table. "Mitch, it's been a very bad week."

"Yes, it has."

"Irene tells me you want out."

Rapp was completely caught off-guard. "I'm ready to move on with my life, sir."

The president looked at Rapp with an unwavering

stare. "What if I told you your country couldn't afford to lose you?"

"I'd tell you I'd already given enough to my country."

The president grinned. There was no intimidating Mitch Rapp. "Yes, you have. No one would argue that . . . especially me. But I'd like you to consider staying on for a while longer."

Rapp felt he was getting sucked into a bad dream. "I'm sorry, sir, but I've already made up my mind. I want a normal life. I've found the right woman, and I'm not going to lose her over a career that I don't even want anymore."

"Are you sure about that?"

"About what?" Rapp wasn't sure whether the president was referring to the woman he'd found or the career he no longer wanted.

The president folded his hands. "Mitch, a man of your talents can't just turn it off and walk away."

"Maybe . . . maybe not, but I'm going to try."

"Well." The president had a big smile on his lips. "I think we may have found a nice middle ground." Hayes turned to the director of the CIA. "Thomas."

"Mitchell." Stansfield's voice was tired and slightly slurred. "I'd like to start by saying that I've been in this business for more than fifty years, and I don't know if I've seen anyone as talented and courageous as yourself."

Rapp looked at Stansfield and replied with a silent nod. The words from the dying legend were worth more than any medal his government could ever give him.

"I have known for some time that I'm dying, and I

wanted to put certain things in order before that came to pass. One of those things, Mitchell, was that I wanted to give you your life back." Stansfield slid a large folder over to Rapp. "This is your official personnel file."

Rapp didn't like what he'd just heard. "I thought it was agreed at the beginning that there would never be any record of me."

"Yes, that was the plan, but things have changed. Some of your exploits over the last several years have been very hard to keep quiet." Stansfield looked at Rapp with his steely gray eyes. "This file is my gift to you and to Irene. I created it with the help of Max Salmen. As your file now reads, you have been an NOC with the Agency for the last ten years. Much of what you did is, of course, not contained in that file or is greatly edited. You are now legitimate, Mitchell."

Rapp was miffed. NOC was an acronym for the Agency's operatives who worked overseas and were not protected by the diplomatic cover of an American embassy or consulate. Rapp stared at the folder in his hands. "Why now? Why after all these years?"

"Because we want you to come inside."

"At Langley?" asked a disbelieving Rapp.

"Yes. We want you to head up the Middle East desk in the Counterterrorism Center."

Rapp looked across the table at Kennedy. He was stunned. It had never occurred to him that they would go to these lengths. It was highly unusual, to say the least, that they would risk bringing someone with his past inside Langley. Kennedy returned his look of disbelief with a rare smile. "Are you sure about this?" he asked.

"Yes," Kennedy answered. "You're too valuable and too young to retire."

Rapp looked back down at the heavy file and shook his head. He really didn't know where to start. The thought of staying connected to the battle was very intriguing, but going inside Langley to suffer the nine-to-five grind was something that he was not so sure he would like. The place was famous for its bureaucratic BS.

"Mitchell," started Stansfield, "there's something I think you need to know. I'm afraid you weren't the ultimate target in Germany."

In light of the fact that Rapp had two baseball-size bruises on his chest he found the statement to be slightly irritating. "No offense, Thomas, but I'm the only person in this room who's been shot this week."

"I didn't say someone didn't want you dead. I said you weren't the ultimate target. Your body was meant to be found next to Count Hagenmiller's. It was meant to embarrass the president, and I think, ultimately, it was meant to ruin Irene's career."

The president's demeanor changed instantly. This was the first he'd heard of this. "What are you trying to say, Thomas?"

"This was not started by the Iraqis or anyone else. This was initiated by someone here in Washington. Someone who doesn't want to see Irene become the next director of the CIA and someone who quite possibly would like to see your administration toppled, Mr. President."

"Do you have some information that you have yet to share with me?"

"No, I don't, Mr. President. Everything I know I have already told you. I have come to some conclusions over the last twenty-four hours that I think point to some big problems."

"Please explain."

"This was not a personal vendetta carried out against Mitchell by the Jansens or someone who hired them to kill him. If that was the case, they would have simply shot him while they were alone in the cabin and been done with him. Instead, they waited until Mitchell took care of the count, and then they made their move. The only conclusion that can be reached is that they wanted Mitchell's body found next to the count holding in his hand the gun that fired the bullet that killed the count."

"But we still had deniability," replied the president. "There is nothing that can officially link Mitch to the CIA or my administration. If Mitch's identity was discovered, Irene was prepared to spread the false rumors that Mitch was a gun for hire. That he'd been hired by the Iraqis to assassinate the count because Hagenmiller was screwing them over on their deal."

"That's all fine unless someone else is leaking Mitchell's real story. Let me ask you this, Mr. President. How many people do you think knew about the operation to take out the count?"

"I would hope very few."

"The four people in this room are the only people who were supposed to know the entire scope of the operation. There were roughly a dozen others who were involved in support roles but had no idea of the complete operation. Someone outside this room also knew what we had planned in Germany." Stansfield paused and took a moment to look at each of the other three. "I know all of you well enough to doubt that you would have been so careless as to talk to someone outside of this group. That means someone else knows about the Orion Team, and I don't mean the deceased Peter Cameron. He was used to get to the Jansens in Germany, but I doubt he was the one who found out what we were up to."

"Then who could it be?" asked the president. "You said yourself that the four of us were the only ones who knew exactly what was going to happen."

"Yes, we were the only ones who knew *exactly* what was going to happen, but there were others who knew the count was a repeat offender. Furthermore, there are people in this town who know about the Orion Team. They don't know what it is called, but they were in on the decision to found it. Senator Clark was smart enough to put two and two together and come to us with his suspicions. There are others who know me well enough to know that I would trust only two individuals to run such a team, Irene or Max Salmen. They also know that you, Mr. President, have decided to take the battle to the terrorists on every front, and beyond that, you throw Mitchell's notoriety over the last year into the picture, and I'm afraid we were caught going to the well one too many times. It should not be shocking to any of us that someone with a limited amount of information was able to figure out what we were up to in Germany."

"But how could they move that fast?" asked Rapp. "I

only learned of the operation seventy-two hours in advance."

"That's what worries me the most. Whoever this person or group is, they have the ability to move very quickly and very quietly."

Rapp looked to Kennedy and watched her stare at Stansfield with her calculating eyes. After a long moment of silence, she said, "It's someone at Langley, isn't it?"

Stansfield nodded slowly. "Yes, I'm afraid so. There could be others outside the Agency, in fact I'm convinced there are, but all things point to a leak somewhere within Langley, and unfortunately I don't have the slightest clue to who it could be."

"Hold on a minute." The president did not like any of this. "What is the motive? Why would someone at Langley want to do this? I thought the one thing we were unified on in this town was the battle against terrorism."

"This has nothing to do with the battle against terrorism," said Stansfield. "It has to do with the battle over knowledge. The battle over who will succeed me as director of the CIA."

"Who will succeed you as director is my decision and no one else's."

"Let me paint a more clear picture for you, Mr. President. I have made a lot of enemies in this town because I have never allowed the brass at the Pentagon or the politicians on the Hill to influence my decisions as director. When they have come to me asking for information, I have always directed them to you or your predecessors. They don't like this. They want someone who will give them access to the Agency's secrets. They know that Irene will do as I have done, and they don't like that. They want someone they can control."

The president looked completely miffed. He wondered if Stansfield was being overly paranoid but was quickly reminded of the events of the last week. There was a foe out there, the only question was who. But still, he didn't want to buy into the scope or the purpose of the thing. "I'm sorry, Thomas, if I sound somewhat skeptical, but I find it a little hard to believe that someone would go to all of this trouble to try to block Irene's nomination."

Stansfield's body was withering away, but his mind was not. Like a grand master in chess, he still had the ability to calculate the ripple effect that could result from one move. "What if I told you the ultimate goal of this person or persons was to topple your administration?"

Hayes was silent for a while. Stansfield had his rapt attention. "How?"

"By exposing first Mitchell and then the full story of the Orion Team. By ultimately linking you to the assassination of Count Hagenmiller."

"You can't be serious. I thought we had the issue of deniability covered."

"We did, sir. That was before we found out there was a leak."

The president let out a moan as he shook his head. He felt things slipping away as he looked at Stansfield's frail body. "Thomas, please tell me you have a plan for dealing with this?"

Stansfield could sense the president's fear. The important thing now that he'd gotten him to recognize the problem was to calm him. "Sir, there is no shortage of people in Washington who would love to destroy me. The only thing that has kept them from doing so is the knowledge that I know their secrets. Those secrets will be passed on to Irene, and I will instruct her and Mitchell how to use them if the need should arise." Stansfield turned toward Rapp. "We need you." The director placed his hand on the newly created personnel file. "This will give you the freedom to live a relatively normal life. You will no longer have to lie to people about where you work. It is my greatest hope that you will take this job. Yes, you have already given enough, and I will never be able to express how grateful I am that you have made the sacrifices you have. When you are confronted with your dark past, Mitchell, you must take comfort in the fact that in the end, you saved far more lives than you took. You are still needed, and I'm not embarrassed in the slightest to ask for your further sacrifice. A man of your talents should not waste them in the corporate arena. You can still make a difference. And the place to make it is in the Counterterrorism Center. I need you there. I need you to watch Irene's back, and I need you to help find the mole." Stansfield paused and looked in admiration at the strong face of Rapp. "If you need some time to think about it, I understand, but please don't take too long." Stansfield smiled. "I'd like to go to my grave with the comfort that you are standing guard."

Rapp couldn't help but grin. It was the first time

he'd ever seen the old spy smile. Reaching out, he grabbed Stansfield's chilled hand. Rapp didn't need any time to think it over. There was no way he could say no to Stansfield. He had far too much respect for the man even to consider turning down the offer. "Thomas, thank you for this." Rapp held up the file. "I will gladly accept your offer."

"Good."

There was a knock on the door. A second later, the door opened, and Special Agent Warch entered the room with a troubled look on his face. The president spun around in his chair and looked up at the man who was in charge of his safety.

"What is it, Jack?"

"Mr. President, I'm afraid I have some bad news. I just received a call from the head of Secretary Midleton's detail." Warch hesitated for a moment, not sure how to continue. "The secretary was just found dead in his home. It appears it was a suicide, sir."

THE FIRE CRACKLED and popped as red-hot embers jumped from the logs. Hank Clark watched with a relaxed intensity from his favorite chair. All of the lights were off in the study. It was just the dancing flames of the fire, his large glass of expensive wine, and Caesar and Brutus, who lay one on each side of the leather chair. Clark was content. Things had not turned out exactly as he'd planned, but there was still time. He looked at it as just one battle in a very long war. As he took a sip of wine, he had to allow himself a smile over the fate of Charles Midleton.

When Clark had gone to Stansfield and the president, he did not think the end result would be the resignation of the secretary of state. Clark's mission was simply to throw them off in case they eventually made the connection between him and Peter Cameron. Clark's cover was already in place. Cameron was a paid consultant for both the House and the Senate Intelligence committees. Now, after Clark had offered his full support of Kennedy in her upcoming nomination, the president would think of him as a trusted ally.

It was a very pleasurable experience watching the Democrats cannibalize each other, especially since it was the Republicans who were usually busy eating their own. It had really been too easy to spin out of the potential disaster. Al Rudin had always been simple to manipulate, but now he was also seeing some weaknesses in President Hayes—weaknesses that had not always been there. Clark had heard rumors after the terrorist attack on the White House that the president had grown more edgy, less tolerant of dissension and petty party squabbling. Now he was seeing it firsthand. Secretary of State Midleton was everything the president said he was and then some, but to force him to resign over this seemed a bit much.

Clark had met with Rudin in one of the Committee's bug-proof briefing rooms earlier in the afternoon. Rudin had whined incessantly for an hour and at one point had attempted to find out if the president had found out about their meeting from Clark. Clark acted as if the accusation barely deserved a response and then launched into a lecture about how Rudin had been continually underestimating Thomas Stansfield for the better part of twenty years. Clark pushed Rudin's paranoia further by asking him, "Why do you think I insist on all of our conversations taking place here, in my own secure briefing room?" The ploy worked. By the time their meeting was over, Rudin was convinced that the CIA had him under surveillance. Clark knew that Stansfield was far too shrewd a man ever to do something so foolish as to put the chairman of the House Permanent Select Committee on Intelligence under surveillance, but it worked on Rudin. Again, the man continued to underestimate his enemies.

Clark had to allow himself a moment of self-congratulation. The way he had manipulated his way out of a potential disaster was brilliant. It was too bad he wouldn't be able to share his role in the secretary of state's resignation with his party's leadership. Someday he might be able to boast, but for now he needed to keep things quiet. He must lie in wait until this storm blew over.

Clark didn't fear many people, but he most definitely feared Thomas Stansfield. The man's intellect and ability to see through deception was amazing. Clark knew that he could not have pulled this off if it wasn't for Stansfield's decaying health. The director of the CIA would have seen right through what he was doing.

Clark would have to make a strong effort to cozy up to Dr. Kennedy and gain her confidence. She would need his help in the coming months. The political battle over her confirmation would be very draining, and she would need an ally on the Hill.

As for Mitch Rapp, Clark wasn't entirely sure. If there was a storm out there on the horizon, he was the lightning waiting to strike. If Cameron had only succeeded in Germany, none of this would be an issue. Rapp would be dead, and the town would be gearing up for one of the biggest investigations in the history of the Congress. The president would be suffering death by a thousand cuts, and Hank Clark would be in the perfect position to launch his bid for the Oval Office. Instead, Rapp was alive, Cameron was dead, and there was no investigation. Clark would have to find a replacement for Cameron. There were several who came to mind, but he doubted any of them could handle Rapp.

Clark took a sip of wine and looked into the fire, searching for a way to deal with Rapp. He'd been staring into the bright flames for minutes when Brutus let out a yawn. The golden retriever lifted his head and stared at his master with his big brown eyes. Clark smiled and held his glass up in a toast to Brutus Marcus Junius. *Keep your enemies close,* the senator told himself. Clark finished his glass of wine and decided he would have to make arrangements to meet this Mitch Rapp.

The dogs grumbled at first, and then, when the doorbell rang, they let loose with the barks. Clark had them calmed down by the time his very important visitor was shown into the study. Jonathan Brown, the deputy director of the CIA, walked stiffly across the room. Clark deduced by the sour expression on the former judge's face that something was bothering him.

Brown, still in a suit and tie, sat on the couch across from Clark. Wringing his hands as if he were Macbeth himself, Brown studied Clark's face for a sign of guilt. He saw nothing, but that meant little. During his years as a federal prosecutor and judge, Brown had seen the guiltiest of people sit like angels through their trials, all the time maintaining their innocence. Brown doubted that Clark would have much difficulty in masking his emotions.

Clark looked at his man and wondered what was wrong. It was Clark who had called this meeting. He did so in order to explain to Brown why he had agreed with the president to back Kennedy's nomination. If Brown had already learned of the deal, it might explain his sour mood. "What's bothering you, Jonathan?"

Brown was tempted to lay down a withering line of questions in search of the truth, but he knew Clark wouldn't tolerate more than two or three. After that, the senator was likely to remind him that if he'd like to leave with his balls still attached to his body, he'd better mind his manners. That had happened once before, and Brown was still smarting from it. "Have you talked to Secretary Midleton this evening?" Brown looked for the slightest sign of guilt. There was nothing.

"No, I haven't, but I heard about his meeting with the president this morning." Clark set his empty wine glass down. "Midleton is to announce his resignation in the morning."

"I don't think that's going to happen."

Clark took his feet off the footstool and sat forward, a look of genuine concern on his face. "What do you mean, it's not going to happen?"

"You honestly don't know, do you?"

"Know what?"

Brown couldn't decide if Clark's reaction thus far was real or fake. He decided he would probably never know for sure, so he said, "Secretary Midleton is dead."

"What?" asked a shocked Clark.

Brown kept his eyes on the man who owned him. "He's dead."

"How?"

"It appears to be a suicide, but one never really knows in this town, does one?" Brown sat back and crossed his legs. "You wouldn't happen to know anything about this, would you?"

The tone in Brown's voice was not lost on the senator. Clark studied Brown for a long moment and then said, "Charles Midleton was an inherently weak man. Everything he got in life was given to him. It doesn't surprise me that he would take his life rather than fight. As to your implication that I might have had something to do with his death, my answer is no, I held no ill will against the man. His career was officially ended this morning when the president asked for his resignation. There was no need for me to do something so risky."

"So you think it was a simple suicide?"

"That would be my guess, but as you've already said, one never knows in this town."

Brown relaxed a little. "Why did you want to see me?"

"We've suffered a bit of a setback, but I don't want you to get upset."

The brief respite of relaxation vanished. "What happened now?"

"I have been put into a position where I have been

forced by Director Stansfield and the president to back Dr. Kennedy's nomination to become the next director of the CIA." Before Brown could get too upset, Clark cautioned, "But don't worry. She will never make it through the confirmation process."

"How can you be so sure?"

Clark grinned. "I think between the two of us, we can prevent that from happening."

"What about me?"

"After Kennedy has been humiliated and torn apart by the committee and the press and quite possibly indicted, I will very quietly whisper in the right ears that you are the only man to clean up the mess. Your credentials as a judge are impeccable . . . you have already been at Langley for a year . . . you will be the natural choice to clean up the mess created by Stansfield and Kennedy."

"And if not?"

"If not, I will take care of you, as I have always said I would."

Brown wasn't so sure. He'd seen the dark side of Clark, and he never wanted to see it again. "Well, I can't say I'm thrilled about this."

"Neither am I, Jonathan, but you have to trust me on this. Once Stansfield is dead, we will be able to move a little more freely, but until then we need to watch our step." Clark rose from the chair. "I think we should have a celebratory drink." The senator ambled over to the bar and grabbed two glasses, filling them halfway with ice and vodka. With his back turned to Brown, Clark relinquished the control on his emotions and al-

lowed a large smile to spread across his face. This was
life; this was the ultimate game. The spoils to the vic-
tors, and to the weak, like Charles Midleton, it was
death. Clark could feel himself growing stronger.
Things had turned out far from perfect, but he had
proven once again that he could maneuver undetected
among the very people he was seeking to destroy. With a
little more patience, all would be his.

Clark returned with the drinks and handed one to
Brown. Holding his glass out, he said, "To your future,
Jonathan."

The two men clinked their glasses, and Brown repeated the phrase to Clark. Whether he liked it or not,
his success was linked to the senator's.

Clark sat back down in his comfortable leather chair
and put his feet up. He took a sip of the cold vodka
and said, "Now, tell me more about this Mitch Rapp
fellow."

ACKNOWLEDGMENTS

IT IS EXTREMELY gratifying to make a living doing something that you love. It is even more so when you are surrounded by people you like, trust, and respect. To my editor, Emily Bestler, a woman of great charm, grace, and intelligence, thank you for taking this book to another level. I hope this is the third of many to come. To Kip Hakala at Pocket Books, your humor, efficiency, and biting honesty are always welcome. To my agent, Sloan Harris, a good friend and a man of real integrity, thank you for keeping me focused. To Teri Steinberg at ICM, thank you for making things run smoothly. To Laurie Cotumaccio, my publicist at Pocket Books, thank you for your persistence and patience. To Steve Kaiser and the rest of the sales force at Pocket Books, I wouldn't be where I am without you. You are the best in the business. To Jack Romanos, thank you for your generosity and support. To Sean and Amy Stone for putting me up and putting up with me. To Larry Johnson for all your insight and stories, and, of course, to those individuals who have contributed to this book and wish to remain anonymous. And to my wife, Lysa, thank you for making me so happy.

Pocket Books
proudly presents

LETHAL AGENT

VINCE FLYNN

Coming Fall 2019

Turn the page for an exclusive look at the next
Mitch Rapp thriller by Kyle Mills.

1

SOUTHWEST OF THAMUD
YEMEN

M ITCH Rapp started to move again, weaving through an expansive boulder field before dropping to his stomach at its edge. A quick scan of the terrain through his binoculars provided the same result it had every time before: reddish dirt covering a seemingly endless series of pronounced ridges. No water. No plant life. A clear sky stained yellow by dust and starting to turn orange in the west. If it were ninety-five below zero instead of ninety-five above, he could have been on Mars.

Rapp shifted his gaze to the right, concentrating for a good fifteen seconds before spotting a flash of movement that was either Scott Coleman or one of his men. All were wearing custom camo made from cloth specifically selected and dyed for this op by Charlie Wicker's girlfriend. She was a professional textile designer and a flat-out genius at matching colors and textures. If you gave her a few decent photos of your operating theater, she'd make you disappear.

A couple of contrails appeared above, and he followed them with his eyes—Saudi jets on their way to bomb urban targets to the west. This sparsely populated part of central Yemen had become the exclusive territory of ISIS and al Qaeda, but the Saudis largely ignored it. Viable targets were hard to engage from the air, and the Kingdom didn't have the stomach to get bloody on the ground. That job had once again landed in his lap.

Satisfied they weren't being watched, Rapp started forward in a crouch. Coleman and his team would follow, watching his back at perfect intervals like they had in Iraq. And Afghanistan. And Syria. And just about every other hellhole the planet had to offer.

The Yemeni civil war had broken out in 2015 between Houthi rebels and government forces. Predictably, other regional powers had been drawn in, most notably Iran, backing the rebels and Saudi Arabia getting behind the government. The involvement of those countries had intensified the conflict, creating a humanitarian disaster impressive even by Middle Eastern standards.

In many ways, it was a forgotten war. The world's dirty little secret. Even among US government officials and military commanders, it would be hard to find anyone aware that two-thirds of Yemen's population was surviving on foreign aid and another eight million were slowly starving. They also wouldn't be able to tell you that hunger and the loss of basic services were causing disease to run rampant through the country. Cholera, antibiotic-resistant bacteria, and even diphtheria were surging to levels unheard of in the modern era.

And anyplace that could be described using words like "forgotten," "rampant," and "war" eventually became a magnet for terrorists. They were yet another disease that infected the weakened and wounded.

An unusually high ridge became visible to the northwest, and Rapp dropped to the ground again, studying it through his lenses. He could make out a gap just large enough for a human about three hundred yards away.

"Whatcha got?" Coleman said over his earpiece.

"The cave entrance. Right where they said it would be."

"Are we moving?"

"No, it's backlit. We'll let the sun drop over the horizon."

"Roger that. Everybody copy?"

Bruno McGraw, Joe Maslick, and Charlie Wicker all acknowledged. The four men with him made up about half the people in the world Rapp trusted. Probably a sad situation, but one that had kept him alive for a lot longer than anyone would have predicted.

He fine-tuned the focus on his binoculars, refining his view of the dark hole in the cliff face. It was hard to believe that Sayid Halabi was still alive. If Rapp had been any closer with that grenade, it would have gotten jammed in the ISIS leader's throat. But even if his aim had been way off, it shouldn't have mattered. The blast had brought down a significant portion of the cavern he'd been hiding out in.

The collapse had been extensive enough that Rapp himself had been caught in it. In fact, he'd have died slowly in the darkness if Joe Maslick wasn't a human wrecking ball who had spent much of his youth digging ditches on a landscaping crew. Oxygen had been getting pretty scarce when Mas had finally broken through and dragged him from the grave he'd made for himself.

Despite all that, the intel on Halabi seemed solid. A while back, someone at NSA had decrypted a scrambled Internet video showing the man standing in the background at an al Qaeda meeting. The initial take had been that it was archival footage dredged up to keep the troops motivated. That hope hadn't lasted long. Analysts quickly dated the images to six months *after* the night Rapp thought he'd finally ground his boot into that ISIS cockroach's throat.

The video had led to the capture of one of the people at that meeting, and his interrogation had led Rapp to this burned-out plain. Word was that Halabi had been severely injured by that grenade and had been hiding out here, convalescing. The sixty-four-thousand-dollar question was whether he was *still* there. The Agency knew he was healthy enough to be going to meetings and raiding al Qaeda for its best talent, starting the process of rebuilding ISIS after the beating it had taken in his absence.

The sun finally hit the horizon, causing an immediate drop in temperature and improvement in visibility. Waiting for full darkness was an option, but it seemed unnecessary. He hadn't seen any sign of exterior guards, and night versus day would have little meaning once he went inside.

"We're on," he said into his throat mike.

"Copy that," came Coleman's response.

Rapp angled left, moving silently across the rocky terrain until he reached a stone wall about twenty yards from the cave entrance. Staying low, he crept along the wall's base until he reached its edge. Still no sign of ISIS enforcers. Behind him, the terrain was similarly empty, but that was to be expected. It was impossible to anticipate the environment inside the cave, and he was concerned that it could get tight enough to make a force of more than one man counterproductive. Coleman and his team would remain invisible until they were needed.

When he finally slipped inside the cavern, the only evidence that it was inhabited was the churned dirt beneath his feet. He held his weapon in front of him as he eased along a passage about three feet wide and ten feet high. The familiar weight of his Glock had been replaced with that of an early model Mission crossbow. His weapons tech had modified it for stealth, pushing the decibel level below eighty-five. Even better, the pitch had been lowered to the point that it sounded nothing like a weapon. Even to Rapp's practiced ear, it came off more like a bag of sand dropping onto a sidewalk.

Crossbows weren't the fastest things to reload and there hadn't been much time to train with it, but he still figured it was the best tool for the job. The quietest pistol he owned—a Volquartsen .22 with a Gemtech suppressor—was strapped to his thigh, but it would be held in reserve. While it was an impressively stealthy weapon, the sharp crack it made was too loud and recognizable for this operating environment.

The darkness deepened the farther he penetrated, but he moved slowly enough for his eyes to keep pace. Based on what had happened last time he'd chased Sayid Halabi into a hole, it made sense to prioritize caution over speed. Mas might have forgotten his shovel.

A faint glow became visible at the end of the passage, and Rapp inched toward it, avoiding the rocks beneath his feet and staying to the soft earth. As he got closer, he could see that the corridor came to a T. The branch going right dead-ended after a few feet, but the one to the left continued. A series of tiny bulbs wired to a car battery was the source of the glow.

One of the downsides of LED technology was that it made hiding out in caves a lot easier. A single battery could provide light for days. But it also created a vulnerability. Power supplies tended not to be as widely distributed and redundant as they used to be.

Rapp reached down and flipped the cable off the battery, plunging the cavern into darkness.

Shouts became audible almost immediately, sounding more annoyed than alarmed. Rapp could tell that the voices belonged to two male Arabic speakers, but picking out exactly what they were saying was difficult with the cavern's acoustics. Basically a little name-calling and arguing about whose turn it was to fix the problem. When all your light came from a single improvised source, occasional outages were inevitable.

One of the men appeared a few seconds later, swinging a flashlight in his right hand but never lifting it high enough to give detail to his face. It didn't matter. From his youthful gait and posture, it was clear that it wasn't Halabi. Just one of his stooges.

Rapp aimed around the corner and gently squeezed the trigger. The sound profile of the crossbow and the projectile's impact were both outstanding. Unfortunately, the accuracy at this range was less so. The man was still standing, seemingly perplexed by the fletching protruding beneath his left collarbone.

Rapp let go of his weapon and sprinted forward, getting one arm around the Arab's neck and clamping a hand over his mouth and nose. The man fought as he was dragged back around the corner but the sound of their struggle was attenuated by soft ground. Finally, Rapp dropped and wrapped his legs around the man to limit his movement. There wasn't enough leverage to choke him out, but the hand over his face was doing a pretty good job of suffocating him. The process took longer than he would have liked, and he was gouged a few times by the protruding bolt, but the Arab finally lost consciousness. A knife to the base of the skull finished him.

Rapp slid from beneath the body and was recocking the crossbow when another shout echoed through the cavern.

"Farid! What are you doing, idiot? Turn the lights back on!"

Rapp yelled back that he couldn't get them working, counting on the acoustics to make it difficult to distinguish one Arabic speaking male from another. He ran to the battery and put the flashlight facedown in the dirt before crouching next to it. The illumination was low enough that anyone approaching wouldn't be able to see much more than a vague human outline.

A stream of half-baked electrical advice preceded the sound of footsteps, and then another young man appeared. He didn't seem at all concerned, once again proving the grand truth of all things human: people saw what they wanted and expected to see.

Rapp let the terrorist get to within fifteen feet before snatching up the crossbow. This time he compensated by aiming low and left, managing to put the projectile center of mass. No follow-up was necessary. The man crumpled and landed face-first in the dirt.

Certain that he wasn't getting up again, Rapp started reconnecting the battery. He was likely going to need the light. Things had gone well so far but, in his experience, good luck never came in threes.

Support for that hypothesis emerged when a man who was apparently distrustful of the sound of falling sand bags sprinted around the corner. Rapp's .22 was in an awkward position to draw, so instead he grabbed one of the bolts quivered on the crossbow.

The terrorist had been a little too enthusiastic in his approach and his momentum bounced him off one of the cave's walls. Rapp took advantage of his compromised balance and lunged, driving the bladed head into his throat.

Not pretty, but effective enough to drop the man. As he fell, though, a small pipe sprouting with wires rolled from his hand.

Not again.

Rapp used his boot to shove the IED beneath the

man's body and then ran in the opposite direction, making it about twenty feet before diving into a shallow dip in the ground. The explosion sent hot gravel washing over him, and he heard a few disconcertingly loud cracks from above, but that was it. The rock had held. He rolled on his back, pulling his shirt over his mouth and nose to protect him from the dust. The smart money would be to turn tail and call in a few bunker busters, but he couldn't bring himself to do it. If Halabi was there, Rapp was going to see him dead. Even if they entered the afterlife together with their hands around each other's throats.

The sound of automatic fire started up outside but Rapp ignored it, pulling the Volquartsen and using a penlight to continue deeper into the cavern. Coleman and his boys could handle themselves.

The cave system turned out to be relatively simple—a lot of branches, but almost all petered out after a few feet. The first chamber of any size contained a cot and some rudimentary medical equipment—an IV cart, monitors, and a garbage can half full of bloody bandages. All of it had the look of having been there for a while.

The second chamber appeared to have been set up for surgical procedures but wasn't much more advanced than something from the First World War. A gas cylinder that looked like it came from a welder, a tray with a few instruments strewn across it, and a makeshift operating table streaked with dried blood.

And that was the end of the line. The cave system dead-ended just beyond.

"Shit!" Rapp shouted, his voice reverberating down the corridor and bouncing back to him.

The son of a bitch had been there. They'd brought him to treat the injuries he'd suffered in Iraq and to give him time to heal. A month ago, Rapp might have been able to look into his eyes, put a pistol between them, and pull the trigger. But now he was long gone. Sayid Halabi had slipped through his fingers again.